D1558736

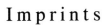

Imprints

Other books by Arthur Janov

THE ANATOMY OF MENTAL ILLNESS
THE FEELING CHILD
PRIMAL MAN: THE NEW CONSCIOUSNESS
THE PRIMAL REVOLUTION
THE PRIMAL SCREAM
PRISONERS OF PAIN

IMPRINTS

The Lifelong Effects of the Birth Experience

ARTHUR JANOV, Ph.D.

COWARD-McCANN, INC.
NEW YORK

The author gratefully acknowledges permission from the
following source to reprint material in this book:
  Houghton Mifflin Company for the excerpt from *Dibs: In
Search of Self* by Virginia Axline. Copyright © 1964 by
Houghton Mifflin Company.

Library of Congress Cataloging in Publication Data

Janov, Arthur.
  Imprints : the lifelong effects of the birth
experience.

  Includes bibliographical references and index.
  1. Childbirth—Psychological aspects. 2. Im-
printing (Psychology) 3. Traumatic neuroses.
I. Title.
BF 713.J35   1983   155.9'1   82-12599
ISBN 0-698-11183-4

PRINTED IN THE UNITED STATES OF AMERICA

Acknowledgments

There have been a number of people who have helped with this book. E. Michael Holden, my scientific colleague for years, has helped revise several chapters and has added valuable information—particularly in regard to the section on Cesarean birth. Nick Barton has helped in the editing and has helped clarify several sections of the book.

I want to thank particularly my editor, Margaret Ryan, for her many, many hours of valuable organization and editorial skills. She has done research, has revised, edited and contributed original ideas wherever necessary.

Finally, my thanks to the patients who were persistent and tenacious enough to maintain their position about birth Primals until I became convinced, despite my own biases. They opened a new world for me and for my future patients.

NOTICE

PRIMAL THERAPY OR REBIRTHING DONE BY UNTRAINED PERSONS CAN BE DANGEROUS. FOR INFORMATION AS TO THE QUALIFICATIONS OF THOSE PRACTICING PRIMAL THERAPY, REBIRTHING, OR OF THOSE WHO CLAIM TO HAVE BEEN TRAINED AT THE PRIMAL INSTITUTE, PLEASE CONTACT: THE PRIMAL INSTITUTE, 2215 COLBY AVE., LOS ANGELES, CALIFORNIA 90064 (TEL. 213-478-0167) *or* THE PRIMAL INSTITUTE OF EUROPE, 10 AVE. PERCIER, PARIS 75008 (TEL. 1-5611332).

To Rick—my pal,
my friend, my son

Contents

III

CATASTROPHIC IMPLICATIONS OF THE BIRTH TRAUMA

IV

THE RESOLUTION OF BIRTH TRAUMA

Preface

Due to the recent flood of books on child rearing, the task of bringing up a healthy child must seem almost impossible to parents. There are so many things that can go wrong, so many things to know about. As if that weren't enough, now we have a book that says that "child" rearing really begins *in the womb,* as early as eight weeks after conception. That period of time is the most crucial of all in setting personality, in determining what diseases one will be afflicted by later in life, and even in determining how long one will live.

What is difficult about this idea is that it is so *intangible.* After all, the events affecting a baby *in utero* are hidden, and so are its reactions to those events. We really can't see what may be harmful to the baby; we can't know how the baby is reacting to what is going on within that special fluid environment. It all seems so mysterious, and parents rightly may feel helpless in the face of this mystery. As if their guilt about how they reared their child at age six, ten or fifteen weren't enough, now they must bear additional guilt about what they did to their child, almost from the moment of conception.

Let me hasten to say that the purpose of this book is not to further complicate parents' lives, but to help them become aware of those prenatal and birth factors that are harmful to their baby. Above all, the purpose is to help parents give their babies the best possible chance for a healthy life. It is also my hope to clarify how we became what we are; to show how those earliest events shaped our attitudes, interests and ideas— as well as our obsessions, compulsions, and our symptoms.

As new knowledge continues to become available, the mistakes we all have made with our children will become clearer and clearer. But we must not dwell on the past, indulging in guilt. We can only look to the future with renewed understanding and a strengthened determination not to pass on those mistakes.

ARTHUR JANOV

I: The Beginning of the End

1

Birthrights: The Beginning of Life

Many of us believe that a newborn infant is little more than a blob of protoplasm, feeling very little, understanding less, reacting hardly at all to its surroundings. Yet the opposite is true. The newborn infant is more fully feeling than he may ever be again; he has a wide open "sensory window" which allows him to react wholly as he may never again; and he is born experiencing his new life without an illusory veil of ideas, which almost undoubtedly will never be the case again.

Most adults cannot comprehend the agony that a newborn is in, even though he may be crying and screaming his heart out. But because he cannot speak, we act as though he hasn't "said" anything. Because he cannot explain himself, we discount his Pain as harmless. We expect newborns to writhe and scream. I think if most babies had words just after birth they would be able to tell us about the harrowing experience they had just been through.

Because the birth trauma has only recently been recognized, almost everyone (except for a lucky few born in "primitive" ways) has suffered from the same Pain and the same unconsciousness. We experienced the traumas of our own births, observed the births of our infants, watched them scream in terror afterwards, and never knew what they were suffering or that we had suffered before them. In a kind of ironic, self-perpetuating cycle, the unconscious Pain of our own births produces more Pain, more neurosis and more unconsciousness. Because the birth trauma is inaccessible, all of us—parents, doctors, nurses and hospital administrators—remain oblivious to the injurious birth procedures being utilized that bring children into the world. Precisely because an important segment of our own reality is blocked from consciousness, we are not conscious of an infant's full reality. Thus we see, but do not perceive; we observe, but do not feel; we watch, but cannot empathize.

To stress the seriousness of the birth trauma may seem like exaggerated melodrama to many adults. It *is* difficult to imagine the Pain involved; to really experience a baby's suffering requires us to get closer to our own suffering—and that may be too close for comfort. This is why the birth trauma cannot be adequately *imagined;* it can only be *relived.* One cannot imagine what it is like to be squeezed for hours by massive contractions; to be blocked in an unyielding canal or pushed back up the canal by a nurse's hands; to be suffocated by an overdose of anesthetic; to be drowned in viscous fluid; to be fighting for air; to be squeezed by a doctor's metal forceps around the head and yanked out unceremoniously—and then to be held upside down in a cold room, spanked sharply by a stranger and removed from the only person a baby knows. What must it feel like to be in a new world, isolated from human contact in a metallic contraption after almost dying; where every sight and sound is totally new and often assaultive; where blinding lights prevent one's perception of this new and strange environment? Indeed, these early experiences become the most memorable—or should I say *im*memorable—of our lives, for no baby can integrate traumatic Pain and keep it in consciousness. That is why the entire birth process, from conception and pregnancy to delivery and post-delivery, can lay the foundation for later mental and physical disease.

How does this happen? What are the mechanisms? We now know that the traumas surrounding birth are engraved as imprints in the developing nervous system of the fetus and newborn. The birth imprint thus determines physiological and neurological response tendencies, shapes later personality and physiotype, and directs the type of pathology we eventually develop. Whether we will be constant travelers, compulsive workers, heavy smokers, overeaters, alcoholics, asthmatics; whether we will be aggressive and ambitious "upbeat" types or depressed and pessimistic "downbeat" types; whether we will be prone to cancer, epilepsy, psychosis or even suicide—may all be predetermined by those first precious hours of birth. Gestation and birth experiences can and do dictate how we act and react for the rest of our lives. Indeed, giving birth in today's world usually means giving birth to neurosis.

I emphasize the birth trauma not because it is the only trauma that produces neurosis, but because it is often responsible for the beginnings of neurosis. I also emphasize it because we are generally unaware of the tremendous impact of prenatal and birth experiences on our lives. Surely if there is any single Pain that starts neurosis in motion it must be the life-and-death struggle of the birth process. This first Pain can and does begin the neurotic split, for it forces the newborn's barely developed repressive system into action to counteract it: the new self is denied access to those deeply buried feelings from birth which were too threatening to integrate. It is this split that we call neurosis, and it is these early forces of Pain that provide continuity to the neurotic personality.

I am not alone in my estimation of the significance of the birth experience. Here is what one researcher wrote in the *Journal of the American Medical Association:**

> The hazards confronting the fetus mount to a climax during the hours of labor. *Birth is the most endangering experience to which most individuals are ever exposed.* The birth process, even under optimal, controlled conditions, is a traumatic, potentially crippling event for the fetus. [Italics added]

All birth experiences are nonverbal. There are no words with which to recall such experiences, for the part of the brain needed to describe experience develops in the individual long after the experiences themselves have been imprinted. That is why no explanation, exhortation or conditioning technique can change the original experience. The Pain is inscribed in every part of the physiologic system, and it is to that precise inscription that we must look for "salvation." It would be as difficult to rid oneself of early Pain through explanation as it would be to rid oneself of language upon request. Both are stamped in early in life and become an integral part of our physiology.

Birth Trauma: Basis for the "Collective" Unconscious

How do the painful experiences around birth get transformed into what we call an "unconscious"? By the neurochemical processes of repression. Most of us cannot remember what our births felt like for good reason. There are chemicals in the brain triggered by Pain to eradicate the memory of the trauma. Note that the chemicals do not rid us of the trauma itself—only of our memory and consciousness of it. Nothing can change the actual imprint of the trauma.

---

*Towbin, Abraham, "Organic Causes of Minimal Brain Dysfunction," *Journal of the American Medical Association,* 217, No. 9, August 30, 1971, 1213.

If there were no system of repressive agents in the nervous system most of us would have either died at birth or we would be awash in Pain nearly all of the time. We would be constantly overwhelmed by a mass of input which would blot out our ability to think, to concentrate, to select what is relevant—in short, to deal with the world around us. There is a collective unconsciousness of the birth Pains because that unconsciousness aids in our survival. This is the true meaning of our "collective" unconscious. I believe the unconscious now posited by theorists and researchers in psychology may well prove to be nothing more than the shared, repressed Pains of very early experience. Freud believed that the unconscious was permanent and immutable because he observed adults reacting to something impelling, continuous and seemingly out of reach. Since he had no tools (no technology) to find and measure what it was, he had to posit an ethereal force (the id) rather than a concrete force (Pain). Indeed, without access to the traumas of one's early life, the unconscious *is* immutable, ethereal and timeless. The Pain *is* endless. It produces the closest thing I can think of to perpetual motion in humans: the "machine" of our bodies is set in perpetual motion by the traumas surrounding birth.

The Issues of Significance and Validity

The encoding of traumas in and around birth has a special significance for several reasons. First, the nervous system of the baby is "naive": the defensive mechanisms are not yet operating at full capacity to blunt and desensitize the baby to what comes in. Second, traumas around birth have an exceedingly high charge value because they are nearly always a matter of life and death. The charge value of the trauma is part of the imprint and retains a commensurate force. In a traumatic birth, the baby's system is in great danger and every ounce of effort is being expended in the fight for survival. The highly charged imprint of that fight is literally an electrical storm which remains in the system as residual tension for a lifetime. Third, the birth imprint is especially important because it is encoded deep and central in the brain and nervous system, and is soon gated over by the developing cortex and by later experience.

We know that birth traumas are significant when they occur, but how do we really know that they occur? What kinds of evidence do we have to establish the birth trauma as a valid phenomenon? There are many types of evidence, both subjective and objective in nature, and much of this book is concerned with presenting it. But one issue is particularly pivotal to establishing the validity of the birth trauma, and that is the issue of *neurological adequacy*. Do the fetus and newborn have an adequately developed neurological system to register, code and store traumas? Many professionals still believe they do not. However, neurological evidence now indicates that the structures mediating Pain are situated lower down in the brain, and develop before birth. Infants born without a cerebral cortex have been shown to react to painful stimuli. We do not need ideas or a cortex in order to suffer.

The eminent neurophysiologist Dr. Paul Yakovlev has written extensively about the maturation process of the human brain and nervous system. He explains the myelinization process, which is the process by which nerve fibers become mature. The sequence or pattern of myelinization is a reliable index of brain maturation, and the inner brain of the fetus is sufficiently myelinated (matured) in the later stages of pregnancy to mediate responses and to code information. Late in pregnancy, the inner brain is also mature enough to mediate visceral responses.*

In short, the newborn infant is a human being with a highly reactive and highly sensitized nervous system. Some areas of its nervous system are fully developed and operative at birth; others hardly, or not at all. The newborn is going to respond to trauma with the most adequate parts of its nervous system. Since there is not a fully developed cortex at birth, those responses are not going to be in the form of words or ideas, but what may well happen is that the traumas and early dislocations in function that do occur will have representations in the cortex after it develops. The point is, while the newborn's system is sufficiently developed to register, store and repress Pain, it is not sufficiently developed to process and integrate it.

That the fetus and newborn can and do react fully to painful stimuli is a basic factor of survival. Pain initiates one of our most primary survival mechanisms. It also makes sense that the fetus and newborn possess the repressive capacities to block life-threatening Pain until their systems are mature enough to integrate it. (Indeed, as will be discussed later in the book, the placental sac is itself a chemical factory producing Pain blunters.) Integration of Pain must await emergence of the higher brain centers, but reaction to Pain goes on from the first few weeks of life *in utero*. Integration of Pain requires consciousness, cognition, and complex neurological functioning; reaction to Pain can occur without consciousness, without cognition, and with only the most primitive neurological structures.

The Discovery: Theory vs. Reality

Is the birth trauma a truth—a reality—or is it just a theory? In truth, I actually *opposed* the notion of birth trauma when my patients first claimed to be reexperiencing their births. I had observed patients reliving their

*Yakovlev, P. I., "Morphological Criteria of Growth and Maturation of the Nervous System in Man," *Journal of Mental Retardation,* 39, Research Publications, A.R.N.M.D., 1962.

birth experiences for two years, and even after they had explained to me what they thought they were undergoing I was reluctant to believe them. My reluctance was corroborated by the neurology department of a local neuropsychiatric institute where I had been informed that no such thing was possible: a fetus's nervous system was not mature enough to react to, code, and store its own birth. Thus, I argued with my patients and suggested to them that their experiences were probably symbolic rather than literal.

In the late 1960s there was no theory in the air about reliving one's birth and so it could not have been "suggested" to these patients. Indeed, my "suggestions" to them actually attempted to counter their experiences. But birth Primals continued. They were happening to too many patients too often to be ignored or minimized. Finally, a neurologist joined our staff, a student of Dr. Yakovlev, who knew that the nervous system of the fetus was capable of coding and storing trauma. We began to see mounting and convincing evidence of this as a result of our own research. The changes that occurred in patients after birth Primals were dramatic and quantifiable. Patients undergoing *birth* Primals as opposed to Primals involving less life-threatening events were hooked up to sophisticated electronic instrumentation. The measurements indicated a significant elevation of all the vital signs during the birth Primal—body temperature rose by three degrees, pulse and blood pressure doubled, and brain wave amplitudes skyrocketed—and a significant lowering of those signs after the Primal.

Through the birth Primal we slowly became aware that what we were observing was a direct relationship between adult symptomatology and the birth trauma. Patients would begin to show a particular symptom—a migraine, an attack of colitis, even the beginnings of a *grand mal* seizure— but with the skillful aid of a therapist, the patient would connect to the original motivating trauma and the feeling that accompanied it. And more amazingly, with the experience of the connected feeling the symptom would disappear. If the person only abreacted (felt the emotion but did not connect it to the original experience) this would not be the case.

We found still more evidence for the validity of the birth Primal. During birth reexperiences patients would not tear or cry; in fact, they could not tear or cry—nor could they talk, scream or move about in the way that babies do. We could only deduce from their fishtailing, salamander-like movements that their whole bodies were being directed by the primitive nervous system of the newborn—a system not yet equipped for the sounds, coordinated movements or the crying typical of a six-month-old baby. Newborns do not cry in the same way that infants cry. That first gasp and wail for life is, indeed, utterly unique, and it remains utterly unique as it is relived.

In observing these birth experiences we watched (often with great trepidation) as anoxia (oxygen deprivation) overwhelmed patients lying unharmed on the floor; we watched as patients struggled to catch their breath, turning red and blue as the early imprint engrossed them— reproducing that very same trauma that had occurred decades before. Some patients could go on for weeks or months with these kinds of Primals before they knew what was happening. It was only after significant resolution of the birth Pain, after almost complete conscious connection to it, that they would know for a certainty what they had reexperienced. It was then that the deepest insights flowed, with an effortlessness, depth and profundity that could not be faked.

We cannot neglect what the patients themselves report about their birth experiences. Hundreds of them describe the same general experience in such a way as to leave little doubt about its validity. We have filmed and videotaped birth Primals, even putting them into slow motion to be observed and evaluated for authenticity by obstetricians. The obstetricians agreed conclusively: the movements, facial expressions, breathing patterns, and sounds were all those of the newborn. While viewing one of these films, Frederick Leboyer, the famous French obstetrician who pioneered the movement for nontraumatic birthing procedures, rose excitedly to declare, "I am vindicated! There finally is the proof!"

We are going to look at the birth experience in terms of its physical, emotional, psychological and intellectual effects on us. We will hear from the patients themselves about what the reliving of an early trauma does for one's life. It will no doubt be surprising to see that what happened to a tiny baby during the first hours of life decades ago can have lifelong ramifications—that most of one's life may be a repetition of that birth event, elaborated and extended through the higher levels of consciousness—but a repetition nonetheless. And it will be equally surprising to see how the reexperience of that event liberates the human system as nothing else can.

The following is the story of a woman named Laura who was filmed as she was having birth Primals. She began the sequence after almost one year of therapy:

Trigger for first birth Primal   My father used to take me fishing. I'd get excited about catching the fish, but when I'd actually see the fish moving around and struggling and dying, I'd get nauseous. I used to feel so badly about it that I didn't want to go fishing any more. I began thinking about fishing the other day and became obsessed about the wriggling and struggling of the fish. This sent me off into my first birth Primal, out of which came many realizations about my life.

*Anger: the proto-
typic response*

Anger has been my lifelong defense. It started in the womb as a means to stay alive. In fact, that aggression was the only thing that kept me alive. I fought and struggled to try to make myself understood at birth—to make it understood *that I was dying.* Later, I began thinking that my mother was very stupid. But really, whenever *anyone* does anything that seems stupid to me, I just go crazy. I get furious when someone doesn't understand me right away. Even if they just misunderstood, I would still think they're stupid. I *need* to be understood with the same urgency that I needed my mother to understand my plight at birth.

I could never tolerate anything over me—anything overpowering me. My body seems to remember something I can't really explain. It just feels like basic survival. I know that I was born not breathing and almost dead. My mother said I wasn't breathing at all and that I was blue. Even the spanking by the doctor didn't help; they had to give me an injection. It must have made me nauseous, because nausea seems to be my first reaction to almost anything. In any catastrophe I get a funny taste which seems to be the dope they gave me at birth. I sort of smell it rather than taste it. As soon as I get that smell I get all fuzzy-headed and confused.

*Nausea: an en-
during birth sensa-
tion*

It seems like I did everything I could to tell my mother I was ready to be born; I didn't know what else to do. And now I never seem to know what to do in certain situations. I think I get confused for two reasons: first, because nothing I did at birth seemed to work; and second, because the shot I got wiped out any ability to think at all, however primitively. It fogged my mind, or what there was of it, so that I couldn't focus or make sense. I've always gotten confused very easily. It doesn't take much to boggle my mind.

*Primal basis for
adult confusion*

I suppose I got confused at birth because I didn't have the brain power to figure things out. Confusion, for me, has always led to inaction. I'm easily overwhelmed and then confused. A big shopping list confuses me; and when I get two orders at once I go nuts. Getting up in the morning means dragging my corpse around all day. I really feel like doing nothing. That's what my body is always saying: "You've already done a lot of work and now you need to rest!" But when I do nothing and waste time I feel like I'm wasting my life, so I get agitated and nervous. I'm pulled in two

Cycle of confusion

Indecision now; wrong decisions at birth

The occult: an answer to "I don't know what to do"

Compounding the original trauma

Aversion to touch: a birth response

Acting out the death and revival of birth

directions all of the time. From the beginning I never knew what to do. My cycle is do nothing—worry—feel guilty—try to do something. I've looked for someone to make up my mind my whole life. I want others to make my decisions because all of my decisions got me nowhere originally.

I used to be into fortune telling, tarot cards, astrology and supernatural phenomena. That was all related to a feeling of "I don't know what to do." At least I could rely on the cards to tell me. I was looking for a divine signal from the heavens. It seems the more Pain I'm in, the more magic I look for. I need something simple and unconfusing from the outside. When I'm miserable and lonely—when I'm not getting along with anyone, when I've got nobody in my life and I just want to die—I start looking at the cards and hoping for a sign. I need the I Ching or the Tarot to drive me away from that pessimism. It's the worst degree of pessimism because in those moments everything is bleak and dark; I have no interests, no goals and no ambition. I just want to rot. I've always been superstitious and relied on mystical things to run my life. Now I see the whole pattern so clearly. I couldn't trust humans from the start of my life so I had to trust things.

I know I've had the lifelong feeling of "Nothing I do is good enough" since birth, when nothing I did do *was* good enough. Then my mother compounded it by never liking anything I did—from the way I made my bed to the way I dressed.

After almost being killed at birth trying to get out of my mother, I then didn't want her to touch me. I was afraid of her; I didn't trust her. Well, since then I have never trusted women nearly as much as I trust men. I never let anyone I don't know well touch me. I have been basically untrusting and paranoid since birth, I think. Touch has always made me nervous, but now I finally know why. *I don't want to be in anyone's grasp.*

It's a funny thing about being born almost dead. I have been acting out that deadness most of my life. Then I get others to "revive" me. I live through their aliveness, their liveliness, their gaiety in the hope that they will bring me out of my deadness. The minute they are gone I feel all blah and dead again. I have acted out a lifetime of being dead and being revived with other people.

Before I came to therapy I had the feeling all of the time that I was going crazy or that I was going to kill

A Primal paradox: feeling bad about feeling good

Second-level constriction: heavy coats

Laura's Primal cycle

Resolving the symptoms by resolving the Pain

myself. I never knew where those death thoughts came from. Even when my life was going well I had those thoughts—in fact, *particularly* when my life was going well. It seems now to be that good feeling just before the hell of coming out. So I get that doom feeling whenever I feel good. I can't let life be good to me. I think a lot of my depressions simply came from the fact that I had a lot of feelings pent up that I never let out; and I never let them out because I never knew what they were. In the first place, they had no words. So it's pretty hard to express yourself when the feelings you are dealing with have no words.

All of my life when I haven't been allowed to do what I want I would just go crazy. Being restricted and enclosed was a way of life for me. In school my mother would bundle me up with heavy coats. Because *she* was cold, *I* had to bundle up. She always kept me enclosed; the coats were just an extension of my birth.

I guess my style has been fight, give up, start to die, fight again. At birth, as soon as I gave up I started to lose consciousness just like in my daily life now. When things get to be too much, I despair, and then I let it all accumulate until I can't struggle anymore. I just want to die. This wanting to die becomes my escape. Then at the last minute I seem to get galvanized again and go on struggling. It can just be something trivial that makes me want to die. Now I see why a trivial thing can set off the old feeling.

I often wonder how to "prove" what I've been through, but I'm not sure that anyone can. The original event is an experience and so is the reliving—there's no thought attached to either one. The "proof" for me comes from the feelings and from the changes that happen after I've felt. For example, whenever I stood in line for a theater I'd get a feeling of overwhelming impatience—I just wanted to smack the guy in front of me. I don't have that anymore and I know it cleared up from reliving my original need to get out and breathe. You can imagine what getting out of an airplane does to me. I know the feeling has always been "I've got to get out of here and if my mother doesn't hurry I'm going to die." My mother couldn't make up her mind about giving birth to me, so I was just stuck with those feelings. Lately, I've had deeper insights. One reason I never got out on time was because she didn't want me—and that was confirmed by her behavior all through my childhood.

The results: "I feel more comfortable now"

I feel more comfortable now. That may not seem very dramatic, but when you've felt unhappy in your skin all of your life and never knew why, believe me, it is a great relief. I also am more open and expressive with people. I see now that there is nothing to be afraid of. I was dominated by that early terror which I projected onto people. I was just scared all of the time. Now that I've felt that fear to its deepest extent, it seems to have gone away. It's like some giant jigsaw puzzle and the fear has finally fallen into place.

Integrating the Pain

I seem so out of control in these experiences in therapy. I just let my body go and it seems to know what it's doing. The minute I try to figure it out or control it, the experience stops. Feeling all of this Pain has given me a better tolerance to it. When I first started feeling in therapy, I would get nauseous and want to throw up. That doesn't happen anymore. The nausea was some kind of original reaction to *any* feeling. I began life with that sensation, and it has been with me until just recently. Finally it is gone. Going through all that early Pain hasn't been fun, but it's certainly nice not to be crazy anymore.

Some weeks later we got the following report:

Reliving the birth

Today I felt like I popped out. Something totally new happened. I began the session feeling cold. I know it was hot in the therapy room, but I was freezing. I also wasn't breathing. I was shivering like mad and blue in the face, according to the therapist. Afterwards I kept feeling, "I'm born, I'm born!" I laughed because I had that feeling while being aware that I was a grown-up.

More insights: "help me out"

Once out I understood more things about myself. As I said, everything in my life was always too much of an effort. In my twenties I couldn't even wash the dishes. I'd just sit around and wait—for what, I wasn't sure. But now I am sure: *I was waiting for mother to do something to help me out.* I couldn't do anything for myself; I mean I did everything I could, and it didn't do any good. So I gave up.

Giving up and just waiting

This had partly made me dependent on others—a kind of nonself-reliance. No matter what I did originally, I did not get what I wanted; I had to wait for "them" to be ready for me. Not being in control of my life, I stopped fighting and just waited. I gave up trying for myself. I didn't know what else to do. I breathed as little as possible because there was no air left—and the pains in my chest are the direct result of my not breathing. Finally my time was due: born blue and not breathing, more dead than alive. But I still had a moment of rejoicing; I was out. I had made it!

"Held down like at birth"

I remember now getting in a fight with my boyfriend. I smacked him on the chest and he grabbed my wrists and held them firmly. Well, I just went nuts. I got panicky and became hysterical. I felt held down again, like at birth, and that is hysteria time for me.

The birth defense in the present: turning blue

What has always helped me is that whenever I started to hit rock bottom I'd get angry and that saved me. I've always known that I was in misery, but I never knew why. I remember when my folks would fight when I was little. I would hold my breath until I turned blue and passed out. That would stop their fighting! I see now how prototypic that response was.

Sex and birth: doing what I didn't want to do

I could never let myself go in sex and so I rarely went to bed with anyone. I didn't enjoy it. I was blocked but never knew it. To me sex was just unpleasant. Now I know what it is: I didn't feel comfortable in a vulnerable or feeling situation. Now that I have opened up to myself, to my deepest self, I can let go in sex, and the pleasant feeling of it tells me how much I automatically couldn't let go before. Sex was related to birth—doing what I didn't want to do; going in someone else's direction. Having sex when I didn't want it would bring up the old birth feeling all over again.

What you have just read are the insights of a woman who has relived her birth. We are going to examine how that is possible, and what the birth trauma is. The idea of events in the womb and around birth having a lifelong impact on our everyday behavior in adult life is so astounding that it requires careful preparation. We will examine birth traumas and events in the womb to show how they are laid down through a process of imprinting that lasts a lifetime. We shall read the stories of many individuals who have relived their birth and the changes that have followed. The birth trauma is the most neglected of traumas, in terms of medical and psychological recognition, yet it is probably the most important event of our lives. Innumerable books have been written on the subject of birth and pregnancy, all of which emphasize the importance of the relationship during childhood of the parent with his child. What has not been emphasized perhaps is that the neurosis of the parent, particularly the mother, is a contagious and transmissible disease. The baby does not *inherit* neurosis from his mother; he has had many months of experience with her before she ever sees him. Neurosis is a powerful adversary. You don't have to do anything to make your child neurotic, particularly in the womb. You only have to be—neurotic.

To conclude this chapter, I want to say again that it is not the purpose of this book to detail the myriad ways something can go wrong during pregnancy. Rather, it is to explore how our later lives are influenced by very early events. In order to do that, we must examine some of the things that can go wrong during gestation, and the ways in which they can go wrong. Some readers, however, may find this material too detailed, and not directly relevant to their lives. If you feel this may be true, proceed to Chapter 3.

2

Nurture or Nightmare:
The Nine Months in the Womb

The womb is one of nature's finest creations. It is an environment of intricate and delicate processes that miraculously coalesce into life. Our time in the womb should be the softest, most nurturing, most protected time of our lives. It should be idyllic. It should be life-ensuring, for every fiber and cell of the womb is geared for supporting, shaping and sustaining life.

Otto Rank believed this was so and his notion became quite popular. He believed that what we were traumatized by was birth; by that sudden thrust into a cruel world which leaves us all secretly longing to go back to that safe place away from life's hardships, back to the comfort, that fluid pillow, that once buffered us from harm. What Rank felt was traumatic was the *contrast* between life in the womb and life in the world. What we now know is that *trauma begins in the womb* and that the difficulty may be in the opposite direction: when we finally arrive in the world we are often leaving behind hardships against which we were helpless. In many cases, the "cushion" of the womb is distorted into a "prison" of lifelong trauma. Pregnancy may be a nine-month nightmare for many babies; and indeed the stuff of later nightmares is inexhaustibly and interminably supplied by these earliest times.

How does this happen? There are many forms of intrauterine stress, many ways in which the developing embryo and fetus can be harmed. Some of these ways are accidental. The mother might be unknowingly exposed to German measles, or to other such diseases. Or, she might be forced to deal with some type of natural disaster while pregnant—a flood, fire or earthquake. These are all situations that are inherently stressful and over which the mother has no control. Accidental stresses will have an impact on the developing baby, but there is no way to foresee or prevent them.

There are forms of intrauterine stress over which the mother *can* have control and which, in fact, the mother is obligated to control. What she eats and drinks, what kinds of drugs she does or does not take, her own personal stress—all are factors that can be controlled to varying degrees. Food, drink and drugs can be controlled totally (provided, of course, the mother has the means to feed herself nutritionally). Personal stress is less controllable. A husband may suddenly inform his wife during her fifth month of pregnancy that he is leaving her, forcing her to deal with the enormous stress of personal loss and rejection plus the stress of being left totally responsible for the life within her. Loved ones may die or become catastrophically ill, businesses may fail, growing children may demand more than the pregnant mother can give.

Forms of personal stress are unlimited, but how the mother deals with those stresses will be quite limited and circumscribed by one underlying factor: whether or not she is neurotic. A neurotic mother (i.e., a mother in Pain) means a Pain-filled womb, for stored Pain infuses the system as surely and as comprehensively as do drugs, alcohol or nicotine. The mother's neurosis predisposes the whole process of entry into life toward a life-threatening rather than life-stimulating passage.

Much of this chapter deals with how far the sciences have come in discovering the relationship between pregnancy and later development. We have discovered a great deal by observing the reexperiences of early birth traumas. Much of the scientific research corroborates what is observed in these birth Primals. It is unfortunate that we must rely on such research to confirm what common sense and instinct should tell us, that the fetus is a being that responds, reacts to and "remembers" its experiences.

It was only when a method was found that permitted access into the labyrinth of the deep unconscious that we could begin to confirm the realities of womb life. Science, finally, is only a footnote to experience. Cold, hard facts are no substitute for experience itself when we are so alienated from our deep, inner selves that we cannot feel for ourselves what the truth is.

It makes perfect sense to start our study of Primal Pain where life itself begins, with the mother, for the quality of the mother determines the quality of motherhood. But the burden cannot be the mother's alone; it must be shared by the father, the family and by society. If, as a society, we put our time, effort and money into creating the most beneficent conditions possible for all pregnant mothers, I am sure that we would have far fewer solutions to seek for a better world, and far healthier human beings seeking them.

Fetal Pain and Repression

The structures mediating Pain and suffering are some of the most ancient in the nervous system. They existed long before other structures evolved to understand or conceptualize them. After but a few weeks of life in the womb, the fetus can react to and store input. The possibility therefore exists that we can become neurotic in the womb; and that is why to think of neurosis in terms of behavior is to think in false concepts. Clearly, we must begin to think of neurosis as a physiologic disease. The Pains that are stored in the womb can be "remembered," but not in terms of the cognitive memory mechanisms we are familiar with. Fetal recall is a body memory. The body remembers, in its own way, and that stored "knowledge" is no less valid than intellectual recall.

Repression is a physiologic process that occurs even while the fetus is in the womb. Internally produced painkillers called endorphines have been found in the placenta, which indicates that trauma to the fetus during pregnancy can be repressed and made unconscious. Thus the fetus has the neurochemical wherewithal to block Pain. The Pain is held down in the nervous system and forms part of the deep unconscious, and so the barrier between the conscious and unconscious begins its life in the womb.

Ultimately, it is the mother's state of being, the kind of person she is physically and psychologically that shapes her child's growth. It is not just a matter of the mother's later overt behavior toward her baby. As we shall see, changes in the mother's body chemistry are imprinted upon the developing fetus and in this way the mother's neurosis (or lack of it) is passed on to her child.

When the baby is born, it will have many characteristics which we previously would have ascribed to heredity. It turns out that many of these traits, personality characteristics and physiologic predispositions have much more to do with the intrauterine environment than with genetic composition. Even when there are hereditary predispositions toward, for example, hypothyroidism, stuttering or allergies, it may still be the quality of the environment in the womb that determines whether or not they become manifest. As long as we did not have access to the womb and birth experience, we could assume heredity was the sole or primary factor determining what condition the baby was born in. Now, in addition to scientific verification, we have another kind of evidence to help us understand the effects of pregnancy and birth—and that is the evidence of people reliving their earliest life experiences.

From these experiences we are discovering that, in a very real sense, neurosis may begin even before the child is conceived. The "genetics" of neurosis—the mechanisms through which it is passed on from one generation to the next—begin with the hidden reasons parents have for conceiving. But what is hidden in the parents unfortunately becomes all too visible in the baby; as neurotic motivations become flesh, their consequences are as visible and catastrophic as any disease or disaster.

Motivations for Conceiving: "A Priori" Neurosis

Does it matter why people have children? Do our motivations for childbearing, conscious or unconscious, affect that minuscule bit of life growing in the womb? I believe so. Research is indicating that mothers unhappy about their pregnancies for whatever reason produce newborns who are hyperirritable and restless, who cry excessively, eat poorly and vomit frequently. It is well and good that these matters are beginning to be quantified, but I don't think we need archives full of statistics to convince us of something so obvious. Every cell in the baby's body, though constructed from the union of male and female cells, is nurtured out of the mother's body. That means that almost anything affecting the mother will have repercussions on the life within. Our motivations for conceiving are literally filtered through the tissues that form both the baby itself and the baby's first environment.

We tend to regard motivation as some sort of abstract psychological state—a province of mind, not of the body. But motivations have precise physical and emotional correlates in addition to any conceptualization of them. In fact, motivations are first of the body. The intellect is the last to have a hand in them; it comes along to articulate what our sensations, feelings and needs are already driving and guiding us to do. Motivation is a result of feeling and body states. That is why neurotic motivations are harmful to the developing fetus. Whatever fears, resentments, pressures, anxieties and egotisms go into the decision to conceive also lie in the tissues that spring from that decision.

A child conceived of neurotic parents is not conceived for itself. From the moment of conception it is being used in the service of the parents' needs—a kind of enforced prenatal prostitution. There are a host of neurotic reasons for having children, none of which has anything to do with producing a healthy new human being. For neurotics, having children too often becomes one more way to act out denied needs and denied Pain.

One of the most common reasons neurotics have children is to produce someone who will be loving; someone the parents can have all to themselves; someone they can be proud of; someone who will need them. The child's value will lie in making his parents feel loved. This may not sound neurotic simply because it is so common. But the child conceived for these reasons has enormous—perhaps too much—responsibility before it even draws its first breath: it is to be its parents' world; to make two complex, unconscious human beings happy; to fulfill their needs in a world where it is hard enough just to get one's own needs fulfilled. However, newborns are themselves composed entirely of need, and so to conceive them out of one's own unfulfilled need is to invite disaster.

Another common motivation for childbearing is to hold together a faltering marriage. Here again the child is conceived under enormous pressure and given a herculean task before it can even move a muscle on its own. The task of this unborn child is simply to solve what two grown, "intelligent" adults could not solve: their own emotional turmoil. What the parents fail to see is that they are trying to turn their unborn child into a solution for their own salvation. A couple might say innocently, "Well, we've been having problems lately and we feel a child will bring us closer together." But closer together to what? They can only come closer together to what is already there: to their own unresolved needs, to their own Pain, to their own neuroses.

A mother who conceives in order to "hook" a man, or a man who unconsciously doubts his masculinity and so impregnates his wife to prove it—both contribute neurotic motivations to their baby's beginnings. The fetus is a product of these motivations, of these combined physiologies. The motivation is a product of a system that is hyperactivated—with altered hormone output, overactive pulse and high blood pressure—because a totally normal system, a system in harmony with itself, is not, by and large, governed by neurotic motivations. The pressure of the mother is not just a psychological metaphor; it is a biological reality.

"Accidental" pregnancy presents the same problem in reverse: the motivation toward *not* getting pregnant becomes the reaction to the unwanted pregnancy. We accidentally create a new human being and then feel nothing but resentment toward it. Accidental babies are usually regarded as intrusions from the moment the pregnancy is discovered. Can a baby really feel worthless in the womb? Yes and no. A baby can feel worthless without knowing worthlessness as a concept. If the tiny, three-week-old embryo can respond to neutral (as opposed to threatening) changes in light and sound in the outer environment, as we now know it does, surely it responds to threatening emotional fluctuations in its inner environment—an environment that no less surrounds and composes it.

What goes on during those nine months of gestation often foretells the quality of relationship the mother and child will have later on. Being ignored or resented in the womb is communicated through an adverse biochemical environment. This usually is compounded later on by more inattention and resentment during childhood; the Primal force then is shaped into fully elaborated feelings of rejection, humiliation and worthlessness. The labels for the hurt are attached much later in life and are finally not really important. It is the hurt itself that counts. Pain is the same no matter what one calls it. It is processed in the same way; nearly all pains (and Pains) are processed in the same biologic manner with the same physiologic mechanisms. Indeed, as our research has shown, no matter what the label, no matter what the name of the Pain, as early Pains are experienced there are characteristic biologic and biochemical changes that occur whether one is feeling worthless or rejected or criticized. The fetus indeed feels Pain, and on some inchoate cellular level it reacts to not being wanted.

A moving illustration of all this comes to mind. In a book called *Dibs: In Search of Self,** Virginia M. Axline recounts her therapeutic work with a child named Dibs who had been diagnosed variously as autistic, schizophrenic and mentally retarded. No one really knew what was wrong with him, only that his behavior was severely disturbed. The story of Dibs is one clear, resounding and published answer to our question of whether a baby can suffer in the womb. I'm sure there are countless similar stories that children could tell if they had the words.

At the point when Axline began her work with Dibs at six years of age, he had been in a private school for almost two years. His behavior was erratic at best and uncontrollable at worst. He spoke almost not at all, sat mute and unmoving at times and exploded into wild temper tantrums at other times. Axline writes:

> His behavior was so uneven. At one time, he seemed to be extremely retarded mentally. Another time he would quickly and quietly do something that indicated he might even have superior intelligence. If he thought anyone was watching him, he quickly withdrew into his shell. Most of the time he crawled around the edge of the room, lurking under tables, rocking back and forth, chewing on the side of his hand, sucking his thumb, lying prone and rigid on the floor when any of the teachers or children tried to involve him in some activity. (p. 15)

No clear diagnosis had ever been made, but both parents believed firmly that Dibs was mentally retarded; this, despite the fact that he would sit absorbed for hours poring over books—as long as no one was present. Axline narrates:

*Ballantine Books, New York, 1964. Copyright © 1964 by Houghton Mifflin Company. Reprinted by permission.

[The teachers] offered him books, toys, puzzles, all kinds of materials that might interest him. He would never take anything directly from anyone. If the object was placed on a table or on the floor near him, later he would pick it up and examine it carefully. He never failed to accept a book. He pored for hours over the printed pages "as though he could read," as Hedda [a teacher] so often said.

Sometimes a teacher would sit near him and read a story or talk about something while Dibs lay face down on the floor, never moving away—but never looking up or showing any overt interest. Miss Jane [another teacher] had often spent time with Dibs in this way. She talked about many things as she held the materials in her hand, demonstrating what she was explaining. . . . She talked about anything she hoped might spark an interest. She said she often felt like a fool—as though she were sitting there talking to herself, but something about his prone position gave her the impression that he was listening. Besides, she often asked, what did she have to lose? (pp. 15–16)

The teachers, the psychologist and the pediatrician were all baffled by Dibs. In trying to evaluate him one day, the school pediatrician had thrown up his hands in despair, saying: "He's a strange one. Who knows? Mentally retarded? Psychotic? Brain-damaged? Who can get close enough to find out what makes him tick?"

Dibs's mother had told Axline from the start that neither she nor her husband would have anything to do with their child's therapy. Axline soon recognized that the mother was not speaking out of harshness or disinterest, but out of her own terror, turmoil and personal restraints. Axline agreed, fearing that any pressure at all would provoke them to terminate Dibs's therapy. After several months of working with Dibs, Axline received an unexpected request from the mother for an interview. Following are excerpts from that interview in which she reveals for the first time what her true feelings were for the child that she conceived. This interview turned out to be the only time the mother would be able to reveal such personal and painful information:

I am so worried about Dibs. . . . Lately, he seems to be so unhappy. He stands around, looking at me, always so silent. He comes out of his room more often now. But he just stands around on the edge of things, like a haunting shadow. And whenever I speak to him, he runs away. Only to return and regard me with such tragic sorrow in his eyes. . . . I feel very uncomfortable when he does that. It is as though he is asking for something—something that I cannot give. He is a very difficult child to understand. I have tried. Really, I have tried. But I have failed. From the beginning, when he was an infant, I could not understand him. I had never really known any children before Dibs. I had no real experience as a woman with children or babies. I didn't have the slightest idea what they were like, really like as persons, that is. I knew all about them biologically, physically, and medically. But I could never understand Dibs. He was such a heartache—such a disappointment from the moment of his birth. We hadn't planned on having a child. His conception was an accident.

He upset all our plans. I had my professional career, too. My husband was proud of my accomplishments. My husband and I were very happy before Dibs was born. And when he was born he was so different. So big and ugly. Such a big, shapeless chunk of a thing! Not responsive at all. In fact, he rejected me from the moment he was born. He would stiffen and cry every time I picked him up!

. . . My pregnancy was very difficult. I was very ill most of the time. And my husband resented my pregnancy. He thought that I could have prevented it. Oh, I don't blame him. I resented it, too. We couldn't do any of the things we used to do together, couldn't go anyplace. I suppose I should say that we didn't, not couldn't. My husband stayed away more and more, buried himself in his work. He is a scientist, you know. A brilliant man! But remote.

. . . Before I became pregnant I was a surgeon. I loved my work. And I had shown promise of achieving success as a surgeon. I had perfected two very complicated heart operations. My husband was proud of me. All our friends were very brilliant, successful, interesting men and women. And then Dibs was born and spoiled all our plans and our life. I felt that I had failed miserably. I decided that I would give up my work. . . .

It soon became obvious that Dibs was not normal. It was bad enough to have a child, but to have a mentally retarded child was really more than we could bear. We were ashamed. We were humiliated. There had never been anything like this in either of our families. My husband, noted throughout the country for his brilliance. And my own record had always been outstanding. All our values had been heavily slanted in the direction of intelligence—fine, precise, noteworthy intellectual achievement!

And our families. We had both grown up in families where those qualities were valued above all others. And then Dibs! So peculiar. So remote. So untouchable. Not talking. Not playing. Slow to walk. Striking out at people like a little wild animal. We were so ashamed. We didn't want any of our friends to know about him. . . . We didn't want anyone to see him. We were so ashamed. And I had lost all confidence in myself. I could not go on with my work. I knew that I would not be able to perform an operation ever again!

. . . I took [Dibs] to a neurologist, one out on the West Coast. I used another name. We didn't want anyone to know what we suspected. But the neurologist couldn't find anything organically wrong with Dibs. Then, a little over a year ago we took him to a psychiatrist, again, not in this area. The psychiatrist insisted on seeing my husband and me for several interviews. This was the only time we ever revealed our true identity to any physician whom we consulted about Dibs. It was a shocking experience. . . .

The psychiatrist told us . . . that Dibs was not mentally defective or psychotic or brain-damaged, but the most rejected and emotionally deprived child he had ever seen. He said my husband and I were the ones who needed the help. . . . I tell you no one knows the terrible tragedy and agony it is to have a mentally handicapped child! (pp. 85–89)

This "mentally handicapped" child had a measured IQ of 168 at the age of six when he was finally able to be tested. And his reading comprehension exceeded what was normal for his age by several years. Dibs's IQ is not important in itself, but it does tell us something about the degree of pathology operating when a child who is born a genius appears to be, instead, severely mentally retarded.

Dibs appears to be a case of severe *in utero* damage. A child is not born reflexively rejecting its mother unless it already has a history of hurt, a hurt derived from maternal rejection transmitted somehow via her physiology. She did not provide a good internal environment for her child, and somehow, somewhere, the baby sensed it.

Dibs's mother's motivations—her reasons for having a child—were transmitted to an unborn human being with profound and lasting consequences. Her Pain distorted the bright spark of life within her, changing it into something unrecognizable from its true, given nature. The damaged child *is,* in a sense, corroboration of the relationship between parental attitude and the psychobiology of the offspring. Infants can be born with such astronomic Pain that they may never be able to integrate it.*

3
The Birth of Neurosis: The Actual Birth Experience

For many of us, birth is the closest we will come to death for the rest of our lives until we are truly at death's door. The possibilities for trauma at birth are multitudinous. Many of these traumas are not obvious because what

*See Appendix A for a detailed and technical discussion of current research on fetal stress and later developmental consequences.

may be exceptionally traumatic for the newborn passes as "normal" from an outsider's point of view.

Birth is an overwhelming experience even when it occurs naturally: the newborn must endure many rapid adjustments, including the powerful movement of uterine contractions, drawing the first breath, undergoing dramatic changes in circulation. Indeed, birth calls for more and greater adaptations than most of us will ever know again.

The difference between a pathological birth and a normal one can be slight; and no one can really tell which it is except the newborn, who will know this only later as an adult—if he's lucky enough to be able to relive the trauma itself. Then he will discover for the first time how it actually was. Meanwhile his body retains the truth of his experience, expressing its Pain in symptoms and neurotic behavior. But because the body cannot communicate directly, we must descend to the lower levels of consciousness where the birth memories are imprinted to get at the truth of that event.

Normal Birth

Let us first take a brief look at a normal birth—paradoxically, a fairly rare occurrence. Contractions in the normal uterus begin from the back and rhythmically move forward in sine wave fashion: a wave of muscle movement advances the baby forward in a smooth way much like a piston in a cylinder. The main pressure from the contractions is absorbed by the baby's feet and pelvis. The contractions are gradual in onset, which allows the baby to prepare emotionally for the journey to come and for the changes from soft to hard contractions.

When all goes well, the baby is propelled smoothly down the V-shaped chute with the head becoming "set" in the uterine canal at the top of the cylinder. As the contractions become stronger the uterine end dilates to make room for the emerging infant. At this point hormones trigger a release in the ligaments between the two halves of the pubic arch, allowing for the regulated descent. The baby's mouth is forward or against the wall of the birth canal. The amniotic fluid that surrounded the baby in the womb is now largely behind him so that it cannot be forced into his lungs. However, there is still enough fluid around him to smooth the way.

As the baby moves toward birth there is an automatic rotation of the head in order to avoid hitting the protruding sacral bone. If the baby's natural descent is somehow interrupted, the rotation—which enables the baby to be in the best position for birth—does not take place and has to be done by the doctor. In a normal birth, one ear should pass lightly over the sacral protuberance. (When it does not, the baby's mouth and nose are mashed against it. This protuberance is rough in texture, which patients reexperiencing the birth trauma describe as a scraping sensation much like being dragged over sandpaper.) Finally, the baby moves down and out into the world.

The sequence of birth is a natural one and should therefore flow. It is by no means a necessarily traumatic event. The massive propelling contractions are not inherently traumatic; they are a biologic necessity. They "stroke" the skin and help stimulate many systems of the body, particularly the urinary, gastrointestinal and respiratory ones. The final major contractions around the baby's thorax help squeeze fluid out and initiate breathing. The rhythm of the sequence or its lack becomes a memory like everything else, and fluid coordination and a sense of rhythm are not unrelated to this memory. What the baby learns in the birth process is how to be or not to be a unified body—a complete human being.

Drugged Birth

Now let us contrast the normal birth with the more usual case—namely, the drugged birth in which the mother is administered an anesthesia of some sort to ease labor pains. As I have already noted, the drug passes through the placental barrier, providing a dose several hundred times too powerful for the baby so that neither the mother nor the baby can react normally to facilitate the birth process.

After administration of drugs, the mother's uterine contractions grow fewer and weaker. Worse, drugs block important neural messages so that the sequence of contractions from back to front is also altered. This means that the baby is less apt to be propelled forward in a smooth way. Most often, it is squeezed and mashed by the out-of-synch contractions—a bit like going through a compacting machine. The uterus therefore acts like a contracting chamber; its movements are strong enough to crush, but not rhythmical or forceful enough to smoothly propel the baby down and out.

Next, the baby's head cannot properly align itself at the top of the canal. This means that the amniotic fluid, which the contractions push forward forcefully, is forced into the baby's mouth, lungs, trachea and stomach. In other words, the baby is being both crushed and asphyxiated; he is, in essence, drowning. Because the baby too is drugged, his respiratory system is weakened (drugs interfere severely with respiration), and he does not have the muscle strength to move to where it hurts less—namely, the proper position for birth.

If the baby were not so heavily drugged it could act instinctively to aid in its own birth. It could flex its muscles so as to push out; it could assume a torpedo-like, well tucked-in position for maximum propulsion; and it could make its body a single unit—chest and belly one entity. With drugs, the body is in a "loose" and fragmented position so that, for instance, the hands and lower arms can be trapped and crushed while the torso moves forward—all because proper coordination is interfered with.

When the drugged newborn is finally at the point of emerging, it often requires external pulling by the doctor to complete what should have been a natural birth sequence. The pulling is often too strong and done from an improper angle—since only the mother's body knows the right one. If the pulling is too fast it may not match the rhythm of the contractions. The baby is thrust against the mother's pelvis; it cannot properly rotate on its own and is scraped along the sacral bone. The baby's head, when finally released and out of the canal, no longer has the cooperation of its feet to push it out and so it may be flopping or even "whiplashed." Often, the baby has to be dragged out by harsh metal forceps. Finally, while the baby is trapped and getting nowhere in its drugged state, it is also rapidly running out of oxygen and its blood system is changing in an attempt to adapt. This is why the baby's face is fully—and unnecessarily—red at birth.

This is a most perilous journey. But the peril may continue even after the baby is out of the canal. How is he received? With brusque handling, cold forceps and metal table, rough towels? Are the lights blinding? Is the baby put into the mother's arms or on her belly? Or isolated without human contact during the critical first minutes and hours? Is the umbilical cord cut too soon so that all of the oxygenated blood does not reach him, thus again making him anoxic? Is he held low so that all fluids will drain out of him? Or is the busy doctor content to roughly aspirate the infant so as to get on with things as efficiently as possible?

These first minutes of life outside the womb are critical, and every event at this time will leave an enduring mark—for better or for worse. We see repeatedly in the words of our patients how each of these minutes forms part of the deep unconscious and becomes the basis for neurotic behavior later on.

The Cesarean Birth

It might seem that birth by Cesarean section would be the easiest and least traumatic way to get born, since the infant doesn't have to hazard the rigors of a long labor or a constricting birth canal but is simply lifted out and into the world. Unfortunately, we have found that traumas to the newborn delivered by C-section are different from—but no less traumatic than—the traumas that occur in a difficult vaginal delivery.

C-sections are performed under two general conditions: either when the mother's contractions are already underway—the mother is in labor—or when the mother is not in labor but is "scheduled" to deliver. Of the two conditions, it is better for the baby if labor has begun before he is delivered. Why? When the contractions are underway the baby is in a readiness state; he is being mobilized in natural, biological ways for the upcoming event of his birth. The period of labor produces vital sign and hormonal changes that gear the baby's system physiologically for birth. He is at least being allowed a portion of his "due process."

When the contractions are not underway—when the baby is scheduled for a certain delivery date either for the convenience of the doctor or the mother—the baby misses out on the entire contraction process. We now know that contractions initiate an important stage of development for the newborn, stimulating the baby's peripheral nerve system which then conducts impulses to the brain, ultimately affecting all key systems. Without that process there may be inadequate activation of the nervous system, and this in turn may affect the child's later development. As mentioned earlier, there are *critical times* in the development of the brain when it must have certain kinds of stimulation in order for it to grow properly. *Critical times* is underscored because the kind of massive stimulation and compression provided by uterine contractions is necessary then and only then; any later kind of stimulation and compression cannot make up for that developmental lack.

Another problem specific to Cesarean birth is that of blood supply. It is most difficult to perform a C-section without lifting the baby out above his blood supply. In a vaginal birth, the umbilical cord is in a lateral position in relation to the baby, but in a C-section the cord is perpendicular to the baby while it is being lifted up and out. It is almost inevitable that some of the blood travels back to the placenta. At that point the baby should be lowered immediately so that blood continues to flow toward him, but even a few seconds of the backward blood flow means that the baby is being asphyxiated—a sensation not unlike what any of us might experience when our air supply is cut off.

There is another subtle trauma involved in the Cesarean. Amniotic fluid has "surface active characteristics" which can make it foam when the baby starts to breathe. Though it may not be obvious that the baby is choking, its lungs may indeed be full of foam. This usually doesn't happen in regular births because the mother's contractions during labor have a kind of massaging motion which drives the fluid out of the baby's lungs. In the C-section, however, the baby's stuffed trachea must be opened mechanically by the doctor. If this doesn't happen immediately he may begin to smother from lack of oxygen, and turn blue.

After enduring all these traumas, the baby is brought out of the womb— but even if he is handled with great sensitivity, he is still almost always separated from his mother immediately, for she has just had major surgery and must herself recover. And to make things easier for that recovery, painkillers are usually administered to her—another source of trauma for the newborn.

There are many reasons for performing a C-section, and those reasons enter into the way the trauma is imprinted. If it is recognized ahead of time that the mother's pelvis is too small for a vaginal delivery, that is one kind of experience: the baby never had a chance to make it out the right (natural) way, he began life "wrong." If the mother has a large tumor blocking the passage that is discovered at the last minute, another kind of Cesarean experience is produced: the baby may have been literally "knocking his head against the wall" from the first moments of life. Breech presentation is yet another. Here, the baby cannot get into the proper position for birth—he presents either fanny-first or legs-first—and both his and his mother's life are endangered. This Cesarean baby comes into the world completely disoriented, literally not knowing up from down. His first contact with the world was backwards, and as we shall see in later chapters, he may feel "backward" the rest of his life. Thus, even within the same birth trauma—in this case, Cesarean—the many possible variations will imprint very different kinds of responses in the individual baby.

We know for certain about the harm of Cesarean delivery by observing the Primals of patients who were born in that manner. These birth Primals lack the fluid rhythm of normal birth contractions. Movements are more random and often more violent. It is as though patients are trying to make up for some developmental deficit by wild movements and thrashings— trying to feel the biologic deprivation which occurred when they were robbed of the compression of normal birth. Indeed, they never seem to have gotten their initial "rhythm," since they were deprived of the initial event which would have primed their bodies properly. The deprivation of this necessary developmental experience is just as catastrophic as over- loading the newborn with too many adverse sensory stimuli. Thus, both the Cesarean birth and the unnatural vaginal birth contribute to neurosis in their own way.

Premature and Late Births

The premature birth is fraught with trauma from every side. Physically, the baby isn't ready to leave the womb and so the early birth usually means serious physical complications—if not a moment-to-moment fight for life. There are any number of studies indicating the harmful effects of a premature birth: everything from brain damage and mental retardation to physical developmental lags, to a greater susceptibility to disease in general. But some of the harmful effects may be due less to the prematur- ity and more to the consequences of the treatment the baby receives in the name of saving its life.

It is perhaps forgotten that the premature baby is, developmentally, still a fetus. As such, it requires all the stimulation that would have been provided in the womb. Most often, however, the reverse occurs. Instead of receiving the increased physical closeness it needs, the premature infant is usually deprived of all closeness in several ways: by leaving its amniotic world early, the fetus misses a period of increased touch within the uterus. Then, after birth, the infant is placed in an isolette and often hooked up to a frightening maze of instruments. When the baby is finally taken home, the family may adopt a kind of "isolette" psychology, being afraid to touch and handle the baby for fear of hurting it.

Dr. Ruth Rice, a Texas psychologist, has been developing methods to counteract the emotional deprivation that occurs after birth for the premature infant. The methods are simple: gently touching and stroking the baby frequently to provide the needed stimulation. To test her methods, Rice applied the touching techniques to a group of premature infants after they had returned from the hospital and compared the results with a control group—a group who received no increased touching. The touching and stroking was done by the infants' mothers. Not surprisingly, the stimulated infants showed significant gains in development. It was also noted that the relationship between mother and infant benefited from the stimulation.*

To explain the method's success, Rice cites studies which have established that tactile stimulation of animals aids maturation of the entire system. A particularly interesting study cited by Rice (Bovard and Newton, 1953) concluded that the early handling of an organism allowed for a normal level of hypothalamic activity that could be permanent, with resulting normal growth hormone production. This finding supports a Primal hypothesis (made over a decade ago) that early deprivation permanently affects hypothalamic activity and distorts hormone production—and that reexperiencing the trauma in Primals can correct the distortion.

Common sense dictates that if the preemie is to have any chance at all for normal growth, it must have a greater than usual amount of tactile stimulation from the beginning. Research conducted by Freedman et al. is instructive here.† Two groups of twins with low birth weights (low enough to be considered premature) were studied. One group was rocked regularly for a period of time and the other group was not. The rocked group gained weight faster than the unrocked group.

The negative physical effects of a premature birth may be visible for years. The preemie's neurologic development is usually much slower than the normal child's, and this may be manifested in developmental lags in

---

*Findings reported in *Developmental Psychology* 13 (1977), 69–76, and the method described in the *APA Monitor,* November 1975.

†Freedman, D. G., Boverman, H., and Freedman, N., "Effects of Kinesthetic Stimulation on Weight Gain and Smiling in Premature Infants," *American Orthopsychiatry Association Presentation,* April 1960, San Francisco.

coordination, balance and athletic abilities. The body seems to take years and years to make up for the early lack. What is not so visible are the emotional "lacks" that have also occurred but gone unrecognized. Now, through the birth Primals of patients born prematurely, we have some idea of what those lacks are; we have some idea of how the premature birth trauma *feels* to the newborn—of the particular Pains imprinted, and of the particular ways that Pain is elaborated in later development.

Being born late is also physically and emotionally traumatic. Because the baby's head and pelvis are larger than normal due to the extra weeks of life in the womb, birth becomes more difficult and traumatic—if not fatal. Indeed, the mortality rate of late-term infants is twice as high as for normal-term infants.

Why is a baby born late? A mother who does not feel ready to be a mother, who is tight and constricted and tends to hold things in, may unconsciously hold her baby in too long. It may be that the combination of hormone secretions necessary for the birth process is delayed due to the mother's own neurosis.

Birth Traumas and Injuries

Fetal deaths associated with childbirth are the fifth major cause of mortality in the United States. And for those infants who live, it is now estimated that one out of sixteen has a recognizable mental or physical defect at birth. It is also estimated that between twenty and sixty thousand birth injuries take place each year which are preventable.

There are, as we have seen, many common sources of injury to the infant during and after birth. During birth, anesthetics and painkillers administered to the mother probably constitute the most common and serious threat to the infant, both in Cesarean and vaginal deliveries. Head rotation via forceps is a common injury during vaginal birth; being lifted above the blood supply is a common injury in a C-section. After either type of delivery, the newborn is usually confronted by sensory flooding, separation from the mother and unfavorable delivery room conditions.

Anoxia (Birth-induced)

There are many causes of prenatal anoxia (oxygen deprivation; see Appendix A). Anoxia during the actual birth process is known to be a leading cause of infant deaths, and is probably the most common cause of infant birth defects. Oxygen shortage during labor or birth produces a state of asphyxiation which can cause mental retardation, epilepsy, cerebral palsy and death. The major causes of anoxia during birth are "Any condition which interferes with the proper exchange of oxygen and carbon dioxide between the mother and the unborn baby. Prolonged or obstructed labor. A traumatic delivery. Too high a dosage of drugs to relieve pain in labor or too deep anesthesia."*

Until recently it was commonly believed that most birth defects were hereditary in origin. That is not the case: "It is now known that much feeblemindedness is directly due to a lack of oxygen during the actual birth process; *anoxia can destroy brain cells in a perfectly normal child during the final moments of birth.*"† [Italics added]

One way this can happen is by strangulation. When external pulling is required by the doctor to help get a drugged infant out, a loop of the umbilical cord can get wrapped around the baby's shoulder or head so that it is pressed against the side of the canal. Strangulation and/or immobilization is the result. The baby is in the position of being in a tourniquet, unable to get rid of its venous blood and also not able to get its arterial blood. Because it is not getting oxygen it is being asphyxiated. The result of this is a desperate attempt by the baby's system to get oxygen to its brain. To accomplish this there is an equally massive vasodilation to permit the greatest amount of blood flow possible. (We shall see later how this particular reaction state forms a prototype for migraines in adult life.)

Oxygen deprivation can be severe enough to cause the baby's heart to skip beats or to stop beating altogether, resulting in obvious birth defects such as mental retardation or cerebral palsy. But more often there are a number of more subtle consequences that go undetected. In later life, however, there may be certain "soft" neurologic signs that are only observable when the person is fatigued: a certain droop on one side of the mouth or eye; a particular but subtle clumsiness; a tendency to stutter or stammer; a tendency to awkwardness and irritability; a developmental lopsidedness of one side of the face or body.

There are also subtle emotional effects tied to oxygen deprivation that will not become manifest until much later—and even then, the causal relationship between the anoxia at birth and the emotionality in adulthood will not be recognized. The repressive mechanisms in the brain (the limbic system) are impaired by the oxygen deprivation; as a child and adult the person is then less able to repress. In stress situations, he may be prone to hysterical reactions wherein he is deluged by early Pain that can no longer be gated. He feels constantly fragmented and overwhelmed—and for good (i.e., neurological) reasons.

These effects of mild anoxia are not brain damage so much as cell damage—damage confined to relatively few, but nonetheless important, cells. Asphyxiation during birth is really a kind of stroke—infant stroke—but because the baby's (apparent) recovery is so immediate, the reality of the harmful effects goes undetected and untreated.

Natural Childbirth and the Family, edited by Helen Wessel (New York: Harper and Row), rev. ed., 1974, p. 203.
†Ibid., p. 203.

Drugs, Anesthetics and Painkillers

It has been assumed that drugs, anesthetics and painkillers were necessary to ease the pain of giving birth. However, recent research findings have established the presence of beta-endorphin, a morphine-like chemical produced by the human system, in the placenta. This means that the mother's body manufactures its own antidote to the pain of childbirth which may, if allowed, reduce her discomfort in the most non-intrusive manner possible. Administering drugs to the mother during childbirth interferes with this natural process and may even result in negative side effects. For instance, the nerve-blocking anesthetics once thought to be harmless for the baby have been found by a UCLA research team to cause damage. Dr. Robert O. Bauer, head of the research team, reported to the California Medical Association Scientific Session in March 1970* that the anesthetics do enter the baby's system in significant levels within only a few minutes of being administered to the mother. He said that such levels might have a harmful effect on the baby's brain if the baby were being stressed in other ways at the same time during birth. Dr. Bauer stressed that it is a myth that certain anesthetics used regionally (in a spinal block) do not pass into the baby. He also said that most doctors fail to realize that local anesthetics are distributed to unanesthetized parts of the body as well.

What are longer-term consequences of drugging for the baby? A study reported in 1978† found that the babies of mothers who received an anesthetic drug called pethidine during delivery were affected by the drug for at least the following year: "For the full year that they [the babies] were followed they were sleepy much of the time, they didn't suck very well, and the mothers spent much more time trying to keep them awake." And Dr. Abraham Lu,‡ Clinical Professor of Pathology at the USC School of Medicine, has estimated that between 50 and 70 percent of all stillbirths and miscarriages are caused by anoxic lesions in the brain, many of which may be drug-related. Along the same lines, Harris Sherline, president of the United Cerebral Palsy Association, warned that the increasing practice of unnaturally delaying birth through drugs is resulting in more cases of brain damage and cerebral palsy in term infants.

Head Rotation and Use of Forceps

It is estimated that physicians use forceps about 90 percent of the time, in normal as well as abnormal deliveries. It is believed, apparently, that the

*Reported in the *Los Angeles Times,* March 11, 1970.

†Reported in *New Scientist,* September 21, 1978, pp. 847–849. (A study by Martin Richards, Medical Psychology Unit, University of Cambridge.)

‡Reported in the *Los Angeles Times,* May 27, 1970.

forceps are both necessary and helpful. In extremely difficult births, the use of forceps may be unavoidable, but is this really the case in most births? Certainly not. In an address at the Cerebral Palsy Institute Proceedings, Dr. Winthrop Phelps reported that the use of forceps, as well as drugs, was implicated as a possible cause of cerebral palsy: ". . . We then must admit that there are birth injuries due to forceps which cause pressure and a fractured skull and subdural hemorrhage. We know also that in this situation you would have cortical damage, and in all probability, spasticity."*

Even when severe damage does not occur there may still be lifelong consequences. When the head is harshly rotated, or is allowed to drop precipitously just as birth is finishing, the birth imprint will be focused in the neck. I believe this is part of the reason that neck tension is a practically universal ailment in adults—because improper head rotation is a practically universal delivery procedure in Western medicine.

Delivery Room Conditions and Sensory Flooding

After going through hours of traumatic birthing experiences, the newborn is often confronted by a vast array of sensory input which usually results in a kind of sensory flooding. The baby is inundated by bright lights and harsh sounds that are experienced as intrusive and overwhelming. Because the newborn's inhibitory centers are not developed as they are in the adult, the baby cannot shut out and adapt to things in the external environment the way an adult can.

The temperature of the delivery room can also be a source of assault for the newborn. The baby removed from a 100-degree womb to an air-conditioned delivery room of 68 degrees is not just made uncomfortable by the abrupt change; more often than not it is in shock. It would be physically shocking for an adult to make such a transition, but the adult can at least recover from the shock. The infant cannot. Indeed, the baby's thermal "setpoint" may be permanently altered by the early shock so that later in life the slightest draft produces an overreaction, a chill, even a cold.

Separation Anxiety

If ever there was a key trauma with lifelong consequences it is the separation of the newborn from its mother right after birth. As if the long birth struggle had not been enough; as if the harsh delivery room conditions had not been enough—the infant is then actually taken away from the one person who has been its entire source of comfort, its entire

---

*Reported in *Natural Childbirth and the Family*, op. cit., p. 204.

world. No wonder so many neurotics cannot be alone: their initial entry into this world was marked by that catastrophic aloneness just after birth when they were placed in a container, alone and uncomforted. If anything, the newborn needs to be held, comforted and touched more now than any other time in his life.

One patient told me that she could be alone if she knew she had a date or appointment later on; otherwise it was unbearable. Her birth Primal "informed" her that she was left alone just after birth (her mother was ill), and she never knew when her alienation and aloneness would end. Now, she *must* know or she suffers that same early panic.

The importance of early mother-child contact or bonding used to be just a theory—but we now have both animal and human research that is establishing the theory as observed and measured fact. In studies with monkeys it was found that early physical contact between mother and baby lowered the levels of the stress hormone cortisol.* What this means is that the baby monkeys without sufficient physical contact were under stress. It is highly likely that the same is true for human babies.

Research on human babies is showing that eye contact immediately after birth is extremely important for mother-child bonding. It was formerly believed that the newborn could not open its eyes and really "see" for days. We now know that is not true. Babies born naturally and nontraumatically are quite able to open their eyes and look directly at their mothers. More, the bond imprinted via the direct eye contact enhances the bonding of physical touch and closeness and adds another, enriching dimension to it.

Breastfeeding is another important bonding experience. There is simply no feeling of comfort and closeness for the infant lying alone in its sterile hospital basinette. Even when the baby is brought to its mother several times a day for feeding, there is still the prototypic experience of being taken away from the mother after partaking of her comfort and nurturance for but a few minutes. (We shall see in a later chapter how this experience of Primal separation is elaborated in many ways in adult emotional life.)

Rough handling is a trauma frequently relived by our patients, and it seems to go hand in hand with the separation terror. By rough handling I don't necessarily mean cruel or harmful treatment, as we might define it. For what an adult observer might view as "efficient" handling or "competent" handling or "detached, professional" handling on the part of the hospital staff, the newborn might experience as cold, unfeeling, and hurtful. The newborn is totally at the mercy of its surroundings. It needs to be loved, not objectively and not efficiently—but in the warmest and gentlest of ways. One patient wrote:

*Reported by H. E. Marano in *Medical World News*.

I had lost the fight at birth and felt totally defeated. Life was against me. I felt I had no control over what was happening to me. During this Primal I felt like I was being jostled about by different people. I was very scared. I'm not sure what the feelings were all about, since there were no scenes or images in my mind. But I would hazard to guess it was the doctor and nurses handling me after birth.

I felt so alone. I cried for help. Where is someone to see how much I hurt? I even felt angry that they could be so stupid to see my crying and screaming and just let me go on doing it. I just wanted someone to hold me gently and let me calm down. Then I felt I didn't want anyone to touch me if it was going to be so rough.

Leboyer Births: A Solution

There is quite a contrast between the traumatized birth and the non-traumatized one. The baby who has had a natural birth is relaxed and undemanding. The parents do not feel harassed; they can relate to their infant more freely. The baby gets more from the very start, all because he was born in less Pain. Paradoxically, the infant in greater Pain usually gets less attention, even though he needs it far more. So winners go on winning and losers go on losing. It is completely unfair and it begins with the beginning of life when the new little person has nothing to say about it. Indeed, unborn children and newborn infants form a silent, and until recently, unrepresented minority. The work of the French obstetrician Frederick Leboyer is changing this. After observing thousands of births, Leboyer began recognizing the mechanical, unfeeling procedures that typified hospital births. He realized, independent of the Primal Therapy movement, that those procedures were painful and traumatic for the newborn. It is interesting that while Leboyer's discoveries stemmed from the observation of birth itself, ours stemmed from the observation of many birth Primals—yet our conclusions were identical.

Leboyer recognized, as did we, that birth need not be difficult or traumatic if it is handled naturally and with care. But final confirmation of his viewpoint came when he viewed our films of patients reliving the traumas he had perceived. Leboyer changed his delivery practices, and to verify the success of those changes one need only observe a Leboyer baby "in action."

Leboyer knew that drugs penetrate the placental barrier and enter the fetal system, so he discarded the use of drugs for delivering mothers. He understood that this giant overdose suffocates the respiratory system of the baby in such a way that it then needs to be spanked into breathing. (Patient after patient has felt the drugs enter his or her system during birth Primals. They go limp, smell something like ether or other drugs, feel a total numbing sensation, become paralyzed and black out.)

Leboyer does not cut the cord until minutes after the birth, thus allowing the baby to continue receiving the oxygenated blood. This makes the first breath of that new substance called air a bit less painful. It helps the newborn get used to breathing slowly. (We have had patients who have felt a burning sensation around the umbilicus during Primals, yet had no idea what the sensation meant. There evidently is a trauma about the premature cutting of the umbilical cord. This premature action affects the amount of oxygen in the system and the infant patient feels that cut-off before being ready to breathe independently. That premature cutting of the umbilical cord forces the baby into a premature state, which makes the first experience of breathing traumatic instead of smooth.)

Next, Leboyer realized that the first screams of the infant in this world were not natural accompaniments to the beginnings of life, but were the screams of terror from overwhelming trauma. So, instead of holding the baby upside down and spanking it—truly a barbaric practice—the baby is immediately placed in a warm bath and then placed on the mother's belly. All of the experiences are soothing.

Leboyer births are carried out in very soft lighting so that the neonate is no longer blinded at birth. After all, there are no lights in the womb. Leboyer himself plays the flute softly while the baby is placed against the warm body of its mother. The baby is massaged and caressed; in all respects his birth has been a joy. Characteristically he opens his eyes—sees—and smiles, something not thought possible by conventional doctors.

There have been no forceps or harsh rotations, no drugs, no noise, no artificial intrusions, no separations from the mother. The baby is allowed a continuity from womb to belly. All is love, warmth, caress and touch. It is difficult to go wrong with this approach—it seems so obvious and logical—and yet to this day Leboyer is still regarded as highly controversial. Indeed there has been great resistance to using Leboyer birth processes in hospitals—resistance, that is, by the medical staff. (In some areas, pregnant women and their husbands have finally pressured hospitals into changing to the Leboyer method.) It seems doctors would rather trust statistical results on births than their own instincts and logic.

I have seen many Leboyer babies. They seem different from other babies. They are bright and alert from the age of just a few months. They are curious and alive. They laugh out loud. They rarely cry; they do not whine. Their eyes shine and they are unafraid. They will reach out to strangers. There is an intelligence in their faces and they have a great calm about them. They are healthy looking. They sleep less than other babies and I believe they sleep better.

And indeed research proves Leboyer babies to be healthier in many respects. In a study conducted by Daniele Rapoport of the French National Center for Scientific Research it was found that Leboyer babies developed faster and better physically than other babies. They began walking sooner; they had less difficulty in toilet training and self-feeding. They did not suffer from colic as did other babies. And, a curious finding: most were ambidextrous.* In general I believe this has something to do with being better balanced. To be well-balanced may indeed have a literal (physiological) meaning. A UCLA study of our advanced patients did in fact find a change in the relationships of the right and left sides of the brain toward greater harmony.

The researchers have had only a few years of study and observation behind them, so we do not know what the long-range effects will be, though it seems likely that the enhanced development would continue. What remains to be seen is the degree to which the Leboyer birth will fortify the child to deal with later trauma and difficulty.

The parents of the Leboyer babies also underwent changes. They felt the birth process was a profoundly moving experience. The fathers had taken an exceptional interest in the birth. The investigators believe that the process strengthens the parent-child bond.

Mothers who have had one child in the conventional way and another by the Leboyer method report a great difference between the two children. My observations of babies who had a Leboyer birth and those who had conventional births compel me to agree wholeheartedly. It seems that babies can take any later trauma twice as well if they have had a good birth. The fragility of the nervous system at birth and the high valence (charge value) of imprinted first-line Pain tend to fracture the system.

What I have said about Leboyer births also applies in some degree to those who have had birth Primals. They have made a more decent birth for themselves in the sense that they have resolved or released some of the harm done by their original birth. After many months of resolving first-line (infant) Pains, these adults are healthier, calmer and feel better.

Obviously, undoing birth trauma is not as good as not having experienced that trauma in the first place. Birth Primals are not the same as having had a sensitive birth. But the changes we see in patients who relive their Pain is another way we know about the great harm done by early traumas. The dramatic changes in personality that occur after birth Primals attest to the reality of a Pain imprinted into the system in its first moments of life.†

*This fact can be interpreted in several ways. It may be simply that the brain is in better harmony and that's how a truly harmonious brain functions—both sides equal. There is evidence of ambidexterity in ancient tribes where it is presumed birth processes were completely natural. There are more tracts leading upward to the left side of the brain (which controls the right hand); so that a birth trauma can overload the ascending tracts, particularly to the left brain which has more tracts to absorb the Primal blast. This may skew handedness toward the right hand.

†See Chapter 11 for a detailed and technical discussion of the neurological mechanisms that mediate the process of imprinting.

4

A Lifetime Script: Prototypic Pain and Its Response

The imprinting of early Pains into the infant's developing nervous system accomplishes two things: first, it sets up a lifelong pool of residual tension, and second, it directs and shapes behavior in particular ways. This means that early Pain shapes both our physiology and our personality. As we have seen, not only are the Pains stamped in, but the entire repertoire of responses and defenses against the Pains are also stamped in.

The early Pains are imprinted as prototypes and the original responses to the Pains are imprinted as prototypic responses. A Pain engraved in the developing brain has caused a groove (or model or template) so that the reaction to that Pain remains as an engraved tendency or pattern.

Thus, when a current situation triggers the early (prototypic) Pains, the original (prototypic) responses are triggered as well. That is why a minor stress in adult life can produce a major migraine headache, asthma attack or a violent outburst. We don't see the prototypic Pain that is triggered by the stress, but we do see the response. The violent outburst or the asthma attack is not the Pain itself, but the reaction to it. The Pain is implicit in the reaction.

The higher the valence of that prototypic Pain, the less strong the external stimuli need to be to set it off. Thus the smallest obstacle in one's life, as for example having to stand in line at a checkout counter any length of time, will make someone who has been prototypically impatient to get out so impatient as to bully his way through the line or demand an extra cashier.

The Trauma Train

The concept of the "trauma train" is worth examining because it helps us understand prototypic responses.

The "trauma train" is a metaphor for the chain of events extending throughout the birth period which ends in a certain way and which causes characteristic reactions. The way in which the birth ends is engraved as a prototypic Pain and the infant's reaction to the Pain becomes the prototypic response.

Thus, if the womb were terribly constricting at birth, and the fetus had to fight to come into life, then the characteristic life-saving response (the end of the trauma train) would be fight, aggressiveness, anger and drive. If the fetus were heavily drugged at birth and could do absolutely nothing except try to breathe, the life-saving response might be resignation, passivity and sensations (feelings)—not yet conceptualized—of futility and despair. The continuity of reactions persists because of the memory trace.

The chain of events surrounding the birth trauma is important in determining the kind of personality one will have later on, but the end of the train—that is, how the birth sequence ends—seems to be of paramount importance, for it is that ending that is fixed permanently. It makes a very big difference if we get off the train in the "fight" mode or in the "passive death" mode, for the brain seems particularly vulnerable at this time to print such information as a kind of permanent program for the rest of our lives. (There seems to be a group of neurons capable of only one-time learning; this group of neurons responds to the conditions at the end of the train and then maintains that response in us.)

Context and the Prototype

The very response which was life-saving for the infant at birth continues on out of context and becomes the basis for neurosis later on. But it is important to understand that the prototypic response is itself not neurotic; it *becomes* neurotic because it persists in situations where it is no longer appropriate.

For example, bronchial constriction was appropriate to save one's life from all of the fluid during the birth process. But bronchial constriction and asthma as a response to an argument between one's parents later becomes life-endangering.

This is true of most prototypic responses: they turn into their opposites and become self-destructive later on simply because they are out of context. Being held back at birth because the doctor wasn't ready is a common practice. The surging forth, the being held back and the subsequent frustration and rage may well become prototypic thereafter. As an adult the person may plunge ahead into projects only to be held back by others who are fearful. Here the surge ahead and the being held back will reawaken unconsciously the birth sequence and the result will be inordinate rage and impatience. Or the aggressive, driving behavior that got one *out* of the birth canal may make one die prematurely from overwork, or make personal relationships extremely difficult. Similarly, the prototypic response of passivity as a life-saving tactic becomes something that can cripple adult life: it inhibits the urge to strive, to function, to succeed, to be motivated.

The prototypic trauma is imprinted physiologically and *will never change* no matter how much one wants it to, how much exhortation or encouragement one receives, or how much conventional psychotherapy one undergoes.

Actually we have many everyday examples of behavior that endure in the way prototypic behavior endures. Anyone who plays golf or tennis knows how important initial attempts are. Once one has learned to swing incorrectly it is very difficult to change. Original learning seems to take on a life of its own which resists any new learning. And the more significant that early learning is for survival, the more resistant it is to change. When that learning takes place in the first minutes of life, one can easily understand its persistence.

Neurosis and the Prototype

The concept of prototypic behavior helps to explain both the intensity and complexity of neurosis. The intensity of neurotic behavior stems from the original survival function of the prototypic response; and the apparent complexity of neurotic behavior—its many forms and manifestations—stems from the elaboration of those simple prototypic responses into very complicated ways of behaving. This happens because each new level of consciousness plays its part in finding "safe" ways to discharge the prototypic Pain.

The important thing to understand about prototypic behavior is that it is a memory of the *beginnings of neurosis*. All the later elaborations and manifestations can ultimately be traced back to those beginnings. That is why the resolution of neurosis must involve a return to the originating prototype, not a futile journey through the mirage of symptoms and distortions that manifest that prototype.

Resolving the prototype will automatically resolve the symptoms of neurosis, but it does not work in the reverse: "resolving" neurotic symptoms will never resolve the prototype nor will mechanical or voluntary changes in behavior change it. It will remain intact and the burden will fall to the different levels of consciousness to find yet newer ways to syphon off the energy from the imprinted Pain.

The Sympathetic and Parasympathetic Systems

The prototype of the birth trauma skews the whole system for a lifetime in two major directions: either toward an aggressive, mobilized tendency, or toward a passive, immobilized tendency. Each of these tendencies is controlled by a different aspect of the autonomic nervous system: the sympathetic or energy-expending system, and the parasympathetic or energy-conserving system. Both systems are modes of metabolic regulation and are governed by the hypothalamus.

The sympathetic system is the workhorse. It galvanizes, mobilizes, alarms and alerts, expends energy and increases the work of organ systems. It elevates temperature and other vital signs such as heart rate and blood pressure. It increases urine production, can produce bowel spasms and churn up the viscera. This system regulates peripheral blood flow so that under anxiety the hands and feet are cold, the face pale. It is this system that triggers secretion of the steroids, the stress hormones. It mediates nervous sweating and dry mouth, high-tension muscle states, taut face and jaw and a higher voice. It is the agency of impulsive behavior. It determines vigilance and pushes toward externalizing behavior rather than toward reflecting on events.

The parasympathetic system, as the energy conserver, is dominant in feeling, in deep sleep and full relaxation. It is responsible for the anabolic or repair functions and serves to lower the vital signs. It dilates certain blood vessels so that the skin is warm, the eyes and mouth are more moist, the muscles more relaxed, the voice lower, with a general slowing of movements. Parasympathetic responses are predominant during rest and during recovery periods following stress.

A healthy person maintains a proper balance between the two states, so that the cycles alternate regularly. However, this balance can be upset by early painful events and one mode or the other will predominate thereafter.

A Theory of Personality

The importance of the sympathetic-parasympathetic dominance is that it provides us with a biological basis for understanding personality development. At last we can leave abstraction and metaphor behind, and replace the vagaries of speculation with the precision of verifiable processes. We no longer need to talk about the "will to power" or the "will to meaning" or the "transcendent function" as theorized bases for personality. Instead, we can talk about the precise ways in which the brain and nervous system react to concrete events, and how those reactions become the physiological basis for the elaboration of personality.

Later childhood events can obviously have a great deal to do with one's personality, but in most cases it is the birth trauma that sets up the lifelong, prototypic dominance of either sympathetic or parasympathetic functioning. For the moment, let's concentrate on just the birth trauma.

When does the trauma end? Is the baby in the sympathetic or parasympathetic mode? Did the trauma end while the struggle was still going on, or when the baby's body began to fail and die? Does it end soon after it begins or after many hours of agony? How does it end—abruptly, or over a long period of time?

Also critical is the nature of the trauma. Too great a dose of anesthetic? Breech birth? Overlong, hard labor? Does the baby get off the trauma train almost dead from drugs and needing to be revived by ice water, drugs, hard slapping, etc.? Is he lifted out by Cesarean? Or is he born still fighting for his life? Has he struggled and failed, struggled and won, not struggled at all? Has he been close to death or for a moment actually been clinically dead? All of this will determine much of the baby's later personality.

How can this be? Because the sympathetic-parasympathetic systems are the substructure out of which ideas, attitudes, values, interest, emotional tone, sexual drive, body shape, ambition, drive and many other psychological characteristics are derived. The prototypic dominance determines the boundaries of our behavior and our personality. It determines what we select out of the environment and shapes our personality. It determines what we select out of the environment to react to, and in fact, drives us to continually act out our past in the present. This is because the dominance is an engraved reaction tendency, but since its cause—the birth trauma—is unconscious, we simply continue to project it and reproduce it.

We act out the sequence of our birth trauma exactly as it was laid down, beginning to end. For example, a patient who could never quite make it out of the birth canal always set up situations in which he never quite finishes anything properly. Another patient who was lifted out by Cesarean section will never let anyone else set the time for her arrival or departure. What each is doing is acting out a lifetime of social experiences based on the prototypic Pain and response patterns—he, not having finished his birth in a smooth and proper way; she, not having had any "say" about when she was born.

Now let's take a closer look at the personality profiles that emerge from the sympathetic versus parasympathetic birth dominance. We must bear in mind that most of us are neither pure sympaths nor pure parasympaths. We combine qualities of both, but tend toward one type or the other. Determining that tendency is more than mere classification for the sake of convenience: it implies that one is more likely to get one type of disease than another, and it tells us a good deal about how a person will defend himself under stress.

The Sympath

A long, hard labor is a common "sympath" birth. For a variety of reasons, the mother tends to be tight and cannot release her baby. She may not be ready to have a child and her system recognizes it, delaying the birth as long as possible. Meanwhile, the fetus is fighting to get out, fighting for its life. It has signaled its readiness to be born by the release of certain hormones. But a neurotic mother isn't communicating well with her baby, even on this unconscious level, and doesn't get the full message. The neurotic mother's system is in conflict; it is trying to release, yet holds back at the same time. The fetus is tortured. It must fight against insuperable odds for life. After many exhausting hours it finally makes it to the outside, only to be spanked into life and then separated from its mother.

What has the neonate learned from all of this? What are his prototypic behaviors? There are many possibilities. The infant who works for hours to get out of the canal is totally mobilized for survival such that this state of mobilization becomes permanent. He has learned to struggle against great odds. He has learned to fight to get what he needs. He has learned that aggressive responses are crucial; that one cannot hang back and expect to succeed.

This learning was not taught to him by anyone; and it is obviously not conceptualized in the newborn as I have conceptualized it here. But the baby *has* learned it from his experience—and that learning is in his body. He has become a "sympath." His sympathetic system has been stamped in as the prototypic, life-saving response. His physiology will tend to be "hyper": fast pulse, high body temperature, high to hyper energy level (hyperthyroidism) and quick reaction tendencies. The psychologic responses of being overly aggressive, impulsive and high-strung will then further elaborate the physiology.

The adult sympath is generally optimistic. He has learned to channel his aggression into more subtle, acceptable forms. He is certain the future will be good *if he tries hard enough* because it was originally. This factor may make him a visionary.

Because the pure sympath is the one who finally succeeded in his struggle, he is most apt to have the personality characteristics of someone who is persistent, ambitious, hard-working, success-oriented, energetic, with little or no tendency toward depression. Perhaps he becomes a hustling salesman. He will not recognize a "no" from a customer. He will not recognize obstacles—a prototypic behavior that saved his life against the greatest obstacle he ever faced. He will be annoying to others because he doesn't let up—just as he didn't let up during the birth struggle. He may gamble in business or at the crap table as a way of fighting against odds. And he will tend to gamble all the more when he knows the odds are against him. He sets up the prototypic situation over and over again so that he can have the same response and try to win. It is a totally unconscious process.

When we wake up in the morning we are still functioning on the lower levels of consciousness and therefore closer to our prototypic feelings. The sympath tends to wake up in a mobilized, ready-to-meet-the-world state: he bolts out of bed because he wakes up in the sympathetic mode just as he did at birth. All of his arousal hormones, including cortisol levels, are quick to increase.

This kind of person works well under pressure. He doesn't collapse from it as the parasympath might. Indeed, he needs the pressure. He creates it if it doesn't exist because keeping the pressure on is a stamped-in experience. For the sympath to be on the go is unconsciously life-saving. He had to force his way out at birth or death would have ensued. Every second was a matter of life and death. The system "remembers" this life-saving reaction and continues it no matter what the later circumstances.

Even mundane situations will evoke the "do-or-die" response. For instance, the sympath may wait until the waiter is at the table before he decides what he wants to order. He then works under pressure to make a choice. Or he waits until the last minute to get ready for a night out. Or he allows deadlines for work or study to creep up on him until he has hardly any time left. Then he mobilizes himself into action.

The tendency to work under pressure is prototypic. But the *form* it takes depends on later experience, as does the strength of the reaction. If as a child the sympath was forced to be prepared in advance, if he was not permitted to put things off until the last minute, then the procrastinating tendency will not be as apparent. But it will always be there. Once the trauma has set in, it alters the metabolism for life. Then one is forced to construct a world to match that metabolism. The sympath walks very fast because his internal motor is running. He talks rapidly for the same reason. Because he is continually syphoning off his energy it keeps him unaware of the Pain beneath it.

Relaxation is a threat to most sympaths. Real rest is beyond them. Since their heart rate and general metabolic rate are high—a permanent pulse of over 80 perhaps—a dialectic process is set in motion. The higher metabolism dictates a more outgoing personality and the more outgoing personality redictates a higher metabolic rate. One feeds the other, and together they synthesize and predetermine physiotype, a personality, a lifestyle—*and a lifetime*.

Following are reports by two patients who express several sympath "themes." In the first report we see a woman who has spent much of her life trying to move away from the constant pressure inside her by literally moving from place to place, and by excessive drinking:

Present-day feeling: "I have to get away"

When I was in Los Angeles I couldn't wait to get out. I was feeling very overwhelmed by the situation I was in—personally and professionally—so all I could think about was getting away on a trip. But when I finally got away on the trip, I kept having the same feeling that *I had to get out* of wherever I was—just as I had felt in Los Angeles.

Acting out an endless cycle

At first there would be a sense of relief when I arrived somewhere, because I had, in fact, acted out the feeling and gotten away. But after I had been there for a very short time the feeling would come up again, and all I could think about was *getting away*. The only relief I got yesterday was in the tourist office buying a ticket to leave, which meant I was moving on. I knew it would be only momentary relief, but that was better than nothing.

It has something to do with everyday routine where there is no movement, no change. Routine to me is a dead environment, and it makes me very anxious. I used to like scuba diving as a way of avoiding that feeling of stagnation: I could get into the fluid situation (the water) and move around and alter my consciousness. But no matter what I did, the pressure pushed at me all the time; the minute I stopped moving it would slop out and overwhelm me.

Rationalizing early feelings in the present

It seems like it doesn't matter what the situation is—whether it's with a boyfriend, a place, a job—I have to get out, leave, do something else. I thought I was "burnt out" on my job, but it was that old feeling coming up again that made me focus on the outside because I didn't know what it was on the inside that was coming up. I suppose if I had no focus on the present for what goes on inside of me I would probably explode. I need to do something with that feeling. If you don't know it for what it is, then you've got to rationalize it in the present.

"It was something inside me"

Until I came close to those feelings I never had any idea that my constant moving around was any kind of acting out. Now it seems like I had to go from place to place to place and still feel anxious before I realized it was something *inside me*. I suppose the same is true for people who are afraid to move around and like to stay in one spot. As long as they stay in one spot, they're never going to know how fearful they are about getting out. They control their fear by staying put; I control mine by moving on!

Drinking to relieve pressure

I used drinking as another way to get away from the pressure and "alter" my consciousness. Getting drunk helped blot out my mind; it "switched off" my brain, and allowed me to stay in a fog and a haze without knowing what was really wrong. The great attraction for me of being unconscious was relief from the pressure. The pressure was always a *physical* sensation to me, and I would have to do something *physical* to drive it away. Booze was one way; moving on was another.

Searching for peace—via turbulence

I spent a lifetime searching for peace and yet got exactly the opposite. I see now that I was always looking for *movement* because I never had that peace and I couldn't stand it. The irony is that real peace probably would have killed me. A peaceful environment wouldn't have matched what was inside me, which was a lot of turmoil; instead, I kept doing things that would match the turbulence inside.

In this second report, we see a young man who has been driven to do things "the hard way" his whole life. His constant internal pressure pushed him into constant struggles, with little or no fulfillment:

Current history

I am 32 years old, and began therapy a couple of years ago. I am broad-shouldered, and have a muscular physique. I did well in high school with compulsory classes, but in the intensive atmosphere of college I spent many helpless hours in front of blank sheets of paper. I have always liked physical work, especially agriculture and construction, but found it hard to take the time to do a well-finished job. I despised successful businessmen who could make a great deal of money by one, carefully considered move.

I have always done things the hard way—always

Doing things "the hard way"

paid taxes rather than getting a good accountant to lower or avoid them, always bought old cars that needed a lot of work rather than buying a decent new model that I could afford. I find it hard to ask anyone for help. In my job I often worked myself into situations of being under a lot of pressure, surrounded by ringing telephones, rather than working quietly at designing (which is what I am best at). I would then feel helpless and unable to make decisions, and would plunge into irrelevant work instead of focusing on what really needed to be done. I would even do things the hard way to relax: walking as fast as possible, or worse, mountain climbing!

Birth feelings: spasms, and a "struggle through syrup"

In a recent session I started having birth feelings in which I went into involuntary reflex spasms. The spasms lasted only about ten seconds, but left me exhausted. What happens now is that I get a feeling about an event in my very early life which is accompanied by a scene, but I am then left with the feeling that there is something more to it. I have pressure in my head, and it feels like very hard work to do anything. It feels as though I have to shake off a great weight or struggle through syrup in order to survive. In sessions I pound my fists and drop into rhythmic spasms of my trunk and legs which are similar to, but much more powerful than, a sexual orgasm. The spasms push my head against the wall. As in the first time it happened, the spasms last about ten seconds, but leave me completely exhausted and breathless. There is no scene, and I feel as though I have been unconscious during the spasms.

Present-day connection: "I have to struggle to survive"

I have made many connections from these feelings. I do things the hard way and take on a lot of physical work as a way of acting out the feeling that I have to struggle physically in order to survive. This has structured my life for as long as I can remember. Under pressure I hyperventilate and my heart rate rises, but I feel helpless and confused because my "natural" response from the early experience is to struggle physically. That's why I find it so hard to sit down and resolve a problem. I can't *just* sit.

Present-day changes: less pressure, more stamina

As a result of connecting to these feelings, I have stopped volunteering for jobs which put me under a lot of pressure; I find myself more able to sit quietly and solve problems; I can take the time to produce careful work rather than rushing about ineffectually. I am also

58   I M P R I N T S

more able to ask for help rather than having to do things the hard way—completely on my own.

When the feeling of being helpless and under pressure comes up I go running. Often, running one or two miles works off enough of the energy to put me into the space where I can connect to my feelings. When I make those connections I even have more physical stamina and need less sleep—from needing a regular eight hours before therapy, I can now function well on only six or seven hours of sleep. Because of this I can cope with late night overtime much better than before.

The Parasympath

Birth for the parasympath is closer to death than to life. For a variety of reasons—breech birth, cord strangulation, a massive dose of drugs to the mother—the baby begins the birth sequence and almost immediately goes into body-fail. In some cases, clinical death actually occurs for a brief, non-lethal interval. Generally, the baby needs a great deal of stimulation to even begin breathing.

The neonate who is almost dead from the birth struggle will get off the trauma train with a parasympathetic dominance stamped into his system for life. His physiology will be "hypo": very slow pulse, low body temperature, low blood pressure, low energy level (hypothyroidism) and slow reaction tendencies. These physiologic states which are the result of an initial trauma and which were life-saving at the time will point the direction for the growing baby in terms of how he will react. This is the kind of infant who starts life lethargic, doesn't cry much, is the "good" baby, very passive and undemanding. It cannot be seen that the reason for this "good" behavior is that the child is overwhelmed by trauma, so overwhelmed that he is in a dazed state for most of his infancy. This child hasn't the energy to be bubbly, laughing, bright and alert as does the child who fought his way out successfully.

All of this, in turn, dictates personality development. The body memory that there was no opportunity for struggle and that response alternatives were nil will be elaborated emotionally and psychologically: the pure parasympath adult is likely to be passive, phlegmatic and pessimistic despite almost any later encouragement. He is more likely to be grim, cautious and conservative, carrying around an almost constant feeling of doom and dread. He feels hopeless and despairing because his early situation at birth was just that. He is constantly looking forward to a doom that has, unbeknown to him, already happened.

This is why the parasympath will see hopeless situations everywhere. He will inappropriately project doom and despair because he is constantly trying to validate a reality that *was*—but is not now—appropriate. Thus, in our hypothetical restaurant situation, the parasympath might frequently (but unconsciously) ask for dishes that are not likely to be available; in personal relationships he might passively provoke rejection; and in work situations he might continually set up failure: all ways of confirming the prototypic message that "nothing I do will be enough" and that "I don't deserve . . . life."

Under stress the parasympath tends toward low blood pressure and slow pulse, replicating the engraved dying response. Taken by themselves these signs might indicate a healthy physical system. But the brainwave activity shows a change toward higher amplitude because the cortex is under stress. These readings mean that the parasympath is more likely to suffer from dizziness, fainting spells and vertigo as well as hypothyroidism and hypoglycemia. He is more prone to migraine. He may live longer than the sympath because of his energy-conserving tendencies, but he carries a great burden of Pain and a constant memory of physical suffering or death deep in his unconscious. He may dream of actually being dead, something the sympath never does.

Anger is slower to build in the parasympath because his system physiologically is not geared for it. It is not, as Freud thought, that he has anger turned inward into depression; rather, he hasn't the physical wherewithal to organize anger as easily as the sympath does. His neurotransmitter and hormone imbalance impede the easy flashes of anger that are so common to the sympath. Again, these are not attitudinal differences, these are profound biological states. The parasympath isn't going to "get over it" and become more ambitious and less phlegmatic just based on intellectual decisions.

In addition to biological differences there are also differences in appearance. The passive person is more likely to look soft physically; his anatomy accommodates to his psyche. He appears defeated, walks and holds himself that way. His system is in "retard" position. The sympath, on the other hand, has a more aggressive stance. He is ready to do battle with even the slightest provocation, his stride is more determined and certainly a lot quicker. If there's a choice of drugs, the parasympath will choose uppers and needs a good deal of coffee to get going in the morning.

Obviously the parasympath is very prone to depression. He wakes up in the morning feeling totally engulfed by inner forces. The subjective experience includes slow heart rate, retarded breathing rate, the feeling that the limbs are heavy or sluggish; the flow of thought is confused, unclear and not very alert. These are already the makings of depression. The idea of death or suicide is often a comfort to the parasympathetic depressive because at least it offers a way out.

The following report well describes the unrelenting feeling of doom and defeat characteristic of the parasympathetic personality. In it, we see the patient's transition from "everything is too much for me" to "I can do anything I want to do" made possible by her connection to very early trauma. We also see how the type of birth she experienced previewed the type of life she would experience with her mother: both were riddled with fear. We have found this is often the case. The birth trauma is a kind of condensed version of the life to come, for the neurosis that produces it in those first hours around birth unfortunately continues with predictable and Pain-filled consistency.

Present-day feelings: "Everything is too much"

I woke up the other morning feeling that everything was too much for me; even the thought of going out to make breakfast or do a few errands for the day was *too* much. I felt utterly overwhelmed, and didn't want to get out of bed. That made me want to cry, so I went to the Institute to try to connect to the feeling.

Second-level dream: impending doom

The first thing that I said was, "It's all too much for me—I just can't do it." Then I cried for a while, and as I was crying I remembered what I had dreamt about during the night. My husband and I were on a vacation and we were going to motels that were out in the country. As we entered the rooms, I would get a feeling that there was danger present—nothing specific—just a very subtle feeling that someone or something was going to hurt us. It felt as if someone were lying in wait for us—a sense of impending doom.

Acting out the doom

As I cried about the dream I remembered how terribly frightened I have been all my life—how I would check my room every night before going to bed by looking under the bed, in the closet, and under the skirt of the vanity table (which, incidentally, I did until I was 21 years old), as well as having a light on in the room throughout the night. I still lay in bed rigidly expecting someone to come and get me and hurt me.

Childhood basis for doom

This feeling led to scenes with my mother where, when my father would go away on business trips, she would make a rope out of neck ties so that we could climb down from the second story in case someone came to murder us. She also would put a stack of old plates on top of the table by the window to be thrown down on the cement below to wake the farm manager in case the murderer cut the phone lines. Then she'd lock the bedroom door and we (Mama, my brother and myself) would all sleep in there together. I was always *so* terrified: if Mama was so scared, then there must be something so big and frightening out there that could *really* kill us. Who could protect us? I couldn't wait for my father to come home and bring some sense of security with him.

My mother was such a hysterical person; she was terrified of everything—authority figures, money, the world in general—as if *everything* "out there" were potentially dangerous and hurtful. Her fear was very infectious.

Birth connection

As I cried about all these things I had been frightened of as a child, I came to a first-line feeling of being born in which I couldn't breathe, and then just after birth when I was left alone. My mother expressed her fear and panic in childbirth by screaming uncontrollably and banging her head against the bedpost. Her terror was communicated to me, and at birth the feeling of fear was further compounded by being left alone when I so obviously needed to be comforted and held. I didn't know then that anyone would ever come to me; I felt a sense of timelessness and eternal waiting. My father said that as he looked through the hospital window I was screaming the loudest—that he could easily hear me over all the other newborns.

The prototype: in everyday life, and at birth

I see now why I have always approached something new with the immediate and all-encompassing reaction of, "No, I can't do it—I'm not ready yet!" My first experience of "new things" was totally frightening: my mother not helping me to get born because of her own fear and terror, and then not being held after I *was* born.

Acting it out: "I can't do it"

No matter what the new situation is that I'm up against, no matter how well qualified I am to do it, I always feel that I can't do it. This even carries over to when I am doing something well that I *know* I can do. I think this is because doing new things puts me face-to-face with my birth and childhood feelings of aloneness and doom. When this feeling is pushing up, I feel that I can't do anything, despite all the evidence to the contrary. That need for reassurance, which never succeeds in reassuring me, is very early Pain rearing its ugly head. The reason no words of truth can reassure me out of that feeling is because it is a birth feeling, and there are no words for it.

Fear and insecurity where no words help

It seems like I have a core feeling of fear and insecurity that is my most central experience of myself as a person. My therapist once said that when I'm in that state of asking for reassurance it's as if I am grasping out all around me, but nothing that is said helps. He's so right. I feel as if I were falling into space and no one is there to catch me. My mind compulsively goes over whatever problem I am having, trying to make sense of it, where there is none. Even after I have understood how to correct a mistake, I am still not satisfied, but continue to think obsessively about it. No words of reassurance help; only feeling the very early feeling makes the obsessional worrying stop. That is why I have always said that feeling a first-line feeling is something that I embrace happily, because the mental torture that I suffer while obsessing is the true agony for me.

Connecting to feelings: "I just want to rest"

I feel so relieved when I make a feeling-connection, because I know it won't be much longer before I can find peace. All my life I have said, "I just want to rest." My body never rests; I am constantly vigilant with a startle reaction second to none. Only after a birth feeling do I feel truly relaxed and sane. So, "I want to rest" is a physical statement as well as an emotional one.

Change in the present: a refinished mirror

After I finished feeling all this, I couldn't wait to get on with the day, and eagerly went about all my errands. The *doom* had lifted! In fact, I even refinished a mirror in my bathroom which an interior decorator had told me was beyond repair. At the time, I had just accepted his opinion. But now I discovered by questioning several people at a paint store that there was, indeed, a way to repair it. In the past I would have never done that—I would have accepted the decorator's pronouncement as incontrovertible fact.

The counterparts of feeling: freedom and creativity

I now see that *feeling* (especially first-line feeling) frees me from the constraints upon my imagination which have held me back from all forms of creative endeavors. In short, before feeling a first-line feeling it seems that everything is too much for me; after feeling it, I am freed to do anything I want to do—*and with ease.*

If I were to tell a person that the reason he does not study the menu until the waiter arrives to take the order or is usually unable to get the dishes he orders might be because of something that happened decades ago at birth, I am sure he would be skeptical. To hear that one's adult behavior rests on a birth trauma is no doubt difficult to accept on many levels. How can it be that someone at age forty reacts every day of his life to something which only lasted a few minutes or a few hours? It doesn't seem logical because we simply had not understood the impact of birth trauma on the nervous system.

It seems like such a small matter—what we do in a restaurant, or wherever; but then neurosis encompasses a lot of small matters. Keeping friends and mates waiting because of the need to work under pressure can be the source of constant arguments; so can constantly making requests that cannot be fulfilled. Waiting until the last second to do work, or unconsciously doing it poorly, can affect one's job and livelihood. The implications of these "small matters" can be vast indeed.

That these small matters are directly connected to the life-and-death matter of birth is now established. We have seen restoration of the balance between parasympathetic and sympathetic functioning begin to occur within the Primal session itself. The sympath comes in anxious and agitated, with all vital functions raised. When the sympathetic defense is strained to its utmost there is a shift, the defense fails, the patient falls into the feeling, and the parasympathetic system takes over. The patient then feels greatly relaxed as the system finally has begun to work in harmony. The sympath's post-session vital signs indicate a shift toward the para-sympathetic side. Conversely, the person in parasympathetic excess in the beginning of a session is able to come up out of his generalized suffering and react to the Pain which caused it. He engages the sympa-thetic system for his expression of the Pain and when the session is over his vital signs will shift toward the sympathetic side.

On a psychological level the normalized balance between sympathetic and parasympathetic modes is illustrated by fewer bouts of depression and moodiness, and fewer extreme highs and lows. The parasympath is able to express his anger and all his feelings more readily, while the sympath has greater possibilities for reflection and calm introspection. The whole system is more moderate. The restoration of balance comes with changing the imprint of Pain which skewed it. Once that is done, the person tends to be neither a sympath nor a parasympath. He is a more stabilized human being. The mentally ill have been called the mentally "unbalanced." Now we see why.

II: The Birth Trauma and the Formation of Consciousness

Introduction

I have pointed out that the painful experiences of the neonatal and antenatal periods are laid down in the deepest layers of the brain and nervous system. Each level of consciousness corresponding to the three key levels of brain development mobilizes against the ascendance of those deep-lying Pains.

This mobilization of the blood, muscle and brain systems is called energy. Energy is a biochemical and electrical force that can be objectively measured. It is something real and material. As long as the birth trauma imprint remains, one or more levels of consciousness will be activated in some way to deal with that Pain. This means the system is in an ongoing state of mobilization in order to supply the energy for repression. Repression is literally an energy-consuming process.

While the Pain from the first-line imprint is repressed, the energy component is not. That energy is discharged in unique ways by each level of consciousness. This discharge of Primal energy into symptoms and behavior forms the implications of the birth trauma on the three levels of consciousness: the physical (first), emotional and psychological (second) and intellectual (third) elaborations of repressed Pain.

We have seen that the physical effects of the birth trauma are the first to be elaborated because of the level of brain development in the infant. These physical effects endure into adulthood and comprise the somatic symptoms, the disturbing sensations and the sexual problems of neurosis.

When the second level of the brain becomes operative between the ages of one and two, the energy can be discharged emotionally and psychologically. In the child this will result in temper tantrums, crying spells, whining fits and any number of behavior problems. In the adult, it will determine overall personality characteristics and emotional disposition.

When the intellect becomes fully operative (around the age of six), it will play its part by converting the energy from the stored first-line Pain into ideas. Those ideas may be the obsessive and manic ones typically associated with neurosis, or they may be more "acceptable" ideas that are extended into philosophical and intellectual systems of thought. Either way, the ideation forms the intellectual elaboration of the early Pain.

Indeed, it is no exaggeration to say that the thoughts that plague us when we're trying to sleep at the age of fifty, the emotions that keep us from concentrating on our work in college, the manic flow of ideas that keeps us from concentrating, even on pleasure—the source of all of these may well have occurred long before we opened our eyes for the first time in this world.

One patient well illustrated how he experienced implications from his birth on all three levels of consciousness. He wrote:

> Since I first began to experience birth feelings, I have become aware of further symbolisms that seem to be related to it:

First-level birth sensations in dreams
> —I frequently dream about being enclosed in some underground canal system which is too narrow to get through. Often I cannot move my feet.

Second-level phobias
> —Being awake, I fear small rooms and spaces in which I can get trapped.

Third-level (language) elaborations
> —My language is filled with phrases such as "I'm stuck," "I feel trapped," "There's no way out" and so on.

The transmutation of first-line energy into second-line emotional reactions and third-line ideas occurs in a slow, insidious way; in fact, we rarely know it is happening. All we are left with after the transmutation are emotional outbursts, manic ideas, phobias and somatic disturbances: indeed, we begin to think that the symptoms or manifestations are "things in themselves." They are not. They stem from a precise yet deeply buried source: the continuing, persistent but *unfinished* intrauterine dialogue with the mother.

Once the nervous system is accelerated due to the Primal force, no measure, technique or outlet can slow it down permanently, short of actual access to those precise imprinted forces which caused the acceleration in the first place. Without that access the person will have to find ways to keep the acceleration under control—through drugs and alcohol, overwork, compulsive behavior, fanatic causes or whatever. These outlets disperse forces that are usually a complete mystery to us, even though they are there just below the level of conscious awareness. The forces remain inaccessible because the outlets, when they are "successful," actually function as first-line blockers by triggering our own internal Pain-killers. These Pain-killers (the endorphines) keep the imprint from consciousness, maintain its well-hidden position, and ensure a continuity of Pain for a lifetime.

We are going to look at how each level of consciousness is altered by the birth trauma and at the specific implications that arise from those alterations on each level. To present the material, we have to look at each level separately, but bear in mind that *the entire person* is altered by repressed Pain, and each level of consciousness is implicated.

People vary tremendously in how they "distribute" the implications of their birth traumas. Some manifest the trauma on all levels of consciousness: they will have somatic symptoms (first-level), emotional problems (second level) and intellectual or fanatic obsessions (third level). Other people will manifest the implications predominantly through one level of consciousness. For instance, a child with strong intellectual capacities may live out the implications of the birth trauma predominantly through his third level: he may grow into a very cut-off scholar, barricading himself behind walls of ideas. This is not to say that the other levels are not affected; they are. But it appears that, for many people, one level or another will emerge as the predominant vehicle for interpreting and expressing the birth trauma.

5
The Balancing Act of Life: The Physical Implications of the Birth Trauma

Primal Pain is not an abstraction. It is above all a sensation. The sensations of birth remain as physical tendencies which become manifest under later stress. When the sensations are chronic or severe enough they can lead to symptoms and disease, to sexual compulsions and disorders and to recurrent nightmares.

The birth trauma hurts physically and in particular places: for some, it means a tightness in the chest and a need to cough; others cannot catch their breath; still others feel a tight band around the head. And there are those who feel a taut or pressured feeling in the neck and shoulders. The sensations can take many forms: a knot in the stomach, palpitations of the heart, a sensation across the face and forehead.

Later in life any stress that is severe enough to upset the defense system will set off these tendencies first. They are the basic tendencies out of which later emotions and ideas are elaborated. The tendencies or sensations will be experienced long before one can get to the Pain itself. And indeed, for most of us, they are experienced over and over again without our ever getting to that original Pain. This is because the sensations have been disconnected through repression from consciousness. One does not feel the entire overwhelming experience of birth but only fragmented sensations. Primals are the connection of those disparate sensations to consciousness.

Physical hurts in and around the time of birth have a way of literally "marking the spot" for a lifetime. In fact, one of the important pieces of evidence concerning the physical imprinting of birth is illustrated by the return of birth marks and bruises on patients reliving their births. These marks recur in the same spots where they first showed themselves.* Physical hurts and sensations from birth do, without doubt, remain physically encoded in the system as latent reaction tendencies and become manifest under the right (i.e., sufficiently stressful) conditions.

It is in fact when the symptoms or sensations are persistent in a patient that we know the Pain is near—constant coughing, a continual lump in the throat, a tautness in the neck and shoulders. The breakthrough of these sensations is known as "first-line intrusion." The way we know that first-line intrusion (which comes from first-line Primal pressure) is indeed a physiologic pressure is that we can see it literally with a blood pressure cusp. As one approaches the Pain in a Primal, the blood pressure continues to mount until it is sometimes well over 200—this, in a person lying still on his back simply reliving a very, very early Pain. The earlier those Pains, the higher the pressure. This is also true for the brainwave patterns. There are significant changes in the electrical output of muscle groups with Primal Pain, as well. Pain is literally a bioelectric force. When we understand that it is an actual physical pressure, a sensation or pressure frozen in time, then the source of chronic migraines, chronic asthma, chronic heart problems is no longer a mystery.

The problem with first-line symptoms and sensations is precisely that they disturb critical organ systems such as the heart and lungs; the symptoms continually stress the organ just as the birth experience

---

*We have shown photographs of this phenomenon in other works. It is interesting to note that birth bruises return in patients who are the most undefended. They seem to have clear access in a total way to the deepest traumas. A person can have birth Primals for months before the bruises reappear. One seems to have to reach a certain critical level of vulnerability first.

stressed it originally. Because these sensations exist as latent tendencies for a lifetime, they eventually can have serious consequences. Rapid heartbeat, for example, will be an immediate reaction tendency to even the slightest stress; eventually that tendency may weaken the heart and result in a full-blown coronary. Thus, the original imprinted stressor becomes a chronic stressor which then leads to serious disease later on.

Sensations

Birth is "sensational" from at least two points of view. First, it is a remarkable event in itself, and so much more when one considers that it can be relived decades after its occurrence. Second, it is literally sensational in terms of the residue of sensations it leaves behind: those very sensations which were traumatic and could not be integrated at the time.

This is called first-line residue. It includes such sensations as choking, gagging, chronic fatigue, localized pains, dizziness, pressure, feeling crushed and suffocated. These sensations will be elaborated on higher levels of consciousness later, but as sensations they also remain "pure" for a lifetime.

Later situations of stress will tend to elicit the prototypic sensations. Someone who fights with his wife may find himself choking or becoming dizzy. A grown child watching his parents fight may suffer from feelings of suffocation which have no organic basis. Or, the sensations can also persist in chronic form such as a kind of endemic fatigue where fatigue is the result of an excruciatingly long birth which became a stamped-in condition. Under later stress the person's first response will be overwhelming fatigue.

It is the Freudian "hysteric" who probably experiences more first-line sensational breakthrough than any other kind of person. Under anxiety he will feel pressured, dizzy, fatigued, suffocated; he will gag, have localized pains, choke. The reactions seem very dramatic and totally out of keeping with reality, but nevertheless they are actual sensations from a long-ago past. They tend to be the first and primary reactions later in difficult situations because they were first and primary reactions at the beginning of life. Their charge value makes them prepotent over any other kind of response.

The so-called hysteric usually suffers from vague symptoms because their origins tend to be both inaccessible and diffused; a general feeling of pressure, for example. The hysteric, above all, is most prone to constant first-line intrusion.

On the evolutionary scale sensations are primary: they are the first-developed and most basic level of life processes. But they soon become elaborated in man by the second and third levels of consciousness. Thus the *sensation* of being crushed at birth may be triggered off by higher level representations such as the *emotional* situation of feeling "crushed" by an overpowering person, or even later by the mere *idea* of crushing. Both higher levels of consciousness have a part in these sensations: indeed, what we once assumed were metaphorical descriptions—"I feel uptight," "I was crushed by the comment"—turn out to have precise and *literal* sources. A person who feels that others are crushing him may have projected all the first-line birth sensations of literally being crushed onto his later relationships with people. (We shall see in a later chapter how in fact many of our everyday expressions are derivatives of specific Primal birth sensations.)

The nature of the sensation being experienced tells us a great deal about the kind of birth trauma and helps us lead a patient toward it when the time is right. I recall one patient crying out, "I'm going crazy—I don't know up from down—everything seems so upside down!" This repetition of "everything seems so upside down" gave us a clue of what was to happen. It did happen that she had a birth Primal in which she relived the sensation of being held upside down by the doctor and spanked—a sensation that was overwhelming at the time and became imprinted for a lifetime. As it began to come into consciousness it reproduced the original disorientation and with that a feeling of "going crazy." The crazy feeling was no more than the disconnection of an overwhelming Pain that had no words or images to depict it.

Indeed, one can see that words are of little use in these early experiences because they were set down long before we had the ability to form words and concepts—long before we could name and comprehend the sensations. Sensations can't really be communicated; they have to be felt in the body in order to be understood.

The prototypic birth sensations may not be severe enough to develop into symptoms that require medical attention, but they nonetheless tax the system in significant ways.

Butterflies

Some people under stress simply have "butterflies" in their stomachs—a mild but total visceral reaction. This again may well be an engraved sensation of fear at birth. Indeed, some individuals have chronic cases of "butterflies": a churning stomach becomes a way of life to which the person adjusts until it mushrooms into something more serious, such as peptic ulcers or colitis.

Drowning

The sensation of drowning at birth is a very common one. Indeed, many of us did almost drown in the amniotic fluid. The terror from that prototypic threat of drowning produces a generalized terror that can be projected onto almost any situation. Usually, though, it will be focused on situations having to do with water. Interestingly enough, the terror associated with that early drowning sensation remains even if the person never goes near water. For instance, it can be triggered in adults who have their mouths and noses covered even for the briefest time and for any reason whatsoever.

Many of our patients have been terrified of water, particularly of putting their head under water. Once the reliving of the trauma has taken place, however, that terror leaves and they are able to learn to swim for the first time.

Generalized Body Experience

For some people the traumatic birth sensations are experienced in a generalized and chronic way—they just don't feel right physically, they are chronically tense, chronically fatigued, easily overtaxed. One patient wrote:

Present sensations	My body has always felt weak and tense and tired. I feel I am constantly stuck in birth feelings and have no energy left for anything else. I was pulled out by
Birth trauma	Cesarean after a very long labor. My body hurts very easily and recovers from physical stress very slowly. (Maybe I've never fully recovered from being born.)
Second-level elaboration	I used to wet my bed almost every night until I was 13 years old; I would get shit from my mother every time, but I never understood why I did it or why she humiliated me for it.
	I am hypersensitive to physical stress. I get overheated very easily. I sweat profusely, and I hate it. I feel that my body is already working hard enough in just day-to-day living. When it comes to doing an actual job, I have to strain myself physically and mentally to just "make it."

Another patient:

	It is always hard for me to talk about my birth Pain because it is practically impossible to convey in words something that happened so long ago before I thought in words. Now the best way to describe what I am
Sensations	feeling is that it is like having a ribbon of spring steel where my bones should be—especially in my upper arms and back. The image of a ribbon of steel is a good one, because while it allows movement (I can move) it also implies a stiffness and rigidity, which I do feel. This stiffness deep in my core constricts my every

Birth history

action and hampers me in whatever I do—be it racquetball, jogging, or creative writing.

I know that what I am feeling is a defense against the awful Pain of my birth. I was a ten-pound-eight-ounce baby, and my mother was a slightly built woman. The struggle of getting out of the womb left me in a Pain no one could rid me of. No person could help me there in the womb, or immediately after I got out. *Maybe* being caressed a lot after coming out would have helped, but my mother tells me I received this. I do not know because I haven't felt it yet, and don't know the quality of the contact. But at any rate, right now when I feel this Pain I can't look for any scapegoat or person to blame—it is just something that happened and that I will have to live through now, in its entirety, before my limbs regain the suppleness taken away by the steel defenses.

Second-level elaborations

The worst problem in living now is the problem my defenses bring up with people. People seem to be restricting and suffocating, like my birth. They grate against my defenses and create a greater burden for me. Many times I just want to be alone because my body is tired of the constant struggle to defend against the Pain, but at the same time I am lonely and if I stay alone I create new Pain in the present. It is a vicious circle, with feeling (slowly and in little doses) the only way out.

The report of yet another patient well illustrates the interface between the original birth sensations and later elaborations of those sensations in generalized body Pain, dreams, emotions and attitudes:

First-line intrusion

I had my firth birth feelings after being in therapy seven months. The birth feelings seemed to come up after periods in which I have strong body Pains in my neck, shoulders and arms which are accompanied by feelings of hopelessness or deadness.

The original imprint

The first time I experienced such feelings I just let myself sink into them, and this led to a sensation of being safe and comfortable inside my mother. The euphoria, however, was short-lived: suddenly I was being forcefully pushed out. I was in much Pain, crying and screaming desperately. I did not want to go—I was not ready, but what could I do against this pushing?

I talked of this experience in post-group, but not until the next day did I have an insight. I have always

Second-level elaboration of the imprint

found it extraordinarily difficult to leave people I am close to. It was no different from the painful way I was forced to leave the good feeling of my mother's womb.

Birth sensations in dreams

For several days after the session I was plagued by more body Pains, with physical weakness and feelings of helplessness. This all led to a most unusual dream. In it, I dove into a river to swim to the other side, but instead of coming up and swimming, I became stuck in a whirlpool. My head and body were being pulled down in a twisting motion, while my feet were above me. In the dream I realized I was doomed unless I did something immediately—I was choking. I gave an almightly struggle and woke up!

Connecting present trigger to past context

Over the next three weeks I experienced birth feelings many times. Often on a Sunday afternoon I would be overcome by the physical symptoms of these feelings. I valued my weekends so much that their ending and my having to go back to work again brought up much sadness. When I let myself feel the sadness of the weekend being over, I would go back to losing the warmth and safety of my mother's womb.

The time came when I had to be straight with my boyfriend about something that was bugging me. Even though I knew it would hurt him, it was hurting me more to hold it back. I had to act. I was talking with my therapist about this when I felt myself back into birth feelings—without any apparent connection to the problem with my boyfriend. The Pain was driving me crazy, and, feeling desperate, I had the impulse to get behind the punching bag. It felt right to be there, banging and struggling in that pushy little space.

Emotional and psychological elaborations

The interconnections: insight and clarity

Afterwards I talked about the experience with my therapist. My head was clear and the words came out easily and simply. Throughout my life I have been quiet and introverted, never able to exert myself— never able to express or demand what I wanted or needed. This was the trigger to the important feeling of needing to be honest, at last, with my boyfriend. I recalled the dream with its prophetic ending where my only chance to save myself was to give a huge struggle. At the time I thought this dream was significant because I have experienced many feelings of having to fight to stop myself from "going under."

Now I had the insight that my birth was so traumatic that whenever I needed to exert myself in the present the old Pain was brought up, which forced my resis-

tance down again. My way of defending against this
Pain had been to be weak or "go dead." This connection somehow freed me to begin expressing myself,
and without a huge struggle. The huge struggle was
from my past and I realized that it didn't have to be
part of my present.

Head and Neck Positions

The precise Pain and its location are not always evident. Sometimes
there are only covert indications: an example would be holding the head
and neck in a certain position to avoid the sensation of Pain that occurred
there at birth. In this way head position—possibly a slight tilt to the left or
right—becomes fixated for life.

Since the site of the sensation tends to be the focus for later compounded stress, the position of the head and neck are often direct
indications of the original birth Pain, literally locked into place. One clear
example of this is found in the syndrome called "swan neck," in which the
neck is hyperextended, pushing upward in a swan position. This can often
be a painful situation, and disappears with the reliving of the harsh
rotation and hyperextension occasioned by the doctors at birth.

One patient wrote:

Sensations	After some weeks of a birth Primal in which I relived some extremely sharp Pains in the back of my head, neck and shoulders, I began to feel a tremendous release of all the physical tension I had frozen there for all of my life. It was as though a huge weight had been lifted from my body—and my psyche. The muscles and
Resolution	tendons around the back of my neck seemed miracu-lously freed from lifelong constriction. I had a new feeling as a result of all this: I felt "inside my skin" for the first time.

And another:

Sensation	In my birth Primals I have always felt a lot of Pain in my face; and in sleep, the pain area is also facial. I feel like the right part is squeezed out. I asked my mother about my birth and she said there was a definite stop
Birth history	during the delivery after which I came out "visibly compressed in the face, especially over the nose." This fits what I have been feeling in my face—what I must have perceived in the birth canal as the complications occurred. My face *was* pressed and I felt danger.

Impulsivity

The impulsive person is also running off a birth sequence. Why is it that no matter what the punishment, no matter how much the person is aware that he shouldn't do something, he does it anyway? Because he cannot control his impulses—literally electrical nerve impulses. They are the Primal forces energizing the system. The impulsive person is a victim of these forces which came into being long before verbalization. First-line forces are *physical* drives against which the neurotic can only array *ideas*. And those forces are stronger than any ideas designed to control them. Indeed, the ideas ("I know I shouldn't eat, drink, exhibit myself, make that phone call, stay up too late, say such-and-such to so-and-so, leave my job, quit school, see this friend or that") are usually too weak to hold back the impulses. This is because ideas are a later development that come along *after the fact*.

It is the first-line forces which move the body into impulsive acts. That is why the impulsive person *does* first and *thinks* later. This is exactly how the brain is developed: impulse first and thought later. The impulsive person is literally someone who is suffering from the impulses of the birth trauma.

A primary impulse in birth is the impulse to move ahead. Part of the need to plunge ahead later no matter what the consequences—without thinking—is that *not* to plunge ahead can recall the trauma of near-death due to stoppage of the natural birth process. Thus, when there is an opening, as it were, the impulsive person simply dashes into a situation. He will agree to do something that upon reflection he doesn't really want to do, or he will buy something suddenly that he really doesn't need or want.

Plunging ahead without thought is one kind of birth analogue. For one reason or another it was necessary for the baby to make a last-ditch attempt to get out, and any possible opening was tried instinctively. In a nontraumatic birth the baby descends in orderly fashion down the canal. In the traumatic birth the sensation of plunging can become an imprinted prototype. Yet although it saved the baby, it does not serve the adult.

The impulsivity in behavior may not be global; one can be more impulsive in one area than another. One can be careful in business and impulsive in sex or inhibited in sex and lavishly impulsive in spending money, and so on.

The point about impulsivity is that a birth sequence is being run off from a time when there was no thought. The entire encapsulated sequence has been transposed into an adult situation almost intact; only the context has been altered. Even though the paroled criminal knows that punishment follows any violation of the law, he will still get into fights which can send

him back to prison. And no matter how apparent it is to the overeater that
that pie or cake will only make matters worse, he will still eat it.

Nausea

Nausea is an example of a sensation that may have occurred during
birth for several reasons, not the least of which was the introduction of
drugs into the mother's system. Later on nausea may be a primary
response to an emotionally or even an intellectually stressing situation. A
person who frequently describes himself as feeling "nauseous" about
things or of finding situations "nauseating" may have nausea as a prototypic response pattern. The emotional reaction of disgust also has nausea
at its base. Indeed, disgust is the second-line (emotional) extension of
nausea. The disgusted person looks nauseated and nausea becomes a
prototype to later psychological situations.

Smoking and Deep Inhalation

One patient got to the root of his heavy and deep smoking pattern after a
birth Primal in which he could not breathe for a long time. He finally took
one tremendous gasp and began breathing. He felt that his need to inhale
deeply was a way of re-creating the Pain of the first breath he ever took. To
him it was a sign of life, for that first breath—though terribly painful—was
the end of the catastrophic trauma of not being able to breathe at all.

First-Level "Stuck"

The sense of being stuck is a physical sensation that often derives from
the birth experience. Again, it has its fibers reaching up into the second
and third levels so that any situation in which a person feels "stuck"—in a
job, in a relationship, in a marriage or even just stuck on a problem
intellectually—may produce an inordinate response due to that physical
sensation and threat of having been stuck at birth.

Suffocation

Fear of suffocating is quite common. It is a component of several
phobias and symptoms. In its milder form, the person may simply feel
uncomfortable or edgy in situations where suffocation could conceivably
occur—in elevators, basements, tunnels, caves.

Frequently, fear of suffocation derives from an actual birth experience
in which there were periods of mild suffocation caused by momentary
oxygen deprivation. This type of experience, when it remains unconscious, can become the basis for quite irrational—and seemingly far-
fetched—fears. One of our patients feared the sight of anything that

resembled a deep hole. He imagined that when people got really angry at him they would tie him up and push him, head down, into a hole until he suffocated. He did not have the slightest idea where such a fear actually came from.

Vertigo

A person's posture, gait and entire kinesthetic sense may also be directly connected to birth, and will change in accordance with specific kinds of birth Primals. One patient, for example, had the sensation of continuous dizziness—a feeling of "falling off the edge of the earth," as she put it. She would often have to fall to the ground and press her head against the grass or pavement as a means of gaining stability and control over the vertigo. In a birth Primal, she relived the origin of the sensation: a displaced presentation at birth, leaving her (as an infant) with a feeling of total disorientation which, under later stress, is triggered. Not knowing what the sensation was really about, she could only describe it as a feeling of "falling off the edge of the earth"—not an inaccurate analogy from the newborn's perspective.

Another patient had a somewhat similar problem:

Sensations and fears

At one time I was working in an extremely tall office building—about 30 stories high—and I frequently had to run errands to different floors by using the elevators. I had felt uneasy about elevators from time to time during my life, but now the feeling became overpowering. I would imagine the chute of dark air under the elevator and feel terrified I might somehow fall down it; or I imagined the elevator breaking down, and I would get very dizzy and sick and have to hold onto the sides of the elevator. I also had several nightmares in which I was in an elevator that was crashing to the ground.

A friend reassured me that there were safety precautions which made what I feared almost impossible, and I began to get a sense that the fear was from somewhere else.

One day in group I was feeling about being alone. I remembered how completely alone and crazy I had felt when left in a mental hospital by my father at the age of 20. I went with the feeling, and suddenly I was a baby, and crying and screaming in terror. My body became rigid and tense, as if it, too, were expressing the terror.

Second-level connection: crazy

I then began to feel that I was falling backwards into a black void. This was the most terrifying sensation I'd ever experienced. I became dizzily and sickeningly disoriented, and cried and screamed throughout. My legs went up over my head, halfway up the wall, so that I was almost upside down. I was certain what the feeling was. After I was born somebody held me upside down. I also connected my fear in the elevator—it was the same feeling.

First-level connection: held upside down

I still get mild sensations of vertigo sometimes, but now I know what they are about. I also know that some of these first-line feelings can't be felt away overnight, but that each time I feel them a bit more, I lose a bit more of the symptom. I also know that this vertigo sensation was what had been pushing up when I was hospitalized, and that having no way to connect to it and feel it in its real context made me very crazy.

Symptoms, Syndromes, and Diseases: The Pathology of Birth

The sensations of birth remain chronic, become focal points for stress and eventually turn into symptoms. These symptoms usually involve the mid-line of the body—the stomach and colon—but the heart and respiratory areas are also common targets. It is generally true that the deeper in the body a symptom is, the deeper in the brain is its originating imprint and the more unconscious its meaning. Severe colitis, for example, indicates, by and large, very early origins.

There is a timetable of symptoms, a schedule which dictates which reactions will be enlisted for Primal wounds. The newborn does not have the facial muscle control to grimace or frown or to look particularly angry or sad. The second level of consciousness is in charge of that. But the newborn is capable of manifesting intestinal and digestive disturbances.

Symptoms are generally commensurate with the amount of underlying Pain. Chronic headaches and blinding migraines are the results of a force. It is a force which is not connected to its source and so must find channels for release. But there is more to the story.

We now know that each of us is a "morphine factory." We each pump out specific kinds and amounts of endorphine (a morphine-like substance) to meet stress. There is a commensurate relationship here. The more severe the stress the more endorphine we produce. To put it another way, the amount of Pain we have determines the quantity and potency of the endorphine we produce. The fact that some endorphines we produce in our own systems are often much more powerful than commercially prepared morphine tells us about the tremendous strength of some of the Pains we deal with. I submit that among these catastrophic valence Pains is the birth trauma.

Endorphines are consumed in the battle against Pain. In a study by Bruno Anselmi (University of Florence), individuals prone to migraine were found to have lower levels of endorphine when they had attacks than when they didn't.* When the attacks had passed safely, their endorphine levels rose again. In another study, rats whose tails were pinched continuously were found to have elevated levels of endorphines. They began to eat compulsively until they were given naloxone, an opiate antagonist, which blocked the painkilling effects of the endorphines. At that point the animals stopped overeating. In other words, *with* painkillers at a high level, the animals developed the symptom of overeating; when the painkillers were blocked, the symptom stopped. Symptoms and endorphines are clearly related: it is not just Pain which produces a symptom but the system's own blocking of it as well. Symptoms are the manifestation of a clash between repression and expression of a feeling. The kind of symptom depends on the focus of the prototypic Pain, hereditary tendencies and the kind of outlets that exist at the moment. When Pain can no longer be contained and/or when organ systems fail in their defense, symptoms result.

Pain produces its own opiates, its own counterforce; thus, one of the ways we measure the amount of Pain in a system is by measuring the amount of these counterforces, i.e., the endorphines. Symptoms indicate that our endorphine supplies have been exhausted.

All of the stress reactions that go along with heightened endorphine release were probably designed by nature to work on a transient basis—for situational stress, so to speak. But once there is an imprint, these stress systems must work continuously, for the imprint makes it seem as if the original situation (such as birth) were still present. That is why we act out the birth analog for a lifetime—because it *is* present. We act out in order to discharge the force and master the trauma. But when that mastering is symbolic rather than connected, we are compelled to do it over and over again.

With higher stress there is an excess of a stress hormone called ACTH, and with that, there tends to be too much stimulation in the gastric area. This overproduction of juices is part of the process of mobilizing the body against danger; and danger in this case is the rise of Pain into consciousness. The danger is inside now, and there is no possible way to run from it, save one: pretend it is not there. One can develop ideas that deny its existence. And, indeed, Pain forces us to do just that, for otherwise we would be feeling it all of the time. But the body goes on processing the event no matter what, and then later one falls prey to a symptom or a disease, seemingly without cause. It is always a danger, this imprint, until the body is able to integrate its force in a systematic way.

Science News, "Endorphines: Down with Migraine Headaches," Vol. 117, June 21, 1980, p. 390.

When catastrophic Pain is laid down early in life the ground is laid for heavy defenses. When the defense system works well, one kind of symptom develops; when it is faulty or overloaded, there is another. High Pain and high repression can leave one with high blood pressure and tense muscles—signs that the pressure is present but contained. As the pressure escapes, one might see migraine or asthma attacks. When the Pain is very high and the circulating endorphines are low, one might see colitis. With a complete overloading of the defense system, cancer (or any other kind of catastrophic systemic disease) or epilepsy might result. The severity of the illness directly reflects the severity of the underlying Pain as well as the inadequacy of the defensive mechanisms.

When a person is confronted directly with his Pain the symptoms cease. We have a choice: bolster the defenses and only temporarily stop the symptom, or face the Pain and rid the system of the generating sources of that symptom. Symptoms, I repeat, arise because one has blocked a critical amount of energy which must go somewhere. Excesses in endorphine production force the system to make chronic responses outside the normal biologic range. Pain is an intruder that won't allow the system to function normally. It didn't originally and it won't now, because it is the same Pain with the same dislocations of function.

But how do we know that it is the ascendance into consciousness of the birth trauma that is the danger? Because as a person gets close to that experience all of his vital signs skyrocket, and more importantly, once arrived into consciousness, the system normalizes in its many functions and symptoms are eliminated. The brain seems to know its enemies and does whatever it can to keep them at bay.

Clearly there is no such thing as a healthy defense. We get sick from our defenses even while they protect us from more severe maladies. The body is always responding to its environment, and what we must recognize is that an early environment—even an environment that existed in the womb—lives on in the system. All of the original sounds, smells, feelings and sensations are alive and kicking in our bodies.

It is quite a leap from being strangled on the cord at minus one hour to the development of colitis at age forty. The only way to find a bridge for that leap is by traveling down the nervous system and feeling that connection for oneself. By removing that trauma from the system, we can see what happens to the symptom. We know then what was truly ailing us. But no one can make that connection for another person; and no one can take anyone else's Pain away.

Now let's take a look at some specific symptoms and their relationship to specific birth traumas.

Angina

A physician whom we treated as a patient came to us with a history of angina. After several months of therapy he described sensations from his first-line Primals: a shortness of breath, a tendency to periodically stop breathing, a tightness in the chest and the mid-epigastral area (which radiates and spreads throughout the chest), a vise-like feeling preventing breathing, a very low pulse and feeling of lethargy, and an overall sensation of dying. There was no active pain, just an ominous feeling that all was about to end. This patient's angina was the summation of all those disparate sensations unified into a single symptom—a form of heart disease.

Asthma

Many specific birth experiences can lay the foundation for a chronic asthma condition later: temporarily drowning in amniotic fluid is one; having the oxygen supply cut off by a twisted umbilical cord is another; being too drugged to take that first breath outside the canal, still another.

There may also be many non-specific traumas—both prenatally and natally—that contribute to this condition. Researchers are finding that this is so. In one report, the researcher suggested that "some children seem to become allergically sensitized to foods while still *in utero.*" In another study, conducted at the Pediatric Allergy Clinic of New York Hospital, asthmatic children were found to have twice as many neonatal complications as non-asthmatic children. The researcher concluded: "Clearly this study shows that a stressful birth significantly increases the chances of a child's developing asthma."*

Our patients have made many connections between their births and their lifelong asthma. One put it this way: "I couldn't breathe at birth and during my life I've had asthma which reproduces the same sensation of not being able to breathe: it kept alive the feeling that I couldn't breathe and reminded me of the trauma I had been through." Another patient who had been plagued by asthma from very early childhood made a return visit home in the course of his therapy. During this time he began to reexperience the original source of that lifelong symptom. Following is his report which illustrates the direct connection between his birth and his asthma, as well as how actual physical birth sensations found their way into his dreams and nightmares, sometimes symbolizing the trauma, sometimes pointing it out quite directly.

*Both studies reported in *Annals of Allergy*, 9/12/77, in an article by Johnstone.

I have suffered from chronic asthma from the age of three. During my adolescence the attacks diminished to the point where I thought I had outgrown it, but by the age of twenty-three the attacks had resumed at full *First-level implica-* force. At that time I had moved back home with my *tion: asthma* parents and entered medical school. The first year of school I was sick only during the winter, but it gradually worsened. By the time I entered therapy four years later, I would have asthma attacks every night, regardless of the season.

I suffered very few attacks from the time I arrived in *Current history* Los Angeles in October of 1979 (four months before I started therapy) until about six months after I was into therapy. But then things began to worsen. In October of 1980 my father offered me a trip home. I was so happy at the thought of going back to France after a year in Los Angeles that I immediately went out to buy my airplane ticket and make reservations for a flight in early December.

Second-level feel- In the two months that preceded my trip, I began to *ings, fears and fan-* be terrified of seeing my parents again. I had literally *tasies* run away from home at the age of twenty-seven, unable to confront them with my desire to go into therapy, not to mention my feelings of loneliness, despair, and utter hopelessness that had motivated the therapy decision in the first place. I was so angry and bitter toward them that I was afraid I would either break down or blow up if I mentioned therapy.

As December drew closer I began to have terrifying fantasies of not being able to cope with my parents, of screaming in a drunken stupor, of savagely bashing their heads against the walls. The worst fantasy of all was one in which my parents convinced everyone that I was insane, committing me to a mental hospital where I would be drugged and locked up, never to come out again. I became very preoccupied with this and spent quite a long time finding ways of coping with my all-too-real fear.

First birth dream One night shortly before I was to leave for France I had a very clear dream of the whole situation. In it I was back in Paris on my trip and about to buy my train ticket to go visit my parents. On the way to the train station I had stopped to see a friend who lives on the 10th floor of his building. We were standing in his living room facing each other. I had my back turned toward his balcony, from which there is a superb panoramic view of Paris. I was saying to him, "I'm afraid of seeing my parents again. I'm afraid they will try to destroy me; I'm afraid they will convince me that I am insane; that they will squish me and shove me into a dark hole, and my mind will be too blurry to escape. I know that this is my birth, and I will have to go through with it before I can get better."

At that same moment in the dream I realized that I had always been afraid of going out onto his balcony for fear I would climb over the railing and jump off, or even simply fall off, because the railing wasn't high enough to protect me (it was actually as high as my shoulders). (When I actually did go back and visit my friend I went out to his balcony and looked straight down the ten floors to the ground. My legs began to shake, I felt weak and terrified, and just went back inside.)

Second-level implication: phobias

My flight was to leave on Saturday at 10:00 P.M. By 3:00 P.M. on Saturday I hadn't packed my suitcase yet, I still had laundry and a few other things to do, and I felt too spaced-out to concentrate on anything. I went to the supermarket and was pushing my cart around, feeling awful. My mind was in a total daze. I often have this feeling in brightly lit supermarkets with the constant background hum. The place was immense and all those brightly colored items on the shelves seemed to be dancing in front of my eyes. My head was aching— there was a pressure right on top and in the middle. I felt a constrictive pressure around my neck, along with a tremendous pressure inside my head. Everything around me was buzzing. My legs were weak and shaky. I had the definite impression that I was never going to make that plane. But I absolutely and desperately had to make it.

First-level sensations pushing upward

I had gone through so many periods of almost delirious homesickness during which I thought of life in Paris night and day, yet any hope of going back had seemed nonexistent. I felt there was no room for me there. I had kept that plane ticket for two months, just waiting, and all of a sudden I was on my way. It was almost unreal. The thought that flashed through my mind then was: *Here I am, 10,000 km. from home, so far that it sometimes seems to exist only in my daydreams; and in a few hours I will effortlessly board a plane that only nine hours later will drop me off in another universe, so very far away.*

Then it clicked into place. I was being born. I had to get out and was being passively transported out into another world that I didn't know. It was just happening to me and I was unable to do anything about it—unable to either push out or go back in. I felt myself hanging upside down, my head pushing on something and not getting anywhere, and my whole body pushing against "it." All the blood was in my head (which accounts for the pressure I often feel in it, as well as for the tightness around my neck—since the blood couldn't circulate back down to my heart). As soon as I made this connection I felt fine—my headache went away, the blood flowed down out of my head, and I was no longer anxious about the trip. I finished my shopping, did my laundry, and packed my bags, all the time delighted by the thought that in less than twelve hours I would be home.

When I first arrived in France I stayed with a cousin in Paris. Here I had another birth dream. In this dream I was completely plastered, and my head was spinning around so fast that I had absolutely no sense of orientation. I was struggling like a fish to come out of a very tight passageway. Soon my eyes began to see light at the end of the tunnel. My vision was still blurred, but my mind began to clear and I distinctly felt that I was lying on my right side. At that moment I realized I was coming out of the birth canal, completely smashed.

A few days later I arrived at my parents' house to spend Christmas with them. I had not seen them in a year and a half. My mother and I stayed up quite late, talking over a bottle of wine. When I went to bed I felt a little tipsy—I cannot hold liquor very well. As soon as I lay down on my bed I felt unable to breathe. For four days I was so sick with asthma that I couldn't even sit in front of the television. I needed several shots of cortisone before the attack subsided.

The day before my departure I began to feel a bit better, until the oppressive atmosphere of my family hit me. I realized there is no gaiety, no laughter. My father is always so serious and silent—I have never seen him break out in a real belly laugh. My mother is always extremely tense, even outright terrified, in his presence. I always felt crushed under the weight of their seriousness—stifled and locked in a hole it seemed I would never get out of.

Asthma and feelings

Since then I have noticed a definite penchant I have for drinking just enough wine to put me into a state of hazy stupor, which I then try to fight off—I really try my hardest to wake up from it. I have also noticed that when I am in this state of lightheadedness I inevitably suffer an asthma attack. I also have asthma attacks when I feel that stifling desperation, that feeling of never being able to survive, of never being able to make it out of the bottomless hole I feel trapped in, and of feeling so crushed and stepped on that I cannot even lift my little finger to defend myself.

"No way out": an asthma attack

In 1974, the year before I entered medical school, my father stopped in Paris to visit me and discuss plans for putting me through school. His plan was simple. I would get room and board if I moved back in with them; and as for the rest, I would have to fend for myself. I flatly refused—the last thing I wanted was to find myself in the middle of their constant bickering. Besides, I had always felt unsafe in their house. My father left Paris and left me feeling helplessly trapped between living in their rigid and cold household, or being abandoned to fend for myself. How could I possibly find the money to put myself through medical school? There seemed to be no ray of hope, *no way out*. I would always be nothing, lost out in the middle of nowhere, miles from the rest of humanity. A couple of days later I suffered an asthma attack.

Born with asthma?

I am beginning to see a relationship betwen alcohol and asthma and alcohol and birth which leads me to feel that my asthma got its start in my birth.

I was born a full-term baby. My mother arrived at the maternity clinic at 5:30 A.M. and I was born at 9:30 A.M. She was anesthetized "at the last moment" (her words). I assume that to mean the moment my head was coming out through the cervix. At 6:00 P.M. on the day of my birth I suddenly started to choke, and turned completely blue. My mother called the midwife, who took me away to the operating room for oxygen. When she brought me back she told my mother she had removed a huge glob of mucus from my pharynx. The same incident occurred again twenty-four hours later. Quite possibly I was born with asthma and this was the end of my first attack, which had been triggered by the anesthetic (as it is now triggered by alcohol) I received as I was coming out of the birth canal.

Colitis

Colitis is an excellent example of first-line trauma manifest physically. Spasms of the colon are one of the few ways the neonate can respond to stress. If enough compounding occurs throughout childhood to reactivate those spasms, an irritable colon leading to a chronic condition of colitis may result.

Colitis is a difficult condition to treat because its tendency is imprinted very early and its associated Pain is all but inaccessible. Colitis is literally grinding oneself internally. It is the result of friction between the forces of *ex*pression and those of *re*pression. It is analogous to grinding of the teeth, a tendency which occurs later and is more associated with second-line trauma. Spasms for the first-liner become prototypic, and may later become entwined with a personality type which "keeps everything inside."

This trauma has nothing to do with words. There is nothing to express except Pain. There is nothing to say that will help. But the agonizing sounds that result from experiencing the trauma which led to those spasms can help resolve the tendency; not one sound but many, for first-line Pains are never resolved in one sitting. The charge value of the Pain is too great for that. In working with patients with colitis, we know that first-line Pain is coming up when their colitis really begins to kick up; at that point patients will almost always go directly into a birth Primal.

Headaches and Migraines

An example of a first-line sensation emerging in later life as a symptom is the pressured feeling in one's head that arises when one is upset. That sensation on or in the head can replicate the birth situation in which the infant's head *was* literally pounding against the mother's pubic arch for hours. The result is a lasting vulnerability to head pressure. We observe how patients automatically butt their heads against a padded wall for hours over a period of months as they re-experience the endless pounding to get out at birth. And let us not overlook the fact that many infants become head-bangers in their cribs. This kind of trauma is more apt to lead to pressure or tension headaches than to migraines. The pressure headache is so common today that it is accepted as an unpleasant but unavoidable part of living. Advertising on television for headache remedies suggests that it is universal. But what is really universal seems to be that struggle of having butted our heads against the pubic arch. Given a natural childbirth I doubt if headaches would be so prevalent. For those of us who had this struggle, almost any stress can set off that birth sensation of taut muscles, head pressure and/or headaches.

Migraines differ from pressure headaches in that they are often the result of oxygen loss at birth coupled with the associated build-up of excess carbon dioxide. The target organs in this case are the blood vessels as opposed to the muscles. The excess of carbon dioxide is a powerful dilator of blood vessels and that dilation is the chief ingredient of a migraine. Adult stress evokes that original loss of oxygen with all its painful repercussions.

The evolution of a migraine is usually two-phased. In response to birth trauma there is first constriction of the blood vessels against the pain. Second, the defense of constriction becomes life-threatening as well, and the body in an attempt to recapture its oxygen produces massive dilation of the vessels. This is the cause of the feeling of great pressure in the head. We then take pills to help the original defense of the vessels, medication known as vasoconstrictors. In almost every case the medication for symptoms is designed to bolster the body's faltering defenses.

The pressure headache tends to be more common and less severe. One patient explained his muscle tension headaches as follows: "The long physical struggle at birth made me stiff and sore in the neck and shoulders, and I've been that way ever since. My head was misshapen and I was born bruised. My headaches always begin behind my eyes." His birth Primals helped solve that chronic focus for tension and clarified why his headaches always began in his eyes. During one Primal he felt fingers pressing in his eyesockets to pull him out. The pressure in the eyes remained as a memory. Stress, attacking the most vulnerable parts first, always began in his eyes, which foretold of the headache to come.

Joint Pains

Another example of imprinted physical hurt came from a patient who at the age of thirty-four had developed rheumatoid arthritis. During his birth Primals he felt the excruciating and prolonged cramping he had undergone and understood that his joints had been marked as vulnerable spots from the time of birth onward. Tension would become focused there, producing permanent Pain in his leg and knee joints. That Pain was actually a memory. Any attempt to massage or manipulate the joints was therefore a futile attempt to tamper with memory. No matter what the temporary relief from massage, the memory and its hurt won out and the Pain returned.

And another:

Birth history   My mother told me that her water broke the morning I was supposed to be born. Then all the contractions stopped until about 6:00 P.M., when they resumed. I was born a couple of hours later.

Reliving origin of symptom

During one Primal I felt how I was in an abnormal fetal position. When I was ready to come out, my legs from my knees to my feet were behind my back. Because of this I suffered great pain in my knees and at one point in my delivery I thought that I would die because my knees were about to break. At this critical moment my legs straightened and I was delivered. Unfortunately, the doctor held me up by my knees (instead of the usual ankle position) and more Pain was added to this area. I had bruises appear on both sides of my knees after one of these birth Primals.

Resolution

When I was a youngster I was told I only had "growing pains" when I complained of sore knees and legs. When I was twenty-one, after the birth of my first son, I went to a clinic for rheumatoid arthritis and was told there was nothing wrong with me. They could not explain the Pain. I no longer have Pain in my legs and knees as a result of my birth Primals.

Thyroid Imbalances

We have seen that a thyroid condition in the mother can be passed on to her fetus during gestation. We have also found that the birth trauma itself can effect an alteration in thyroid functioning, even when the mother's thyroid was normal during pregnancy. A drop in the mobilization of the baby's entire body so as to conserve its energy at birth and save itself by not fighting can be accompanied by a drop in one of the mobilizing hormones—namely, the thyroid. Later on a continuous drop in thyroid—hypothyroidism—can have serious consequences for one's general health and can affect, among other things, hair texture, general energy level, skin tone, bone development and weight gain and distribution.

Upper Respiratory Disease

The origins of such chronic ailments as bronchitis, sinus congestion and sore throats may lie in one's birth experience. Following is a report by a patient describing her discovery that this was indeed the case.

Symptoms

Through feeling my birth I have found the origin of several symptoms I have been plagued by throughout my life: nasal congestion, bronchitis and sore throats.

Primal connection

Before I felt the birth connections to these symptoms I developed such a huge swollen gland in my neck that I had to go to an emergency room for treatment. The doctor didn't know what had caused it. About a week later I had a Primal in which I was a tiny baby with some fluid in my throat that was threatening to suffocate me. In the feeling, I cried and retched. There was something in my throat that shouldn't have been there, and I am sure that the mysterious lump was a forerunner to the feeling. I have had to feel this feeling a lot and it still has not gone completely.

Before these Primals I get a build-up of phlegm in my nasal passages and am constantly trying to clear my throat. To feel the feeling I have to lie on my side— there really is phlegm in my throat in the present and I could choke in the present if I stayed on my back. I cry fiercely, making a sort of "Oh, oh, oh" sound, and with each "Oh" I am trying to push out more of the alien fluid. It is a life-and-death struggle; it takes up all my energy and sometimes ends with a horrible scream.

Symptom resolution After I feel these feelings my nose is clear and I can breathe freely for the first time in my life. One morning I lay in bed just breathing—just enjoying the sensation of the air rushing, unobstructed, into my lungs. I am convinced that a lifetime "stuffy nose" originated in my birth experience.

It also makes sense to me that later in life whenever things went wrong—when my brother died and my father left home—I would get bronchitis. (In my medical treatment I would have to lie on my stomach and cough up as much phlegm as possible.) These times of extreme stress triggered memories of my birth and produced a birth trauma symptom—trying to keep from dying from some fluid in my windpipe.

Born with a sore throat? Then the feeling took a slightly different turn. Before I connected to it, though, I had a very sore throat. In my Primal I was a tiny baby and I was crying about the Pain in my throat. At one point in the Primal I felt something going down my throat and scraping the back of it. Whatever this was it hurt me a lot. I cannot know for sure, but it seems likely that since I had fluid blocking my windpipe they may have tried to remove it with some kind of instrument. I also cannot be one hundred percent sure yet, but it is possible that my frequent sore throats may be coming from this. I hope so, because then when I've felt enough of the feeling I won't have to suffer from them anymore.

Sex and the Birth Trauma

Sex is another way that many of us deal with first-line Pain. Whereas the sensations of sex are not sensations from the birth process, the convulsive tendencies in sex may be. There are those who need convulsive release through compulsive sex. Their Pain has been so great that only compulsive sex with its massive release through orgasm is enough to keep the overload at a manageable level that allows them to function. If they are not able to do this, there is nothing else on their minds but sex.

What is really "on their minds" is first-line pressure reconverted by the same part of the brain that handles pressure—the hypothalamus. Once this reconversion of Primal energy into sexual energy has taken place the ideas and impulses for sex set in. It is again a case of the proper sensations and feelings in the wrong context. Since sex feels good and seems so obvious a need, most neurotics who are compulsively sexual have no idea that they are neurotic. They just think they are hypersexed. But what they eventually discover in their birth Primals is that their compulsive sexual "needs" are really first-line *Pains* reconverted and discharged sexually.

One patient who was insatiable in sex (who also had an enormously high tension level) suffered from high blood pressure whenever she didn't "get enough." The pressure simply took a biologic detour. Outside of epilepsy sex is the only way one can produce physical convulsions and discharge a large amount of convulsive tension very quickly. Very often convulsive Pain requires frequent, convulsive sex. If sex is not possible, the massive energy can be released piecemeal—tics being one way, stuttering another. Those who have had a number of birth Primals have considerably reduced needs for sex. Those outside of therapy who cannot have sex when they want it find themselves uncomfortably close to their Pain because for the moment they are deprived of an outlet. (It is the same thing as the smoker who smokes the minute any tension comes up. The smoking takes the edge off the Pain and thus prevents the person from ever even recognizing that there's a relationship between the need to smoke and imprinted Pain.)

No theories or hypotheses are necessary to "prove" the relationship between sex and the birth trauma. For the patient who has had a birth Primal and then reports great and unexpected—and, I might add, unsuggested—change in his or her sex life, the experience is sufficient proof. Improvement in sex after birth Primals happens with regularity to many hundreds of patients. The reason is clear: sex and neurosis are both of the body, not just the mind. Sexual behavior is embedded in that neurosis and reflects it; the deeper the neurosis the more likely there will be a problem with sex.

The primitive part of the nervous system that mediates sexual functioning also mediates the birth trauma. The birth trauma and birth Primal often deal with convulsions, and the blockage of those convulsions often means the diminution of sexual response. Interestingly enough, we learned of this relationship after the fact: liberating the convulsions of birth seemed to enhance the responsive convulsions of sex. This has proven particularly true for women, who have reported feeling freer and more lubricated sexually following birth Primals than after any other kind of Primals— including those dealing directly with sexual inhibitions set down by parents. The explanation is simple: there is a widespread shutdown of the body when terrible Pain occurs at birth. This shutdown, when compounded by sexual constraints later on, leads to various kinds of frigidity or impotence in which almost no sexual sensations occur during intercourse.

In addition to the general shutdown there are also the more specific contributions of birth trauma to sex functions. For example, one patient had a Primal in which she struggled to the point of death in the canal. She had been born anoxic and blue. The stamped-in memory/experience was that before one comes alive there is death (or near death). The connection she made to her sex life was that when she was about to climax—to really come alive and enjoy herself—she went "dead." She suddenly shut off. She could never understand why, since her parents had been quite liberal about sex. She also made the discovery that this was how she dealt with her whole life. Whenever she was on the verge of success with her boyfriend, whenever she had a very good time, she had to do something to ruin it. Happiness scared her; she had to go through agonies first. She would pick a fight and then make up, then get along and feel good and then start the whole sequence over again. She was the absolute victim of her birth in her relationships. The irony of her situation was that the closer she got to life the closer she was to death. She was trapped in a "no exit" situation. She also realized that her violent headaches were the result of that ineluctable conflict. She continually ran off the birth sequence symbolically, always one step removed from herself.

Many women report that at the zenith of sexual excitement they go dead. Some women do well until penetration and then go dead. "There is something about the womb that is a reminder," reported one woman. Another felt that it was simply too much stimulation and so shut down. Another felt penetration as aggression, an assault against her person, still another as submission.

These are all second-line compounds of the birth trauma in which all was prepared for birth, the baby was "excited" sensorily for its adventure and its system was in a state of readiness. Then suddenly all closed up and shut down. The baby who was about to succeed and feel alive sensed that the mother (given an anesthetic) no longer had any life in her body. The baby became confused and terrorized—which later becomes the prototype for shutting down in sex. The birth trauma may then be compounded over the years by parents who are intolerant of enthusiasm and excitement, and whose main response to any kind of exuberance is to silence the child. Together the two experiences—one lasting minutes or hours, the other lasting years—synthesize the repression into a formidable determinant of feeling and behavior.

Men and women in the throes of birth Primals often become *less* sexual for a time. As noted previously, re-experiencing the birth trauma does not happen in just one session. For most patients, birth Primals extend over a period of several months. This means that the unleashed aspects of the birth trauma will require heavy repression as the leashed aspects are integrated. The system can take only so much Pain. Sexual orgasm during this time period frequently leads to a birth Primal immediately afterwards. It occasionally happens that the orgasm is preceded by birth concomitants such as gagging, coughing, inability to catch one's breath, etc. One patient wrote:

> I've found that the stronger the orgasm is, the stronger the Pain is. It's as if that pleasure brings instant Pain. I often find myself holding back from fully enjoying the orgasm because of the Pain it so often brings.
>
> When I focus on the feeling it feels like I am choking to death, and while I am choking I am fighting to stay alive. It really feels as if I am going to die, and I'm so scared because I know no one will come to help me. I fight and fight and fight, choking on my own phlegm, and then the feeling stops—I am exhausted.

For the patient in the process of having a series of birth Primals, having sex is really tampering with the repressive system that has marched in to shut off the Pain from the previous birth Primal and allow respite until the next. That often doesn't stop patients from sexual activity, but for a time it can be unpleasant. It seems the more one pushes down against the birth trauma the more one is either frigid or impotent. The more one opens up to it the more sexual one becomes.

Sex is a sensation, first and foremost. In humans it is also mixed with feeling and emotion. If both sensation (first-line) and emotion (second-line) are repressed, then the two elements essential in sex are simply not available. All that is left are third-level performances and renditions of how one *thinks* sex ought to be. Sex on this level is a sham.

It may be that there was no birth trauma—no first-line shutdown—only second-line prohibitions of sex via parental warnings and the like. In that event the sexual problem if it exists is not going to be nearly as severe. Its treatment will have nothing to do with birth. Conversely, it is possible that a bad birth occurs in a family in which the child experiences no later sexual inhibitions. Here too the problem will not be as deep as it would with second-line compounding; nonetheless the birth trauma will have to be addressed to resolve it fully.

Sex is an impulse. In many ways it is similar in quality to a Primal. In both the sex act and a Primal experience there are few words, there is a great upheaval of sensations and emotions, and a build-up of tension leading to climax and release. Both processes must evolve naturally; one step cannot be superimposed on another—one cannot make a performance out of either process—and neither the sexual nor the Primal release should come too soon or the feeling will be cut short.

It is for all these reasons that there is a kind of inverse relationship between sex and Primals: the more Primals the less need for compulsive sex. This is no more than saying the obvious, which is that Primal energy is often released in sex, and in this sense it is "contaminated" by it. The rerouting of Pain into sex is an automatic function such that the individual is rarely aware of what is happening. He or she feels a "sexual" pressure when it is much more likely to be Primal pressure rerouted. The release feels good, as does any release of tension. As one patient noted:

> The violent curling and thrashing of my spine, and the enormous need to thrust forward, the waves of gags and the powerful contractions to force fluid out of my lungs, those volcanic feelings that wanted to come shooting out of me into life all found release in sex. Sex has always been for me a matter of survival. A fight for life. A kind of dominate or be dominated. And of course I always tried to get my partners to react the way I wanted them to react. I also noticed that I usually screamed at the top of my lungs when I had orgasm. And I always thought it was sexual and now I know what it really is. I don't think my sex was very harmonious in the sense that I was always working against my partner, somehow a recreation of my birth. I had to have sex all the time because somehow it kept me alive.

The relationship between Primal and sexual upheavals is evident in any number of patients who report tears and crying during or after orgasm. They know now what they are dredging up with sex and they also note how remarkably similar the sounds are in both experiences.

Sex and Need

Much first-line trauma occurs during the perinatal period around and just after birth. These are critical periods for the newborn when needs must be fulfilled as never again. Two needs in particular are related to later sexual problems. The first is the need for touch, the second the need to suck. The baby must be touched and caressed immediately after birth. He must have the mother's warmth almost continually during this time; otherwise all the touch in the world will not be enough. Why? Because needs are in force at certain times in human development and must be attended to then and only then. To be left alone immediately after birth and then held a great deal three weeks later does not undo the Pain from that initial—and critical—deprivation.

This tells us why the neurotic can never be loved enough. He was not loved when he should have been. All of the rest of life is but a poor substitute; a symbolic ploy to the unconscious to try to "pretend" that the fulfillment has really occurred. One can never prove undying love to the neurotic because it will have to be "proven" again and again with reassurances in constant demand. What many people want out of sex is that touch rather than sex. They want the warmth, protection, love, closeness and reassurance that touch brings and the price they are willing to pay is sex.

The second need that is related to sex is the sucking need. The baby needs a long period of sucking the breast, both for nourishment and for fulfillment of the sucking need itself. There is no substitute for fulfilling this need at the proper time. One can suck on breasts for a lifetime, be fixated on them forever, have all the sucking one wants as an *adult* and never eradicate that original need.

The relationship between lack of breastfeeding and compulsive sex is direct. Both men and women who have relived that need discovered that throughout their lives the thought or sight of ample breasts was terribly exciting; and of course what is "exciting" in the sense of stimulating to the system is unfulfilled need. It incites like nothing else. It also leaves a residue of orality that Freud wrote about—the need to smoke and suck on cigarettes, or preferably a large cigar; the need to eat too much and talk too much are obvious sequelae. Compulsive oral sex is not the least of these residual effects of early oral deprivation. Because there are critical periods for fulfillment, breastfeeding—with its perioral stimulation to areas around the mouth—is a very important experience.

Birth, Sex and Identity

Sex doesn't mean just lovemaking. It involves a complicated sense of identity as male or female. We cannot function fully in the sex act if we don't feel good about what sex we are. One patient wrote:

> I felt *not wanted* at birth because I was not the boy that my parents wanted—I was just a girl. Up until my teen years I struggled to be a boy. At that point my struggle became "wanting to be a woman." I became interested in boys. But I was a failure as both a boy and as a woman.
>
> Since therapy at age thirty-nine, my breasts have finally developed. Ironically, this happened over a period of time in which I was feeling intensely about *wanting to be a boy*. My whole body has since changed. I still weigh from 115 to 120 pounds, but I seem more

relaxed—less taut—all over, and my hips are softer and fuller. I even walk differently—more fluidly.

Premature Ejaculation

The man with premature ejaculation is another case in point that relates sex and birth trauma. Ejaculation reflects the amount of pressure released. When the sum total of the electrical impulses, particularly those giant ones from birth, are evoked in sex, the pressure for release is enormous. Men with insufficient higher-level control will ejaculate too quickly. One reason for that lack of control is the lack of solidity of the third level due to a lifetime of first-line birth intrusion. The ongoing intrusion, because of its original force, prevents proper cohesion of the third-level in adulthood. So the energy of all of the traumas from birth onward is released in sex. Obviously premature ejaculation also has such second-line components as a fear of women, but much of the problem has nothing to do with sex at all. One can analyze it as a fear of women, fear of sex, fear of displeasing, fear of disapproval of performance etc., and still never fully resolve this problem. One can, it is true, help a bit by dealing with some later childhood aspects of it; one can controvert bad sex education, but it is not a profound approach.

Circumcision

The originating prototype of birth trauma isn't always restricted to birth itself. Circumcision shortly after birth can also cause prototypic Pain. Later threat or stress can set off anxiety or pain focused on the penis. In an unconscious way, a man may try to use his penis to discharge tension. Early in life this can take the form of bedwetting; later, of compulsive masturbation and sex. Or he will make an unconscious connection that by manipulating his penis he can avoid anxiety. Thus he may avoid having sex with a partner. This will be particularly true if second-line compounding involves fear of the mother and later fear of women. Then the way to avoid anxiety would be not to have heterosexual experiences.

The point is that a prototypic trauma such as circumcision can focus Pain and its reactions on the penis. The penis becomes the symptom. Sex clinicians or other symptom-treating professionals might focus treatment on the penis without recognizing its connection to very early Pain. This is something that neither patient nor therapist could even guess at without access to the deeper levels of consciousness. The prototype sets up a permanent focus—in this case, the penis—as well as a characteristic way of reacting. The prototypic situation has a permanent directive effect, which means that there is no profound personality change to be made without resolution of the prototype.

One patient wrote:

I had a first-line feeling come up after about five months of therapy.
The trigger was a paper cut I had gotten at work from the edge of a
cardboard box. For the remainder of the day I was obsessed by the
thought of being captured in a war and somehow having my penis cut
lengthwise, from the tip downward.
    After work I lay down and let myself feel a sensation around my
penis, although I wouldn't say it was exactly a cutting feeling. But
after that I didn't worry about being cut anymore. My fear in the
present involved having the tip of my penis cut, while the Primal
involved a feeling around it—about an inch back.

Homosexuality

No one can say at this point that the birth trauma "causes" homosexuality, but it has been our observation that the homosexuals we have seen in
therapy have had catastrophic birth histories. Gestation experiences
together with the birth trauma may bias male-female sex hormone relationships permanently, leaving certain proclivities or tendencies. These
tendencies may shape the way a person responds to later events so that,
for example, the loss of a father or a mother may be responded to in a
different way—a more feminine way in the male, a more masculine way in
the female—than for someone who has had a different birth history. The
implications of this are not only that the level of Pain is significant in
homosexuality, but also that the traumas involved in many cases may be
very early, even prenatal, events. That would help explain why some
homosexuals feel that they were "born that way," and why those individuals would face great difficulty in feeling and resolving the origins of their
homosexuality.
    The roots of homosexuality are deep indeed, and to think that one can
treat it in adulthood by encouraging a person to go to bed with someone of
the opposite sex is to take a superficial approach. We also know that in any
given family two children with the same parents will respond quite
differently to the parental situation. One sibling may become homosexual
and the other not. Of course, they will have many other early experiences
that will also shape them. But it is clear that children react differently to
their world from very early on. That is because there is already a rather
lengthy history of experience in the child that predates his relationship
with his parents. This early history in the womb and at birth may be quite
different for each child, and thus may make each a different kind of person
before they ever meet their parents in the world.
    By retrospective observation we know that hormone output is shaped
early on. We see men begin beard growth in their thirties as a result of

therapy and first-line Primals; we see breast development in women as a result of their Primals. We can assume that early Pain has interfered with hormone output and balance because altering Pain levels produce changes in hormone levels. We note, too, that in some cases homosexuality has been reversed by removing Primal Pain. This reversal usually occurs only after a long period of first-line Primals. The logical conclusion, then, is that homosexuality is a deep-lying tendency, a total personality state, not confined to sexual behavior alone. I have long contended that homosexuality is a problem of need rather than sex. It is a case in which need gets sexualized rather than the other way around. In instances of prenatal and birth trauma, need gets sexualized in the most primary way possible: physiologically by altering hormone balances.

Each of us has a personality that is partially shaped by our birth experiences. As part of our entire developmental history we have certain sexual preferences. Those preferences are part of our physiology. Our personality, homosexual or not, is found in every cell, membrane, muscle and bone. We are shaped organically, which means that we do not grow up "normal" and then "adopt" homosexuality. That tendency has been imprinted from the earliest days in the womb.

More often than not, the person who turns to homosexuality as an adult has had much compounding stress and Pain throughout childhood and adolescence. For example, one male homosexual patient had the additional problem of having suffered from insufficient breastfeeding and later from a lack of affection from his father. As a result he was "hooked on sucking"—penises. Whenever he saw a man his first impulse was to want to suck. Further, he had to make the man come. An insight from one of his birth Primals was that he experienced the other man's orgasm as sucking milk from his own mother's breast. In acting this out unconsciously, he found excitement in his partner's ejaculation.

As the birth and post-birth traumas begin their ascent after one year in therapy, he began to have nightmares in which a penis would turn into a breast. These dreams foretold of feeling and memories to come. As the original need to suck his mother's breast surfaced, the need to suck penises began to diminish. This required months of Primals dealing with the deprivation of both needs—the lack of breastfeeding and the lack of fatherly affection—needs deprived for many years and composed of thousands of experiences condensed and compressed into a few intense feelings. Within the unity of those few feelings lay the multitude of experiences which told the same story: "You have no mother and no father . . . no one wants you . . . no one wants to hold you . . . no one wants to love you."

It is interesting that this patient often smacked his lips unconsciously when he Primalled about his father. Unbeknownst to him he was simply transferring the sucking reflex from his mother—who *didn't* fulfill that need—to his father—who *might* fulfill the need. His mother had been ill from the beginning of his life. There was no hope there. His father offered at least the possibility of love. Unfortunately it remained only a possibility. *But need never allows hope to die.*

We can see with this need to suck how futile it is to deal with a disorder such as homosexuality on the verbal level. There is no exhortation or insight, no conditioning in the world that can alter the original need. Needs evolve genetically and are fundamental to survival. The patient's homosexuality was an attempt at survival and had that special force behind it; that is why its compulsion was so strong. It was an attempt to fulfill a genetically encoded survival need, albeit symbolically, because the body always veers toward its needs, no matter how hard external forces try to push it elsewhere.

Another male homosexual patient reported his lifelong fear of women and, of course, of his mother. Whenever he began to have sex with a woman he became apprehensive, wanted to flee, and felt as if death were impending. In his birth Primals he felt the connection between not being allowed out of the womb on time and the feeling that his mother was "against" him. In a very literal sense her body had acted against his efforts to be born. In sex, getting close to the womb evoked the same threatening feelings and drove him away from women. He had almost died in the womb. This unconscious memory was an important force, later compounded by lack of warmth from his mother and ultimately manifested in homosexuality.

Following are extensive reports by two French patients who lived and experienced both the homosexuality and its connections to early trauma. The first report was written by a woman who had been in therapy for thirteen months.

Loneliness: "inscribed in my skin"

My first birth Primal felt like a fissure was seared inside of me, and now all kinds of things are pouring out. Above all is the feeling of a terrible loneliness. I remember a book, *The Well of Loneliness,* about a lesbian, and it is an apt description.

In my Primal yesterday I became aware that whenever I am held I feel like a small child, the child who should have been held a long time ago. The moment I am in the arms of my lover (who at present is a woman), I am myself—but "myself" as a baby and a child. I want comfort and protection; I want to stay in the embrace forever. Being held is what I have wanted more than anything. The loneliness of not having had it feels as if it were inscribed in my skin—that constant ache of never having been touched. During this feeling my hands become deathly cold.

Childhood connection

To help me go with this feeling my therapist embraced me. Suddenly I felt panicked—no room to breathe. I began to feel suffocated and I fought physically to get out of the embrace. It felt like I was being suffocated by my mother who later in life seemed to need me more than I needed her; and tried to make up for a lifetime of not touching me by now squeezing me very hard and holding on very tightly.

Birth connection

I suddenly felt confused—I wanted to be touched but I was also overwhelmed by it. Confusion then turned into anger, anger at being deprived and then suffocated. The front of my head felt funny, vulnerable. I turned onto my stomach and began to move rhythmically and involuntarily, with my head feeling more and more vulnerable. I started pushing against the pillow with my head in such a way that I made a pocket. The pocket then clicked into a womb feeling; I was swept away, suffocating, not able to breathe. My head felt like jelly; I felt helpless and trapped. I was sure I was going to die. There was the urge to push and the wanting to give up at the same time. It was too painful. The feeling finally ended, and I felt a relief.

Present-day elaborations

I came out of it—it had felt almost like a kind of violent coma—with the immediate perception of the parallels between my birth and some of the structures I have built around me—my life patterns. I realized that I have left a string of unfinished things in my life. I have studied art, literature, psychology, and am now doing ceramics. I am usually good at things I attempt, but then a pressure builds up inside of me and I quit and go on to something else. At birth the physical pressure was so strong, so life-endangering, that I kept giving up the push to finish and get born. I needed physically to run away from this agony, to flee to safety, but it was not possible. Now I do it symbolically when I quit my projects halfway through. Also, there was too much physical stimulation without any actual warmth or caressing throughout my birth. And it has been like that ever since. I never had physical contact that was reassuring and comforting. It was always "pressure," smothering and life-endangering.

Birth trauma and sexual "preference"

It set up my aversion for any kind of tight embrace, particularly in sex with the man on top and me pinned underneath—it is completely intolerable. Being with a woman in lovemaking is gentler for me. A woman's embrace is lighter, less restricting, less physically overpowering. I am not under a man's control. It seems that in every cell of my body I carry the imprint of the terror of having fought for my life at birth.

Childhood (second-level) compounding

I suppose my sexuality was formed to a degree at birth. It was compounded throughout my life by my mother who used to beat me for masturbating as a child. She told me that it would cripple me, that I'd become retarded, etc., etc., all from touching myself. When I had to have my appendix out at the age of seven she told me it was punishment for masturbating. I wasn't touched and I wasn't allowed to touch myself.

I remember my mother touching me warmly at certain times—whenever she diapered me she would cup my vagina in her hand and say affectionate things to me. I needed more physical comfort as I got older, so I masturbated; I masturbated and got beaten.

Reliving: from fear to "life-saving" connections

I am full of fear. These connections are life-saving for me because before my life was just so many fragments. I had all of these terrors making themselves felt in the present without any understanding of their origins. My only reality was fear. I think I turned to women out of this fear and, funnily enough, the fear at birth—the constriction, being overpowered, being held in and held back—all seem to be important in why I turned away from men. I have never been able to be "under anyone's thumb." I think these Primals will save me from a lot of unfinished projects, too much failure and maybe from a detoured sex life.

The next report was written by a male patient:

I was born in 1951 to parents who were small farmers. I started therapy at the Primal Institute about four years ago because of homosexuality, and I now work in Europe as a teacher in economics and social sciences.

Early discovery of a difference

I was about four years old and was having a walk with my grandmother when I asked her to explain the difference between men and women. As she did, I somehow realized that I could not function within that pattern, that there was something wrong in my mind about that: I needed something from a man that you were supposed to get from a woman. I did not know then, of course, that there was a special name for that, and I didn't worry too much about it.

When I started school I simply avoided girls, which was not difficult since we were not allowed to sit together in class and also had to play in different areas. I was mostly interested in studying and in being first in class, to please my parents. I did not get very much acquainted with the other boys; I felt different and "special." They were talking a lot about girls and I was not interested; in this area I felt inferior to them.

Discovery of "deviation"

Then at the age of ten I found a book about sexual deviation titled something like "The Third Sex" and I started to understand a little more about what was wrong with me. And I was worried. At school I wanted older male pupils to help me and take care of me. I felt lost except in class. At ten my parents put me in boarding school; I felt like I was dying.

I used to go to the restrooms during breaks when the older boys were there, and seeing their genitals fascinated me. From that time on I became addicted to men's rooms. I used to go to these places, watch penises, walk out, walk around for a while, then come back again. I was a "penis addict."

Death of the father

When I was 21 my father committed suicide. The farm broke up and the family scattered. I started having relations with men at an emotional as well as sexual level. It was quite easy for me to meet a lot of homosexual men, and I had many different lovers. Sometimes the relationship lasted just one night, sometimes several weeks or months.

Acting it out

The first time I sucked a penis, I became very excited and it made me feel good. At the beginning these experiences were fantastic. I was feeling so released; being with a man made me feel at peace, and I had dreamed of that for such a long time. Later it was not so good and I had a sense somewhere deep inside that it was not real, that I was destroying myself.

First long-term homosexual relationship

Then I had one lover, Daniel, for two years. We really liked each other but there was always tension between us. We would split up and then our need made us come back. He was a nice person and kind; he was like a father for me. But I never seemed to get what I wanted from him: of course, he could not give me what my father had not given me in the past. I realized that if I could not get what I wanted from Daniel, then I would never get it from any man, because Daniel was the kindest of all the men I had been involved with.

The hopeless paradox

I had come to realize through a kind of self-analysis that something was wrong with the life I was living. I was caught up in a paradox that made me feel hopeless: I was looking for a man who was masculine and able and willing to give me affection; but, being a homosexual himself, he could not fulfill my needs because he was just as needy!

I decided to give up sexual relations with men. I suffered over that choice, but fortunately Daniel and I were able to remain friends. Then I read *The Primal Scream.* I cried and basically understood why I became homosexual. Months later I came to The Primal Institute for therapy.

Childhood trauma

I have felt many feelings about my parents not loving me and not being interested in me. My mother was always distant and treated me very roughly even though she was anxious to be perceived by the neighbors as a good mother. One day in a session I was crying about my mother. I had a great deal of feeling in my body and my hand was moving close to my mouth like I was masturbating a guy to get his liquid. Suddenly in my mind the penis turned into my mother's breasts. I stopped crying, astonished by the realization. I had been breastfed one or two days and then fed with a bottle.

First birth feeling: from a penis to a breast

Overwhelming birth need to suck

Another time, while a friend sat with me, I felt a sequence of prolonged physical struggle like I was coming out in birth, and I felt a terrible need in my mouth for sucking. The feeling was overwhelming. I grabbed my friend and wanted to suck him all over, which I had often felt when I was having sex with men. The feeling was: I have such a need that I am ready to suck anything.

Re-creating the birth pressure

Recently at work I received a bad teaching schedule, contrary to the one I had requested. It made me feel rejected by the administration. I went to a room to feel that, and soon it became my parents against me during my childhood and then my mother against me, this time in purely physical terms, in the canal during birth. All my life I have experienced outside reality—other people, events, circumstances—as being against me, as pressure. It is becoming clear to me that I have moved through life the same way I moved through the birth canal, experiencing everything as a source of pressure no matter what, re-creating pressure "around" me even when there is none. It is almost as if I needed to have such pressure on me at all times to prevent myself from feeling the real, original pressure.

Family dynamics

A kind of vicious circle developed between my

parents and me from the beginning. When my mother was pregnant they had many expectations for me, that I would be the continuation of the farm. It was very important to them as Europeans, with a farm handed down from their ancestors, to have a son who would take over. And there I was, crying and demanding from the start. They thought I was an abnormal child—and they told me so all during my childhood—which increased that sense of everything being "against me." When my brother was born a year and a half later, they preferred him because he was a happier, quieter child.

Demanding "from the start"

Most of the attention I got from my mother when I was small was when she fed me—mostly forcing food into my mouth since I had no appetite—and when she removed my diapers and cleaned me. I have had feeling about wanting my mother to hug and touch *all* of me, not just my rear. Being touched there made me very excited during homosexual relations. I became focused on my mouth and my ass, which is not surprising since I was actually treated more like a tube than a human being.

Childhood rein- forcements

When I was small my father paid attention to me, played and talked with me, and carried me on his shoulders. But as his marriage deteriorated, which it did very quickly, he withdrew inside himself. He became depressed, mentally absent, lost social interests and stopped seeing his friends. And he stopped paying attention to me. Then in boarding school I only saw him on the weekends. My brother stayed home and became his helper on the farm. One Sunday morning my father got up very early to take my brother fishing, leaving me behind in the darkness of my bedroom. I have often cried about that scene, because it sums up a lot of my feelings.

Relationship with parents

So even though I got very little from my father, I longed for more of the affection he had expressed to me when I was small. And my mother was so cold that there was no hope on her side. Later the message was as clear as if it had been written on my mind: that closeness and love was possible only with a man. When my father killed himself, I was lost, sad and in need, and it was only then that I began acting out homosexually.

Father's suicide ini- tiates homosexual acting out

In my life now, I no longer feel a need for homosexual relations. Homosexual fantasies may come up when I am tense but disappear after feeling the source of the tension. It is now very clear to me, when I see a

Resolution   homosexual man who would have fit my fantasies, that
I am in front of a person in pain and need, a person who
obviously could not fulfill my need for a father.

My relations with women have benefited a great deal
from the therapy. I had never had sex with a woman in
my life. I was afraid that I would not be able to handle
such closeness and that I would faint.

After two years of therapy I started having sex with
Homosexuality: a   women and got pleasure out of it. Now social and
way to survive   sexual relationships with women are common experiences in my life. I knew that it was something real that
I wanted to have. I am starting to live daily with my
girlfriend—a situation that had always looked like an
impossible dream. I may still have difficulties in my
relations with women for a long time, especially in
letting go completely during sex, but these difficulties
become smaller to the degree I feel the feelings involved. At least now I can use my time and energy to
fulfill my present need. I do not have to look for a man
to give me what my father did not give me, or avoid
women because my mother hurt me. I realize now this
homosexuality was the way I found to survive a lack of
love.

Childhood Trauma and Adult Sexuality

There are some catastrophic events in childhood that can be equal to or
greater than the valence of first-line birth trauma in distorting later sexual
response. Incest and rape are two examples; death of a loved one another.

Incest which has been repressed and ascends toward consciousness has
the same power as birth to disrupt the mind and produce either the feeling
of going crazy or insanity itself. The rise of both birth and incest memories
have the same catastrophic, depressing effect that makes one suicidal.

One woman lost her beloved father at age five. She had been very close
to him. That one experience left her with a lifelong fear of being left after
being open and close to a man. The closer she came as an adult to a loving
man, particularly in sex, the more shut-down she became. That experience for her was a very high valence because it, too, involved survival.
The intolerable feeling was that her father was gone forever.

Social Implications of the Birth Trauma in Sex

Most professionals today believe that the answer to sexual problems
lies in sex education. But sexual behavior really has less to do with sex
education (or miseducation) than with nonsexual traumas which have left
their mark in the body. This is not to say that sex education plays no role,

because it certainly does. But in terms of the relative charge value of the traumas affecting and suppressing bodily function, poor sex education on the second level of consciousness—no matter how traumatic—is no match for the birth trauma. The pain voltage of an admonition against "fooling around" is rarely equal to the Pain voltage of birth trauma; and it is voltage, ultimately, that one is suppressing in the body through increased electrical activity in the brain and with alterations in biochemical patterns.

We must remember that an early Primal trauma creates a literal electrical storm in the brain. It is "capped" by the various repressive gating mechanisms of the central nervous system but its energy forms a perpetual fountain dispersed here and there. We each then find ways to literally discharge electrical impulses. It is difficult to keep this in mind when we talk about human beings because we seem to believe that we're above being simply matter with electrical energy.

Sexual orgasm involves a complete release of feeling. In a repressed individual that release is not possible: there is an ongoing clash between *release* and *inhibition* in the body, quite apart from the sexual component. Sexual activity simply heightens that conflict; and while it does provide some release, it is not the complete release that occurs when repression is not present.

Because release is global, any total release tends also to release Pain. No wonder so many of us smoke, cry or feel slightly anguished or depressed after having sex.

Sex is but a condensed version of all of one's neurosis and one's life. It is a concentrated dose of one's internal reality because during it intense feelings are on the ascent and immediately available. These same feelings are there in us with or without sex, but what the concentration in sex does is bring up the entire sequence and its *irr*esolution within a short space of time. Like a dream, it is a kind of time-lapse camera. Indeed, sex is the "royal road to the unconscious."

I believe that one factor in the detachment of sex from emotion in so many people is the disconnection among the levels of consciousness. If we live in our heads, we will have a hard time feeling our bodies. If we are stuck in birth feelings our ability to develop emotional attachments will suffer. To suppress our emotional lives leaves us with only the raw and partially suppressed sensations of sex.

Feeling the few but intense Primal feelings that get attached to countless and diverse experiences literally unlocks our "memory bank." In some respects, Primal feelings constellate into something like a "black hole" in space that sucks everything within its radius into it. The Primal "black hole" sucks in experience after experience, compounding the feeling until its force is enormous. That is why one can only experience parts of it at a time. Each new scene taps a minuscule part of the Primal feeling.

The consequence is this: We cannot suppress what our bodies contain and not suffer sexually. To convulse from long repressed Pain means to be able finally to react convulsively in sex.

Dreams and the Physical Implications of Birth Trauma

One of the best ways to understand how birth sensations remain in our systems is through dreams and nightmares. Here we often find the feelings of being choked, pressured, stuck, suffocated and crushed. We can suffer birth sensations in our dreams for decades and never know their source. There is always a "story" in the dream to justify the sensation but that is simply the work of the second level of consciousness. Yet whatever symbol is provided by a higher level of consciousness, it is the sensations themselves that reflect the real event in one's past.

One patient, for example, had constant nightmares in which he felt that he was dying. He had to wake himself up to make sure he was still alive. This was a re-creation of how it felt to come out of birth—into life, confused and overwhelmed by the experience.

This patient also constantly had the image of having his head pulled over a fence by the "enemy" and then learned that he had been born in an upper-brow presentation, with his head thrown back in a locked neck position. This image as well as the nightmares were resolved by his birth Primals. From this we see how it was the deeper imprint that produced his sensations, not the apparent "story line" of his nightmares.

Another patient, born Cesarean after a very long labor, reported:

> I used to have a dream when I was very young that someone was sitting on my chest. The pressure in my chest comes back periodically, and then I know it is the birth Pain coming up. I used to think I had an ulcer the Pain was so intense.

There is little interpretive cortex at birth to make sense of traumas. And even if there were, what is being done to the newborn really makes little sense. With the later development of the cortex one is forced to "guess" at what has gone on in the remote past, down deep in the nervous system, to a different cluster of neuronal cells. That guess is usually wrong. The function of dreams is like that guess. It makes up a story in retrospect; and indeed its function is *not* to tell the truth but to disguise it. The real story is much too painful to be told directly.

I shall now discuss a few nightmares that everyone seems to experience at one time or another. If they sound familiar, we must ask why. What is the basis for the commonality? What is it about our experiences that makes us all have such similar nightmares?

Stuck in a Tunnel

The nightmare of being stuck in a tight tunnel or shaft is something many of us have had. Those sensations would not be evident in us unless there were a memory circuit to produce them. There is. It is the memory of being squeezed too tightly in the birth canal. And, as with the nightmare, that is an experience many of us have had.

It may seem like quite a leap to assume that the experience underlying this common nightmare is a birth trauma, but I wouldn't posit it had not so many hundreds of patients relived the Pains and resolved the nightmares. I remember my own nightmares of being stuck in a washing machine and revolving around the center core of the machine in a very thick fluid. I couldn't catch my breath. That was truly a "birth" nightmare.

Light at the Tunnel's End

Accompanying the dream of being in a tunnel is often the feeling of seeing light at the end and trying to get to it. The symbolism is obvious— literally seeing the "light of day" at the end of the birth canal. So many children need to see some kind of light on when faced with going to sleep in a dark room because their memory of the birth trauma is near the surface.

Inability to Scream

Many of us have had nightmares in which we can neither speak nor scream. In fact, we cannot make a noise. This is because the level of brain organization which predominates during the deep sleep nightmare has no words. The second level of consciousness is involved in making up a story for us that makes our terror rational, and then the first level sees to it that we cannot scream or open our mouths. That is the sensation at birth— being unable to open our mouths. The suffering that goes on in the womb is all in silence. The baby can kick and move but it cannot call out for help. The child may then whine for years because he couldn't really scream out directly in the womb.

Car with No Brakes

Here is a classic birth nightmare from one of our patients:

I am driving my car and find that I have no brakes. I can no longer control the car, and it is going faster and faster. I begin to feel totally helpless and I think that I'm going to die. The car flies off the road and I fall and fall. I think to myself, "What is the best position to get into to avoid being hurt?" I get into a fetal position, feeling this is the last second of my life. The car starts crushing me from the crash, but it is crushing me softly. It is like there are cushions around me that don't leave me any space. I can't breathe; I feel trapped. I wake up breathless and in terror.

The sensations of not being able to catch one's breath, of being crushed, of falling and of terror are very much those of birth. The story, in fact, is not far from the actual birth sequence. The feeling of "no brakes" and of falling mirrors the birth experience of being moved by powerful contractions and of being literally unhooked from a stable position and moved downwards. The dream sensation of being crushed softly while in a fetal position reproduces the birth sensation of moving from the uterus into the birth canal.

Another patient reported:

In my dream I was driving a car and I wanted to stop. My brakes didn't respond—I pushed the brakes on and on without success. It was an awful feeling not to be able to stop. It seemed somehow that I was falling into space without being able to hold onto anything at all. All this happened in a split second.

Then I had the feeling that my mother pushed me out very quickly before I was ready—before I could "apply any brakes." This has affected my life so that whenever I talk to people the words come out of my mouth like I came out of my mother—extremely quickly—without enough time for careful thought and reasoning. My whole personality has always been impulsive.

The "brakes" *are* literally off in the dream state: the third-line braking or inhibitory system has "gone to sleep" (inhibition is the central function of the third line). Feelings then get out of control and one *feels* out of control. Certainly the most uncontrollable experience we have all had is the birth experience. In a birth with any trauma whatsoever, the over-riding feelings in the fetus are of helplessness and terror. It is exactly those feelings that appear again in the nightmare.

Stop the Battle

In the battle nightmare themes of attack, chase and enemy predominate. One patient reported:

I am on a ride at Disneyland. It's on a track and there is a whole long thing that keeps winding around and curving. I am in this machine on the track and I believe I've found a safe place. Outside of the machine the Germans are fighting the Americans. I'm the only one safe. The Americans are trying to kill me by trying to push me to fight against the Germans. I feel the pressure of them trying to get me to move. The machine goes around the whole course. Just when I think the ride is finished and everything is going to be okay, it starts all over again. Suddenly it stops and I feel that if I stay there I'll die. I have to get it to move or I'll die. I start moving.

This was a recurrent dream for the patient. The fact that it was recurrent and fear-provoking meant that it was an unresolved situation with strong feelings and sensations attached to it. The patient had a birth Primal after this dream in which he felt that he had to fight the whole way through the circular passage, and was seeking a safe place to stop. The point in the dream at which it was no longer safe was paralleled in his birth experience by a deadening of the mother's body by drugs. Then the "machine" (his mother's body) stopped and he was trapped. He felt he was going to die (his mother was totally unconscious), even wanted to die but was unable to. There was no choice but to go on—to "start moving."

The pressure of the Americans trying to get him to move was an interesting bit of symbolism, since most of the people around him later on tried to get him to do one thing or another, but he couldn't bring himself to do anything. He spent a lifetime feeling both pressured and lethargic. In anxiety situations he found it difficult to catch his breath because the pressure focused on his chest. At bottom, the pressure he felt to get moving is symbolized in the conflict between the Americans and the Germans; he is being pushed to fight against great odds. And in his birth, there were great odds preventing his escape.

Many of us who do not have these kinds of nightmares nevertheless have certain panic buttons related to the same sensations. If, for example, something is put over our mouths even for a fraction of a second, there can be instant panic. The old sensation of suffocation is triggered, making the reaction to momentary restriction inordinate. The same panic can be triggered by being rendered helpless either physically (by being held down) or psychologically (by being placed in a situation in which one can do nothing). Most of us aren't aware that we are feeling the panic feelings from our births.

It is noteworthy that many patients who have never consciously felt symptoms of birth, or who never had birth-sensation nightmares, begin to do so later in therapy when they are much less defended. Accessibility of the birth trauma depends on compounding. If the childhood was filled with trauma that taxed the whole defensive system, the child will be riddled with birth nightmares, and will always remain close to those sensations. If the childhood was not so traumatic, then the first-line latent forces will remain buried and will be more inaccessible later.

Conclusions

Repression of traumatic birth sensations results in a total shutdown of body responses. That is why feeling Pain liberates joy by reducing repression throughout the entire system. Sensations are the basis for emotional flavor. There is no emotion without sensation, and no attitudes or ideations that are not derived from some emotion, however remote the connection. The sensation of impending death at birth is a global one, and the repression of that sensation is no less global.

I suppose if there were one overarching sensation in neurosis, it would be that feeling of deadness, lifelessness and emptiness. So many people today feel that life is gray, uninteresting. This is often the result of repression, a repression that began with the beginning of life. It seems that the earlier the need for massive repression the more likely the person is to feel dead. One can often tell the "amount" of repression by the "amount" of life in the voice. One patient who was blocked at birth had a voice that sounded like it was coming from the depths of a tomb. Undoing massive repression literally puts life back into the system so that it once again looks and sounds alive.

There seems to be some great knowledge of the body that offers up Pains in a precise sequence depending on their weight, force and ability to be integrated—an order preordained, forged out of millions of years of evolution, that results in a physical intelligence that has nothing to do with "mind" as we know it. The body seems to "know" what it can take and what it cannot.

The treatment of sexual problems in particular must take into account the dialectic unity of Pain and pleasure. They are both feelings. In order to feel one, we must be able to feel the other. That is why neurotics who have a sudden moment of joy, such as winning a contest, often cry. Pleasure dredges up the Pain. That is also why those who are in Pain cannot feel, can't feel pleasure either. The suppression of Pain can sometimes lead to a deceptive "pleasure," but pleasure is not simply the absence of unrepressed Pain. It is an active feeling in itself, a state of its own, and the birth trauma is what starts most of us out totally unable to feel it. Reliving the Primal Pain finally clarifies pleasure. Pleasure is an affirmation of life, of all systems working in harmony. Once freed of those forces which have mired us in agonies, we can feel something entirely new—real pleasure.

Primal demons at once keep us from feeling pleasure and at the same time turn us onto an eternal search for it. We become hooked on demonology because we must believe that there is some kind of magic force driving us; especially since it is beyond our imaginations that it is the power of birth that is moving us. That force, always springing up from its original source, makes us believe that there must be a mystical power that can exorcise our demons and finally free us. There is indeed something that can free us. It is neither mystical nor magical. It is simply reliving our Pain.

6
Trapped in Time: The Psychological Implications of the Birth Trauma

When there is too much Pain from early trauma and the first level of consciousness can no longer contain it, the second level will take the overflow. The second level deals with emotion and personality, and much of what we experience as adult behavior will be permeated by the ways in which the second level disperses that early Pain. These dispersements are determined by the specifics of the birth trauma itself, and constitute the psychological implications of it.

Psychologically, the Pain will shape and direct such personality characteristics as ambition, dependence, independence, mobility, immobility, indecisiveness and the like; and it will establish the emotional disposition by which we react to the world—optimistically, despairingly, rebelliously and so forth. The Pain will produce emotional outbursts and rages in some, and in others it will be the driving force behind phobias and compulsions. In the body it can result in tension, stuttering, tics, shakes and tremors. And in everyday adult life, it can work its way into relationships, marriages, lifestyles and careers.

This is quite a long list of ramifications, but again we must keep in mind that it is a list of symptoms and manifestations. Indeed, there seem to be as many second-level extensions of the birth trauma as there are people who have had birth traumas. This is as it should be, for each person is unique and reacts uniquely. The unifying element that saves us from what could be a hopeless maze of unique reactions is the Pain. The Pain is the common generating source to which we return for resolution.

Let us talk first about the notion of unconscious meaning. How can something have meaning and yet be unconscious? A Primal birth Pain has a specific meaning that is encoded at the time it occurs. As the individual develops, the meaning is woven into all aspects of consciousness. Although that meaning cannot be conceptualized until there is the brain capacity to do so, the meaning exists nonetheless: it is inherent in the experience itself. Meanwhile, as those cognitive capacities are developing, an entire history with one's parents is also unfolding. More often than not, it is a history that provides further unconscious meaning for the original birth trauma.

For example, one individual whose mother was never there for him may interpret his birth trauma as: "There was never anyone to help me. Mother never helped from birth onward." Another may experience that same trauma as: "She made me work for everything I got." This interpretation will be the one of choice if this indeed happened later on. The trauma, in short, is wound into an entire historical configuration; it is not an isolated and disconnected phenomenon.

To be born prematurely has many unconscious meanings for the baby, some of which may be: "I am not ready for this," "I'm not being allowed to finish," or "Don't let me go." It is a *physiologic* meaning. As we develop and can think things out, that specific meaning becomes incorporated within and attached to current happenings. The meaning projected onto the present-day event is the very same meaning that was there at birth. That is why a patient reliving a second-line Pain such as "She was never there for me" or "Don't leave me—don't let me be alone" can eventually be led back to the first-line trauma of being sent out of the canal prematurely. Once the second-line component of the feeling is resolved, it allows the person to go deeper into its connecting links.

One of our patients was making a speech when he was told by the moderator that he was running over his limit and would have to wrap it up. The patient became acutely anxious, but somehow could not leave the stage. He had to say everything he had prepared. Later he had this insight from a Primal about being premature: "You took my time away, Mommy." The speech was the unconscious analogue of the birth process. The man attached a specific unconscious meaning to being stopped in the middle of a speech: to stop an ongoing action (birth) meant possible death. To put it another way, the physiologic imprint from birth (to stop is to die) remained in the system and became reattached to an unrelated psychological experience—in this case, being stopped in the middle of a speech. This man *had* to run off the whole speech sequence, just as he had been driven all his life to finish compulsively everything he began down to the last, minute detail. When he finally felt the real context of his compulsion, he was able to eradicate it.

Perhaps it is easier to understand the notion of unconscious meaning in terms of childhood (second-line) Pains. So many of us, for example, cannot take criticism. We defend, blame others, deny, or whatever, all to keep from feeling we did something wrong. For some of us, even mild criticism is enough to trigger loss of temper or severe depression. Why such a dread of being wrong? Because it has unconscious meaning. That meaning is, "They don't love me." We cannot accept the reality of being wrong now perhaps because we were constantly criticized for being wrong as children, and that meant our parents didn't love us. Or the meaning could be, "I can't take any more. It's too much." Having been criticized constantly in one's youth makes any additional criticism when we're grown up intolerable—the last straw.

To be criticized now takes on the same meaning. The original childhood Pain is unconsciously transferred onto the present. The current event has an added meaning; it is no longer the thing in itself. Added meaning is, in fact, a hallmark of neurosis. The difficulty is that what is added is deeply unconscious.

The true knowledge and interpretation of early trauma—its unconscious meaning—comes with its total reliving. It is then that the deep-lying, motivating forces behind all later behavior are uncovered for the person, who will then have such insights as, "I see now why I have despaired over the smallest setback"; "I see why I've been so pathologically competitive—I needed to be ahead of everybody"; "I've always felt battered by life, have been easily hurt, and now I know where the battered feeling comes from."

The psychological consequences of the birth trauma are always unconscious by definition. That is because it is the function of the repressive system to protect us against the Pain and keep us unconscious. Nevertheless, we *are* affected. The unconscious meaning of the birth trauma does not just pop up in an isolated experience and then retreat innocuously back into the unconscious. Rather, it penetrates most aspects of our lives and interfuses all levels of consciousness. It is a force that helps shape personality traits and characteristics; that energizes and selects emotional disposition; and, as we shall see later, that influences ideational and ideological preferences. Finally, it is that very unconscious meaning that motivates and rationalizes our values, our ethics, and our entire lifestyles.

Trauma-Induced Traits and Characteristics

The transmutation of first-line energy into traits and characteristics involves a channeling of a precise amount of Primal pressure. Thus the characteristics will have a force and unrelenting quality about them commensurate with the degree of trauma imprinted. Someone who is "burning with ambition" is literally burning up energy from repressed Pain with his ambition. Someone who is "as tough as nails" is literally burning up that same energy by being compulsively independent.

Ambition/Lethargy

Ambition is an excellent example of how this works, for it is a physiologic quantity of energy directed into the psychological arena. The Primal feeling of pressure at birth is frozen in time and continues in two ways. First, the amount of pressure in the original Primal feeling will constitute a general source of energy for the person—the child never stops moving for a moment; the adult is constantly "on the run." Second, the feeling of pressure is established as a quality of experience—an experiential prototype—and is later channeled into a specific personality characteristic: ambition.

The ambitious person always has new plans, new projects, new things to do, new ideas for the future. He cannot rest content but must constantly generate all sorts of schemes, goals and causes to make money, to get ahead, to improve himself, to improve his family, to improve the world. Ambition becomes an obsession, but it is a subtle—and socially acceptable—form of obsession. His "obsession" happens to coincide with a predominant value in the culture.

In an ironic dialectic interplay, ambition is not only a means of releasing pressure through an excessive amount of activity, it is also a means of keeping the pressure on by focusing on an unending series of goals toward which one must continually strive. The mind literally races to keep up with the pressure, the true source of which is completely unconscious. If the ambitious person did not so occupy himself with a continual stream of external concerns, he would feel that pressure for what it is and either "explode"—have a nervous breakdown—or ultimately feel the Pain. Ambition is thus both a means of discharging Primal energy and at the same time a means of rationalizing the manic quality of that energy. After all, such a person reasons, there is nothing wrong with wanting to "get ahead."

The ambitious person never relaxes, even "at the top." But he cannot not relax because he is ambitious; he is ambitious because he cannot relax. He literally needs the external pressure because the internal pressure is already there and demands a rationale.

We do not refer to "ambition" in reference to the newborn, but it should be clear that he, too, has one overriding goal: to "get ahead and get out." His whole psychology is geared toward the future because the future holds the key to survival. Later, when a mind is developed, when the neocortex is adequately matured, the individual can become "ambitious."

So many of us have that need to look forward to something and feel a vague dis-ease, a vague malaise, when we are bereft of projects, parties or whatever. The focus has to be on future aiming, future striving, because the original struggle toward the future—toward getting out and getting ahead—was absolutely life-saving. To relax would be experienced as *not* getting ahead; that is, it would threaten the original prototypic survival pattern of focusing on the future as a means to escape and final survival. To relax thus takes on the first-line unconscious meaning of "to give up the struggle and die": relaxing threatens us with the intrusion of that early Primal birth Pain, Pain that would have meant death had the newborn succumbed to it.

It is clear why conventional psychotherapy cannot succeed in cases dealing with psychological problems such as excessive ambition. To sever ambition from its Primal roots is to sever it from its cause and from its potential cure. To try to condition *in* relaxation or to meditate *away* the excessive pressure is a useless exercise; the cause is not touched, and the energy will simply be rerouted and redressed. Thus the person may let up on his job, but become fanatic about his golf or his jogging or his stamp collection. The Pain will continue to take its due.

Obviously not all ambition is sick. There must be a balanced amount of healthy ambition in us, or we would never move forward. And that is precisely the problem with individuals whose births were blocked or drugged. They develop the very opposite of ambition: a kind of despairing, what's-the-use attitude (the baby's efforts *were* useless in getting him out), a looking backward in life instead of forward (because the forward direction was literally blocked at birth), always bewildered about what to do next (because the baby's natural instinct about what to do next to get born was repeatedly overruled). Later, life seems pointless, any effort a waste of time, and the thought of self-help impossible.

This is the kind of infant who starts life lethargically, who doesn't cry much and is a "good" baby. He is passive and undemanding in the crib because he hasn't the aggression to be demanding. He ignores his own needs; for example, he doesn't eat with relish but with phlegmatic resignation. He is dazed and overwhelmed in every sense, and the bubbling, laughing, bright spirit of a healthy child is noticeably missing.

In many cases the transition out of the sac was disastrous, so there is a continuing tendency later on to retreat to the known, to hold onto the past—an attitude of conservatism and an abhorrence of sudden change. These people are not comfortable away from the "womb." They are not adventurous types. If they travel they soon want to return home. They don't want to change jobs, homes or points of view. Their surroundings become the placental sac and they construct a safe milieu within which they operate. (Some patients have literally reconstructed that early environment by becoming expert scuba divers who say that they feel much more comfortable in the sea.)

The person with this kind of birth trauma will prefer routine—not because he is an inherently organized person—but because any change or deviation in routine will only seem for the worse. The future will be tainted by a vague sense of doom because the "future" at birth was an agony. The person will tend to avoid "free-floating" situations in which limits are not well circumscribed and every eventuality not well considered. But, again, the doom or disaster that the person is trying so hard to avoid by his meticulous planning has already taken place; and while it cannot be undone, it can at last be resolved.

At the very start of life these babies may have all but given up in the absence of help. Hence, the complaint, "I need someone to help me out." But help *out of what?* Many of us were *not* helped at birth—our mothers were too drugged to take an active part in pushing us out of the canal. That lack of active participation can be experienced by the infant as what we later term rejection.

We all needed a helping hand. What we were often treated to instead was harsh forceps which hurt terribly. Whether or not the doctor and mother meant well doesn't matter: the infant experiences not intentions but realities. Good intentions are never prepotent over the Pain of forceps, suffocation and strangulation.

As a result of these types of experiences with *not* being helped, many of us argue later with our mates or friends because they won't help us out enough. We make unreasonable and unnecessary demands for help, again transforming and converting the original Primal feeling. Certainly we may need help from our friends from time to time, but often our need is inordinate, and our reaction to lack of help too strong.

One must be careful, however, not to oversimplify. Not everybody who struggled in the womb is ambitious. Many, many shaping experiences in childhood are needed to produce excessive ambition in the adult: Parents who are very ambitious for their child, who foster a highly competitive atmosphere, who constantly push the child to get ahead, to make it. Compounding is always very important: It takes energy from the first level of consciousness and shapes it psychologically. But the starting point is birth: The type of birth trauma imprinted predetermines the types of psychological tendencies that will be available for later development.

Dependence/Independence

The characteristics of dependence and independence are also frequently related to birth. Obviously, the newborn has neither trait when he arrives in the world, but what he does have is the experience of either being helped or of being helpless during birth. The Primal imprint of that experience may determine the predominance of one characteristic over the other as the personality develops.

Depending on the birth sequence itself, later one will act out either against being helpless and dependent, or will act out the helplessness and dependence in clear form. Which direction the person takes depends, again, on later compounding and the particular birth sequence itself. If the child has parents who do everything for him so that he never learns to do anything for himself, he may continue to act out being helpless. If the child gets little or no help, he will act out against the helplessness because he understands that survival is in his own hands. He never gets the chance to feel helpless and consequently will be very intolerant of those who act in any way helpless and dependent.

The predominant characteristic that emerges from the birth sequence can be further affected by cultural factors. Obviously, the degree to which the characteristic is accepted and supported culturally will have a lot to do with whether the adult views it as healthy or neurotic. Independence, for example, is like ambition: it is one of the culture's top-rated qualities—for men. This makes it easy to pass off excessive independence in a man as a virtue instead of recognizing it for the type of neurosis it really is. In a woman, however, healthy independence may be viewed as sick, whereas excessive and neurotic dependence may be encouraged. Similarly, the man who does not fit the macho mold may be viewed as dependent and unmanly, when in fact he is neither—he is simply a feeling person.

This intersection of culture and neurosis further compounds and confuses the problem. For when the culture's values coincide with the neurotic behavior and oppose the healthy alternative, the person's defenses can become even more difficult to penetrate. The added cultural reinforcement rationalizes the real need even further into the unconscious.

The characteristic of independence may begin at birth when one has to do it all oneself, without any help from Mother. The absence of help from birth onward may cause an individual to deny his need for help altogether—to "tough it out" instead. Even the infant can develop an attitude of not letting anyone help him . . . eat, get dressed, play, crawl or walk. The feeling from birth of having to do it all oneself remains as the underlying substratum out of which all later attitudes and ideas are differentiated. The original feeling is simply represented and rerepresented on different levels of the brain.

The "independent" adult may successfully block his need, but both Pain and need will eventually wear his system down. This person's thoughts fall back on the rationale: "I don't need anyone's help—I can do it all myself." Need is exacerbated through lack of fulfillment, then twisted. Such a person may get angry if anyone does try to help him out. Allowing himself to be helped brings up the Primal Pain and produces anxiety, so being independent and "tough" becomes a necessity and is rationalized as a virtue.

If this person becomes a father, he won't want his children to be helped out either. He will insist that they make it on their own, that they "tow the line," "stand on their own two feet," long before they are of age to do so. The children cannot even ask for help without eliciting a sarcastic answer, a frown or a disapproving look. They, too, soon learn to be "independent." They, too, will suffer from lack of fulfillment of need. The father will also have many *ideas* about how bad it is to help people out which he will pass along to his children. The cycle proceeds: Father cannot help his children because he himself was not helped right from the start. Since he won't allow himself to be helped, his need remains. If he could gain access to that Primal need, he would be able to allow himself to be helped, and he would be able to help others out. One patient wrote:

> I have felt what it was like to roll over from my back to my stomach for the very first time in my life. I was alone and that is what made it frightening. The pleasure was in the exhilaration and need to experience this new movement. It could have been a completely satisfying event had someone been there with a gentle hand to allow me to do it safely. Even though this may seem like a "small" feeling, it has helped me in my "now" life. I can feel when my children need encouragement and help in trying new things, and I am more able to offer them a helping hand.

Helping someone out would be literal in the case of a mother having a baby. The feeling that "I've never been helped out and I can't help anyone else out" is bound to affect the kind of childbirth the mother experiences.

The "independent" child may act tough: he will act out his need to be helped, but behind a barrier of toughness. The child and, later, the adult will be demanding and unappreciative, always making people feel as if they have not done enough for him. The need and vulnerability beneath this tough exterior will not be apparent at all. He will go on demanding of others and will not be able to recognize when he *is* being helped. And there will never be enough help to quell that early Pain and need. That is why neurotics need more and more. They are filling needs symbolically, and symbolic fulfillment is a very light meal.

The Pain of birth can give one the feeling that nothing good comes from the outside. This later elaborates into a false independence based on a distrust of everyone: "Don't let anyone have power over you . . . because when they do, they hurt you"; "Take fate into your own hands and do everything on your own." These attitudes may become still further elaborated in work situations so that the person feels he simply cannot tolerate a boss supervising and ordering him around. Or, if he has to work for someone, he'll make sure to arrange it so that no one tells him how and when to work. This is all part of wanting to do things *his* way and not anyone else's—which means Mother's disastrous way. It is also a way of re-enacting that early sequence in which help was not forthcoming: pretending not to need help protects one from that unconscious helpless feeling. By *not* allowing help, the issue never comes up—and neither does the Pain. Again, compounding is necessary on the other levels of consciousness in order for these tendencies to become characteristic responses in adult life.

There are endless variations of ways we find to act out in denial of that birth feeling of utter helplessness. One of our patients used her career as the vehicle for denial: she achieved a yellow belt in karate in Denmark, and became an instructor in self-defense for women. There was some realistic basis for this career choice because rapes were increasing throughout Western Europe, but she soon began to realize her stronger, personal motivations. She felt in her Primals that she was acting out against the terrible helplessness she had experienced at birth. Indeed, she had become counterphobic: throughout her life she had fought against the terror of appearing helpless in front of anyone. As a result, she became very domineering and masculinized. She built an entire superstructure *over* the need by converting it into its opposite. But beneath it all was a newborn not being helped by its mother.

A man who felt this Primal helplessness discovered that he had been counteracting his feeling by trying to be totally help*ful* to absolutely every one of his patients (he was a physician). After a birth Primal, he realized he didn't have to be the savior of the world; he didn't have to have an answer for everything.

Another patient who had to have answers for everything finally understood why he had become the intellectual he was: he needed never to be caught without some kind of information in order to maintain a semblance of control over his life. Information was a way of fighting against that helplessness of *not* knowing. He wanted to have all the answers so that he would never be hurt again—but again all on an unconscious level.

Yet another patient, a doctor, became a specialist in terminal cases, unconsciously looking for answers about how to keep himself alive, but instead putting all his energy into keeping everyone else alive. The fact that he chose terminal cases as his specialty was an indication of how terminal his own needs had become. It was a matter of life and death, just as it had been originally—at birth. Obviously, the work this man did was real and valuable, but the motivation behind it was unconscious. Even though he continued the same work after therapy, he did it with a different feeling. Now his own motivations were clear because he finally got clear on his own needs; and now too he was free to really help others because he had finally helped himself.

Some people act out against the helpless terror from birth by continually defying it. One patient had become a race car driver, thereby re-creating his terror but in a situation over which he had total control. The closer to death he came the calmer and more alive he felt. Another patient, again a doctor, had a similar feeling: the more catastrophic the situation, the more life-threatening the surgical procedure, the calmer he became. He said that he thrived on this kind of excitement. It became a continuous cycle of re-creating the birth terror and then mastering it. The notion that finally one is in control is soothing, because originally one was totally in the control of others.

Fighting against Primal helplessness leads people into a wide range of irrational behavior. Patients have noted that in situations of helplessness, such as being cheated and knowing it, they would do things unconsciously that they knew were useless and counterproductive in order to keep that feeling down. One patient told me how he had pursued a law suit that cost him a great deal of money—knowing full well at the time that it wasn't worth it—because he could not tolerate feeling helpless. The old feeling kept him from making a proper appraisal of his current situation.

On the other side of the coin we have the baby who had to succumb at birth. The reaction to the Primal helplessness will be quite different later on. The adult may actually want someone else to have all the power. He may want to be the victim. He may want to act out being helpless and dependent. This kind of person needs a boss and a mate to tell him what to do. As an infant this person was helpless and was a victim. The peculiar circumstances of his birth made it impossible for him to act in such a way as to gain power over his destiny. His passivity helped save him and was imprinted as a life-saving response. Later he might develop a fateful attitude—"what is meant to be is meant to be, and there isn't much anyone can do." This psychological attitude stems from a strictly physiologic experience; it is a cognitive (third-level) representation of his early (first-level) experience.

If the neonate had to defer at birth, if he was the helpless victim of the powers that be, that tendency—deferring to the powers that be—becomes an encoded response organized below the level of conscious awareness. He may grow up to believe in authority and be ready to obey just as he was ready to defer to power and "obey" at birth. He is still being born, as it were; and he continues to react as if the birth were still going on. One patient wrote:

Waiting instead of asserting   I have found that my tendency to stand back and wait instead of going out into the world to get what I need for myself is also connected to my birth. I feel that I will not be able to take the conflict that would

Waiting as the only alternative at birth

arise if I were assertive, and that it's easier to get things done by just being good and waiting.

I know from what my mother has told me that my birth took quite a long time. I was her first child, and the labor lasted eleven hours. I started to come out at about 11 P.M.; my mother said that she was very sleepy at that point and the nurse had to keep waking her up and telling her to push. It's not surprising, then, that I have had birth feelings about getting no help from my mother, and that I gave up trying to get help and just waited for something to happen. *Waiting* was the only alternative to forging ahead and feeling the Pain of not being helped. My first neurotic shutdown of Pain happened before I was fully born.

The helpless person also may wallow in his need for help, convincing himself that lying around waiting for others to do things for him is quite healthy, and that, in fact, it is his right to expect help from all quarters at all times. He may constantly back himself into impossible situations which require help from others, not realizing that the kind of help he truly needs is not in the present.

The response of being dependent and passive may become reinforced by later parental tyranny. But it can also occur without it. Indeed, the aggressive baby may react aggressively no matter what the later environment because aggression meant survival and life. Similarly, passivity may become a habitual pattern without a great deal of second-level reinforcement. This is because the prototypic response patterns are usually *self*-reinforcing: to react passively makes others have to be more outgoing and aggressive, which in turn reinforces the passivity.

As an adult, one may marry a person who will provide this counterbalance. In fact this is often the case. Neither person is aware of the seesaw dynamics they are carrying out; they just become part of an unconscious scenario, part of a bad and very repetitive play with no end, in which the characters are so stylized and "set" (the behavior is literally *set* by the prototype) that the whole scene is tiresome beyond description.

One patient had gone to a marriage counselor, feeling that her husband always "held her back." She complained that she was always unable to do what she wanted, that she was forced into a dependent role, and that no matter how hard she pleaded or fought, she felt controlled and held back. After a number of birth Primals in which she did indeed reconnect with being held back, she could finally separate the past from the present. She no longer was forced to project onto her husband a trauma that had happened as she first entered this world. Until that time the marriage was turbulent because she was awash in the past while focusing on the present.

But, of course, a neurotic has no other choice. To have focused on the past would have meant a connected Primal, and for that she needed help.

Another patient who had been held back at birth grew up feeling that she was always wrong and that she would never be believed. Her report shows how birth feelings intrude upon present experiences, and how properly utilizing those experiences can lead to freedom from the past:

The birth trauma: pushed back

Three years ago when I was attending a mock Primal center I had my first birth Primal. In it I felt ready to be born—I had pushed and struggled my way through the birth canal to the cervix which was dilated and ready to allow my passage to the world outside—but someone on the outside was not. I felt two fingers on my head pushing me back and keeping me inside—thus denying my first basic right of being born. The following day I was in agony; I couldn't move my head and the pain in my neck was excruciating.

Unlike here [the Primal Institute] where reality prevails, the mock center offered no reality; feelings were not integrated with one's present life and every word one uttered was "an old feeling"—the present ceased to exist; it had no meaning or connection to the past.

At the time, the birth Primal connected to having been told I was a phony and a fake, but the knowledge made no difference to my life until three months ago. At a post-group one night one of the therapists made a remark about me which I felt was inappropriate in view of my history. It was important for me to express how I felt to her, and so the following night in post-group I did so. It has always been very difficult for me to express what I feel is right to anyone—friends, lovers, and especially, of course, to my mother. There were many times with my mother that I felt she would kill me for opposing her, if she ever lost control.

Confronting a therapist

So, confronting the therapist filled me with fear, terror at exposing myself, terror at not knowing how she would react, but I had to do it.

I confronted her, and before I could furnish all the details and reasons of why I was right, she said, "You're right, Jan, and I'm sorry." I felt a little stunned and cried. Then something changed physically inside of me, and it wasn't until I was at home that I realized what the change was. When the therapist said, "You're right," it was like I was free; the pressure in my head was gone at last. I was left with all the reasons why she was wrong, and I didn't need them; it was as though I needed those reasons to act as a buffer around

Being right and being free

my head so I wouldn't feel the brick wall and the Pain of being stopped and not believed.

At that instant when she said, "You're right," I did not have to defend against not being believed—I didn't need the buffers because I *was* right and I *was* believed

Insights and connections

without any need to find justifications and reasons. This connects to many instances throughout my childhood and adult life—not being believed was death for me and I have rarely taken the chance of being assertive and standing up for what I believe to be right, because the Primal feelings, until now, have stopped me.

In closing, I'd like to say that I'm really glad that you therapists are not perfect, because the chance I had through an error gave me the opportunity to be real and true to my own feelings.

Another patient relived being held back at birth because the doctor had not arrived in time. As a consequence he felt both helpless and held back, and realized that he had contrived his life to justify the feeling that "people were holding him back." He always had excuses for why he didn't do things, for why he didn't buy this property, or make this deal, because "they" were holding him back. There were many problems with his wife because he began to blame her for keeping him from getting ahead, and whenever she put any impediment whatsoever in his way he became rageful. The marriage was in serious trouble until he found out that it was primarily a birth sequence that was the problem.

Patients with domineering, controlling mothers often have birth Primals about the fact that they have felt held back by women since the time of birth. They either chose women friends who were controlling so that they continued the struggle of being held back, or they chose women friends who were totally passive and who couldn't possibly hold them back from anything they wanted to do. In the end we will each choose one course over another depending upon our later life experiences, but it is not a free choice: either choice is neurotic because it is Primally determined.

The helpless feeling from birth can also involve death or near-death feelings. One patient who had a birth Primal about struggling in the birth canal until he felt near death uncovered his lifelong pattern of letting everything accumulate until it was all too much, until he was completely overwhelmed, then feeling he wanted to give up and die. Another person who had the same kind of birth trauma had a different reaction: he let everything go until the last minute, then galvanized himself into action because he was in a crisis. He focused his entire life around crises. He bought books on the coming financial disaster, on the coming earthquakes, on the inevitable ecological chaos, and planned his life according to each predicted crisis. He read just enough to keep himself in a constant panic state, just like he was at birth. He reenacted the helpless feeling by making everything hopelessly critical. Because he never had control over his own inner destiny, he spent his life trying to gain control over outer, disastrous destinies—truly an attempt to symbolically master old Pain.

And yet another patient who also felt in a constant state of crisis had a birth Primal in which he was pulled out at the last second by the doctor. As an adult, this man had never been a strong person because his prototypic behavior was to rely on others. Whenever he got into a difficult situation he would immediately look for outside help to come along. At the point of crisis, the point that recapitulated the near-death experience, he would just freeze and wait.

How the prototype works in relation to later experience is obviously quite complex. There are no simple rules or clear-cut categories. For example, a person can have dependence imprinted on the first level of consciousness as the prototypic birth response, yet have independence developed and nurtured on the second level by caring parents throughout childhood. Thus we have counterbalancing factors which have to be taken into account in assessing overall personality. In the above case, subsequent influences could overcome the prototype and the result would be a fairly self-reliant individual.

Second-Level "Stuck"

I have discussed how sensations which are the first elements of a total Primal feeling remain pure throughout our lives and become ramified emotionally and intellectually as the brain matures. Thus the sensation of being stuck in the canal elaborates into the characteristic of being stuck throughout life. The person may become "stuck" in anything he attempts. Some people act out being stuck by being unable to leave the house, and may even develop a phobia about "going out." Others are stuck in their jobs or stuck in their marriages, and don't know how to get out because they are continuously re-enacting the original experience of being stuck. They never feel truly free because their feelings are not of freedom, but of being stuck. *Stuck* is the prototype, the mental blinder. If by chance they do free themselves from a bad job or a bad relationship they will manage to get themselves trapped in another situation where that feeling will be dominant again. In other words, the lifestyle is so contrived as to rationalize the unconscious living out of that very early imprinted sensation.

Being stuck in the canal can lead to a variety of feelings depending upon how the situation was resolved originally. If the baby had to be pulled out it may be that the adult is left with the residual feeling of waiting constantly for someone to "pull him out" of a bad situation. It would never-occur to this person that he could pull himself out of situations. It is not within the realm of his possibilities because it wasn't originally. This pattern also leads to stifled creativity and lack of imagination.

If the baby were heavily drugged and then also had to be pulled out to start its life, the residual feeling in the adult may be a need for a great deal of excitement in order to feel alive. But one will never feel truly alive until one has resolved that early drugged, near-death situation. After that, one can feel joyful and exuberant without being dragged down constantly by that early imprint. One patient wrote:

Current trigger	I move furniture for a living. One morning my buddy was tired and not feeling well. We had a particularly hard day's work ahead of us. I thought, "Well, it's up to me to carry the day because my buddy's not up to it." The trouble was, I felt pretty lousy myself—no energy—so I went to a pharmacist and bought some caffeine pills before we started work. (I had used caffeine pills sometimes when I couldn't get speed before therapy.)
Birth feeling: stuck in canal with no help and no way out	I had a birth feeling shortly after that day. In the feeling I was stuck inside of my mother—stuck in a black elastic tube with no way out, having no rapport with my mother, and thoroughly exhausted and frustrated by the feeling of not moving forward. In the feeling, I felt completely suspended in a void—with no memory of the world—the womb—I had just left. It was obvious that my mother could not or would not help me. It was up to me to do it, but I was completely exhausted. I had fought for her attention, to no avail. Nothing I did seemed to work. The more I tried, the more stuck I got.
Insights	I realized by buying those caffeine pills I was trying *to borrow energy from outside of me* to get me through the day's work. I was trying to get that physical help I had never received from my mother during my birth.
	After many more birth feelings I realized that my use of drugs before therapy had been an unstraight way of crying for help. The feeling was, "I don't want to help myself—I want you to help me, Mommy"—which goes back to being stuck in the birth canal.

Still another patient wrote:

Whenever I wanted to go shopping I always hesitated before buying something, especially something I could not afford. My husband always objected and I always flew into a rage because he claimed I "bought over my head" while I believed that I "couldn't make a move without somebody stopping me." He gave me no freedom and I felt stuck. I found out that I couldn't make a move in the canal for many many hours and I suppose that buying over my head is just the symbolic way of getting the freedom I never had.

This spending too liberally actually was a symbolic way of gaining the freedom she could not feel, and of course she would become instantly rageful when anyone tried to curb her impulse.

For some, the feeling of being stuck translates into "I can't get going, I can't get up in the morning, I don't seem to have the motivation to pull myself out of things." Encouragement and exhortation by friends will be a very poor technique for getting out of that deep feeling, and one will need it constantly to get going at all. It's also the kind of feeling that makes one need to be invited out by others instead of initiating and organizing things oneself. It's the need to be cajoled, to be bolstered, to be drawn out. Again, being drawn out is an almost literal message from birth.

Then there are those people who always have great beginnings but poor finishes; they begin countless projects and never finish any of them. This is often a birth analogue—the start was all right but the finish was bad: the baby got stuck. In fact, not finishing projects as an adult can be a way of avoiding the terrible feelings of having had a bad finish at birth. And here we see again how character traits such as lack of organization and lack of stick-to-itiveness are not genetic, but stem from a specific kind of birth sequence.

Of course, there is also the opposite tendency: the compulsion to finish everything, never stopping short of one's goal, because to stop originally had catastrophic implications. The urgency of survival actually may be the motivating force behind cleaning the kitchen before one can sit and enjoy a cup of coffee. In another slight twist, one may need the pressure of "things to do" because one needed pressure originally to make it out of the birth canal. The variations are myriad.

One patient noted that the relationship with his wife was bad for years but that he felt he could never do anything about it. The idea of alternatives simply never entered his mind. They were living in a small, dark apartment and he never felt that he could move. He could never change any of his circumstances. It all seemed like too much effort. The dark, cramped atmosphere of the apartment actually brought him into his birth feelings one day after many months of therapy. He began feeling very tight and restricted and then a panic feeling set in. He felt as though he was loosing total control and that his body was being torn apart. He said:

The horror I felt at that time was beyond life and death. I needed to end the tremendous pain. My body started to give up and then like a miracle the pressure disappeared and I was born. But I was left with feeling stuck all of my life. I wrote my mother to ask her about my birth and she told me that when she came to the hospital she told the nurse that she believed I was on the way. The nurse refused to believe her. When they realized that my mother was right they held me back until everything was ready. I have always felt that I was controlled by forces bigger than me and I have been mystical about unseen forces "out there" for the last decade. I always thought that any real change happened because of some miracle and not by any effort of mine. So I was real passive, always thinking that what I did never counted. In my dreams even, I was always in some kind of mine shaft, never able to crawl out.

The feeling of being stuck no longer controls my life. I can now do something about the conditions of my existence. My blood pressure is dropping to below normal and now I can even take the elevator even though the stairs tend to be tempting sometimes.

Getting Through

Another variation of the stuck theme is "I can't get through to you." Why is it that we use the metaphor of not getting through to someone when what we mean is not being able to make them understand us? Perhaps it is because in trying to make someone understand us we evoke an earlier experience in which we needed the kind of understanding that would have enabled us to be born with ease. That was a time when getting through had a literal meaning. It was vital in regard to physical communication with the mother through the wall of the womb, and it was vital in regard to pushing through the birth canal to the world outside.

A further extension of the same theme is the feeling of not being able to get through the job, the homework, the week, the relationship. Having a long struggle ahead brings up the old feeling of not being able to contact the mother easily. Monday morning blues is a good example—there is dread that Sunday is over and that the struggle must begin all over again.

In Primal Therapy we separate the present symbol from the past feeling so that the person can finally feel what it really was he couldn't get through. Until he gets to that original feeling he will continue to overreact whenever someone doesn't understand him—shouting his favorite lament, "I can never get through to you!" And he will continue to overreact to any project or challenge that faces him—again with his favorite lament, "I can't get through this!"

Once the early feeling is felt, however, there is no longer dread over long-term challenges or commitments. The person can now set himself a goal of completing college, for example, without the continual worry that he'll never be able to get through it. Feeling that original Pain can transform a person who constantly gives up into one who willingly sticks things out.

The following report well describes the stuck feeling and its offshoot of not "getting through" as the patient experiences it in the present (third level), and then in the original birth sequence (first level). It also shows the direct interface between birth feelings and present problems—and how feeling the original Pain can bring about touching and important changes in one's current life.

First-line break-through

I started my therapy in April of 1976. After a month I began to experience birth feelings, but I didn't recognize them as such. One time I just felt a need to get out of the group room during group. I had no reason—I just felt myself saying, "I've got to get out of here." Another time in group I just lay very still and felt dead.

The dialectic: from feeling Pain to feeling "great"

Eight months into therapy I was in bed and let myself feel very closed in. I curled up tightly as I felt this. A day or so later I felt great, and the idea of going out and being with people seemed incredibly natural. Usually I have to drive myself to socialize and do so only after months of being alone and realizing how horrible my aloneness is. One day at work, a few days after feeling this closed-in feeling, I was eating at a

Changes in behavior

table in the lunch room. I realized I was not taking part in the conversation at the table, and saw a table with people I thought I'd rather talk to. I simply got up and went to the other table, and as I did that I felt very powerful in making my life more desirable. This incident may sound minor, but it isn't—before I just would have remained in the situation in which I felt alone.

The birth sequence

During my fourth week in therapy, I did a lot of first-line work. One time I started trying to push my head through the [padded] wall to get through it. I couldn't, and started to beat on it. However, I soon felt that this didn't fit my feelings, so I moved away from the wall and flailed at the air. At this point I felt late in being born; I felt clearly how I couldn't get out of my mother's womb when I wanted to. Beating on the wall didn't fit. As a baby I felt my mother's womb all around me, so in the Primal I flailed at the air, I didn't beat on the wall. I did want to push my head through the wall, though, as I had wanted to get my head through my mother's birth canal originally. After struggling for a while, I gave up.

The prototype and its undoing

This has been typical of my life for as long as I can remember. I tend to give up on getting what I really want. *A few months earlier when I had made more effort to be with people, I was doing it as a result of having felt my tendency to give up on what I wanted in the beginning.*

"I can't get through"

In a post-group session a few months ago, I got into a lengthy discussion with a therapist in which I tried to get him to understand me and be the way I wanted him to be. I wasn't successful, and when I saw nothing was going to come from the conversation, I just got out of it. I had learned from previous experience that some people will just never understand me.

However, when I got home I got into my Primal box and continued to try to make the therapist understand me. I thought this was a father-thing, and I tried to let it go back to him. Then, out of the clear blue sky, I hit the wall and screamed, "Mommy, let me out of here!" I cried for a while, and then lay down with my mind totally clear of the struggle situation I was in. I had felt third-line feelings about trying to get people to understand me, but this was the first time I had experienced the birth feeling beneath it.

Interface between third and first level

Last week I tried to meet a girl I saw on the bus. We both got off at the same stop. I was going to ask her to have coffee with me. I said, "Excuse me," just to get her attention. She didn't even look at me. I was amazed that I didn't feel bad or stupid, or anything like that. It was nice not to have those feelings come up. Then in a few minutes I suddenly felt, "I try so hard and nothing works." I started to cry right on the street. I'd felt enough of the third- and second-line connections so that the only feeling to come up in this situation was the first-line feeling from when I tried so hard to get born and nothing I did worked.

Birth prototype

I have found that my initial experience in life—that of trying hard, finding that nothing worked, and giving up—affected how I reacted to all later traumatic experiences as well as to how I react in the present when I want something. Even if I Primalled away all the second- and third-line Pain, I think I'd still give up too easily on getting what I want if I didn't reexperience my birth. Specifically, *feeling second- and third-line Pains changes my relationships with people; feeling first-line Pain gives me the energy to go out and form those relationships in the first place.* [Italics added]

Functions of the three levels

Struggle

Still another common life scenario is the struggle theme. Often the baby who struggled so hard during birth will arrange his later life in such a way that everything is a struggle; he will not allow things to come easily because life itself didn't come easily. This type of person will grow up and have children whom he won't allow to play or relax without having done their myriad of chores first. He will constantly put obstacles in front of himself and his family because struggling against and overcoming obstacles is his prototypic experience. In this way he compounds and reinforces his own birth trauma until it becomes an inflexible pattern.

One of our patients had an insight into why she always fell in love with losers: she needed a real struggle. She married an alcoholic and tried to reform him, finally giving up when the odds were overwhelming. This again was a re-enactment of the birth sequence. She could never recognize that it was almost an impossibility to cure her husband's alcoholism since he himself was not motivated. He had given up, but she could not give up.

Another patient wrote:

Birth cycle: fight and defeat

After 16 months of therapy I have slowly begun to feel a birth feeling which seems to rule my life and lie at the base of my neurosis. It is the feeling that I constantly have to fight for my life—that I have to fight all the time to stay alive. I experience this fight in my day-to-day life just to stay on my own two feet. My natural—or I should say neurotic—inclination is to give up and not fight. The cycle goes: fight, get nowhere, give up, want to die, not want to die, decide not to die, and fight again, get nowhere, etc., etc. The cycle goes on and on. Along with this is the feeling that it doesn't matter what I do—I don't get anywhere, so why try, why fight; I may as well give up and die. But I want to live, desperately.

The dialectic: positive changes in the present leading to painful feelings from the past

The more I take care of myself in the present the more I feel this feeling. Taking care of myself makes me feel how hard it is, how there is no one to help, how alone I am. Getting my life together means starting to really live in the present and to feel the old feeling of fighting to live as just that—an *old* feeling.

What has led me to be able to begin to feel this horrible feeling? Several positive changes in my life: building a relationship with someone I care for, acting out my Pain less, and taking better care of myself, which includes wearing nice clothes instead of dressing like a slob; fully supporting myself momentarily in-

stead of constantly running short and needing to bor-
row from my father; keeping a clean apartment instead
of living in a mess; and taking a nice vacation.

Focus on the present as inroad to the past

At my six-month interview my therapist told me to
focus on getting my present life together; then I
wouldn't have to *try* to feel feelings—they would just
come. I knew he was right but I didn't want to listen,
because getting my life together seemed too hard a
task, too big a struggle. I just wanted to *feel,* and then
have my life fall into place. But I have learned the hard
way that it just doesn't happen that way—either in
therapy, or in life in general.

Notice, again, the continual interplay between feeling the original Pain
and making positive changes in one's present life.

In the next report, the patient describes how being a "night person" is a
continual re-enactment of the long, hard struggle he underwent at birth:

Birth prototype: lifestyle as a "night person"

I have made some very interesting connections to
how my birth has affected my everyday life. The
insights have to do with the way I go through the day—
a pattern I have repeated daily for as long as I can
remember.

I am a night person. I hate the day with its strong
daylight. I usually get up in the morning as late as
possible and go to bed at night as late as possible. I love
the evening hours.

Each day starts in the same manner for me: when I
wake up in the morning it is the worst moment of the
day. I feel very bad and defenseless every morning,
knowing that I have a long struggle ahead of me to get
through the day and finally reach the evening when I
know I will feel better. As the day goes by, I feel better
and better; and when the night finally comes, I start
feeling really good and safe. I reach a peak of feeling
good at bedtime—and that moment when I slip into my
bedsheets and feel the warmth and security of my bed
gives me so much joy that I get nice feelings all over my
body. Then I relax completely, and sink into a forgetful
sleep.

I never knew why each day of my life was like this;
or even that there was anything unusual or restrictive
about loathing 12 out of 24 hours in the day. Then I felt
a couple of birth feelings and became more conscious
of how the imprint of my birth affects my everyday
life.

The birth trauma

What I felt in the birth feelings was a long and agonizing struggle. Incredible pressures smashing my head and back. My mother couldn't help me at all. I was stuck inside, and I knew I could count only on myself to get out and live. So I did all the work myself, pushing and pushing for several hours until I was completely exhausted. At that point I gave up because there simply was nothing else I could do.

I eventually got out alive. I'll always remember that one feeling where I am lying on my back, sucking my thumb and slowly going to sleep. The struggle is over, I made it! I'm out and alive. I'm safe, and now I can relax and let myself go to sleep and forget it all! That moment felt so good!

Re-enacting the trauma

I go through each day exactly the same way as I experienced my birth. In the morning the struggle is yet to come—my birth is beginning and I'm apprehensive about the struggle—and the closer I get to that moment when I will relax and go to sleep, the better and safer I feel. As the evening comes and bedtime approaches, I feel more and more relaxed and safe. More and more myself, too.

Later on this pattern was reinforced by the fact that every evening before bedtime, my father would give my sister and me one entire half hour of his valuable time, playing with us and telling us stories. That was the only half hour in the day when he would take care of us and we would really look forward to it every day.

"Born that way"

So I am a night person. In a way, you could say that I was "born that way"!—but not in the sense of genes and heredity. It is truly amazing to me how my birth experience has had such a great impact on my everyday life.

Staying Put; Moving On

The ways in which the unconscious meaning of the birth trauma impels us are numerous and highly individualized. For instance, to one patient "staying put" meant staying in a safe place (the womb). The birth struggle to survive had involved staying put, and that translated in later life into not taking an important job that meant moving to another city. Even the thought of the transfer produced an anxiety attack. This man *had* to stay put. Here was a birth sequence being triggered some thirty-five years later, unconsciously determining a crucial life choice.

Another patient had the opposite response tendency. He felt in his birth Primals that he was a "mistake." In his adult life he acted out the trauma by continually changing jobs—by *not* staying put—thus hoping to avoid what he feared his employer would eventually discover: that he had made a "mistake" in hiring him.

Still another patient was asked to transplant some shrubbery from one part of a garden to another. In doing the job, she felt an inexplicable amount of anxiety. In her birth Primals she felt that the original transplantation from womb to life—compounded by numerous transplantations from city to city as part of life in an Army family—had all been so traumatic that any kind of transplantation in the present re-evoked those early Pains.

Therefore, while survival means staying put to one person, it may mean death to another: getting out of the womb and moving on will mean survival. And again, both variations will be acted out throughout life.

Going Back

One patient got into a birth Primal after a seemingly minor second-line feeling. She was experiencing feelings about how she never liked to "go back." History bored her. She hated it when she forgot something at her house that made her have to turn around and go back. She didn't feel anxious when she had to go back, just annoyed—a little too annoyed. She felt on the second level about this, about how her parents were never satisfied with whatever she did and made her go back over everything. Then she slipped into the first level: getting out of the canal was everything; going back was death—the origin of her adult behavior pattern.

The reverse of this negative feeling frequently comes from Cesarean births. Many of our Cesarean patients have the feeling that they must go back to where they started in order to feel complete. They have a general feeling of incompleteness—that nothing is "settled" in life. And, indeed, there *is* something to go back to; there *was* something left incomplete; there *was* a developmental lack that is unsettling. Some very important part of growth and development was abbreviated in their birth experience. One is truly not complete when the birth sequence is not completed naturally.

A slight variation on this theme was expressed by a patient who had been stuck inside the birth canal: he always wanted to go back to that time before the trauma:

A doomed future and an idyllic past	For nearly two years after I began therapy I felt there was no future for me. My life was in the past. One day a song triggered a memory of an idyllic scene from my life several years earlier. In the scene I was with the girl I loved, feeding ducks by a river. At first, I didn't understand why the memory made me cry so much. I

"I can't go back"

had been daydreaming about being with this girl by a quiet country river, back in the summer of 1972. The therapist encouraged me to describe the scene in detail—the water lilies, the wildflowers, the sunshine reflecting off the water, the bird songs—even the breeze and scents of summer.

As I did so I became increasingly upset. The therapist asked me why. "Because I can't *go back* there," I said. "That's right," she said, "you can't go back." I went directly into a feeling. Just before I got totally stuck at birth I had a fleeting memory of life as it had been in the womb—of life shared—a life I could not go back to.

Resolution

I still think of the experiences I had with that particular girlfriend as the best time of my life; but the difference now is that I'm not looking back. The feeling of doom in the future has dissolved. I'm facing a future, and I'm glad I'm alive. Maybe I'll fall in love again—this time as a man who wants to share his life with a woman—not as a baby struggling to return to his mother's womb.

Getting Ready; Leaving

The "getting ready" theme takes several forms. One of our patients who had been born prematurely would always get a sudden pang when asked to go somewhere or do something. He would feel a subtle hesitation and a need to gather himself together first. After reliving the birth sequence he had the insight, "I'm not going to go anywhere you want me to go; I'm going when *I'm* ready." The feeling was, "I'm not ready when you're ready," and he had acted out that hesitation all of his life. He could never be spontaneous as a result. Whenever anyone set a date for him he would always be late, even when it came to pleasurable situations. He would be the last to join in on anything. He had to do things in his way, in his time.

Another patient, born too quickly, wrote:

The trauma: born too fast

A week after I returned home from Switzerland [the Primal retreat held in 1980] I was sitting one evening in a kind of blur of tiredness. I was still very open emotionally from the retreat, and I suddenly began to feel/remember being born. It was a kind of split-second Primal of incredible intensity: I was in the birth canal and being pushed out too fast *before I was ready*. I felt panic; I wanted everything to slow down to my pace; I wanted to control what was happening to me; I desperately wanted to stop *until I was ready,* but I was not being allowed to.

A flood of insights

The feeling was over in a few moments, but I was flooded with insights that extended over several days. I realized, in a flash, that my life has been dictated by two major birth feelings:

(1) *I'm not ready yet!:* everything is going too fast for me—I can't keep up—slow down to my pace; and

(2) *I can't stand this pressure!*

I had felt the second feeling about pressure in birth Primals before, but it has never been resolved; I still crack up when I'm under too much pressure at work. The connections I felt over the first feeling are still actively affecting my life some three weeks later.

Being late as an acting out of not being ready to be born

The first feeling has helped me to understand why *I'm always late.* I am never ready on time because *I wasn't ready to be born.* My habit of tardiness was one of the reasons I gave for wanting to do Primal Therapy, as my job had been threatened repeatedly by my inability to get to work on time. But work hasn't been the only problem area; any time I have to "get out of" the house by a specific time I simply cannot. Even on the weekends, it is sometimes three or four o'clock in the afternoon before I am ready to do anything.

I see now that I act out "not being ready to be born" the whole time. Everything I do, I do slowly—always holding back, taking my time. If I am rushed into anything which I cannot prepare for, I get panic-stricken and cannot function. Every aspect of my life—work, relationships, sex, interests, travel—is affected by my feeling that *I never have time to get ready.* Talk about prototypic experience! It seems I have spent my whole life saying, *"I'm not ready yet— wait for me!"*

Resolution and improvements in current life

Since I made these connections I have experienced improvements in my life which seem out of proportion to the nature of the Primal (after all, it only lasted a few minutes): I have been on time for work every day but two; I have been able to leave the house without having to tidy it up; and I have been able to have friends in without becoming panic-stricken about not having vacuumed the carpets or washed the dishes. I haven't had to "be ready" first.

These may seem like minor changes, but they have

made a tremendous contribution to my being able to feel relaxed.

Yet another patient who was premature had the feeling that she never wanted to say goodbye; she never felt ready to leave anything, starting with the womb. This feeling caused her great difficulties in many areas: in leaving her boyfriend with whom she wasn't getting along, in leaving her apartment where she was unhappy, and particularly in leaving that comfortable womb at birth. Because she had been forced to leave the womb before she was ready, she never felt ready for anything as an adult. She discovered that she didn't like to say goodbye to the night and so would stay up very late; then she didn't want to say goodbye to the morning so she stayed in bed very late. In general her life was controlled by that early event. She could never leave what she was doing to do something else without a great deal of anxiety. She had to fully complete an activity from beginning to end, and any interruption would produce irritation or even rage.

Switching

Another characteristic arising from the Cesarean birth trauma is an intolerance for unexpected changes; switching plans of any kind triggers inordinate anger and anxiety in the person. The conventional therapist might label the problem as "arrested development of the ego" or a "fixation of the ego at the infantile stage," and other such elaborate concepts. We have found a far more direct cause, however, in the Cesarean birth experience. One patient wrote:

> My worst Primals involved the switch of being born Cesarean after trying so hard to be born the right way. To this day, if someone switches plans on me without my knowing it or being involved I am immediately thrown into a first-line Primal about it.

And another:

> Gradually, after two years of feeling these birth feelings, I am better able to stand and switch; that is, having something planned suddenly changed. I used to get quite angry and upset and terribly afraid when this happened. My reaction now is much less severe.

Another offshoot of switching plans is changing directions. One Cesarean patient wrote: "I still have no sense of direction and I believe this is directly connected with my birth." She could not direct herself in the present because when she tried at birth she was stopped and forced into the opposite direction.

Indecisiveness

Depending on the nature of the birth trauma, it is possible that a long labor in which none of the baby's efforts brought success will lead to a later characteristic of indecisiveness. If struggle yielded nothing, the later reaction may be, "I can't decide anything for myself—I have no decision power." This then becomes the prototypic response throughout life. It is a *biologic* experience of indecision rather than a *cognitive* inability. The person cannot make up his mind now because when he did, in the most important issue he ever faced, it did him no good. This Primal experience of failure sets the stage for an a priori feeling of ineffectiveness: one feels defeated before ever taking the first step.

Such a person might let his parents, and later his friends or mate, make up his mind for him on both major and minor matters. He will see what others order from the menu and then order the same. The more others take over his daily decision-making, the more reinforced the prototype of being indecisive becomes since the directive influence from birth is paramount. In the "clash of wills" at birth, it was Mother who predominated.

Following is a report by a patient who reexperienced the disastrous effects of triggering his own birth, and how this had impeded his ability to make decisions—literally, to make his own moves—ever since:

Trigger for birth feelings: a visit home

The first time I reexperienced the beginning of my birth was when I was going to go home for a visit after a year of therapy. Visiting my family involved traveling many thousands of miles away from the Institute. As my departure date drew near, I became increasingly anxious and afraid that it would all be too difficult—that I would not be able to cope with seeing my parents. I made sure I had several addresses of Primal people in the area, but the feeling that it would be too difficult persisted.

One day I went to the Institute and lay down in the large group room to feel. I began to feel my anxiety about leaving this environment in which my feelings were understood and it was safe to be just the way I

The birth trauma: from joy to horror

really am. I cried about not wanting to leave, and eventually this strange new thing began to happen. It was as though everything went black and quiet; I was curled up in a ball barely aware of anything. I then lifted my head in what felt like a rather joyful exploratory movement, but instead it triggered a hellish process that I would have done anything to avoid. I was in the womb, and my move to leave triggered off my birth process. After I had felt something of how it felt to have inadvertently set off this horrendous chain of events, I realized why I had been so afraid of leaving the Institute. The Institute had been my womb and I was sure my move to leave it was going to produce some awful calamity. Not surprisingly, I realized after feeling this that it would not be *that* hard, and, in fact, I coped with the trip successfully.

Indecisiveness: acted out as a child, imprinted as a fetus

It truly amazed me when I connected another of my feelings to this start of my birth. I have always had difficulty making decisions. Whenever I make a decision I feel it is the wrong one. I originally connected this back to my decision at age 8 to go to boarding school. My parents had offered me the choice of going "next semester or when you're 12," and I thought about it for a while and then surprised them by saying that I wanted to go the next semester. But when it came to that moment when my mother actually left me at the school, I changed my mind. I cried and screamed to try and make her take me with her, but it was no use. I had made what seemed like an extremely costly mistake, and it was, but the surprising part is that this exact feeling goes back to my birth. The first movement I made with my head turned out to be a mistake, and I would have done anything to remain safe and secure in my mother's womb. The message seemed to be, "Don't make a move on your own."

Trauma-Induced Emotional Response Patterns

The intense emotions felt by the neonate in and around birth remain in the system and eventually emerge as the emotional implications of the birth trauma. The intensity of the emotions will be commensurate with the degree of trauma imprinted, in the same way that personality characteristics reflect a commensurate Primal force. Often we hear parents say, "He was just *born* with a temper!" or "She was a moody baby from the start." We now know that what we once thought was genetic is primarily experiential: We are not born with an angry or anxious disposition in our genes, but almost universally we *are* born angry and anxious.

Anger and Rage

One of the emotional consequences of a long, hard labor is a general feeling of rage and rebelliousness. Many patients report that mad frustration of not being able to get out—it simply infuriated the neonate. He utilized his rage to fight his way out; and his rage pulled him through. One can see these rageful movements in birth Primals, with the wild thrashing and gnashing, the uncontrolled body movements and fury in the faces of patients. The rage is life-saving.

Whenever a person with this kind of birth trauma later hears "No you can't!", a resonating chord is struck: the sensation of birth, when the mother's body was saying "No you can't . . . get out," is reactivated. That physical experience of not being able to do what you want and need to do at birth becomes a physiologic prototype, drawing other similar experiences into its orbit. Later, the command "No you can't!" may set off an inordinate rage and a *biologic* need to act anyway. That need *to do it anyway* meant survival at birth, so there is going to be a tremendous force behind a person's rage and rebellion in the present.

Even a simple frustration such as having to wait in a slow-moving line for a theater showing, waiting to debark from an airplane or having to wait for a meal to be served can bring up the birth anlage. That is when the rage comes up. And as noted earlier, what was initially a life-saving reaction now becomes a negative or even life-threatening behavior.

One of our patients described an incident which typified for him the relationship between his birth and his rages. He was riding in a car once with his mother when they become stuck in traffic. He angrily told her to "get going" even though she obviously couldn't go anywhere (they were directly behind another car) and clearly it was not her fault. Nevertheless he screamed "Go!" and then punched her.

The survival valence of the need to "get going" (in birth) made him act irrationally and violently. That same feeling may be in all of us, but those who are better defended may just get irritable and curse. In the above case, the third level was bypassed entirely; the man just began punching (a first-line reaction) because he was overwhelmed with urgency by the upcoming feeling—and no amount of rationality could supersede its potency.

Another patient, born Cesarean, describes a more typical reaction:

> I used to get very angry whenever anyone would cut in front of me—either in a line or in a car. I would get outraged, feeling "they" were holding me back and cutting me off. Anger and irritability have been major modes of acting out for me, but now happen rarely. Usually there is just fear underneath the anger—fear that I connect to the terrible fear I had of my mother at birth.

(Notice how being "cut off" was the Primal trigger—not so surprising, since being "cut off" and out of her mother's womb was her Primal experience.)

When a person has a birth Primal and feels the rage over his frustration at not being allowed out, he may finally be liberated to express anger in a rightful, positive way:

> Since experiencing and integrating birth feelings I am much more spontaneous in asserting and expressing myself. I can "go for" the

things important to me without the past fear. This is also directly related to being able to express anger in the present for the first time ever. I knew from the wonderful feeling that overwhelmed me after I expressed my anger that the Pain was endurable, and I was getting well.

Getting in touch with that prototypic rage which the neonate rightfully felt at birth is liberating. The person finally understands why his first reaction to every frustration was anger—even as a very young child—until it was punished or beaten out of him. His parents might have rationalized, "He's always had such a temper—just born with it, I guess!" Not so. The temper was part of the aggressive response at birth. It was a response provoked by circumstances. Being "hot-tempered" may in fact begin in the womb. Another patient wrote:

My birth was a long, eighteen-hour struggle. I felt that there was no way out, but I could not stop struggling because to stop was to never get out. I was frustrated and scared by this long wait. I did not know what was happening, and I was simply born angry.

Many of our patients have never expressed rage as adults. They typically suffer from the suppressed symptoms of rage—headaches, rashes, allergies—until they descend to that first-line Primal rage at birth. It usually has been decades since they have been able to express and feel fully the early rage. Feeling the rage finally liberates them from it, rids them of their symptoms, and frees them for the first time to assert their wants and needs in a healthy, non-manipulative way. Another report:

Rage, migraines, and birth

I still don't think my life is in good enough shape to feel the total Pain of this feeling that I have to constantly fight to stay alive. The migraine Pain is pushing on me most of the time, telling me my Pain is there. But still I must fight in my everyday life to make it better, so as to feel this feeling, so as to *live* my life. How angry it all gets me that I have to go through all this just to be the person my parents took away from me. It seems like such a waste of time and energy. I feel so used and abused.

The stage I am at now is just being very angry at having had it so hard my whole life. I hate the fact that I have to fight to live. Lately I wake up in the morning, and within fifteen minutes of getting up I have what I call an "angry headache." I've always noticed that I get these headaches when I am particularly angry. The headaches are located on my left side: my left temple, eye, neck, and shoulder. They are similar in Pain to the migraines which I get on my right side, but a bit less intense. The first thoughts that enter my mind are, "Shit! Here we go again—fight through another day."

I feel even angrier since I went on vacation in the Caribbean and had three wonderful days when I didn't have to fight. I just lived. I realized then what I had missed out on my whole life. I am furious. My only consolation is that I know once I get past this tremendous outrage, I will go deeper into the feeling and slowly resolve it.

Resolution through feeling: the only hope

One patient who had a birth Primal about rage realized why he was so combative and argumentative, and why he could never admit that he was wrong. For him, the unconscious meaning of succumbing to somebody else's argument was death. He had not succumbed to the opposition he had felt in the birth canal, and he could not succumb now; he was absolutely impenetrable in terms of new ideas. The leitmotif was *not* succumbing to anyone else. That theme suffused his life in various ways, one of which was to play "devil's advocate": since he was an intellectual who loved to debate, he set it up so that he could not lose even an argument. There was a great Primal stake in winning.

Another patient had a most battering birth. He came out bruised and misshapen, his journey down the canal a harrowing one. Later he discovered that he had always been ready to fight anyone who even brushed against him slightly. He already felt so bruised that the slightest touch made him wince, triggering his rage and aggression. His pre-therapy rationalization had been that he was simply a "touchy" person who didn't like to be jostled.

Worthless, Ugly, and Unwanted

Rage is also often compounded by feelings of worthlessness. When we speak of feeling worthless as adults invariably there is a Primal connection and a feeling of Primal rage associated with it. One patient had been feeling for months how her parents had made her feel worthless by frequently criticizing and humiliating her. There seemed to be a whole childhood of reasons to account for her adult feelings. Yet the story did not end or begin there. Eventually she felt that the origin of her worthless feelings lay in the fact that even at birth no one had cared whether she lived or died. Among many insights, she now realized that her sudden rages at her husband for supposedly not giving her enough money to spend on clothes for herself had a Primal origin: She unconsciously wanted him to give her the attention and care she had been deprived of from birth onward. Money became the symbol for the Primal love she never got, and her husband became the target for the Primal rage she never expressed.

From this example we see why it is not enough to connect to the childhood sources of these feelings when there is a deeper, birth connection. Each level of consciousness is unique; the child is not the infant. In a sense we are talking about two separate persons, and we need to relive both. How the infant experiences that rage and worthlessness is substantively different from how the child experiences it. That is why each needs a time to "speak," and each has its own needs.

Can a newborn feel ugly? One patient wrote:

> When I was born I felt that my mother did not want to look at me. As a result, I have always felt ugly—and therefore *was*. My mother verified the fact that she did not want to look at me when I was born because I had been bruised on my forehead and nose after my dry birth. Also, the nurse had painted black marks under my eyes to protect me from the bright lights and this added to my "ugliness." During my life it has been a constant struggle for me to try to look pretty. Now, when I'm feeling good, it just doesn't matter that I am not pretty. Something seems to show in my face when I am happy, because at those time people like to be with me.

In the next report, the patient connects his feelings of being ugly to the treatment he received immediately after his birth. The birth trauma of being stuck in the canal was made even more traumatic by what followed it:

Prototypic feelings

Often when I'm alone my Pain comes up because when I'm lonely I feel badly about myself. At the bottom of it I feel like some kind of sub-human abomination. I feel hurt and ugly.

Hurt: *rough handling*

The *hurt* originates from the very rough handling I received from the hands of the doctor who delivered me. His hands grabbed my head like pliers; he twisted me around, yanked me out, and swung me around into an upside-down position. My welcome into the world was something like getting punched out by a steam hammer.

Ugly: *doctor's cold detachment*

Ugly comes from my first minutes after birth. I sensed the doctor's cold detachment—he had no sensitivity whatsoever to my pain. I was handled like an unfeeling object. I was dumped on my back, away from my mother who no longer existed for me.

Present-day trigger: My nervous system suffered such a pounding that I
The Elephant Man experienced it in a Primal as feeling mangled and monstrously distorted. The monstrous feeling came shortly after I had seen the movie, *The Elephant Man* —a film about a monstrously ugly yet feeling human being. As a newborn, my feelings were smashed. Too much Pain. In the Primal I experienced feeling as hideous on the inside—in my nervous system and brain—as the Elephant Man had appeared on the surface. *I felt like he looked.*

The entire sequence Then I experienced the whole sequence even more clearly: I'd just come from a paradise inside my mother's womb, only to be stuck for what seemed like an eternity in the birth canal where all my efforts came to nothing; on top of that I was suddenly battered and tossed about and abandoned like a piece of bruised meat. It was quite a bring-down. I felt like an ugly, unwantable creature.

Being stuck in the birth canal frequently sets up a Primal basis for feeling worthless and unwanted: clearly there is something that obstructs the baby from coming into life and that something can be the mother's own reticence and fear. But whatever the cause the baby only knows that it is being blocked; it is not getting an "all-signals-go" response. This experience may be elaborated later into a shy, withdrawn and generally "held back" personality.

Usually our later feelings of worthlessness or ugliness do have an early physiologic base. If to be stuck in the canal means *biologically* that one's most urgent need to become alive is not responded to, is ignored, then any later neglect—in the crib or as a five-year-old—will be elaborated into the feeling, "No one cares about me; I must not deserve to be cared about."

Being "ignored" in the womb and at birth means having one's needs impeded, counteracted or altered. Such an experience lays the foundation for a prototypic response of worthlessness to any later stress. It shapes the later feelings of rejection in accordance with the earliest, prepotent experience. The labels may change—from feeling "creepy" as a five-year-old, to feeling "like shit" as an adolescent, to feeling "worthless and inferior" as an adult—but all are variations of Primal.

A neonate doesn't think "However hard I try, I get nowhere." He doesn't think "I am ugly"—but he has had an *experience*. He will have to wait years to put a name to that experience, but it is the *experience* that counts. Putting a label on a suit is not the same as the suit itself. The rock bottom of any experience is that specific experiential process that gives us the feeling of feeling.

Adult Separation Anxiety

When the newborn is not put with its mother right away, a feeling of catastrophic aloneness is imprinted. Some patients report this birth feeling in adult life as an overwhelming emptiness, coupled with a chronic anxiety. Indeed, separation anxiety is frequently at the bottom of compulsive behavior. One patient felt that he compulsively filled himself up with food as a means of hiding that emptiness. Another woman felt that she had to be filled up with penises, the basis for her nyphomania, as a result of that very same feeling. She had to feel "connected."

If the baby is left totally alone after birth (which has been the common practice) and is abandoned in a variety of ways during early childhood, then the feeling of loneliness and the stark terror over being alone will be interpreted later as abandonment. If that same birth trauma of separation occurs but the parents are warm and kind and there for the child later, then the anxiety will be considerably lessened and there will be less of a drive to be with other people constantly. As always, the interpretation of the birth trauma will be very different for the person in whom it was compounded during childhood from those of a person who suffered little compounding.

One patient wrote:

Primal aloneness

After my birth (which took 18 hours) I was left completely alone. That really hurt after all the physical Pain I had just been through. All I wanted was comfort and contact.

Acting out against the aloneness

After feeling the Pain of that first separation in Primals, I understood much about how I had lived. As I grew up, I would constantly organize social things—childhood gangs when I was small, and sports activities as I grew older. I would do anything to avoid being alone.

I also couldn't stand it if someone didn't like me. I have spent my whole life avoiding making people angry with me. I was always the "good guy," telling jokes, making people feel comfortable, etc.

As an adult I continued to try to make everyone happy, even at the expense of my wife and kids. My married life was crazy, as I always felt tied down and wanted to be free—*but I absolutely did not want to be alone.*

Even the act of going to bed alone in a dark room

would activate that fear and Pain. I always fought against going to bed as a child, and when I grew older I would masturbate or drink to help me get to sleep as quickly as possible.

We see quite clearly the effects of early separation from the mother in adults who were born prematurely. One patient wrote:

The trauma: pre-maturity

I was born a month and a half prematurely, with a heart defect, and was put in an incubator for two months. I survived against all odds, and primarily against my mother's wishes.

When I entered therapy, I remember that Dr. Holden [the neurologist for The Primal Institute] and I talked about the reasons why I had survived. He said that, in time, I would find out what had kept me alive.

Infant compounding

My mother has told me that I wasn't touched very much in those early months of my life because, she said, "You cried too much when handled." I was even fed without being touched hardly at all. At the Insti-

Overwhelming feeling of waiting

tute, I relived being left alone in the incubator, and the first feeling that completely overtook me was that of *waiting*.

Reliving the trauma

At first I didn't know what I was waiting for, but in my enclosed cubicle, it felt like life itself. It was terrifying to be so alone, shut inside that thing and so tightly bound with covers—it was hard to move. Everything in me felt like giving up, except for that crazy feeling of *waiting* for something or someone.

One night as I was screaming my heart out in the room at the Institute, someone suddenly opened the door: instantly I felt my whole body tense in expectation. The door closed again and I was back in my misery. When a therapist came out of nowhere I asked her to touch my forehead very softly, and then I knew—I felt it: *the hands*. Sometime, a long time ago, another pair of hands had stroked my head while I desperately tried to reach out, to touch. My whole being just ached to be touched.

Waiting to feel the hands *for 28 years*

But the hands never stayed long, so I just waited for them to come back. After feeling for a few months about expecting life from those hands, of feeling that those hands were my lifeline, I finally felt that they were not coming back. With that cold realization, I decided that I wanted to die; there were no more reasons for me to go on living.

It has taken me 28 years to feel that waiting for a pair of hands to touch me and keep me alive.

I can't say that I have stopped waiting entirely, but the search for someone to make my life better is over. And subsequently, I am now in the process of taking charge of my own life.

*Giving up the strug-
gle to enjoy*

One more thing. Some time after feeling about that early trauma, the overjoyous, overreactive little girl in me died as well, and for the first time in my life depression has settled in. It goes hand in hand with loneliness and helplessness, which until now I was never able to feel. It seems that a lifelong struggle of enjoying myself and never feeling depressed and alone was related to that Painful, early memory. I realize now that I usually acted in exactly the opposite way in which my Pain lay. Maybe now I can really begin to enjoy living.

Doom

When beginning anything new many of us are prone to the feeling that something terrible is going to happen—a feeling of impending doom. That overriding feeling that everything is doomed makes its victims unable to take happiness; unconsciously they cannot stand to "make it" because in their birth they just barely "made it" out. Something terrible has *already* happened, only they aren't aware of it. They are in a constant struggle to be happy because struggle was their first and prototypic experience. Ironically, these people will go to lectures and weekend seminars in order to "learn" to be happy. But we cannot teach the adult to be happy, just as we cannot teach the newborn not to cry. Feelings are not taught; they simply *are*.

The feeling of impending doom is likely to happen when the person really feels good. The locked-in imprint is that Pain always follows pleasure—the birth analogue. Indeed, some people will actually make themselves feel bad the moment they start to feel good in order to have some control over that feeling of impending doom. The unconscious dictum seems to be, "If you are feeling good, look out!" Many of us feel good and then suffer a vague apprehension that it won't last. We usually contrive ways so that it won't. Of course, the good feeling in the womb didn't last either.

This doom-and-gloom scenario gets compounded by the fact that many parents can't stand seeing their children having fun, goofing around, doing "nothing" but enjoying themselves. They manage to find something "constructive" for the children to do instead. There is a great fear that fun and relaxation will spoil us. No wonder so few of us can relax.

The feeling of doom is frequently related to Cesarean births. Most Cesareans are planned, scheduled events in which the baby is truly the last to know what is happening. Birth is very abrupt, and the baby has no time to prepare for the sudden transition from womb to world. Thereafter, the person with this kind of birth trauma isn't going to feel good about any sudden transition. Transition may signal the doom of total helplessness and literally of being in someone else's hands. Worse still, that prototypic transition involved major surgery—a trauma in itself—so that the last comfort the baby "remembers" systemically was in the placental sac just before birth. The transition out of that sac was disastrous for the newborn so that later there is a tendency to retreat to the known, to hold onto the past—a conservatism and an abhorrence of sudden change of any kind.

As I have pointed out, the person with this kind of birth trauma will prefer routine—not because he is an inherently organized person—but because any change or deviation in routine will only seem for the worse. Being afraid to try new things isn't just a superficial attitude; it is a memory of survival. The future will be tainted by a vague sense of doom because the "future" at birth was an agony. The person will tend to avoid situations in which limits are not well circumscribed and every eventuality not well considered. But, again, the doom or disaster that the person is trying so hard to avoid in the present by his meticulous planning *has already taken place.*

One Cesarean patient wrote:

Feelings of doom and failure

Another more recent problem for me has been intense feelings of failure because I had nothing to do with getting born. I feel a deep sense of not being able to do anything without help and symbolize on the therapists for this help. I always feel doomed to fail and set myself up in various ways in the present to do exactly that—ways which are not yet very clear to me.

Death in the womb

I am very suicidal lately and must take drugs and stay close to the Institute because of the feelings of not wanting to live—which I realize is really not wanting to live with *this Pain.* I guess I am trying to finish my death in the womb. I live in the future with a terrible sense of dread about it, and cannot live in the present without getting frantic.

And another:

Progression of Primals

I have been in Primal Therapy for one year and my Primals have gotten progressively deeper. From the three-week intensive when I first learned to let myself cry again, through my fourth week to now, my feelings go deeper and more intensely than ever. For a time I wondered where all of this would end up. After every Primal I used to think, "How much deeper can I go—how much more intense can the Pain get? What is the source of all of this suffering I am going through?" In the past, I used to think that there was something really wrong with me. There was, but I never understood why, or what to do to change it.

Birth trauma: tried but failed: Cesarean

I've only had birth feelings recently but they seem to explain a lot to me. I've caught a glimpse of the answers to a lot of questions I've been asking myself for the past 10 or 15 years. I am beginning to understand why I am the way I am. My birth was Cesarean and my mother tells me I didn't want to come out. I think and feel that I tried my best and hardest to be born, but my mother tensed up and held me back. I must have tried so hard that I think I nearly died. Knowing the way my mother is, I am sure that her body tensed up out of fear and anxiety.

The prototype: "Everything has always been hard"

Everything has always been hard for me. The smallest tasks were frequently overwhelming for me (and sometimes still are). Physical situations are always extremely difficult. I can remember as a teenager in high school always wishing I could start everything all over again: classes, school days, assignments, school years, relationships with fellow students . . . my whole life! I wished that I could do it right this time. This hope was the only thing that kept me going. Instinctively I knew that better parents and better circumstances would have made a world of difference. Unconsciously (I thought) adopting this attitude, my miserable life was doomed to failure. Everything I tried to do failed miserably. There came a point when I just gave up even trying because I always knew (or expected) the outcome to be the same. The story of my life is based on my beginning. My birth was hard—my whole life has been hard.

Phobias

Phobias are a complex phenomenon. They contain both psychological and intellectual implications of the birth trauma: they have the emotional component of fear as well as the intellectual (mental) focus on whatever is feared. In phobias the emotional content predominates; the idea or object is really secondary. Obsessions, on the other hand, are an example of the reverse: they also contain both second- and third-level implications, but with the third level predominating.

Many of us do not recognize that we are phobic. Yet any fear which is inordinate and inappropriate and which has a compulsive quality to it can be considered a phobia. That vague stab of apprehension when someone closes a door behind us, sealing off "escape," is an example of what I mean. Anxiety at having to wait in line to get off an airplane is another. The feeling of relief at having aisle exits available in a theater also reveals a phobic attitude.

Infants are not phobic. They do not have the brain capacity for it. However, they *can* be fearful. Later, the stream of underlying first-line fear can be channeled by childhood experiences into a specific fear of heights, elevators, snakes or whatever.

The emotional component of such phobias will be very much like the emotional component of certain kinds of fearful dreams, and indeed a recurrent nightmare has much in common with phobias in terms of the mode of handling the birth event. Both rationalize the emotional component into an appropriate image; and in both the emotional component predominates but is enclosed and disguised by the images.

While childhood Pains which compound the birth trauma are also important in the development of phobias, the nature and degree of the birth trauma itself can prescribe the content and severity of the later phobia:

> I am a jet pilot who became more and more phobic flying in formation, particularly in cloud banks. It got so bad that I really had a tough time flying. Recently I've had a Primal which clarified and resolved the entire thing for me. Being in a cloud bank did not allow me to have the sensation of *motion*. It was like a static state which reminded me exactly of what happened to me at birth. Lack of motion really did mean death then and the feeling in the cloud bank was exactly the same.
>
> I remember as a child always drawing angels with wings and always having fantasies of being an angel with wings who could fly. I now realize that the feeling of being trapped and stuck was at the bottom of so much of my childhood imagery and my choice of profession as an adult. It caught up with me, however, in my phobias.

Fear of Heights

The fear of not being rooted solidly to the ground can come from birth when the baby found itself in strange positions without any natural orientation. This is often the case in breech birth, and most commonly occurs when the newborn is held upside down just after birth.

One patient relived feeling totally disoriented in coming out of the canal; then he felt a rapid loss of support and a sudden thrust downward as he was allowed to drop a few inches into the doctor's hands. These birth sensations left him with a residual fear which later took the form of a fear of heights.

Another patient feared overpasses, bridges and narrow highways in the mountains. It all seemed a classic case of fear of heights until she had her birth Primal and discovered that the true feeling inside this phobia was not so much a fear of heights as a fear of "no exit." Being on a bridge or narrow mountain road triggered off the feeling she had experienced in the birth canal of "I'm going to die and there is no exit."

Fear of the Dark

The almost universal childhood fear of the dark has an obvious relationship to birth: How many children, who are still so close in time to their birth experiences, fear the dark? Very many. And though it seems that many of us outgrow that fear, we don't—it is just more buried as we grow older. Some of us never outgrow it at all. One patient wrote:

After I had several insights about my birth experience, I talked to my friend about it. My friend subsequently called to say how she was now able to connect her terror of the dark with a vague feeling/memory she had always had about being in a dark "room" with a light far away that she had to aim for. She now recognized this as her birth experience, and that she's been having Primals (without knowing what they were) about it all her life. She also realized that her whole life has been a pattern of striving to reach particular goals, of trying to "make it"—out of the dark.

Children who must have the light on in order to sleep are suffering acutely from that dark period just before they saw their first light of day. In a conditioning paradigm, it seems that dark represents agony and light represents respite—for it was in the light that the agony stopped; it was in the light that breathing began; and it was in light that the first comfort from Mother became evident.

Claustrophobia

Claustrophobia is a fear that is harder to rationalize, especially when it is highly generalized. One patient who had been squeezed in the birth canal was fearful of tight places as a child. As an adult it translated into a fear of elevators and psychologically into a fear of any "tight" situation she felt she couldn't get out of.

Another patient became anxious when confined in any space. Not only was he claustrophobic in small spaces, but any prolonged containment such as sitting in a classroom produced an agitated state—no felt Pain, just a need to get out. Recess at school was always a tremendous relief to him. As an adult he had to take outdoor jobs. He interpreted his birth trauma mainly as one of confinement. He was also confined a lot later on: he wasn't allowed to play after school but had to come straight home to do his chores. These events became the second-line links to first-line trauma.

As mentioned, the birth feeling of confinement leads to claustrophobia not only in the physical sense but also in the psychological sense. One patient wrote:

> After having several birth Primals I was telling my mother about them and she recognized that her claustrophobia is from her birth experience: being crushed in a tiny space and unable to free her arms; she also saw that she acts this out by getting herself into situations which she can't "get out of"; she said she always feels "stuck."

Another example of psychological claustrophobia came from one of our staff members. She began complaining about the "lack of room to breathe in here [the Institute]"; "there is not enough space to grow"; "I need more space for myself"; and "you're closing in on me." While there may be a kernel of truth in these types of statements, they are usually blown out of proportion by the birth anlage. That is, they are *in* proportion to the original Pain, but out of proportion to the current situation. Interestingly enough, the staff member became discontented with the Institute's *psychological* space just as she began her birth Primals in which she re-experienced the literal lack of *physical* space she had had during her birth. After these Primals the Institute suddenly seemed freer to her, more permissive and open. She could "breathe" again.

Doom and Disaster Fears

Many people who develop phobias find ways to make sense out of them. One patient, a Californian, recalled reacting to his mounting internal pressure before entering therapy by deciding that California was going to fall off into the ocean from an earthquake. So he packed his things, gave up his job and moved to Arizona. California may one day fall into the ocean. But whether that happens or not, this man's ideas and his move were phobic because they were prompted by a feeling of terror and doom from his past—not by the real threat of disaster in the present.

At the time, this patient did not realize how phobic he was because many other people shared the same idea. The possibility of an earthquake was a great "hook" on which to hang all sorts of unconscious Primal pressure. (Not surprisingly, some of these individuals previously had been part of the "acid" generation, and nothing releases catastrophic birth fears so quickly as LSD.)

In Primal Therapy, this patient experienced his feeling of doom and disaster in its real context. He could situate it in the past where it came from instead of projecting it into the future and developing a phobia. He could weigh the likelihood of an actual earthquake and react to it as a remote possibility rather than as a pressing inevitability. The real inevitability that had caused this man to literally flee *was* a natural disaster; but it did not involve the geological instability of California—it involved the Pain of his birth.

The following report shows the relationship between the development of phobias and the presence of repressed, catastrophic Pain. This patient's traumatic birth was compounded by severe childhood trauma, and the phobias became for her a comparatively "safe" means of experiencing an otherwise devastating amount of Pain. In her report we see the descent into ever earlier levels of consciousness as she experiences the present-day hook for her disaster phobias first in her husband's Pain (third level), then in the childhood memories of her mother and father (second level), and finally in a "type of feeling that [she] could not connect to any picture or memory" (first level):

Fear of planes

I have always felt terrified in a plane. I was terrified of the emptiness beneath the plane, and felt as though it were going to lose its balance and fall, non-stop. I would sit still and frozen, holding my breath, not moving a muscle, and wanting to scream at the stewardesses to sit down and not move either. To make matters worse, being in the airplane also would bring up another of my biggest phobias—claustrophobia.

Fear of enclosed places

I would feel claustrophobic in any place such as a room, elevator, bus or subway where I could not see a window that I would be able to open if I needed to. Immediately I would have trouble breathing and would become afraid that I would die. I felt the same way on some days in Los Angeles, when the smog was very heavy. Even when I was outside on those days, I felt as though I were trapped under a huge blanket covering the whole city.

Fear of earthquakes

Another of my phobias was a fear of earthquakes. Even if I only *heard* the word *earthquake,* I would become terrified. For a long time I thought my fear was completely realistic, and that people who were not scared were just crazy and unconscious. I was terrified that in an earthquake the earth would open up and I would be swallowed by the ground or stuck underneath a building.

Other feelings connected with earthquakes were: I could not depend on the earth to support me; I would be completely powerless over its movements; and it could happen at any time without warning—I was completely at its mercy. In my fear I also could feel physically the sensation of how I might be burned in a fire caused by the quake.

I had all these phobias when I started therapy. They got worse and worse as I got deeper and deeper into my old feelings. I want to describe a few of the key Primals that I have had concerning these phobias and how they related to my suppressed childhood Pain and to my buried birth Pain.

Current connection to earthquake phobia

The first Primal started me on my way. I was driving to a private session at the Institute when I heard on the radio that an earthquake was predicted. When I got to my session I was able for the first time to make a connection between my fear of being swallowed by the earth and my fear of being swallowed by my husband's Pain. At that time my husband was in a lot of Pain and not doing anything about it. His hopelessness was driving me crazy; I felt constantly pushed down, squashed and suffocated by it.

Childhood connections

As I was crying in the session I began to remember how my mother behaved throughout my childhood. She was always expressing a lot of Pain, crying or laughing hysterically, complaining about everything, never really satisfied, almost always sick physically. On top of all that she attempted suicide several times. She made me feel as though things would have been better for her if I had been different, more caring. I felt as though I were carrying her whole weight on my shoulders—like she was taking up all the space; I felt I was being forced to repress any feelings that I had. It seemed I had no right to exist. For example, when I would say, "I'm tired," she would answer, "You're too young to be tired!"

Feeling the "ground underneath my feet"

This old feeling was part of the reason it was so difficult for me to stand my husband's Pain. For a time, these connections relieved the pressure that was also behind my fear of earthquakes. I found myself a lot more confident in the solidity of the ground underneath my feet. I remember driving back home after the session, looking at the buildings, the trees, the sky—the entire scene was so much more vivid, real and beautiful now that I was rid of the fear that it could all fall apart in an instant.

Later, another earthquake warning helped me to make a new connection about some painful experiences that I had already Primalled about previously. In the session I was crying about an earthquake coming; I felt completely trapped by the possibility that I would not be able to get out of Los Angeles before it struck. My therapist asked me if I had ever been locked up in my life. At first I answered no; then after thinking about it for a minute I said, "I was never really locked up *physically,* but I remember *feeling* trapped." I again felt what it was like living with my mother and stepfather, how I could never do anything that *I* wanted to do, how they systematically refused anything I asked for. They chose my clothes, my food, my pastimes, everything. And I hated everything—the clothes, the food, the pastimes! But there was no way to fight back because they always found very good justifications for their refusals. They said they wanted me to be well-educated, well brought up, and that they knew what was best for me. They made me feel that everything I wanted was wrong and that my wants meant nothing at all. If I said I did not like a dish we had for dinner, my stepfather would force me to have a second helping.

Earthquake phobia and severe childhood trauma

Until recently most of my Primals have been about the period of my life after the age of six when I lived with my mother and stepfather. They mostly involved feelings of being trapped, alone and hopeless. Within the last five months I have been Primalling about feelings from my life before I was six when I lived in many different foster homes. The Primals also involve feelings of being trapped, alone and hopeless. My mother put me in these foster homes because she and my father were getting a divorce, and she was working and had no time for me. Except for my first foster-mother with whom I lived until I was about two years old, I don't remember any other foster-mother loving, or even liking, me. The two last foster homes I lived in were run by women who terrified me. My needs (even basic physical needs) were absolutely denied. One woman would allow me to use the toilet only following her preplanned schedule—even when I needed to use it so badly that I was in physical pain. She limited how much water I could drink per day: during hot weather the maximum was one-half cup! She also often hit me with a whip.

Being around her and the foster-mother before her was a constant threat. I could never understand what would make them so angry with me; I just got used to living in a constant state of terror, always expecting a terrible punishment to fall on me at any time. When one of these foster-mothers would just enter the same room I was in I would feel pain in my stomach, shake all over, and get dizzy. It was like walking in a mine field. I have had many Primals about these experiences, but even deeper Primals involved feeling abandoned by my parents—like I had nobody at all.

Early body sensations

Later on in therapy I got into a different, even earlier, type of feeling that I could not connect to any picture or memory. It was just body sensations—I felt like a tiny animal lying on my back, naked, having no words. It was like every single part of my body was screaming in its own way with Pain and need—need of being touched and held. It felt like I was in a desert, alone and devastated. I was crying and screaming but there was no emotion, just the feeling of needing something I did not have. It was earlier, deeper, more painful than emotions like sadness. But once again, as in Primals from later in my life, I felt trapped—and now even stronger than before. My body felt so wracked with pain that I wanted to fly out of it.

Desertion by father

The last feeling I would like to describe happened a few weeks ago. I was lying in the dark and started picturing the scene when my real father came to say goodbye to me when I was not quite two years old. He got down on his knees and said to me that he was leaving, but would come back. I was standing in front of him, and his hands were holding my arms. I did not say anything. I saw his body walking away from me, even though I kept looking down at the grass that was so green. I remained quiet at the time. Again in the feeling, there was not really any sadness—mostly emptiness and a sensation of dizziness.

Memories of mother

That day I went to buddy with a friend because I had gotten very sick—bad sore throat, pain in my ears— just in the same way I used to be very sick when I was a little girl. After crying for a while about my father leaving I started talking about the times when I was small and got very sick—how my mother used to come, pick me up and take me home [from the foster home]. In my memories I had always believed that it was wonderful to be with her and that she loved me. In this feeling for the first time I remembered how she was then—her body was moving around my bed—she was serving me my meals, doing everything that needed to be done, but I started feeling like she was not really there. It was just her body, her actions, but inside I felt very strongly that she did not care.

I realized that the reason it felt so good to be home was because I was *away* from the foster homes and *away* from the danger. I could just lie down and relax in the warmth of my bed. At that point in the feeling when I felt like the struggle for survival was over, I started feeling the emptiness so huge inside of me. Immediately I experienced a birth sensation: tremendous pressure like a circle around my forehead, as if fingers of a crazy person were trying to make my head burst. The pressure went down to my eyes, to my nose. It was so unbearable that I had the urge to push forward. The whole sensation lasted just a minute or two. I moved forward because of an unbearable pressure: it struck me that it had been that way my entire life.

Reexperiencing birth sensations

I always wanted to go back or away or escape, because whatever I was doing, wherever I was— whether I was four, ten, twenty years old, or even now—I always felt this pressure. For example, each year around April (the month of my birth) I would have to go away. The need for warmth would push me to give up everything I was doing at the moment and go away to a foreign country where the weather was very warm.

The prototypic pressure

I have always felt like it was hopeless and meaningless to take a step, and I now realized why I would never take a step on my own or for myself—until I was too scared of getting hurt or punished for not doing it. That is the way I functioned in school, at home with my parents and in my adult life, too—postponing everything until there was no other choice but to do it.

Myriad act-outs of the trauma

I can hear myself saying a million times, "I did it because I had no choice." It was partly that feeling that drove me to Primal Therapy. Through my Primals I have come to understand why I was always emotionally unstable, always financially unable to support myself; why I would always begin something but would give up before I could finish it; why I could never rest or relax; why I always moved so fast and put myself in so many crazy, dead-end situations. All of a sudden, it felt like all the pieces of a puzzle fell into place so that everything I had gone through during my life made sense.

Phobias: defense against the real *danger*

I created struggles, symbolized on things and people, developed phobias and saw danger all around me because it kept me from feeling the devastating emptiness of what *had* been the *real* danger: being left in those foster homes by my parents when I was little. I also realized that the danger and the trapped feelings I experienced in the foster homes helped distract me from feeling this emptiness and rejection when it first happened. It also kept me from feeling the even more devastating *physical* emptiness I experienced at the very beginning of my life because of not getting the *Birth connection* touching I needed. Because of this deprivation, I disconnected my body from the reality of its sensations, making myself physically insensitive.

I understand now how being on hashish and similar drugs in my twenties—giving my body that drug-induced access to strong sensations—must have brought up all the Pain of what I did not get back then, and that is why it made me feel so crazy.

Resolution

Now I can be independent without feeling constantly like I am going to die. My fears of earthquakes, planes, etc., have practically disappeared. I would still get scared if an earthquake struck, but nothing more than what is normal in such circumstances. I no longer put myself under a lot of pressure, like I used to do all the time. It seems the more I feel the original pressure, the less it plagues me in my present life.

The slightest statement by a mate or friend can give rise to the phobic attitude, just as the most neutral situation—riding in an elevator or sitting in a theater—can give rise to the phobic anxiety. If the disproportionate anxiety doesn't come from the other person or from the elevator or theater, where does it come from? It must lie in the past, in the body and the brain. While the focus of the phobia may be fortuitous, certainly conditioned by life circumstance, free-floating fear is neither fortuitous nor genetic: it simply has left its precise home and wandered toward other places where it adheres. So though it seems farfetched to contend that all these diverse fears may stem from a single imprint, one has to understand that the energy—or perhaps the fear—becomes an enduring force that must find an outlet until it achieves resolution.

Phobias and phobic attitudes become automatically transformed by birth Primals, not by any attempt on our parts to persuade the patient this way or that. It is indeed useless to try to argue against fears and attitudes that are but a conversion of the original birth feelings into present-day defense mechanisms. For ultimately, defenses yield only to internal connection, never to external attack.

Counterphobias

Phobias have a companion—the counterphobias. Counterphobias stem from the same fears as do phobias; what differs is the person's reaction to those fears. The phobic knows he is afraid. He doesn't know what he is really afraid of but he does know he has a fear. The counterphobic doesn't even acknowledge his fear. He unconsciously overcompensates for the buried fear by being overly fearless. This is because the fear is so great that recognition of any fear at all threatens evocation of the ultimate fear. So, the opposite stance is taken. The counterphobic shuts off all fear and then works to re-create it again under controlled circumstances. He becomes a race car driver, a sky diver, a stuntman, a downhill skier, a mountain climber. It takes extremes of danger for this type of person to register any fear at all. Primal patients who finally do feel their birth terror lose all counterphobic, "toughing-it-out" behavior. They finally become themselves—after spending a lifetime of driving motorcycles, driving cars fast, swimming unsafely—by first letting themselves be the scared little boy or girl, the terrified newborn or infant. And, of course, one secret aim of counterphobic behavior is to be in touch with those baby fears.

Images as Implications

Once the second level of consciousness is fully developed, the Primal force is able to impel production of images, and this in turn means nightmares, tortured artwork or possibly hallucinations. There will be night terrors that conjure up fearsome creatures, dreams with terrifying situations and "no exit" endings. There will be drawings or paintings filled with awesome, bizarre figures, even though the person has no awareness of what they really mean or the force behind them. In the most extreme cases, there will be hallucinations in which the vividness of the images literally impels them into life—a life of psychosis.

A recurrent nightmare is related to early imprinted Pain and is good evidence for prototypic reactions. Dreams are just another way—the second-level way—we handle the imprint. But we act on that emotional force every day of our lives.

Nightmares can be excruciating. The Pain, however, doesn't come from the nightmare—the nightmare comes from the Pain. An engram imprinted in the first seconds of life can persist in our dreams for six and seven decades. The persistence of nightmare is the most conclusive evidence of the imprint, and the resolution of the nightmare through the reexperience of Pain is the most conclusive evidence of how imprints are resolved. The recurrent nightmare helps us understand prototypic Pain and prototypic response better than almost any other phenomenon. For we can see in the nightmare how Pain fixates, directs and circumscribes our reactions. Nothing we can do will change it; nothing will lower its intensity. We are simply victims of the unconscious Pain which shapes and controls even our dream states. One patient wrote:

> Birth feelings made me realize the source of all my dreams about amphibians, fish, rivers, canals, crocodiles and sinking ships. The Primals helped unravel the terror of my childhood nightmares where no imagery was sufficient to symbolize the terror of a shattered nervous system.

And another:

> I should have know how important my birth experience was to me, as my recurring childhood nightmare was of being hurled along a tunnel in the grip of huge tires and feeling totally overwhelmed and terrified.

The emotional force of the nightmare tells us something about the force of Pain at work in our unconscious all of the time; for it is always there, sometimes better gated than other times, but never altered, no matter how many times we have the same nightmare. The primal force is an active energy source that directs our waking behavior and can burn up whatever food we take in so that we cannot gain weight. It comes out at night when we descend down the brain hierarchy, but it doesn't sleep during the daytime either. It does its work deep in the system far from waking consciousness. The only time the "monster" gets close is in anxiety states or psychosis. One patient wrote:

> Many times I feel like an old, worn-out man ready to give up and die. I think I nearly did die at birth. I have had a recurrent dream where I am suddenly facing certain death. In it, I am usually falling endlessly, and the feeling so overwhelms me that when I wake up my heart is beating furiously and I am sure that what happened in the dream is true and real.

Why is it that we behave the same way in our nightmares decade after decade? Why is it that we go on being in terrible anxiety year after year over the same kind of dream story? Our responses seem to be predetermined. The responses of our "enemy" seem predetermined as well:

whether a burglar, a Nazi, or an alligator, they always do the same thing—chase and attack. Dream enemies are unrelenting because the unconscious Pain is unrelenting.

If we are in charge of the dreams that we ourselves produce, why are we so powerless to stop our own self-created enemies from pursuing us? Unfortunately, the "we" in charge of the dream is on a lower level of consciousness beyond the control of the third-level intellect. The persuasive powers of the conscious mind are useless in the dream state, just as they are against any lower-level force. It turns out that there are several "we's": those of sensation and emotion as well as intellect. When they all get together and work in harmony, we are integrated human beings. Until then, we suffer from prototypic reactions over which we have no present-day control, stemming from prototypic Pain over which we had no control long ago.

Second-Level Body Implications

We now find that symptoms we once thought were caused primarily by second-line (childhood) trauma often have first-line (birth) connections. This is not so surprising when we realize the persistent force beneath these symptoms.

The unceasing repetition of facial tics for a lifetime is one example of this force or energy, for clearly no one is born with a tic. A lifelong pattern of stuttering is another example. There may or may not be some key neurological deficits involved in the speech center, but it seems that it takes Primal trauma to make the symptom overt in many cases. The periodic electrical Primal force seems to intrude into speech patterns, disrupting them and preventing smooth expression. Stuttering is a symptom that results from conflicting impulses of expression and repression, generated by two opposing streams of consciousness. Even if what is being repressed is nonverbal, purely Primal energy or rage, it still intrudes onto the verbal level. Or, the child may be repressing verbal material—his disappointment, his feeling criticized, not listened to, etc.—and stuttering is the compromise. We have seen stutterers who have radically improved when they could finally express themselves in Primals.

What does birth trauma have to do with stuttering? A particular type of birth trauma, such as strangulation on the umbilical cord, sets up a target area of vulnerability which may be compounded later by family experiences to produce stuttering. The pressure from the parents to talk reactivates the child's target area of trauma. The valence from the birth trauma together with the emotional pressure to talk produces an overload resulting in broken speech. (With different compounding experiences the strangulation trauma would not result in any type of speech problem at all, but in a chronic sore throat, in asthma or in a fear of being closed in. As always, it is the individual's unique matrix of experiences that elaborates the birth trauma into one symptom or another.)

If birth trauma is implicated in stuttering, there must be a specific memory filtering into consciousness that later inhibits speech. But how can a completely nonverbal, indeed preverbal, memory of being strangled at birth later affect a completely verbal function such as speech? In *Primal Man,* Dr. Michael Holden explained:

> Can a child transiently asphyxiated by an umbilical cord around his neck, or by a compressed loop of umbilical cord, form a memory of it? The reported responses of patients during Primal Therapy suggest that such memories are formed. The relationship of asthma or stuttering to such an event is quite congruent with the adequacy of the neural structures integrating the functions of the trachea, respiration, and the larynx in the newborn. Each body part is woven into integrated function by the action of the nervous system. It would be nonrational to say that the trachea "remembers" transient strangulation during birth, but there is neuroembryological evidence that the functioning unit of trachea and newborn nervous system is a reactive, adequate system; one potentially capable of "learning" from an exceedingly intense stimulus.

In other words, there is a body memory of what happened; and there is adequate neural development to encode and process the experience into a memory, an engram, or an imprint. Memory is not simply the province of the "mind"; it is a holistic state, and each level of consciousness participates in it. The trachea does "remember"—not metaphorically, not anthropomorphically, but cellularly.

Body and mind are one and change as a unit in response to an experiental therapy. Indeed, one would have to be suspicious if all we found were the psychological changes reported on our questionnaires without the accompanying physiologic alterations as well. It would be one more sign that the body was out of sync with the mind, and that the therapy was out of sync with both.*

---

*We have measured the emotional and psychological effects of birth. See Appendix B for a full discussion of our findings.

7

Mind-Set: The Intellectual Implications of the Birth Trauma

What we learn through repression is how to alter reality. We convert real events into derivatives. Thus, on one level we can change Pain into sexual energy; on another level we can siphon it off via emotional outbursts; and on still another level we can convert that energy into ideas. Ideas derived from repressed early Pain form the intellectual implications of the birth trauma. Their job is to keep our beliefs, philosophies, ideologies and politics consistent with our internal, repressed reality. It is a cycle. Birth and early childhood events forge our personality characteristics and emotional disposition, and then we justify and reinforce all that by adopting ideas, which further entrench our state of being. In this way, a neurotic beginning generates self-perpetuating consequences.

A person having neurotic independence as a strong personality trait, for example, will also have strong *ideas* about the utter necessity for and virtue of independence as a way of life for everyone. This person may strongly believe that people must make it on their own; that the welfare system is nothing more than a capitulation to weakness; that socialism is the downfall of the world; that only the fittest survive; that poverty is deserved; that "an eye for an eye" is how it ought to be. These ideas simply elaborate the person's defenses on a cognitive level, and are commensurate with the strength of the Pain.

The Nature of Ideas

How does all this happen? The first thing to remember is that the brain innately moves toward internal consistency, be it neurotic or otherwise. A consistency based on pathology seems better than inconsistency and contradiction.

The neocortex or third level of consciousness deals with all aspects of cognition: with logic and problem solving, with ideology and philosophy, with concepts, hypotheses, theories; with delusions and illusions, with perceptions and misperceptions. Put all of these elements together and you get a fully operative intellect playing its part in the neurotic balance by converting Pain into ideas.

These ideas may be the tenacious, obsessive and manic ideas clearly associated with neurosis; they may be the simple but diehard beliefs of the farmer or laborer; or they may be the intricate and complex ideas that are woven into philosophical and intellectual systems of thought. In any case, the ideation is the cognitive extension of the early Pain and may constitute the cognitive implications of the birth trauma.

Obviously, not all ideas in the world derive from birth or childhood traumas, but many ideas that people have *about* the world are often distant Primal elaborations. How can we tell a neurotic idea from a nonneurotic one? By its valence, by its tenacity, even by its syntax and grammatical composition.

One person, for example, might hold so passionately to the idea that capitalism is the solution to world problems that his blood vessels pop out at the mere mention of socialism. He simply cannot discuss the pros and cons in a moderate, detached way. Here, the valence or reactive level of the viewpoint gives away a Primal stake.

Another person might be less emotional but no less inflexible. While maintaining a composed and "detached" state, he might simply but intractably refuse to consider any alternative ideas. Here, the tenacity of the stance indicates deeper forces at work.

A third telltale sign can be purely linguistic in nature. With or without valence or tenacity, a statement can reveal a Primal stake simply by virtue of the pronouns, modifying adjectives and grammatical qualifiers a person uses. For instance: "*Everyone* on welfare is lazy"; "*All* politicians are corrupt"; "The *whole* world is falling apart"; "*No one* is safe from threat"; "There is *nothing* we can do about it"; and so on. Sweeping generalizations and all-or-nothing attitudes are almost always energized by Primal Pain—and frequently an important part of that Pain is birth-related.

Sweeping generalizations result from the generalization of Pain that becomes necessary once it has been disengaged from its proper connection. The power is "sprayed" indiscriminately so that later, for example, a hatred for Mother turns into the entrenched belief that all women are cruel. This generalizing tendency ends when specific connections to Pain are made.

Generalization occurs on all levels of consciousness. It is not solely the province of cognition or ideation—it is just easier to spot there. Feeling rejected and worthless because a waiter or salesperson was a bit distant or impolite is an example of emotional generalization. A tendency to bruise or injure easily may be an example of generalization on the purely physical level: one patient had an inordinate tendency to bruise at the slightest bump until she felt the inordinate but *specific* bruising at birth. In short, all levels—the physical, the emotional and the cognitive—work to balance and "distribute" the Pain.

Since the Primal imprint is an electrical-chemical energy source, the ideas which result from it are thus based on a real physiological force. This force is what makes them fanatical, tenacious, implacable and manic. Experience does not change the ideas. The person goes on thinking the same thoughts despite experience; or worse, experiences are contrived to reinforce the Primal prejudices.

Insomnia is another manifestation of Pain converted into third-level ideation. We have had many patients who have suffered from insomnia for years because ideas descend upon them in bursts so that they can never rest. The moment they try to sleep there is that inevitable, unceasing flow of thoughts. Actually it is not the ideas that are unceasing—it is the energy that impels them. Ideas only accommodate the Primal force.

The Primal pressure that makes thoughts race "like crazy" contributes much to the makeup of the zealot and the fanatic. The pressure is encapsulated within an ideational system, but surges forth with a strength that compels the person to follow his ideas with the same violence that gave rise to them. One cannot get through to the fanatic because one is dealing with an unyielding, obdurate force. The Primal overload has been rechanneled into the present, into ideas. The neuronal circuitry has been rerouted and converted, and the result is an implacable stance where reason dare not tread.

The force of this reroute largely determines the force of the ideas and the stubbornness with which one adheres to them. The only way to change the ideas is to tap into the original force. The insight therapies have an impossible task here, because they are using ideas to combat ideas when the problem lies elsewhere. The force continues to function no matter how rational and dissuasive the arguments.

The link between current obsessive ideas and the original Pain is often obscure and literally circuitous, but it is the clue to the Pain—if the person is willing to pursue it to its source. If the idea can be considered a *clue* rather than reality itself, then there is hope—both for the person in Pain and for the therapist who is treating him. As one takes the Primal trail into Pain the first stop will be later childhood; next comes early childhood, and then eventually the force is traced down into the earliest minutes of life. One patient well described the interface he experienced between his third-level ideation and his earliest, first-level Pain:

Original trauma	Below the feeling of fighting to live is another feeling, one rung down the ladder, which I have felt only slightly. I have gone back to the feeling of being stuck when I am being born. I have to fight my way out of the birth canal. Finally my head is out but the rest of me won't come out. This feeling is such an analogy to my
Third-level connection	life: my head is always *out*—I'm always thinking, thinking, thinking, but the rest of me is inactive. My body doesn't feel connected to my head. I so often live in my head, and only recently started to feel my body as a cohesive part of me.
First-level connection	Back to the feeling, "I feel stuck." My neck hurts. It hurts even as I write about it. It feels as if someone is pulling on my neck and it's very painful. My head is swaying from side to side and my voice lets out small wails of being very scared. Again I am fighting for my life and there is no help. I even have to be born on my own. My mother does not help me out. That has been a constant theme all my life—no help, fight on your own. It seems like my head eventually took over the whole battle.

Philosophies

Some of the most interesting connections our patients make are between philosophies they've adopted as adults and birth traumas they had experienced as infants. I suppose these types of connections are the most compelling because they are the most unexpected. For one thing, philosophy is so far removed from the realities of day-to-day life, let alone the raw realities of Pain and trauma. For another, philosophy is surrounded by a mystique of purity: it is considered the inner sanctum of scholarly pursuits, safely removed from the contamination of unconscious motivations and unconscious Pain. Who would ever think that, more often than not, the philosophy is actually a disguise for and a defense against those very motivations and that Pain.

Existentialism

One of our patients had become an existentialist in her teens. It was the philosophy of despair—a philosophy precisely derived from the parasympathetic imprint that had begun her life. The philosophy made rational an inchoate, ineffable feeling that had been with her since she could remember. She was ideally suited for it, and when it came along she adopted it as naturally as a duck takes to water. Her misery had been transmuted into ideation before it ever became a conscious state—and the ideation thereby kept the misery at bay.

The transplantation of the birth trauma onto the cognitive level is again illustrated by a patient who had spent years in search of her "identity" under the guise of scholastic pursuits. She had been a philosophy major in college, specializing in the study of identity.

In her therapy, she realized that as an only child she had felt rejected and "like a piece of furniture at the dinner table" because her parents rarely spoke to her. During the Primal sequence, she came down first to those childhood feelings of not being recognized by her parents and, subsequently, to the struggle of a long labor. From this came the insight that her existence had never been acknowledged; even in the womb, even in the throes of birth, her desperation had been ignored. So, her search for identity was uncovered for what it was: a struggle to feel who she was and, indeed, to feel whether she existed at all. She realized that she had converted the Pain of not having her presence acknowledged and her identity reinforced into intellectualisms and philosophies, and that the strength of her search had lain in the strength of those imbedded Pains.

Laissez-Faire

Another patient connected his laissez-faire philosophy of economics to his birth. The gist of the laissez-faire approach is total freedom without control: let the economy go however it's going to go without too much interference from the government. The patient realized that "total freedom" had such strong appeal for him because his birth had been just the opposite: as that tiny, defenseless baby trying to get born he had been very controlled and very held back by his mother's uneasy condition. He had had no freedom to follow his own birth impulses; he had been forced to subordinate them to the stronger force—his mother. Later, he latched onto a philosophy of economics that expressed exactly but dispassionately what he needed. But while the philosophy was dispassionate, his need to defend it was not. He had a tremendous (unconscious) stake in maintaining it, even in the face of new facts. That is why people so often don't want to be bothered by facts—facts interfere with what is being defended.

Totalitarianism

The experience of yet another patient shows how birth Pain is elaborated on both second and third levels. Rage and political philosophy may seem far removed from one another, yet as this patient relived her birth, it became clear that both had emerged out of the same Pain. She had had a frustrating time trying to get out of the womb. A tumor had blocked her way, and she was finally pulled out by Cesarean section. This experience established a prototypic pattern of rage and defeat in response to any later frustration. As a child and an adult, she would become outraged the minute she had to wait for anything—and then she would want to just give up. She expressed the feeling of wanting to surrender in the face of challenge as "I can't go all the way." And, indeed, she had not been allowed to go all the way at birth—she had not been allowed to complete her own birth impulses naturally.

As a young adult she cultivated a political philosophy that viewed democracy as an outmoded form of organization. Her "reasoning" was that in a democracy you cannot get the job done when you want to: "It's too slow and cumbersome." She didn't like the idea of everyone having to have a say; she couldn't stand waiting for all those points of view. This ideological superstructure was later clarified by the feeling, "I can't stand not being able to do what I want when I want." That was the Primal context.

Expressions of Birth Trauma in Literature

Conscious or unconscious references to birth trauma abound in literature. It is outside the scope of this book to provide such a survey, but I would like to quote a particularly pertinent passage from Henry Miller's *Tropic of Cancer:**

The same story everywhere. If you want bread, you've got to get in harness, get in lockstep. All over the earth a grey desert, a carpet of steel and cement. Production! More nuts and bolts, more barbed wire, more dog biscuits, more lawn mowers, more ball bearings, more high explosives, more tanks, more poison gas, more soap, more toothpaste, more newspapers, more education, more churches, more libraries, more museums. *Forward! Time presses. The embryo is pressing through the neck of the womb, and there's not even a gob of spit to ease the passage. A dry, strangulating birth.* [Italics added]

Images of birth trauma can also be found in poetry. The poems our patients have written try to put into words the wordless experience of the birth traumas they have undergone. One patient wrote:

I came into this world throwing out tentacles
Millions of sensitive filaments

*New York, Grove Press, 1961, p. 240.

Reaching around to feel the warmth, the light, the air,
The smells, the touch of hands,
The music and movement of life,
Searching for nourishment and smiling eyes,
Hoping to meet the feathery leaves and the sea,
The softness of a round and gentle universe.
I found myself stared at
By an ugly, powerful lightbulb,
Fell into a cold, antiseptic space,
My head cut open with one blow,
Rough hands threw me away
All bruised
Until my tentacles withered and grew inward.
I lay on my back pretending
I was not feeling
As I had cut my contacts with outside
And presented to the world
A smooth, round, tentacle-free figure.
Not until late at night
When everything went still and safe
I would split my belly open
Take out my tentacles
Alive with memories, pulsating with fear and anger;
They talk to me
Of the death and premature burial
Of my feelings.

And another:

Pushing slowly against shreds of flesh
Breathing blood and darkness
Heaving and crushed out of shape
Losing count of my limbs
And beheaded at regular intervals
Waiting at the gates of life
For a helpful hand
To drag me out of my tomb.
Thus I spend days and years
Hoping for the great event
Which will fill my eyes with light
My lungs with air
And I in turn will fill the world
With songs and love.
Waiting is all that ever happens
I fight it with sobs and writhing
Or with a deadly frozen stillness

Howl into deep muffled tunnels
Which only brings my own voice back to me
And count the ticks of my heartbeat
With quiet rage
Hoping that one day
I might lose all desire
To be born.

Intellect, Curiosity and Confusion

We have observed some of the more obvious cognitive results of the birth trauma in how the intellect is shaped. When a mother has been drugged, the fetus comes out half dead and numb. As a consequence, there can be a stamped-in sluggishness and a lifelong lethargy which affects later mental acuity. The prototypic reaction might be an overall lack of alertness. On the other hand, another baby that came out less drugged and fighting all the way may come through the birth trauma being very alert—alert to all possible dangers. This can result in a hyper-alert state which can literally "cause" a higher level of intelligence; or rather, the hyper-alert state "causes" the person to fully but neurotically utilize every ounce of intelligence inscribed into his genes. The prototypically sluggish person would not be energized enough to do this.

Curiosity

Curiosity is part of the formation of intellect. Some schools of psychology even contend that there is a separate curiosity drive—some kind of innate, motivating force that compels us to search and question. One patient who had a Primal about her birth gave us an insight into the origins of certain types of curiosity. She had suffered from a prolonged and difficult labor from which she emerged half dead. She was then held upside down, spanked, taken away from her mother and put into a special crib. She had gone through all this trauma in a total confusion of sensation. She had been bewildered, not in any intellectual sense, but *organismically.*

Later she became an avid reader, a collector of trivia, an insatiable gatherer of information. She *had* to know everything. It wasn't just a desire—it was a compulsion. After a year of therapy she reexperienced the feelings of being born, and felt and understood her confusion and bewilderment. She knew then that her "curiosity" was from that birth experience. Her later need to know so much was an unconscious effort to master the bewilderment of the early experience. The compulsion of her curiosity "drive" was thus a reaction to a painful situation—a third-level attempt to cope with it—and lessened considerably with the reexperience of the original feeling.

Confusion

We must understand that confusion around the time of birth is quite common. Events are taking place for which the baby has no name, no precedents and no control. He hasn't the equipment to order, label and understand all that is happening. He can only suffer from it. That is why so many of us become confused under later stress in life. We revert to our prototypic reactions. This is particularly true when first-line Pains are inadvertently triggered, or when someone is fairly far along in therapy and has access to perinatal Pain. Temporary confusion is common at this juncture because first-line Pains, when imminent, defy conceptualization. As they come up there is no way to put them into language. We can only experience those Pains in their own terms. For an intellectual used to conceptualizing everything on the third level, this is difficult to do. Intellectuals have a hard time accepting and adjusting to the idea of preverbal Pains. When you live only in your "head" it is hard to believe that there are other levels of reality besides ideas; better to array the evidence against the notion of preverbal imprints than to run the risk of facing it.

There are many ways we can react to early confusion, depending upon later experience. One person might fight it by trying to know everything; another person might succumb to it and stay hopelessly confused. The latter course is more likely to be taken by someone whose later life was also very confusing: moving all the time, new stepfathers, inexplicable rages by Mother and so on.

Confusion can lead to a psychologically dependent personality—someone who needs direction about almost everything, because the slightest input confuses him. This is the very opposite of the kind of hyper-alert person who is constantly scanning his environment to protect himself against that early confusion. His eyes search out every aspect of the situation as he frantically but unconsciously tries to maintain control. Unfortunately, the situation he is really trying to control is and *was* completely uncontrollable.

A patient who used to be a compulsive listmaker wrote:

Third-level symptom: listmaking

> I'm an obsessive. The true meaning of the word became clear to me only after I had felt several related birth feelings. I've always been very rigid and afraid of change. To cope with that I became a listmaker: I made a list, each and every day of my life, of the things I had to do. I rewrote the lists constantly, adding new items or changing the order in which they had to be done. I projected my lists up to a week in advance. I created a system to indicate which things really *had* to be done

and which were only "bonus" activities. This system included methodical underlining, circling, and starring various items on the list. I even wrote down what I ate each day, with the total calories I consumed.

Defensive function of symptom

As I write this now, it seems quite bizarre, but for a long time the system kept down Pain and made me feel in control of my life. The price I paid was waking up daily with severe anxiety about what I had to do, and not really enjoying anything I did.

Obsessing about feelings: another third-level symptom

My obsessiveness extended to non-list concerns as well, but still revolving around things I needed to "do." The concerns were: my failure at being open or friendly to new people, especially men, and at saying how I felt, especially when angry. A thought would enter my mind, such as: "Ed's constant talking is irritating me." Then I would obsess about telling Ed. Important here are the words *obsess about*. Rather than just tell Ed how I felt, and have done with it, I would think about it for hours or days trying to figure out *how* I should say it. In the end, I always said what I needed to, but I became so *un*-spontaneous and uptight about the situation that my delivery was inappropriate and the exchange seemed anticlimactic.

In some ways, therapy initially became another "thing" for me to obsess about. Through my feelings, though, I've learned that my obsessiveness is an attempt to *hold onto*—a thought, a plan, an idea—but it is always a *holding on* in the face of horrendous Pain.

Original trauma

The first inroad I made into my obsessiveness and rigidity, and my first step in letting go of it, came after a feeling I experienced of being terribly jostled around and frightened in the womb. I felt aimless, unending

Present-day disconnected sensations of the birth trauma

turbulence, and the fear was agonizing. Afterwards, I understood why I had always feared light planes, roller coasters and fast motion in general. The few times I had ridden a roller coaster, I felt only mortal horror, while my friends squealed with glee and excitement. I remained speechless with fright, and thought of nothing but when the ride would end.

Connection and resolution: "The beauty was astounding"

Two weeks after this Primal, I took a helicopter ride with a friend into the Grand Canyon. I loved it, even when the pilot turned the plane on its side. For a split second, my old terror came up—the holding-on, brittle feeling I've always had. Then I recalled the Primal and said to myself: "You know now where that feeling belongs. You can let go of it and enjoy the ride—go with it." And I did. The beauty was astounding, as was the sensation of movement. It is a memory I'll always treasure.

That happened five months ago. Since then, I've had

many Primals about my birth which have clarified my obsessive behavior to me. The most profound feelings I experienced were those in which I felt excruciating physical Pain. My body felt as if it were being cracked at the waist, with sharp discomfort in the small of my back and in the pelvic region. I know no facts about my birth, since both my parents are dead, but from my feelings I know it was extremely painful. (I suspect the Pain was caused by my mother's tightness, as she was

an extremely tense woman.) After these Primals, I understood that I developed listmaking to try to manage the pure, raw, physical Pain I had to cope with. Lists were my only way of staying sane, of making sense, of *holding onto* reality.

I stopped writing all lists, except for grocery shopping, about one and a half months ago. I no longer write my calories down either. It is wonderful—I feel quite liberated. The very thought of writing a list now makes me cringe.

I've recently had more insights about my inability to

"let go." The only drug I ever took was marijuana. I was too afraid of losing control to take anything else. It was good I never did—my neurosis kept me sane until I could get help. I believe now that if I had taken LSD, or a similar, mind-altering drug, I would have gone crazy. I could not have dealt with the early Pain it would have forced up.

The last, and best, insight I've had from all this: I've never been able to let go and enjoy my life until very recently. I have *held on*—even to my Pain, as that was all I had from the very start.

Primal Expressions

Many expressions used in everyday speech make literal sense when viewed in relation to birth experiences. We say, for instance, that a person "lives over his head," that someone "always takes the line of least resistance," that another goes into things "feet first." People are described as "headstrong," "pushy," or "all turned around." They have "a great weight on their shoulders," or they "don't know whether they are coming or going."

These expressions or "Primal slips" often reveal unconscious Primal feelings, and just as often, unconscious Primal *birth* feelings. They are so much a part of our cultural idiom precisely because of the number of past experiences that we all have in common.

Nick Barton, Associate Director of the Primal Institute in Los Angeles, well described Primal slips in an article for *The Primal Newsletter.** Following are edited excerpts from the article:

Many of our metaphorical phrases are not just whimsically or accidentally chosen. Indeed, looked at in the context of our early years, their meaning is not metaphorical at all but entirely literal. Remarkably, so many of these expressions seem to derive from specific, *physical* experiences.

If someone asks a friend, "Help me out," one assumes a simple call for assistance. But why not "Help me on" or "Help me above" or just plain "Help me"? The preposition *out* may be used because it recalls an event where the person had to be physically helped out from surroundings that were actually restraining, physically. If one thinks of a baby trapped helplessly in a constraining birth canal as its mother tenses up against delivery, one can understand the subsequent choice of words. Perhaps birth was impossible without external assistance, or seemed impossible. This memory is so powerful and so formative that it influences the manner of expression of an adult.

Typically, an expression like "Help me out" is used in a *nonphysical* predicament. It might be a financial, social or work situation. The point is that there may be absolutely no present evidence of physical constriction and yet the selection of words clearly implies one.

. . . The use of physical metaphors in nonphysical situations is a sign of a number of things. It is an indication that certain events during early childhood stay with us as a permanent influence, even molding our forms of speech. In his various predicaments, an infant only has the option for physical expression such as struggling, crying, chewing, kicking, etc. And those predicaments are assimilated at the physical level. Later, in situations which *symbolically* provoke memory of an early unresolved situation such as being trapped at birth, *mentality translates that physical imprint via the already symbolic medium of language into a variety of psychological expressions.* The use of physical metaphors to convey states of mind illustrates the continual interrelationship of the various levels of human consciousness . . . By careful attention to a patient's choice of words, a therapist can get an idea about what is really going on underneath the patient's ostensible meaning. He can determine how close to certain types of feelings the patient is by noticing a propensity for certain idioms over others and by noting repetition of the same phrases. In

*October 1979, Vol. II, No. 2.

treating them as literal he may help a person to the real source of his feeling. Words and phrases can be the key to otherwise obscured experiences of the past. They are indeed tell-tale signs. It seems to me that we can rely on people to tell us where they really are (even chronologically) whether they mean to tell us or not.

The concept of the verbal slip is nothing new to psychologists. The fact that people have secret thoughts and feelings that are only inadvertently expressed was discussed by Freud. The difference being drawn here is that they can refer back beyond the capacity for speech or ideation to very early development, to preverbal, physical states and experiences—experiences that many theories do not even consider formative. We are not talking just about leakage or restrained thoughts and emotions, but about *the translation and projection into and through language of actual, physical, infantile experiences that are registered in consciousness at a much deeper level.* In addition, a "Primal slip" usually provides a context for the repressed material. That is, it indicates that the person is responding not just to hidden forces but to a specific kind of repressed memory or event.

The following chart provides a list of common idiomatic expressions and the possible birth events from which they may stem. Italics are used to emphasize the tendency to use a *physical* word or term to describe a *nonphysical,* usually psychological, situation:

IDIOMATIC EXPRESSION	POSSIBLE BIRTH CONTEXT
I'm *stuck* . . . in this problem, in my job, in my marriage.	Baby stuck in the birth canal during birth.
Everything is *closing in* on me.	Tension or constriction in the birth canal.
Everything/everybody *gets in my way.*	Tumors, umbilical cord, pelvic arch, forceps, doctor's hands.
I can't *get going.*	No help from mother; stopped by drugs; strangled by cord.
You're *holding me back.*	Mother tensing against delivery; doctors or nurses delaying birth to conform to schedules.
You're *pushing me* too far.	Mother trying too hard to get birth over with; or, the baby's movements overtaken by labor-inducing drugs.
There's *no room to breathe.* I need *space.* I feel *trapped.*	Birth canal constricting; not enough room for easy passage; actual blockage by tumor or cord.

IDIOMATIC EXPRESSION	POSSIBLE BIRTH CONTEXT
I'm under *pressure*. These are *pressing* matters.	Generalized sensation in birth.
There's a *weight* on my shoulders. That's a *load* off my mind. You're a *pain in the neck*.	Specific points of pressure and/or injury during birth.
I have to *feel* my way . . . through this new job.	The baby literally feels its way out.
I'm being *pulled* in all directions.	Restraint from mother's body counteracted by pulling from doctor's hands or forceps.
I'm *drowning* . . . in work, in problems, in sorrow.	Excessive amniotic fluid causing partial suffocation.
I'm *gripped* by . . . pain, fear, depression.	Actual grip of the canal, rough handling by the hands of doctors or nurses.
I can't *get through* to you. I can't *get through* this . . . job, weekend, marriage.	Baby's birth signals not heeded by a drugged mother; constriction in the birth canal; passage blocked.
I don't know which way is *up*. Everything is *topsy-turvy*.	Turned around the wrong way before birth or held up by the feet after delivery.
I do everything *ass* backwards. I go into things *feet first*.	Entry into the world: breech birth.
Support me.	Someone to hold the baby securely.
I'm . . . losing *touch,* out of *touch, detached*.	May refer either to losing contact with mother after delivery, being placed in incubator, or not being held enough later.
I'm *hungry* for love. I feel *empty*. I'm *starved* for affection.	When love meant food—the right amount at the right time from the right source—but instead baby was subjected to scheduled and bottled feedings.
I'm always *sucking up* to people.	Unresolved need to breast-feed.

"I'm leaving my wife because she leaves me *no space* to breathe" was the pre-therapy complaint of one patient, who did indeed leave his wife.

Later, after a series of birth Primals he saw that he had overreacted in relation to her. She was controlling, it was true, but it was intolerable and unworkable because of his first-line Pain. In a way, he wasn't really overreacting; rather, he was reacting to an old event in the present.

Another patient was having a great deal of trouble with her husband with whom she had gotten along previously. She complained in her therapy session that he was beginning to "crush her" and "suffocate her." She said that his domination was intolerable. She would pack and leave under the slightest pretext. She simply had "to get out!" The most minor event was able to trigger such overreaction because she did, indeed, have to *get out*. It was too much for her to stay in the current situation just as it had been too much in the original trauma of birth where she had suffocated, not being able to get born. It had been a life-threatening situation.

"I feel like the walls are closing in on me" was the statement of one patient, and again the choice of words was both direct and literal. He could not sustain relationships because this old feeling was always intruding. He always had to "move on," "get out from under," "break free," and the like. There were no walls closing in on him in his adult life, but there had been walls (the birth canal) that closed in on him at birth.

Yet another patient began therapy with the notion regarding her marriage that "no matter where I turn I see no way out." This feeling plagued her for months until she connected to her original birth experience of being trapped—with no way out.

It is interesting that such ideation never seems out of context at the time we use it. I believe that is because we are responding to a prepotent reality. That reality is foremost in our minds because for the moment the lower-level truth *has* moved to the forefront: It is the baby's brain that takes over and the adult's brain which tries to adapt. The baby doesn't think "No matter where I turn I see no way out" when he is struggling to get out of the canal. But when the ideational brain is sufficiently matured it will take that memory and put it into words. Since the average person is totally disengaged from the context of the memory (his birth), the complaints often seem exaggerated; not to the user, however. He is making a kind of sense, at least in terms of his inner life. He believes that so-and-so is not giving him a way out because that is the feeling he is dealing with. Only the feeling didn't come out of so-and-so's behavior—it came out of an internal force. It was superimposed on this other person and at that point became neurotic.

We have observed how frequently a single sentence or phrase will suddenly flash into a person's mind when coming out of a birth Primal. The sentence then becomes the basis for a flood of insights.

One patient came out of her Primal with a sign flashing in front of her that read NO EXIT. She realized that the sign was symbolic of her whole life. She never could find her way out of things: she couldn't get out of a bad marriage, a bad job, a bad location—all because she constantly but unconsciously re-created that specific *no-exit* feeling. She trapped herself continuously.

Another patient came out of her Primal with the sentence "It's never enough." The insight was that the struggle of birth had not been enough to get her born, and that prototypic experience was then later compounded by parents who never felt that what she did was good enough. This feeling prevented her from doing anything right because she already felt that nothing she could possibly do would be enough—*to get born.*

Still another patient came out of a Primal with the sentence "It has to be." After reliving the birth sequence she understood the absolute necessity for struggle: it had meant survival from the very start. She had to fight to get born; she had to fight to stay alive. The fight *had to be.* She made everything a struggle and a hassle, her life was never simple. But nothing was ever quite right, despite all that effort. That's what made her life neurotic: she had the right feeling in the wrong context. She had become *un*natural from the very start of life because the natural progression of her birth process had been prevented.

Conclusions

It should be clear from what I have written that ideas and their context are often two different things. To think that neurosis is a psychological malady which can be cured with psychotherapy—a therapy primarily dealing with ideas—is to take a most superficial view, not only in the conventional sense but in a deep biologic one as well. Ideas are anchored in an obscured primordial past. They bob to the surface like buoys, each painted differently, each with its own characteristics—yet each attached firmly to the same foundation. Our ideas don't vary much in content or drift easily into new areas because they are held fast by chemical bonds every bit as strong as the chain links on an anchor. Those chemical processes, together with associated electrical ones, are both real and strong. They change only when the foundation is addressed.

We have found evidence of this in two independent neurologic studies of Primal patients. It was found that after eight months of therapy there was a shift in the balance of voltage between the right and left hemispheres of the brain. There was a movement toward greater balance or harmony. Thus when the repressive barriers of feeling are lifted, the brain also moves automatically toward harmony. Or, to put it another way, facing reality— being real—makes one harmonious. Indeed, the bodily system *in toto* appears to be nothing more than a miraculous, harmonious concert; a symphony that plays in tune even without a conductor. Left to its own workings, everything comes together. But any alien force, whether a microbe or Pain, becomes a strident note forcing the orchestra (the system) to compensate. Certain sections must take over and readjust. The orchestra goes on playing but some sections are weak and cannot carry their proper load. Others are intrusive and must be curbed. In the case of the brain, a hemisphere must adopt a job it wasn't intended for. It must overwork, and we see this in the amount of power or voltage it uses in its daily operations. This power diminishes radically and permanently with the lifting of repression. Eliminating Pain disengages those circuits that mediated all unreal thoughts made necessary by trauma. The area of the brain freed from its unreal task can rest at last, and this repose shows on our electronic instruments. Having dealt with reality, it can now leave unreality and go back to the real work of living.

Ideas are the farthest removed from early preverbal experiences. Both in the evolution of the species and in the development of each individual's brain, ideas were and are the last to emerge. This doesn't mean that ideas are necessarily distortions of reality. In an integrated person, the neocortex is directly connected to the two lower levels of consciousness so that the ideas produced by it are accurate representations of those lower-level realities.

Ideas generated to quell Pain are the most distant products of that Pain. First-level visceral products and second-level feeling and imagistic products are all more closely related. Ideas generated to quell the Pain from imprinted birth trauma go even farther into the psychological stratosphere. Fortunately, a neurotic's ideas do not exist in a vacuum: they are enlivened and substantiated by a Primal force that in one way or another—at one time or another—reveals their true heritage. And that heritage contains its own undoing once it is revealed.

III: Catastrophic Implications of the Birth Trauma

Introduction

The deeper and heavier the force of stored Pain, the greater the potential for catastrophic reaction later on. There is always some kind of "seepage" from early imprints that lets us know it is there. Sometimes we can simply tap our feet or drum our fingers to release the excess energy. Other times the energy and its repression is of such magnitude that there is no release, and the pressure on the system becomes enormous. It is then that catastrophic reactions, both physiological and psychological, appear.

Craziness is a defense against Pain. The body has many ways to go crazy and we can be "crazy" on any level of consciousness. Thus, cancer may be a kind of physiological or cellular insanity; epilepsy a kind of neurological insanity; and psychosis a kind of intellectual insanity. In every case the body and mind are trying to accommodate to the Primal force, a force which has caused severe dislocations of function on the level involved. When these defenses, as extreme as they are, don't work, the person may be pushed to the most catastrophic defense of all: suicide, killing the Pain by killing the self. Disconnection of Pain from its context can lead to only two alternatives other than suicide—the symbolization of the feelings via bizarre ideation, or their somatization via a catastrophic physical disease. The biological components may be the same, however: higher than normal vital signs, characteristic hormonal changes (including an increased amount of the stress hormones) and alterations in the levels of circulating biochemical repressants (such as endorphines). This shows us that although cancer, epilepsy and psychosis are different diseases, they are at the same time really only different manifestations of the same Pain. The manifestations differ because each level of consciousness deals with the Primal force in a different way. But they all can be the result of the very same energy flow.

What has the birth trauma to do with disease and suicide? We have found that the more serious the symptom, the more likely the generating force is birth and pre-birth encoded trauma. It is possible, however, for shattering events in early childhood to equal the birth trauma in degree of damage, but the events usually must involve survival. In any case, the brain is more equipped biologically at this later stage to handle the trauma.

An analogy to how our immune system works might be instructive here. When the naive human system comes into contact with antigens or allergy-producing substances, it does not immediately produce antibodies. Instead, the body begins the manufacture of specific antibodies in relation to the specific antigen so that the next time it encounters this foreign material, the body "remembers" the early assault and produces the correct antibody to combat it.

This is probably what happens with all kinds of somatic and psychologic defenses, including the most severe ones. Early on, the infant has very little defense against assault. The early events—the traumas before and during birth—cause the beginnings of the production of those inner combating materials, particularly the endorphines. Later assault produces first the memory of the original assault and then the production of whatever is needed to meet the current assault. This means that later defenses are based on memories of the original assaults. When those original events are catastrophically severe, the defenses the person develops will be equally severe, even when outer circumstances don't appear commensurately traumatic. That is why it is so hard to comprehend something like cancer or psychosis. It is so incomprehensibly severe that it seems as though it came from "out of the blue." We can't relate to such illness precisely because the catastrophic Pain it is expressing is still deeply unconscious. And as long as we can't relate to it—can't locate a cause within ourselves—we will have virtually no control over it.

Obviously, not all diseases are caused by Pain, but research is slowly establishing that many may have purely psychosomatic origins. Cancer and psychogenic epilepsy are two such diseases. As for suicide, there is no question of its cause. But psychosis is a different story. Some believe its cause is biochemical, others hereditary, still others, environmental. Interestingly enough, they may all be right, from one vantage point: psychosis does cause severe biochemical imbalances, it is "transmitted" prenatally via the environment of the womb and it is reinforced in childhood via continued trauma.

8

Born Into Madness? The Contribution of Birth to Insanity

Because psychosis involves a dislocation of thoughts we think of it as a mental disease—a disease of the mind. Yet we are not clear about what "mind" is or where it is located. Its manifestation, it is true, is ideational in nature. But we must confuse the way in which the illness is expressed with its essential nature.

The neocortex, the general store of ideas, is a late addition to the brain. Ideas reflect the workings of lower processes, but they do not generate those processes. We see how bizarre or psychotic ideas evolve out of early and lower-level imprints as patients come close to birth memories in therapy. Ideas become strained and strange. Conversely, as the lower-level imprints of the birth trauma are resolved, psychotic ideation recedes. This constitutes clinical evidence for the direct link between the birth trauma and the brain's attempt to deal with that trauma via ideas.

Ideas do not exist in the void. They are not independent entities. They are the final way-station of our sensations and emotions. Ideas describe our state of being and allow us to communicate. If that state is overwhelmed by early Pain, the communication is garbled. That is because the only "sense" it can possibly make is an internal one. Psychosis is simply the rationalization process taken to the extreme. "Somebody is out to get me" may not correspond to anything rational going on in the present, but it may well be linked to actual events from childhood when parents were hurting the child, whose only recourse at the time was to repress the Pain.

Psychosis may also correspond to the birth event, during which the newborn is hurt for no reason. In later life it thus becomes easy to "imagine" that one will be hurt for no reason. If the womb were a hostile environment—and if we understand neurosis as the right feeling in the wrong context—then it is easy to see that the early environment has forged certain kinds of negative thoughts and attitudes. Getting "too close" to people means that one can be "crushed" by them. The idea that "someone is out to get me" may make no external sense, and have no basis in current reality, but it becomes utterly rational when placed in Primal context. A history of hurt impels those ideas and only now do we know how far back that history goes.

To try to dissuade someone from a deeply rooted idea, an idea not really rooted in the thinking, ideational cortex, can only make someone more unreal and neurotic because the idea is the last tie to the feeling. We know this because by giving certain kinds of pain-killers to a person—drugs that work on the *lower levels* of the brain—strange or psychotic ideas often disappear immediately. The ideas are right; the context is wrong. Psychotic ideation thus seems to make as much sense as the actual experience.

The Cause of Psychosis

It is not bizarre ideas that make someone crazy; it is the cause of those ideas. We must not confound manifestations of disease with their generating source. Another way we know that Pain is the cause of psychosis is that in dialysis the blood can be "washed" and changed. This washing often temporarily removes psychotic symptoms. The hypothesis is that certain chemicals which mediate Pain are removed from the blood system during dialysis.

Pain can be an "alien intrusion" in the sense that it prevents normal functioning. Being held back at birth, being prevented from crying—either can cause Pain. Such intrusions—be they physical or psychological—force the system to compensate by veering away from its normal development and function. The intrusion of Pain may eventually trigger the emergence of a defense system or "antibodies" in the form of psychosis. The function of psychosis is thus to absorb and discharge the lower-level dysfunction through the vehicle of bizarre ideas and images.

But it is not just Pain that is the cause of psychosis; it is also the degree of disconnection from it. Disconnection forces us to deny what really happened and substitute something different. The child whose parents tell him repeatedly that their violent fights are "normal" and shouldn't upset him must then come up with another reason for feeling so desperately upset. There is an inverse relationship here: the less validation the child receives for his feelings in the context in which they occur the more disconnected and bizarre the "reasons" for the feelings will become. Thus, if the child is forced to deny his real fear of his parents he may then transform it into a fear of his teachers. If that fear is still discounted and belittled by his parents—"Oh, Johnny, that's just ridiculous, your teachers won't hurt you!"—the child will be forced to search even further for "reasons." He may then come up with "I can't go to school because I'll die if I use the toilets." And so on, until there is a thoroughly distorted mind. And all because the child's original, rightful feeling of fright and terror in response to parental violence was flatly denied.

Psychosis as Energy

If the lower levels can absorb enough of the Primal energy there will be no psychosis. If migraines, high blood pressure, colitis, epilepsy and ulcers can discharge some of the energy it may stave off psychosis. Many of us stave off psychosis a lot of the time. The workaholic is an example. To sit still drives him "crazy"—not an arbitrary choice of words. Alcohol pushes down Pain, as do cigarettes.

The fact that this energy can be discharged through exercise, through physical manipulation, abreacted through screaming or shocked out of the system with electroshock indicates that Pain is a global energy force. It is an electrical event that is commensurately diminished by "busyness." Thus the electrical force of the musculature, when diminished through exercise, also helps diminish the tendency toward psychotic ideation. That is why pre-psychotics who come in for therapy may be asked to jog a mile or two before their sessions—to dissipate enough energy to temporarily lower the overall Pain level and allow them access to the "Primal Zone."* Here is clear evidence for the fact that we are not solely dealing with a *mental* illness: changes in the electrical output of the muscles or the brain directly affect how we *think*.

One graphic way to actually see the energy and force of Pain in psychotics is to observe their birth Primals. It is a force that pushes up the brain-wave amplitude by hundreds of a percent; that raises body temperature within minutes by three degrees; and that doubles blood pressure and heart rate. Since the patient experiencing a Primal is lying still, in a pressure-free environment, it becomes evident that whatever pressure

---

*The Primal Zone is the zone where feelings can be felt, where Pain and repression are balanced in favor of an ascendence of Pain toward consciousness without overwhelming it. It is the zone where healing occurs.

explodes from him during that time can only come from *within*. This tells us about the relationship between the energy in the birth trauma and the energy in psychosis as nothing else could. The activated brain is to be expected judging by the work it must do to deal with the Pain.

Perhaps the "Big Bang" notion of the universe would provide a good analogy here. The reverberations of that event resounded throughout the cosmos and constituted measureable electrical energy. Within the human system the energy of the original "big bang" (the birth trauma) is distributed throughout the inner cosmos (the body). Anything which disrupts the distribution of energy interferes with the balance of the system. Any artificial changes in this distribution, such as massage to ease physical tension, will cause a temporary release at best, and at worst, will redistribute the energy elsewhere. The body always copes in the best way it can without outside help. The increased electrical activity in an adult muscle system, when permanently reduced through birth Primals, testifies to the "big bang" notion, and how this manifestation in the muscle galaxy gives us a window into history. Psychosis, too, points to a history unexplored.

Psychosis arises when the chemico-electric pressure "in the head" cannot be diminished. We need ideas (in the head) to go crazy with, and that means we need a mature ideational mind for psychosis to occur. Psychosis as we know it is the last evolutionary alternative for discharging excess Primal energy. Animals do not have this luxury. They cannot spin a web of ideas to diminish their Pain. But the dog that bites everyone in sight because it has spent its lifetime tied up and mistreated is nonetheless exhibiting its own form of psychosis.

Psychosis as the Ultimate Defense

Psychosis is the last thing that the brain can do with the Primal onslaught. It must not be tampered with without regard to its underlying forces. Those forces are the ways in which the system maintains its equilibrium. One must always consider this biological homeostatic balancing principle before addressing any symptom or behavior as a discrete entity. Psychosis is able to discharge enough Pain to keep the person's vital functions operating. Ultimately, it is a defense against death, which makes it all the more dangerous to tamper with. If the person cannot go crazy—if the ultimate defense fails and connected feeling is not possible—then death is the only alternative. We cannot sustain disconnected, undefended Pain as an ongoing state of being. Recall one patient's description of how she felt after joining a spiritual community and "giving up" her anger:

We had gurus who told us that it was bad to get angry so I stopped getting angry; I stopped letting things bother me. In a way, I see now that *that attitude was like a death sentence for me. Anger was the one defense that kept me alive*—my anger and my fight. When I gave that up in the name of spirituality, I became defenseless. I stopped eating and dropped to ninety pounds. I got deathly ill. My hair started falling out and my skin turned yellow. I didn't know what was happening to me, but *I felt like I was slowly dying.* (Italics added.) I had given up the only thing that kept me alive—my anger.

Conventional treatment of psychosis can be dangerous precisely because defenses are blocked or altered without attention to the need for a feeling connection to the Pain that is being defended. Without his defenses, the psychotic is left in a very precarious limbo. The bizarre but well-defended world he is familiar with is altered, but the real inner world of his Pain remains inaccessible. He can't go "down" into his feeling reality or back "up" into his psychotic reality. He is truly in a no-man's land.

We can imagine, to a degree, the danger of such a situation by taking a less extreme example. Say we are hurt or humiliated by a friend or associate. At the point where the hurt begins to hit us, our defensive system swings into action to rationalize, counter, and attenuate the hurt. The deeper the hurt, the stronger our need to rationalize it will be. Usually it is not a question of choice. It is a matter of the body and brain automatically moving to minimize suffering.

If, however, our defenses against that hurt suddenly are blocked, we would be thrust into a jumble of emotion we could neither understand nor integrate. What was a relatively minor hurt then becomes an unbuffered assault to a system undefended. Unless we know how to connect to the Primal source of that hurt and thereby give it meaning, it will simply continue to bombard us. Meaning opens the door to healing; feeling provides passage through it.

Psychosis, Violence and Birth

In the case of psychosis we are talking about years of unceasing agonies which have continually flooded the system. Tampering with defenses against those agonies is literally playing with dynamite: the power and force in disconnected first-line Pain is explosive and can be tremendously destructive. We have only to look to our prisons to see that. Psychopathic and psychotic behavior are really two forks in the same road of early, catastrophic Pain. The pent-up violence from the original frustration of not getting out of the canal—a trauma with high electrical valence—plus the compounding of years of emotional deprivation can sow the seeds of either psychotic or psychopathic behavior later on. Violence against a person can begin at birth and will find its release at one time or another.

Not surprisingly, research is beginning to correlate adult violent behavior with early infant trauma. Sarnoff A. Mednick, Director of the Institute of Psychology in Copenhagen, reported in *Psychology Today** on an extensive research study of 2,000 Danish males born in Copenhagen in 1936: "Of 16 men who committed violent crimes, 15 of them had the most horrible possible conditions at birth . . . and the 16th had an epileptic mother." Dr. Mednick concludes that "it is very possible that we are on the track of conditions that make some contributions to impulsive criminality."

Dr. Mednick's research team also did an extensive study of schizophrenic children. He found again that adverse conditions during pregnancy and birth complications seemed to have contributed significantly toward the later mental illness. Seventy percent of the disturbed children in the study had suffered one or more serious complication during pregnancy or birth: anoxia, prematurity, prolonged labor, strangulation by the cord or breech birth. Mednick concluded that "pregnancy or birth complications damage the body's ability to regulate stress response mechanisms."

In our own country, recognition of the important lifelong effects of traumatic birth experiences has come from a rather unusual source—a state legislator. John Vasconcellos of San Jose, California, has suggested that modern birth procedures are a possible cause of crime.

As reported by the Santa Barbara *New Press* in 1979, Vasconcellos believes that a change in birth practices could produce a long-term reduction in tendencies toward crime: "An infant immediately traumatized at birth may well be conditioned toward violence." He advocated adoption of the Leboyer method on a wide-scale basis and proposed research into the connection between birth and later violent behavior as an alternative to the traditional policy of finding "more and better ways of repressing and controlling ourselves and each other."

Psychotic Ideation and the Brain

The relationship between birth and psychotic ideation strikes us soon in therapy. The pre-psychotics we treat often begin their birth Primals very early in therapy—too early, in fact—and must be detoured around them for some time until they have the strength to integrate the Pain. To achieve this detour, we sometimes administer tranquilizers which function as first-

*April 1971, Volume 4, p. 11.

line blockers so that some of the lesser charged traumas can be dealt with.

What is really happening is that the first-line material with its enormous charge is constantly intruding upon the second and third levels of consciousness. The patient is overwhelmed to the point where he cannot focus on one scene or one feeling. Cohesion is lost. Often the second level is also overloaded with compounded childhood traumas so that it is of little help as a defense. This leaves the third level bearing most of the brunt of first-line intrusion. The cohesion of the third level becomes increasingly disrupted as it is forced to recruit more and more neurons to deal with the assault.

If we can imagine the third line as a puzzle put together (which is cohesive), and if we can imagine lower-line Pains thrusting upward against the puzzle to disrupt its organization and cohesion, we may get an idea of what the problem is in psychosis. The result of that force or thrust is that the intellect fragments, leaving many pieces totally disconnected from one another. There is no longer one cohesive picture. When there is that lack of cohesion in psychosis the person attends to each separate perception or idea as an isolated experience. There is no overall structure to unify thought and perception. That is why the psychotic may start out with a perfectly clear notion and then go off into bizarre babblings. Psychotic ideation is one clear way we know that massive Pain is on the rise or close to consciousness.

The problem in recovering the birth trauma is that the ideational mind must come to terms with an event down deep in the nervous system; an event that pre-dates the development of the very ideas that must be utilized to understand it. The experience makes "no sense" without access to the original happening; it simply could not be otherwise. To be lying in a comfortable room in therapy and to be suddenly plunged into an overwhelming feeling of death and doom almost always makes a person feel initially that he is going crazy.

What the ideational mind must do in a Primal is "let go" of its functions and trust the lower levels. The experience of the feeling itself provides all the logic one needs; and indeed, after the experience of the feeling the third level automatically reconstitutes to provide the logic and concepts needed to communicate the feeling. The point is that the "logic" of the feelings must be felt. That logic is inherent in a *connected* feeling. Trying to impose ideas over feelings is superfluous; in fact, it is when one tries to surround Primal, nonverbal feelings with ideas that one goes crazy. There is no concept, no attitude or stance to take toward the experience. It is what it is and must be taken as such. To do otherwise is very much like trying to steady a block of ideas on a volcano. The blast of feeling scatters and fragments the ideas so that what you are left with are scattered notions, fragmented thoughts and the ashes of a psychotic break.

Neurotic vs. Psychotic Ideation

It is a fine line, that boundary between neurotic and psychotic thought. To misinterpret a situation is usually neurotic. To fabricate a situation is another matter. The patient who left his wife because "she leaves me no space to breathe" perhaps misinterpreted his reality. His wife did tend to dominate; yet his reaction was inordinate due to the Primal anlage—there was literally no space to breathe at birth. But to imagine that "the Mafia is planning to suffocate me" is to arrive on the psychotic plane. There is a qualitative difference between the two kinds of ideation. "The walls are closing in on me" or "I've got to move" are examples of repressed birth Pain producing neurotic ideation. But "They are conspiring to seal me in my room" is psychotic. The common neurotic complaint that "everyone is putting too much pressure on me" may be an overreaction caused by the high level of inner pressure. Feeling the Primal pressure tells the neurotic person how disconnected her reaction was. The psychotic, however, can usually take no pressure at all. Even having to select clothes in a department store can become overwhelming.

The crazy idea never seems that crazy to the person who is genuinely psychotic. He is responding directly to an urgent inner reality. For him the context is real since he is living in that past and not in the present. It is the primitive baby brain that has moved to the forefront accompanied by its history of memories. The third-line or adult brain is simply there trying to make sense of the memories. If the memory could be connected directly to the consciousness, it would a Primal. But the event is blocked from its direct route and therefore becomes symbolized. Those events are so far removed from any current reality that naturally any explanation or rationalization of them seems bizarre. The verbal mind is putting ideas on an event that had no ideas. It is making conceptual a nonconceptual experience. It cannot make any "sense." And it shouldn't.

Psychosis and Sleep

Because of all the overload on the third level, psychotics have rare periods of deep sleep. This is another indication that the forces behind psychosis are on the first level of consciousness. Deep sleep occurs on the deepest level of consciousness. We have observed for many years that chronic insomniacs often suffer from first-line intrusion, and that patients with first-line Pain on the ascendance will suffer first in the area of sleep.

Brain-wave amplitude during deep sleep is characterized by large, slow waves. Repression now is at a maximum to keep any intruding Pain from breaking into consciousness and disrupting sleep. Without this natural repressive process most of us would be unable to sleep. The psychotic, lacking a proper defense system, is in a chronic state of first-line intrusion. It is in the forefront all of the time. Deep sleep means that first-line Pains are well sequestered, and that is not possible for the psychotic.

The person whose unconscious is disrupted by consciousness—that is, the person who *cannot* become deeply unconscious—is the psychotic. He has lost the wherewithal to repress and thus the wherewithal to sleep. The person who is suddenly thrust into consciousness by night terrors is experiencing first-line energy bursting upward through the repressive barriers. And usually the nightmare just before the abrupt awakening is characterized by first-line concomitants: inability to catch one's breath, a crushing or squeezing sensation, a feeling of drowning or suffocation, a trapped feeling and the sensation of imminent death.

People who have taken LSD may also have sleep problems for years after they have stopped using the drug because LSD disrupts the natural repressive systems. One needs a "quiet" brain to sleep, and this is not possible when it is being bombarded with stimulation from within. In sleep one is reversing evolution: the third level drops off first, then the second level and finally one "lives" on the first level. When the third level is peppered with first-line forces, the mind races instead of remaining tranquil, thus preventing sleep. It is racing to cope with the intrusion. Ordinarily, the lower level gating systems would function properly and sleep would be no problem.

The psychotic, the insomniac and the person with night terrors are all descending in sleep to a nightmare *already lived*. The descent is into reality. But before a direct linkup can be made in sleep, repression sets in.

Different Types of Psychosis: Different Diseases or Different Illusions?

Psychotic reactions are reactions to imprints. Depending upon one's prototypic tendencies and one's life history, those reactions will differ. Thus there is catatonic schizophrenia, manic-depressive psychosis, paranoid schizophrenia, etc. These are not different diseases, or even different subdiseases. They indicate the same massive Pain and the same massive dislocation of function, but in varying ways.

The catatonic schizophrenic is reacting to his Pain in a somatic way by paralysis of the body wall; the manic-depressive is reacting on the emotional level by way of extreme and uncontrollable mood swings; and the paranoid schizophrenic is reacting in ideational (intellectual) terms by way of bizarre and distorted thoughts.

Indeed, much depends on the original birth prototype. When there is a great surge toward life at birth interrupted by a massive shut-off from drugs resulting in a near-death experience, the basis may be laid for manic-depressive mood swings in later life. Of course, this tendency would be greatly reinforced by a volatile family atmosphere, but that original birth imprint of polarity between up and down—between life and death—may be the determining factor.

The pressure (energy) behind both polarities is the same. Depression is the body's attempt to push down the force of Pain; what one feels in a depression is the labored effort of the body to accomplish precisely that. Mania takes over when repression finally fails; now the mind and body (behavior) truly go wild; the person gets as "high" as he was "low" the day before.

There is a sense of inevitability in manic-depression. Mania is usually followed by depression, and depression will often regenerate the mania. This is because the manic-depressive cycle can be tied up with the birth cycle—replicating the "up" of imminent life followed by the "down" of drugs and near death. That is exactly what happened originally, and that is exactly what will be replayed for life. The manic-depressive becomes accustomed to holding down any good feelings out of fear of what is to come.* Happiness always brings with it the memory or sensation of death and depression. Indeed, mania and depression are the flip sides of the same coin of birth trauma.

Paranoia is another example of Primal pressure.† A difficult birth followed by a childhood of criticism and haranguing can easily leave the adult believing that people on the street are saying bad things about him. What happens here is that the child is forced to repress all those harangues—"Can't you learn anything!"; "Why are you always so slow!"; "Why aren't you like your brother!"; "You're just no good!"—to get by, but is eventually forced by the internal pressure to project it all somewhere. And it is easier to believe that strangers on the street dislike you than to believe your own mother did.

Without the enormous pressure of birth the child might have grown into a neurotic adult who complains constantly about how much everyone pushes him. But *with* the birth pressure he can be pushed into psychosis, now believing that anyone who looks at him wants to hurt him. The content is real—it is merely out of context. "People" did say bad things about him—but the people were his parents and the time was twenty or thirty years ago. The newborn has no way of knowing or understanding that the Pain he is experiencing is unintended. It should be no surprise that such Pain can lead straight to paranoid tendencies in adolescence and adulthood.

*The drug lithium (commonly prescribed for manic depression) accomplishes exactly that: it smooths out the highs and the lows, allowing the individual to exist in a "gray zone" of neutrality as a defense.
†Again, it is likely that the specific type of family pathology plays an important role in determining the specific type of psychosis that later develops.

Ideas are never "diseased." They can, however, reflect a dislocation of the mind's function, and that is the nature of disease.*

Paranoia is not just a mental illness. There are clear biologic changes such as the change in stress hormone levels, for example. We are dealing with a diseased *system,* which is why its treatment cannot be confined to mental concepts.

One patient who had been left alone for hours after birth, compounded by a childhood of rejection, began to have a delusion after his wife left him that there were people in the television set who were telling him what to do. They were talking directly to him. The old feeling was, "I'm all alone and no one cares." The people in the television set had cared. That man's delusion disappeared once he had felt both his birth agony of being left alone and his childhood Pain of rejection.

Another patient who was born Cesarean after two days of labor wrote:

Present-day feelings

I talked with my therapist about what had happened during the week and that I felt I had no control over my life. I began to take the feeling of having no control in the present back to being in the womb and having no control over what happened to me in there.

Reliving the struggle of labor

I was inside my mother, again trying to get out, again feeling her hatred of me, hurting me. I started pushing, trying to get out. The therapist helped me by pushing me into the corner with a pillow. My back hurt. I started to choke on fluid. Then I felt exhausted and unable to go any further—the anguish of not knowing

"Going crazy" in the womb

what was happening. I had had a previous Primal in which I felt I had actually gone crazy in my mother's womb, right before I was born. It felt like an electric shock right up the middle of my forehead and really hurt physically. I know that this is true. I went crazy because I was just too tired to fight anymore. I felt like I was dying at birth, and have had many suicidal feelings throughout my life. I just wanted the Pain to stop.

Getting back to my birth. I rested a bit after the initial fight. Then I began to feel something totally different. I felt as if I were being pulled in the opposite

Reliving the Cesarean trauma

direction to the one I had been trying so hard to go in. I felt very helpless and terrified. I told the therapist I felt

*An analogy from biology comes to mind. A microbe entering the system causes many subsystems to begin battle. The body becomes mobilized toward this end, and changes in function occur to accommodate that mobilization. There is a change in the number of white cells, a change in heart rate, in skin tone, in blood circulation, etc. Over time the strain on the subsystems causes a breakdown of normal organ function, and it is that breakdown that we call disease.

like I was in a river which was carrying me down-stream while I was trying so hard to hang on to anything to keep me from going that way. I got very frightened. The therapist held out her hand to steady me and told me it was a feeling, but that I needed to feel it more. I asked her to stand me upside down on my head. At first, I helped by holding my hands on the floor, but then I went with the feeling of being upside down and just let go. How the therapist ever managed to keep me in that position, I'll never know. It was terrifying. Then I flopped down and really cried. I was out of the womb. I was so scared and exhausted. I lay there gurgling and choking on fluid. I felt very ex-hausted. Two days of labor later I had at last been born.

Childhood com-pounding: adult paranoia

I know now why I have always felt like I was a bad girl. My mother used to show me the scar. I was a bad girl, never did anything right, was constantly criti-cized, but still kept on trying to please her. All for nothing. She never, ever loved me or wanted me even from the beginning of life before birth. I think that is why I have always been very paranoid and could not separate my Pain from everyone else's, just like I could not separate myself from my mother.

Psychosis, Religion and Mysticism

What is dangerous for the psychotic is banding together with others who have the same or similar problems. Joining religious and mystical groups can prevent the psychotic from ever really getting well. Why? First and foremost, the psychotic is a person with death present in a most immediate way: the birth imprint of near-death. Religious and mystical notions make death manageable, palatable, even nonexistent: your body dies but your soul lives on; or, you will be transported into a better life where rewards are finally forthcoming. Such notions are very appealing to the psychotic, indeed, to many people; they have enormous power. Much of that power comes from the so-called transcendent nature of the notions: conve-niently, they are not based on proofs but on "givens." These givens are easily fixated and institutionalized into ideas which serve as automatic repressive mechanisms. Thus the person with ascending birth Pain can blot it out with a preordained doctrine. That doctrine will prevent his ever really connecting to his Pain, and thus to reality. He now has what I call "benign psychosis."

The role of ideas is very important in adult psychosis. We do see psychotic reactions which apparently occur without the use of ideas—

childhood autism is an example. But as adults we tend to use ideas to go crazy, for ideas are the most recent evolutionary tool developed by man for coping. In psychosis, however, the neuron system is stretched to its limit, which is why the ideas it produces seem so far-fetched, so "off the wall."

Two elements—repression and disconnection—ensure a fixed symbolization of the Pain and a reinforcement of unreal ideas. To tamper with the ideas is to tamper with the defense, all of which threatens to bring the Pain closer to consciousness. These ideas have a Primal stake and can allow for a rising above reality, *literally,* in the brain. They permit someone to go crazy in a sane way, or at least in a culturally defined, acceptable way—a sanity redefined by the group. The group provides guidelines for the behavior of its novitiates and channels the psychosis within those confines. The person no longer feels alone in his insanity—and thankfully, for otherwise the mental hospitals would be fuller still. (They may be as full as they are due to the failure of mysticism and religion to contain insanity within acceptable boundaries.)

The function of a false idea is to hide reality. When an inner reality is prepotent, the ideas are held to that inner reality despite any kind of current alteration in circumstance and they take on a force and tenacity commensurate with the feelings. The ideas become as strong and inflexible as the imprint. When one argues with the idea, one is really arguing with history and there are no good arguments that will change that.

Ingmar Bergman said in *The Seventh Seal,* "We make symbols out of our fears and call it God"; and John Lennon wrote, "God is a concept by which we measure our Pain." The notion that there is a force out there stronger than the individual who will help and direct him is not very different from the psychotic (and non-religious) delusion that there is a force out there stronger than the individual who is out to hurt him. The context is roughly the same; only the nature of the feeling changes. The same inner force is at work; it is an inner force projected externally, each with a slightly different twist. If God were constantly trying to "hurt" instead of "help," the person would more likely be adjudged insane. The birth trauma occurs unconsciously, but we manufacture God and heaven consciously. The notion of God is not only there to quell our Pains but to fulfill our key, unfulfilled needs (to be listened to, protected, watched over, loved, etc.). It is the notion that begins to produce the endorphines that literally answer our prayers for surcease. The idea of God is the real power; yet we imagine that the relief is the workings of a deity. We ourselves bring on the relief by fiats of faith and hope. Those two psychological factors arise out of Pain and suppress it. The power is inside of us; positive belief has the power to tranquilize.

The true power lies in the Pain, which when felt alters misdirected belief into disbelief. Belief in others and in things evaporates with the Pain. A person who has felt himself deeply can now believe in himself. For all the things we believe in—the deities, the mystical notions, the former lives, the after-lives, etc.—are things that somehow fulfill us. We want an all-powerful being who won't let anything bad happen to us, who will balance the scales and see that justice is done, who will see that our enemies are punished and that good deeds are rewarded.

The psychotic is right about a "force"—only it is a Primal force, not "out there" but deep inside. Since there is no way to imagine that such a force exists inside of us—particularly since it is repression's task to make sure we don't know about it—it must be projected outside. When felt, that force dispels notions of an omniscient benefactor and malevolent attacker alike. That force may take months to feel, or perhaps years.

No longer overloaded by history, the person lives in the present and is a feeling person. That is the definition of a healthy individual: someone who can feel . . . someone whose first instinct is not to repress.

Infantile Autism and Primal Pain: A Case Report

The causes of infantile autism (a type of childhood psychosis) are complex and not fully understood at this time. Probably it involves a combination of both structural (brain) damage and massive Primal (first-line) Pain. In 1974, we received extensive communications from the mother of an autistic child, indicating in a most moving way the critical role of Pain in autism.

At the time we received the letters, the mother and her eight-year-old child lived in Virginia; unfortunately, they were never able to travel to Los Angeles. What had prompted her to write was an "episode" with her son that had been the most terrifying, agonizing and ultimately therapeutic event she had ever experienced with him. After the episode the changes in the child were so marked that his mother felt she at last had found an inroad into his autism. That inroad was Pain and its expression.

Obviously we cannot draw conclusions from the experiences of one child, but the point of presenting this case is to make concrete the very real price of early Pain. We can only deduce that, since expressing the Pain resulted in reduced autistic behavior, the autism was connected to that Pain in an important and possibly critical way. The boy's medical records indicated that his birth had involved three and possibly four major traumas that were gross enough to be noted and included in his medical file. It is also highly likely that several other traumatic events occurred from the baby's perspective that went unnoticed and unrecorded.

Following are excerpts from Mrs. K.'s first letter, in which she describes her son Jason's developmental history and the episode that prompted her to write (their names have been changed to protect their anonymity):

Dear Dr. Janov,

The enclosed information may be of interest to you and to your Institute. I feel I should inform you that I had not read any of your publications prior to my "experience" with my son, although I had discussed "Primal" with a friend, due to the fact that my son had never really cried. I have attached my son's medical records along with pictures of him at different ages relating to pertinent situations.

I believe the other records will show that between the ages of two and five Jason did not talk. Speech had started before the age of two and then just stopped. The very strange thing that did occur was the fact that Jason would hum the "Star Spangled Banner"—every chorus, but no words. I had mentioned this to various professionals, but received many "odd" looks, and therefore discontinued any further discussion of my son.

During this time period speech was not necessary between my son and myself. Jason would come to me and I knew what he wanted. On one occasion I tried giving him a glass of milk instead of the orange juice that I "knew" he wanted. The child threw the milk in my face, along with the glass.

Although Jason was not talking, my mother and I noticed that he could read. We were quite sure of this by the time he was three years old. Mother and I worked constantly with him, and indeed did get the child to start saying words. Jason was admitted to private school, where his older brother and sister went, because of his "reading" ability. Although he had started talking more, I noticed that he talked *at* me and not *to* me. I was so sure that my son would be "OK" after we had gotten him to talk. There was speech, but no thought or expression. After Dr. G. had finished his evaluation, reality hit hard. I had nothing more than a trained "puppet." There are some things we know, but to really admit it openly is another thing.

I have not gone into Jason's "temper tantrums," "rages," etc. I am sure that anyone familiar with the autistic child is already well aware of the violence involved. It is the most pathetic situation I know of. It is so evident that these children cannot help what they do.

To get back to the matter of my "experience" with my son. I went to the Bruno Bettelheim Orthogenic Clinic in Chicago seeking . . . help? answers? who knows? The important part is that on my return trip I stopped at Shands Teaching Hospital and met with a Mrs. C. on the previous recommendation of Dr. G.

I spoke to Mrs. C. about many situations involving my son. I told her of his inability to cry. Then I proceeded to tell her about something that would "just happen" when I could feel him on the verge of tears. I also explained that when this did occur, I would feel myself literally "freeze" inside. I seemed to be afraid of what would happen. It was then that Mrs. C. assured me that it could not hurt my son to cry. I explained that I was somehow afraid of losing what I had. You see, even a trained "puppet" was better than the nothing I had before. Again, Mrs. C. assured me that I could not hurt my son by getting him to cry, and advised me to cry with him.

I also explained that I could not make this happen. It did not occur on every head banging. When Jason would get to the point where I felt he was really on the verge of injuring himself, I would slap him very hard, just once, and then hold him in my arms to comfort him. At this point I would sing a lullaby and he would curl up in my arms like a baby. This is when he reached the point of near tears.

I returned home that same night, and I do contribute part of what ensured to my own mental state—I was exhausted and my defenses were down. I learned a long time ago that my son would "use" emotions like weapons, and therefore kept myself prepared this particular night. Jason at first appeared happy to see me. But I had been home just long enough to change my clothes when he started in screaming, hitting, and head banging. It became increasingly worse until I had to slap him. This time was different, though. I didn't become frightened and just continuing singing. Jason tried to get away instead of allowing himself to be comforted like before. He really got violent. On different previous occasions, he had made some strange little moaning-like sounds at times. But it wasn't the same this time. He kicked and screamed and fought to get away from me, at which point I noticed what seemed to be some wetness around his eyes. I remembered what Mrs. C. had said and continued holding him and singing (if you can call it that). Jason was still kicking and fighting, but also began to make some very unusual sounds. If you do not believe this next portion, I don't blame you. The sound turned into something else. Something very horrible. Had I not kept Mrs. C.'s reassurances in mind, I don't know what I owuld have done. These sounds that came from my son were the most horrible—inhuman—I don't know what to call them. I have never heard anything like it, and I cannot relate any sound that could be similar. My son did indeed start to cry, but the sounds continued. It was not until he began sobbing that they began to diminish. Yes, I did cry with him. As to how long he cried, I really don't know. It could have been a half hour or an hour. I did not plan this, nor did I keep track of any time.

About a week later, I had gone to the store and my son had an accident at home. He had hurt his finger, and he really cried. When I returned home my mother and daughter were both amazed and couldn't wait to tell me how Jason had cried when he got hurt. We were delighted. My son got hurt and he cried!

The original "episode" occurred in the early part of April. I have enclosed a picture of my son taken in June. It shows my son with his two upper front teeth still very much intact, with no evidence of his second teeth coming through. About a month and a half ago, he lost his two upper front teeth and the new ones are already through. This was my reason for phoning your Institute—to find out if you indeed have medical facts proving glandular changes occurring in the body after experiencing a highly emotional traumatic experience.

My son is not only experiencing physical changes, but mental as well. My "puppet" is no more. He has begun to express his own thoughts. He was at Shands this past Monday and Tuesday for another evaluation. When the time came for my son to draw a picture of a person, this was the final test for me. Up until this time the only thing he could do was to write the word *person*. Not this time—this time he drew a person—crude, perhaps—but he drew one.

There have been several other occasions similar to our first episode, but none quite as intense. Once, when I knew I could not go through it, I asked my mother to hold onto him and keep singing until he cried.

I don't believe words are necessary to express how I feel.

Mrs. K. included extensive medical histories and developmental evaluations with her letters. Jason's birth history records that he was delivered by Cesarean section (first trauma) after a full-term pregnancy; that he encountered a "drastic loss of weight" (second trauma) after birth; that Mrs. K. showed a positive serology—venereal disease—at the time of delivery, as did her newly born son (third trauma), for which he was treated with penicillin for eight weeks; and finally that he "may have had a transfusion for an Rh-negative factor (possible fourth trauma) immediately after birth. And, as I said before, these are only the traumas known from the medical point of view. What it was like for tiny Jason we cannot know. The fact that from early infancy onward he was frequently ill and had much difficulty sleeping indicates, to me, the after-effects of a very painful birth. In her second letter to us, Mrs. K. summed up her son's story in a few sentences: "To go into a detailed explanation I would have to begin eight years ago. The story of my son would be quite lengthy. It took me eight years to realize what the 'difference' was with Jason *from the time he was born*. There was no warmth." [Italics added]

Over the next year, Mrs. K. continued to send us reports of her son's progress. In her experiences, that progress seemed directly related to his growing ability to cry. Slowly, crying replaced the violent tantrums, and "normal" behavior began to replace many of the autistic traits.

Three months after her first letter, Mrs. K. writes:

This past weekend Jason had a good cry. He was getting overly tired. We had probably over-done the day with activities, and when I pulled into the driveway he was fussing. He told me he was going to bang his head on his knee. I told him, "OK," and he did—but ever so lightly. I held out my arms to him and began singing, and Jason merely had a good cry. He came into the house afterwards, bathed, and went to bed—smiling.

And almost a year from her first letter:

Although some time has passed since I last wrote you, I thought you might be interested to know of Jason's progress. He was discharged from Shands on June 19th, and his progress is so remarkable that many of the doctors have called it quite "unbelievable." I find it most amazing that our medical profession can sit back and be so amazed at Jason's progress, and yet when I mention Primal, I have had several responses that "we must take a conservative approach." Well, I suppose we still live in such a closed-minded society that even living proof isn't enough.

Changing Psychosis: The Ultimate Therapeutic Challenge

For the psychotic, ideational change alone is a dangerous and precarious approach. It must rely upon the most noncohesive and unstable part of the person—his thought processes—as the very vehicle of change. Psychosis is therefore the ultimate challenge for any therapy because it is the ultimate distortion of human nature. That distortion is a process that begins with birth and germinates throughout childhood. Birth is probably never the sole cause of psychosis, because nothing exists in a vacuum. A child who has an extremely traumatic birth and is then raised in a loving and supportive family is not going to become psychotic. But another child with a similarly traumatic birth and an unsupportive family may. Conversely, the birth may have been fine, but the childhood so shattering that psychosis results without significant birth trauma.

Profound change in personality should mean just that: a profound change in the entire system, body and brain alike—a change no less encompassing than the profound pathology that created the psychosis to begin with.

A change in ideas must be reflected in the body or that change is only "skin-" or "cortex-deep." Any real change in ideas must evolve out of the individual and his history. Deep access and full connection are what ultimately anchor ideas in reality rather than in psychotic ideation.

9

The Long Reach of Birth: One Road to Cancer and Epilepsy

The notion of a link between catastrophic illness and personal trauma is not new. Recent research has correlated specific illnesses with specific types of personalities so that it is now common to speak of a cancer personality profile, a heart attack profile, and so on. What these correlations suggest is that the ways in which people react to stress and trauma determine the type of illness they incur. But what determines those characteristic ways of responding? And what establishes a valence of Pain so high that catastrophic illness is the observable correspondence? I have attempted to propose answers to these questions from a new perspective. While I am not saying that all illness is caused by trauma and its repression, I do think we may soon find that the somatization of Pain over a lifetime of experience acts as the single most common yet least understood etiological factor.

Cancer

Supporting evidence linking Pain and cancer has come from several areas, one having to do with our own immune system and its surveillance function in relation to disease. It seems that cancer cells appear periodically in everyone's body but are usually destroyed by white blood cells called lymphocytes. When the immune system is overloaded by stress, however, it does not function well and the cancer cells are allowed to grow and reproduce.

Our current knowledge indicates that Pain is directly related to endorphine output and this in turn alters lymphocyte production. It is this lymphocyte output that we are now researching; but it seems reasonable that the blockage of Pain changes the immune surveillance system which may in turn predispose one to a higher risk of cancer.

Steven Locke, a Boston University researcher, reported that in a study of college students, those who coped poorly with stress appeared to "suffer deficits in cell-mediated immunity against certain disease."* He suggested that those individuals who cope well with stress display what he termed an active "Natural Killer Cell Activity" which goes into action when the body is threatened by abnormal cells (such as cancer).

The procedure Locke and his colleagues used was to extract white blood cells from both good and bad "copers." They then exposed the white blood cells from both groups to leukemia cells. Each leukemia cell was tagged with radioactive material. It turned out that the "Natural Killer Cell Activity" was highest in the good copers. In other words, the good copers had a better functioning immune system and were thus less prone to disease.

In yet another experiment by the well-known stress researcher Hans Selye, rodents were placed on slippery mounds so that whenever they fell asleep they would fall into a water tank. Their sleep thus constantly interrupted, the animals became chronically fatigued and stressed—and developed cancer along the pituitary-adrenal axis that secretes the endorphines. Cancer developed because the environment was demanding too much of the animals' organ systems; in other words, the need for endorphine created by the outer stress stretched the pituitary beyond its capacity. It is not so farfetched to say also that the excessive endorphine output called upon to meet inner Pain forces the system to make continuous responses outside its normal range, also resulting in disease.

The importance of the research cited is that it is not Pain alone which produces catastrophic disease but the response of repression to that Pain. It is becoming clear that symptoms are mediated by the very chemicals called in to combat Pain. As I have said, there is no such thing as a healthy disease. Defenses lead to disease. It doesn't seem to matter whether the result is psychological in the form of neurosis or psychosis, or physical in the form of disease: both result from increased endorphine levels. What all this may mean is that lowering the internal endorphine levels by extracting

*Science News, March 11, 1978, p. 151.

Pain from the system can be a specific preventative against the progression of cancer. Until we take Pain out of the system its repression may well be fatal.

Epilepsy

The kind of pressure the psychotic contains within him is no different from the pressure we see in psychogenic epilepsy. Nothing more vividly depicts the convulsive storm left by first-line trauma than a seizure. The *grand mal* seizure represents a massive release of energy that has been stored via repression. The magnitude of the seizure is usually commensurate with the magnitude of the Pain being repressed. A *grand mal* seizure simply externalizes and concretizes those specific quantities of energy.

Epilepsy shows what can happen when birth trauma is compounded by numerous childhood traumas: the body reaches a point where it can no longer integrate the Pain. With enough repression of feeling, the pressure can become severe enough to trigger a sudden, random and massive discharge of energy—neural-electrical energy. It is the way the brain "lets go," just as shaking and tremors are the way the body can let go; or diarrhea is a way the viscera let go. It is again the same Primal force we are dealing with. The brain simply does the only thing left to do in terms of defense. It releases enough tension to keep the person free of symptoms for a brief time, until another convulsion erupts due to the resurgence of imprinted Pain. Indeed, the slightest trigger—a clap of the hands, a flashbulb or a car horn—can bring on a convulsion.

The connections between Pain and epilepsy and between birth trauma and epilepsy have become increasingly clear through the work we have done with epileptic patients. They learned to heed the signals of the beginning feeling of a seizure (the prodromal aura) so that instead of going into the seizure, they Primalled. Primals that come out of the beginnings of a seizure are as intense as the seizure would have been, and almost always involve life and death sensations of choking, gagging, drowning and gasping for air.

Following is a report by one epileptic patient who felt that in his Primals he was "allowing myself to convulse, bit by bit."

Birth imprint   In my helplessness while drowning in the womb I felt I couldn't move or cry out or scream; I was dying; I was tensing up against my extinction, and I knew it. This tensing up has become my lifelong sensation, as has the feeling that something terrible is always about to happen.

In one session I was gagging and choking with my head and nose pressed into a pint of mucus on the floor that had just come out of me. I suddenly had the insight that what I was going through was exactly the same process that happens in my epileptic convulsions. In this insight I discovered that I was allowing myself to convulse, bit by bit, a little gagging at a time, so that I was actually reexperiencing the terror of my birth slowly and deliberately. I was feeling the Pain instead of closing down against it. I realized that it was closing down against Pain that produced my epileptic seizures.

The tritest situations would seem to trigger off those old buried feelings; they would rush up in a massive *grand mal* seizure and I would have convulsions totally out of control. In short, *my epileptic fits were really birth Primals in disguise.* That lifelong feeling that something terrible is about to happen was true—except that the something terrible *had already happened:* I had almost drowned at birth. By sampling the feeling bit by bit, by trying it out, by testing it, by drowning a little bit at a time, it didn't seem so terrible after all.

After weeks of birth Primals I decided to phone my mother and ask her about my birth. I shouldn't have been so astonished to find out that I was born a "blue baby"—I was born suffering from oxygen deprivation and heavily anesthetized so that the doctor had to swing me around and spank me a great deal to get me going. I couldn't assist in my own birth because I was drugged. I couldn't even try to discharge the mucus in my air passages.

I felt as though I had passed through a very serious illness with these Primals, and now I was convalescing. My sex drive dropped to zero for a while, and I felt absolutely neuter. I have been off Dilantin without a seizure. The well has been tapped. I now have my whole painful childhood ahead of me.

Another patient wrote extensively about his epilepsy and how it changed in therapy:

Before I entered Primal Therapy I was epileptic. I had hundreds of seizures, dating from when I was about seven until I entered therapy at the age of twenty-one. I passed out in classes, at work, at play, before friends and family, at the dinner table and while asleep.

Seizures as a way of life

I always felt acutely aware that I passed out because I was miserable and unhappy. If I couldn't handle it I passed out. Seizures made sense in the context of my life, so I gradually just accepted them. By the time I came to the Institute I wondered why everybody made such a fuss over the fact that I passed out a lot. Shortly into my first session I found out. I could scarcely even talk about my family and my feelings without starting to seize. I'd get a sickly, doomed feeling with a horrible

Seizure sensations

sensation in my guts. An electrical buzzing/tingling sensation would displace the horror, starting in my genitals and bowels and rising from there. Sometimes I could feel my interior organs slide against the abdominal wall. The buzz would crawl up through my guts to my diaphragm and to my throat. Often I'd try to hold it back, but the effort seemed doomed. The feeling had to be real: it was right there. With this realization, the buzz would rise further. Before therapy, the buzzing would become general just after it reached my throat.

The step from seizing to feeling

My vision would become black and white, then black, as I passed out. In my sessions, when the buzzing reached my throat I'd be able to say the feeling, drop into my old tearful horror and feel better. Exactly as I dropped into the feeling, the buzzing (the seizure) dissipated.

Primals v. seizures

This must have happened at least a hundred times over my first year and a half of therapy. There are a few distinctions between Primals and seizures. After a Primal I "come to" feeling relatively clear about what happened. I understand my life in a new, clearer way. After seizures I wondered where I was. I'd have a thick buzz left in my tongue, and a bad feeling in my guts. I'd feel as if there had been *something* I'd forgotten, somehow. Thinking about feelings leads to concrete, useful changes in my life. Thinking about seizures often led me to pass out again and again. I am conscious during my feelings. I've heard other patients worry about being aware, during their feelings, of other events in the group room. But it is that same awareness which makes sense out of the old experience. Were they completely unaware, they'd be having a seizure.

My Primals have a cumulative, beneficial effect on me. After nearly two years of therapy, my life has improved beyond recognition. Seizures simply got me beyond the next few minutes of life, and at a considerable inconvenience. As my therapy progressed, the pre-seizure symptoms before feelings became less pronounced. A few months ago I had a light tingle in my abdomen before I had a deep feeling. Since then there's no buzzing at all. What seems to remain of my epilepsy is just that I cry frequently and that my feelings attack me quickly with little or no warning. I often find it difficult not to feel even when it's inconvenient. But even that is changing.

I now know just why and how I became epileptic. I seized because I was in massive Pain. I was almost constantly scared. I had daily migraines—my head hurt almost constantly for three years. My whole body was wracked with Pains. Nothing pleased my crazy mother or helped the hurt much. Recently I remembered lying in the garage at age nine, pretending to be a baby and suddenly seeing the old scenes from my infancy. This was not atypical. I had constant nightmares, sometimes several per night. I'd wake feeling flesh over my face. Once, two years before therapy, I had a complete birth feeling. In my life, there was no way to pretend for long that being smart or athletic would make me feel good. Everything hurt. Death seemed close at hand.

But many suffering people become violent and/or crazy instead of seizing. My seizures were the result of my specific Pain. I've had dozens of Primals about times I passed out. I'd pass out as I began to realize that I was deathly sick and hurting, that nobody found me worth helping and that there was no point in even trying. The first seizure I remember happened when Mom screamed at me for smashing my funnybone on the dinner table. As I came to—I still couldn't see—I heard Mom say, "Now quit playing on the floor and eat your dinner." I tried to say I'd "fainted," but she cut me off. So I ate my dinner.

Later I passed out frequently in classes, where lecturers regularly spewed nonsense over me, oblivious of my agony.

My next series of seizures occurred when I cut my finger carving a jack-o'-lantern. I stood in the hallway, holding up my bloody hand for Mom to see, hoping she'd help me. She looked horrified and angry. She said I should get to the bathroom: didn't I realize what the blood could be doing to the floor? I took two steps into the bathroom, looked at my ashen face and bloody finger against the hospital-white wall and flopped across the linoleum. Mom would stand me up just as I came to, say "Now just *stand* there, I'm going to get some paper towels." I'd keel over as she left. This was repeated several times. I felt sure I was dying.

In scores of Primals I've lain on that floor, asking for help and asking to see Dad and my brothers. Especially I cried, "Mommy, hold me!" It seemed that the only thing that had ever made me feel good was Mom's warm presence. She left, as on that day in the bathroom, and I "died." She left and I "died" over and over again. Subsequently, I passed out whenever it became too obvious that I was hurting and that nobody cared enough to help. So I passed out with migraines, stubbed toes and bad dreams. Almost any Pain would confront me with the reality that nobody much loved me.

Passing out because "nobody loved me"

Had I some decent outlet for my Pain, I would surely have used it. My brothers all fought my mother, each in his way, and none of them had seizures. Why did I?

The answer is in my horrible experience as a baby. I felt that I was dying, and experienced the physical equivalent of "Why fight it?" I cried for ages in the crib until I was exhausted and asleep. I gave up on my mother ever coming. The need for rest overwhelmed any hope of being fed. *Then* she came and woke me to feed me. Why fight it? Twice now I've had feelings in which I felt sure I'd drown. And I gave up. Another time I felt myself lying in a white hospital room with white walls and an itchy bandage over my seared penis with nobody around, scared to even cry because the last time I'd done *that* they came and cut me. Why call for help?

Baby Pain and epilepsy

In all these events I felt that there was no hope, that I was dying, and that I'd be better off just letting it happen. The first situation in which I encountered this was birth. When the contractions started, they nearly broke my skull. Something must have happened to the cord, because soon I was getting no air. The womb went static and vibrated instead of contracting. I tried to breathe but my face was flush against flesh and all I could do was create horrid changes of pressure in my chest. I tried to thrash, to *change* something, but the walls were insanely strong. I longed to feel once more

Birth and epilepsy: born almost dead

the comfort of the womb's nurture. (Later I would lie in my room with the bass up on the stereo, curled under a blanket and rocking/vibrating. But then it was nowhere to be found.) I gave up breathing and started to die. Presumably I was born almost immediately thereafter.

I've been told that the whole process took under an hour. It was called an "easy birth." I wonder for whom. I felt that I was dying; that the dying process had begun. The process carried the feeling of dying, of passing out, that exploded into my later seizures. It also set the pattern for my headaches, and for repeated failings throughout my life. Nobody would love me anyway, so what was the use? I just wallowed in whatever sensation seemed most comfortable. Since it seemed, inside, as though I had just a few minutes to live, I never lifted a finger to cause anything. I'm dying, so why wash the dishes or comb my hair? I didn't even think, for the most part, of simple, direct palliatives like narcotics or suicide. My system tended just to sit back and more or less just let the Pain attack.

Seizures: infantile and fetal memories

I now recognize that many of the thoughts and sensations that occurred during the rise of a seizure were literal and nearly complete infantile or fetal memories. Seizure-like tingling used to accompany prolonged and inescapable natal memories on several occasions when I was a child.

The vital part of all this for me is that overwhelming, barely repressed feelings caused my symptoms and that by feeling I shed the symptom. I now deliberately find things to make me feel good. That is, I'm really living, instead of constantly dying.

I want to make one more note. For the most part, my suffering caused my seizures, not the other way around. I wonder how many elileptics under medication are being done a service. Of course, there are social advantages to not convulsing. Social attitudes are pretty negative. And I'd be terrified of passing out now. But I have no idea where all that Pain would have gone had I not seized. It's a shame that most of the medical profession can only help someone who has seizures *act* well, instead of helping him feel and integrate the Pain that causes the seizures.

Feeling the Pain: an end to epilepsy

Several months after writing the above account, the patient was involved in an auto accident which triggered still deeper connections to the real source of his epilepsy:

A couple of days ago I had the first deep feeling in the month following my auto accident and the most direct connection to my epilepsy ever.

First seizure in two and a half years

Breaking my sternum in the collision triggered my first seizure since I started therapy over two and a half years ago. The seizure was different. For the first time just as I came to I was aware of the typical shuddering that had been mimed and described for me over the years by my mother, teachers and friends.

In the month that followed without deep feeling, I felt close to passing out several times, something I had not experienced in well over a year. The night before I finally Primalled, I had two nightmares about auto accidents—my first. When I awoke, my chest was still sore to the slightest movement and I assumed that I remained too damaged to feel. By that afternoon I was in so much visible Pain that I took a friend's suggestion and went to a room just to cry a little.

Reliving the accident

Straightaway I sobbed about having nobody to help me or to care for me. I bound my hands over my chest, where the sheer physical Pain severely limited my breathing. I saw my mother hanging over me, grimacing as in previous seizure scenes. Suddenly I was flat on my back on Electric Avenue in Venice, the scene of my accident, asking "Where am I? What happened to me?" Strange people stood over me, staring. "Somebody take care of me!" . . . "I can't move!" I screamed and groaned. Fluid ran from my eyes, nose and throat and gathered in puddles across the room. I saw the blood flow from my mouth and nose onto the sidewalk. I bellowed like an animal. I felt I was dying. My chest and pelvis convulsed alternately. The spasms in my chest had a strange fractured dissonance. They were fast and arrhythmic, like my breathing after the collision. The details of the accident unrolled sequentially, like an uncut film, from my shuddering as I came to on the sidewalk, the crowd and the paramedic's questions, to my grating bones on the X-ray table.

I tried to murmur "Oh God!" (my only words at the time) but produced only fluted hiccups and spurts of fluid. Even the memories and considerations I'd had of previous seizures returned in perfect order. Occasionally I'd sit up with exclamations of how horrible it all was, how there just *had* to be someone there to *help*. Finally my chest convulsed, my arms and legs shot spastically in front of me as I saw the car cross the center line of the street and smash into me once, twice, again and again. I opened my eyes in my broken,

squealing car and moaned that I had nothing left. I felt
a light tingle in my fingers and I was on the sidewalk
again. It was so horrible to be unable to breathe! My
ribs seemed to just rattle in my chest without order or
meaning.

I kneeled in the room. There was no air and the walls
seemed close. My head throbbed in my hands like dead
weight. Blood seemed to slosh around in my head. I
flopped down and had my friend press his hands into

Descent into birth

my right eye and the back of my head, where the Pain
was worst. I shuddered, quit breathing completely and
began unified S-shaped contractions. The womb
formed around me. I have felt before how the umbilicus was not pumping enough, how I tried sucking
through it and it seemed empty. I even recall trying to
breathe in the canal. But now there was just NO AIR.
My body was flailing away at this massive womb wall,
through no effort on my part: I was passing out, dying.

Birth convulsions
identical to seizures

No point *trying* to breathe. The convulsions became
progressively quicker and less synchronic. The pattern
of convulsion was identical to the descriptions of my
seizures I had pried out of witnesses over the years and
which I had experienced in feeling and in the moments
of convulsing on the sidewalk in Venice.

My friend, who has seen mine and other birth feelings before, had removed his hands from my head.

Epilepsy: prototypic
re-enactment of a
pre-birth experience

Later he would ask me whether I had been conscious
for the duration of the event. His impression was that
he'd seen a seizure. My assumption is that I passed out
in the womb. Later in life, when I'd hit a crisis, I'd feel
so hopeless I'd reproduce my whole seizure/dying
scene to the point of wriggling through the same
convulsions.

What we must understand is that the pressure that erupts so suddenly
and convulsively in the *grand mal* seizure is always there. The seizure
simply occurs at the point when the brain can no longer contain the
buildup. It is a very graphic sign that repression has failed. It is no
different quantitatively than when thoughts go "wild" from pressure in
psychosis, or when cells go "wild" from pressure in cancer. The massive
quantity of energy is the same; what differs is the form of experience into
which the energy is routed.

10

The End of the Line: Suicide as a Solution to Birth

Despair. Hopelessness. Helplessness. Doom. A bottomless feeling of "What's the use?", "What's the point?", "No way out." These are the central feelings in the urge to kill oneself. They are also the key feelings surrounding a traumatic birth. Possibly the closest most of us will come to death is when we first come to life. The experience of having come very close to death at birth may leave one with death feelings against which one fights for a lifetime. The memory of the near-death experience is an imprint just as any other memory is. It, too, can become a prototypic reaction such that thoughts of death become prepotent over constructive thoughts whenever later stress occurs.

When ideas of death habitually come into one's mind it must be assumed that the ideas reflect lower-level forces at work. Suicidal thoughts are the products of those forces, however, and not the cause. The idea of death or suicide is often a comfort because at least it offers a way out. People want to die when they see no way out, and when all else fails they can kill some of that Pain by merely thinking of death. They feel there is no way out but death because they are experiencing the original birth feeling on a completely unconscious level. In the immediacy of the situation they cannot discriminate between feelings which are from the past and those which are in the present. That is why a person may not even consider leaving his or her spouse, despite the fact that the marriage is a nightmare for both of them. Bound by the past, no alternatives can be seen in the present. Life was hell and it still is. It is not surprising that the only solution seems to be suicide—not to leave, not to change, not to create a new life for oneself—but to die. Death is a solution now because near death was the only "solution" to birth trauma. Death becomes stamped in as the answer, and given the right circumstances it becomes the only solution to life's problems. It beckons release from the Pain. The point is that first there is despair, and then there is suicidal despair. I submit that suicidal despair—despair steeped in death feelings—is most often a memory of near death.

In the following report we see how suicide became an obsession in thought and action as a "solution" to Pain laid down at birth and reinforced throughout childhood:

Prototypic trauma: immediate separation

I have just learned how important that first day of life is. My mother was sick and I was taken away from her right after birth. She also neglected me the rest of my life as well. But that first day on earth I was so alone and terrified. I needed so desperately. And then not being touched for days afterwards left me half dead. I needed so much, and no one was there so I just switched off. She never touched me later either, so I never came alive. I needed to be touched for life, but I wasn't, so I felt and acted *un*lively.

Suicide attempt: blood as Pain

I actually slashed my wrists twice. Once I did it, I thought, because I had lost my boyfriend. I looked into the mirror and saw the blood, and it felt like a heroin rush. I never felt so calm in all my life. The blood was my Pain gushing out and finally I could *see* it. And maybe, I hoped my mother would also be able to see it at last. Maybe she would finally see my agony and do something. Hold me, touch me, give me what I have always needed!

A "vacuum" at birth

Re-experiencing that first day of my life was like being in a vacuum. There were no loving hands to make me feel safe and secure. No one can imagine the panic of the newborn during those first precarious moments—especially, as in my case, if the terror causes the baby to cut off and seem unaffected.

Dream symbolism: a nightmare of falling

There was no support of me, literally, and sure enough, my lifelong nightmare has been of falling and falling. I would always have the nightmare when I was left alone to sleep, so I had to sleep with someone near me all the time. Otherwise panic would set in—that original aloneness.

Suicide: a message to Mama

I have been obsessed by death. I wanted to die instead of living half dead. When you're dead you feel nothing. Bliss. Suicide for me was bliss. I have always acted out: "Your baby is dead, Mama, look! I want you to know it, but you don't. You won't open your eyes until I'm bleeding on the floor—until you can see me lying there completely alone and half dead like I've always been. Although you never saw my blood, Mama, it was my way of showing you that you killed me."

Added trauma

Suicide as the only solution

Resolution via feeling

I've been told that I was taken out of the birth canal with forceps because I started to die during labor. To come out in that way after all the other trauma and then to be left alone was really inhuman. Those hours were a lifetime for me. What a reception into life! No wonder death felt like the only solution. Fortunately, I've gotten over the need to slash my wrists. I've felt that agony of those first moments and I don't have to act it out anymore. Now only the thoughts of death remain, but they are just thoughts—there is no force of feeling behind them.

Suicide and the Primal Prototype

The parasympath is far more prone to suicide both in thought and action than is the sympath. This is because the parasympath birth usually involves a near-death situation in which the newborn had no options or alternatives other than to bear the trauma totally. The parasympath baby had no other choice at birth than to react to the threat of death in an inward and passive way. This leads to a reflective personality state where one can only sit, wait and think about the Pain.

The sympath baby, on the other hand, began life fighting (there were options available to fight for), has become accustomed to it and as an adult will struggle and fight away from depressive or suicidal feelings. The struggle helped him survive at birth, and through that experience he has learned to run—from Pain, from suicidal thoughts, from anything that reminds him of defeat or death. He will not be actively suicidal unless all avenues of escape, all avenues of release, have been shut off: if he loses his job, his wife, his health—if there are no other possibilities in the world, then this kind of person will finally consider suicide on a conscious level—but only then.

This is not to say that the sympath personality is immune to death impulses in everyday life circumstances. The impulses are simply not

conscious. That is, the sympath may not preoccupy himself with conscious thoughts of death, but he may so preoccupy himself with work that
the work becomes a slow, unconscious act of suicide. It is interesting that
the people who literally work themselves to death even after they have
had heart attacks are the ones for whom struggle meant life and not death.
Yet in a transposition that takes place later, the unceasing struggle means
an early death, even though it originally meant survival.

Triggering and Coping with Suicidal Birth Feelings

There are two ways in which birth feelings get triggered. The first way
occurs when overwhelming events in the present leave one feeling hopeless: the loss of a long-held job, failure in school, the death of a loved one,
divorce, separation, illness, etc. These current life traumas activate
residual birth feelings so that a situation that should be viewed as difficult
or stressful is now viewed as hopeless and impossible. Instead of feeling
sad, frustrated or depressed, the person feels suicidal.

The second way in which birth feelings get triggered is through the
intentional evocation of them. When this occurs prematurely, obsessive
thoughts of suicide may result. As we shall see in the next chapter, this
often happens in rebirthing therapies in which patients are directed into
birth sequences "cold turkey." Even when the descent into consciousness
is slow and methodical, an individual touching upon birth feelings may
become depressed and not know why. Since he is not going through any
outward trauma, the feelings do not make sense and he feels overwhelmed
by them. It feels as if the Pain will never end. It is not unexpected that one
might have suicidal thoughts during these periods. Out of our Primal
patient population, 17 percent made at least one attempt at suicide before
therapy. And I would guess that almost 100 percent of our patients are
confronted with suicidal feelings at one time or another during therapy
which they don't act upon.

The closer the Pain is to consciousness, the more likely it is that the
impulse will be moved into action. With less "braking" of the impulses—
that is, with less symbolization of the Pain—the more likely it will be acted
upon by direct physical assault. That is why many patients experience
transient suicidal feelings as they approach first-line Pain. That is also why
the patient must be made aware that those feelings of doom, despair and
utter hopelessness are part of a birth feeling which is being experienced
without proper connection. Because the patient is awash in the feelings,
he needs help straightening out the past from the present if he is not to
become a danger to himself. It is at this point that the therapist must
evaluate the patient's readiness for the birth experience. Has he gotten a
good deal of childhood material out of the way? Does he have a strong

enough ego with which to integrate the experience? Or does he need more defense-bolstering? Often, we choose the third option, which is to retard the reliving for a time until we are sure the person can take it. But we also know that he may have suicidal feelings periodically until he resolves the Pain.*

Case Reports

Patient after patient has reported the feeling of death during sleep and the need to wake up to make sure they are still alive. Again we see evidence of the prepotent, internal reality: those spells of terror are simply fragments of the original experience breaking through.

One can see from this why trying to talk someone out of a suicidal impulse is not an effective approach. The system always veers toward its imprint. One may talk away, exhort away, plead away those tendencies, but the minute the exhortations stop the system veers again toward the disconnected memories of death—memories that reside in brain tissue deep down in the nervous system and have nothing to do with words or concepts.

The following report describes a patient's experience with the unexpected breakthrough of death sensations in the present and his connection of those sensations to his past. In the report we also see how it is the patient's own internal connections that bring about resolution, not the exhortations or arguments of a therapist:

Present-day trigger: crashing waves

A couple of months ago I came close to having a fatal accident. I went swimming when the waves were much bigger than usual. I decided to swim out past the breakers to where it was calmer. I did so, swam around a bit, and then turned and headed for shore. Unfortunately I didn't time it right and soon saw a huge wave not far behind me. It crashed down on me, pushed me under and left me breathless and fearful. I was not far from shore and soon felt the sand under my feet, but the swirling water was taking all my strength as I fought to get ashore. I looked around and another huge wave was almost on me. I was scared but also calculat-

Breakthrough of death sensations

ing how much strength I had left. The wave broke on me and again I was pushed under, but this time a strange feeling started to rise. I felt that death was very

---

*One of the ways we may help the person is with the use of first-line blockers—the tranquilizers that work on lower-level activation. The person must take enough of the drug to hold down the overactivation of Pain but not so much that he cannot feel. Clearly, the dosage must be determined by someone who is an expert on both the action of drugs and the "action" of Primal Pain.

close; I was weak and could not fight all this power. Surrender seemed so easy, so *right;* death seemed so welcoming and so ordinary. If I gave in, I would be dead—just another event in my life. Then I thought how ludicrous—how insane—for me to die in such circumstances, but a few yards from the shore on Venice beach.

All these thoughts took but a few seconds, after which I again fought and pushed upwards. I cried out as I surfaced so that someone nearby would see me if I were caught by another wave. Luckily I wasn't. I stumbled ashore weary, shaken, and breathless. I felt that I had been in a situation the like of which I had never experienced before, and did not wish ever to experience again. I told a few people about the incident, and then didn't think much more about it.

Continued break-through: "danger and the nearness of death"

In the next week or so I was working on roofs. On two separate occasions, as I came near the edge of the roof, I had strong sensations of danger and the near-ness of death, and again the feeling and even the desire/ temptation to surrender—to fall voluntarily to my possible death. I had not had such feelings on previous occasions when I was high up somewhere.

Some weeks later I had a session and was talking about the great pressure I felt from the present circum-stances of my life. I started to talk about the waves and soon I began crying. The therapist asked me what had made me cry, and I said, "The massive power of the waves—they are so strong and I am so weak." I cried

Second-level con-nection: pressure of waves—pressure of parents

quite a bit, and then talked about the pressure of work and felt that. I then recalled how I had felt a similar overwhelming pressure as a teenager when I realized how much I was not getting from my parents, and how much I *would not be able to get,* ever. This latter feeling was the worst—that I needed so much and couldn't get it. It felt as if I were trying to escape from my life's circumstances; there was no escape, and the pressure just pushed me down so that I could not rise up and be myself. I was surprised and glad to make the connection between the pressure of the waves and the pressure of my parents.

Beginnings of first-line connections: getting through

I also had the feeling of wanting to bash my head against the [padded] wall to get through to my mother, and I did this. The next few weeks I felt much, much stronger and more capable. Also during the next weeks the feeling (which had been occurring occasionally in the preceding months) of wanting to ram my head against the wall and just push through became stronger. The feelings were quite intense; sometimes they were just wordless feelings of anger and frustration. When I did speak, I either wanted to get through to my mother, wanted to touch her, or wanted to convince her that I was not bad.

Beginnings of specific birth connections

Now I sense a connection between the awful pressure and strength of the waves crashing down and threatening me and the intense pressure I often experience when I feel about my mother. I sense that a lot of it is linked to my birth—maybe I'm wrong—I have not gone very far into these feelings, but it seems so to me. I have a feeling that even though I fought, I felt beaten and ready to surrender. This was certainly the story the rest of my life with her. She made everything difficult, was always critical, and never gave anything.

Needed balance between first- and second-level feelings

Although the experience with the waves stirred up feelings which allowed me to make some important connections, I was swept back to very early feelings which bypassed how I felt later on in childhood. I began, when I felt bad, to jump back to this earliest period of my life and have first-line feelings, without, however, fully connecting. It just felt good to have the feelings. I got away from feeling badly. Now, though, I am trying to verbalize the feelings and thereby make more connections. This is working well, and I am better able to integrate the new feelings.

As with all Primal imprints, the death imprint has different unconscious meanings for different patients. It can mean escape, surrender, victory, defeat, weakness, strength and so on. It all depends upon the total context—the total life history.

One man had the insight after his birth Primal that trying to kill himself was really an attempt to save his own life. He wanted to come near death, make that last desperate telephone call for a friend to save him, and be saved—just as it had happened at birth. We have found that people who had been asphyxiated by drugs at birth often have that same impulse to take massive amounts of asphyxiating drugs and then make that final call to be saved.

Another patient came out of his birth Primal with the insight that suicide was his means of conquering death. He had always had an inner feeling of foreboding and doom, and the thought of suicide was his self-assurance that he could control the ultimate doom: "Death is not going to come and get me—*I'm* going to get it!" It was his way of conquering the helplessness of the agonies around birth.

Still another patient felt the idea of suicide made her strong: she could be active about death instead of being passively confronted with its terror. It seems that for many people, suicide is a major defense against that feeling of Primal helplessness that feels so catastrophic that even death is better.

I have pointed out previously that the baby's responses to the birth trauma are also imprinted as prototypic patterns. One interesting aspect of the near-death imprint is that the later tool of suicide is often closely related to the original kind of near-death experience. A patient who relived being strangled on the cord had always had the impulse to hang herself when she thought of suicide. Another patient who had been butted up against the pubic arch during birth had the impulse to kill himself with a blast of dynamite, and indeed he even stored dynamite in his garage for that fateful day. The image in his mind was to hold a stick of dynamite to his ears in order to blow the pressure out of his head. What he really wanted was to get rid of that catastrophic pressure at birth.

Dynamite was the tool of choice for yet another patient (from Switzerland), but for an entirely different reason. In a personal letter to me he explained:

Tool of choice for suicide: dynamite

Remember in Champery when we were talking about why people would use certain methods to kill themselves? I said that if I ever wanted to kill myself I would only do it with a pack of dynamite—by blowing out my brains. You asked me if I knew why, and I said I didn't. Well, I know now.

Suicidal impulses

The other day I felt so low and then it occurred to me that I had my gun just standing there in the corner of my room . . . I saw myself taking my gun, going to the roof of the apartment building, and shooting myself in the throat. All of this was very clear. I saw the moment when I pulled the trigger and the split second after when I realized (and *felt*) that this is it: *I am dying.*

Primal connection

Then I realized, that's it! That's why I want to use dynamite—the split second. With dynamite, there is not even a split second. The moment it goes off, your brain is disintegrated. There's no possibility that I might feel, even for a split second, "I am dying."

That's the point! I don't want to feel: DYING. My real, original self doesn't want to die; I just don't want to feel the agony of my tremendous loneliness and hopelessness.

Birth trauma

We also talked about "commensuration." I don't know when I was dying as a child, except that my parents told me that as a baby the umbilical cord had wrapped around my neck three times, and with three separate knots to boot. They assured me, though, that I was not born blue, and that my birth "was an easy one"!

Another patient who had a compulsive drive left in him from being driven out of the birth canal said that he thought he would work himself to death. One Scandinavian patient had the impulse to go down by a lake and freeze herself quietly and effortlessly. In her birth Primal she reexperienced the horrible exhaustion she felt from trying to get born. The effort at birth had been imprinted, and after that everything became too much for her. To counter that feeling she wanted to just fade away—to simply stop feeling all that exhaustion. She didn't want any work left in her life—not even the work of trying to kill herself.

Another patient wanted to take pills to kill herself—the pills could give her the rationale for feeling so utterly exhausted. One man who felt himself aspirating fluids and drowning at birth had the impulse to swim out to sea so far that he could not get back—and thus die by drowning. The idea of drowning was further attractive to him because he did not want his body to be found. He discovered the reason for this was that his body had been in such Pain after birth that he would rather not have any body at all. That way he would not suffer. And a woman who had always been called "pushy" relived pushing to get out of the birth canal; she always had the feeling when on a balcony that she would be pushed off, to her death.

Conclusions

The major way people choose to attempt suicide is with painkillers. This is not by accident. People are trying to kill the Pain, but by one means or another happen to kill themselves as well. Most of the suicide patients we have treated have said that if they could have killed the Pain, they would not have needed to try to kill themselves. It just so happened that their Pain and their selves were inextricably joined.

We have found that deep, first-line Primals make a significant difference in the resolution of those suicidal impulses. Those who relive the death experience in and around birth seem to finally resolve that fixation on death and suicide. What is clear here is that feeling horrendous Pain is not the real danger, as some claim. On the contrary, not feeling it leaves one in danger of ever-present death and doom feelings.

Childhood trauma naturally plays a significant role in later suicidal impulses, and those impulses are attenuated by the resolution of childhood Pain. But it seems that full resolution of the tendencies is almost always linked to first-line forces—for it is those forces that predispose and presensitize one to suicidal impulses in the first place.

It may seem odd that those few minutes around birth can determine whether or not one will consider suicide as a serious alternative at a later age, but the Primal evidence is convincing that this is the case. Attempts at suicide are attempts of the system to go back and get close to that death feeling. It's a way of recovering that original physiological experience in which the baby first came close to death in order to get into life.

What this means is that suicide is really an attempt at healing. It is really an attempt to conquer death. It is, ultimately, a testimony to the power of Primal Pain: one would rather be dead than feel it. And not so accidentally, feeling the early death allows us to leave those suicidal feelings behind, forever.

IV: The Resolution of Birth Trauma

11

Cast for Life: The Imprint of Events Around Birth

Before we can understand the process by which the birth trauma is resolved, we first have to understand the way in which the brain is organized to engrave those events. Let us take a brief, nontechnical look at the structure of the brain so that we can better understand how and where Primal Pain is laid down.

The brain is organized in three concentric spheres or zones: inner, middle and outer. Each sphere is made up of specific sets of nerve networks which have their own consciousness and memory storehouse. Each is responsible for a different area of functioning.

The inner zone of the brain is what I call the first level of consciousness; it is the innermost brain and its job is to mediate all visceral functioning. Pains which occur before, during and for several months after birth are first-line Pains; they occurred at the time the first level of consciousness was developing.

The middle zone of the brain forms the second level of consciousness and is the level that mediates and processes feelings and emotions. Second-line Pains are those which occurred after the age of about one year when the second level began its development. Childhood emotional traumas are stored here.

The outer mantle of the brain forms the third level of consciousness, and is the last level to develop. This is the area of the "intellect" where first- and second-line events are given meaning through language and symbolization. Third-line Pains begin at about the age of six and are the least traumatic to process.

Birth Trauma and the First Level of Consciousness

In order to understand the effects of birth trauma on the newborn, we have to take a closer look at the first level of consciousness, for that is the only level that is adequately developed at the time of birth.

The first level of consciousness controls visceral functioning and involves the portion of the brain that mediates responses in the mid-line of the body: the heart, respiratory muscles, bladder, stomach, blood-forming organs and hormonal regulation. Anything which affects the first level will affect those functions. The responses, whether of the stomach, lungs, heart or colon, will be registered with a permanence and durability greater than all subsequently learned behaviors. We react with our physical systems before we can scream, scream before we can communicate with sounds, communicate with sounds before we speak words and speak words before we know their meaning. Each function is dependent on the development of the nervous sytem. The most primitive reactions deal with the ancient mid-line of the central nervous system which controls sucking, swallowing, gagging, choking, breathing, gasping, digesting, eliminating and crying. Dislocations occurring during the development of the mid-line system can produce later anorexia, asthma, colitis, compulsive vomiting and ulcers. Any painful event occurring before and around birth will be reacted to in terms of the system which is adequate and functioning at the time.

The newborn and the fetus can respond to threat only with visceral functions. The heart can speed up, blood pressure rise, breathing become faster and stronger, gastric secretions multiply and so on. All of these bodily reactions are behaviors, though they are physical rather than verbal responses.

First-line traumatic pressure usually manifests itself in hyperactivity and hypermotility of the baby; he is more active, has highly irregular sleep patterns and spits up constantly. Thirty years later this very same energy source will result in insomnia, obsessions, compulsions and overwork. It is the force that makes someone drink or smoke or gamble incessantly. Any impulse will do, since drinking and other "impulsive" behavior is no more than the conversion of those early electrical *impulses* into psychologic behavior. The behavior is compelling because these impulses pre-date psychologic inhibition of a developed cortex by years.

Discharging Primal Pain

It is the viscera and deep inner organ systems of the first level of consciousness which act to generate and increase the energy output of the organism. This is in contradistinction to the other levels of consciousness, which serve to utilize and therefore decrease energy states. The second level, which controls body wall action, performs work which expends energy, and the third level, which controls mentation, also utilizes energy for its work.

What this all means is that infant Pains which affect the first level produce a chronic hyperenergetic and hypermetabolic system. The first level, which controls and regulates metabolism, must actually overwork in order to process the Pain. Thus it is pain and not necessarily genes that initiates a hyperactive metabolism. It then becomes the lifelong job of the other two levels to discharge that excess energy in one way or another.

Each level discharges excess Primal energy in order of its development. Early on, when the system is not fully developed, the discharge is almost totally visceral (first level); as physical and muscle coordination and emotional expression develop, the energy can flow into body wall or muscle release (second level) where we can become tense physically so that the muscles are tensed up; and finally, when the neocortex (third level) is fully developed, ideas can absorb and discharge the energy.

In adulthood, energy release travels the same routes; first, the body will handle a current trauma viscerally, then in terms of the muscle system and finally, when those two systems are inadequate, ideas will take over. Each succeeding level acts as a barrier of defense for the next; if there is first-line pushing, the second level will try to take care of it and there will be emotional outbursts, tantrums or nightmares. Later there are racing thoughts. It is an upward-moving succession. The intellectual whose life is in his head can often develop coherent systems of thought and cover well the first-line Pain—so well that he is forever unaware of the drive behind his intellectuality. Those who are not mind-oriented and who are exceptionally tense physically can fall back on the body for discharge of energy—compulsive marathon running might be an example.

So, we have a birth trauma blocked through repression, which then sets up an excess of energy in the baby's system. This energy is progressively channeled into the viscera and later will be called anxiety; funneled into the muscle systems and called tension; and eventually converted into ideas, which become the obsessive-compulsive thoughts of the neurotic. These three modes of handling the same Pain are not different diseases; they are simply different manifestations of the same disease. As the human being evolved he developed different capacities to handle adversity. The three levels express man's evolution. He has become more sophisticated in dealing with his world. Under enough pressure he can now become "psychologically" ill.

Of course, second- and third-line traumas will exacerbate the problem. They will add to the general load of Pain. But these levels of Pain are more accessible. Because they have occurred later in the brain's development and do not deal with birth, the charge value of the Pain is usually not life and death, and is therefore far less than first-line Pains. Losing a job can be excruciating but it can never be as painful as being sent to boarding school at the age of six. Being sent to boarding school, while often horrific, is usually never as traumatic in terms of the Pain and tension laid down in the system as almost dying by being strangled on the cord at birth. One reason is simply that the brain provides more wherewithal to handle trauma as it develops. It permits more response alternatives. The adult can complain to his wife or she to her husband. She can smoke, drink, take tranquilizers or get on the phone. The child can do a lot more than the infant who can do absolutely nothing but bear the Pain. The infant has one alternative. Either feel the Pain or repress it. In another strange dialectic, if he represses, he must go on feeling it. That is, he must go on experiencing it unconsciously.

The traumas which occur on any level of consciousness remain in the system as reverberating circuits of Pain. These circuits of Pain galvanize the body against danger—the danger of consciousness. First-line Pain accomplishes this by stimulating the output of chemical pain-blunters known as endorphine. Usually, the output is commensurate with the amount of Pain involved. First-line Pains cause the production of morphine-like substances which can be one thousand times more powerful than commercially prepared morphine. When the chronic Pain is too great, however, endorphine production is inadequate to the task; shattering Pain can then reach consciousness prematurely and insanity or death can result. Thus, the human system is designed to maintain unconsciousness (by imprinting the Pain rather than feeling it consciously) in order to preserve its integrity.

Imprinting

There are three critical factors involved in the imprinting of early trauma: input (or quantity), response (or quality) and timing. All three factors converge to imprint or encode Primal Pain as a physical reality in our bodies.

Input and Response

The imprint of the birth trauma involves two forms of memory: the memory of the event itself, the context and its sensations; and the memory of the quantity of Pain involved. These two memories occupy different neural circuits. Excessive input is shunted into those parts of the brain genetically designed to deal with overload. Thus, the information is *not* relayed via a relay station (known as the thalamus) to the cortex where it could become conscious. Rather, it is channeled into a kind of reservoir and then relayed to parts of the brain that could respond appropriately. This usually involves the limbic system and the alerting (reticular) system, which together mobilize the body. The energy reverberates within the limbic system for a lifetime. Thus, the "mind" doesn't ever know what is going on down below, but the body does, and it responds appropriately. We become "souped up" and don't know why.

Whenever a Pain is engraved into the nervous system, the response to that Pain is also stamped in. Thus, prenatal and natal traumas have both a quantitative and qualitative effect. There is the input or overload (quantity) of Pain which is registered and processed on lower levels of the brain; and a registration of the response to that input (quality) which becomes fixed and determines the type of behavior later on. The Pain and the response are a unity which becomes prototypic so that under any later stress the original response pattern is automatically triggered.

The memory of the input of Pain is in the form of residual tension or energy which has a certain valence and reverberates throughout the body to be absorbed by one system or another: be it the blood, muscles or the brain. This process can be measured: an electromyograph will show undue muscle tension and a blood pressure test will show elevated pressure.

The amount of compounded energy (quantity) determines the strength and tenacity in the later neurotic response, while the kind of situation and response (quality) shapes the direction the behavior will take. Massive drugs to the mother (the input) which almost killed the fetus will stamp in a passivity and lethargy (the response) for a lifetime. A long hard labor (the input) in which the newborn had to fight tenaciously for its life will stamp in aggressiveness and drive (the response) for a lifetime. The input and the response are twin aspects of the imprinted trauma, and we shall see later how both aspects must be relived in the way they were engraved in order to release the effects of that trauma.

Timing

Timing of the input is critical in determining the degree of trauma. A particular input of Pain during the time when the nervous system and its hormones are just being organized is going to have a much more devastating effect than that same input months later. The earlier the trauma the greater the effect on later function and development (and the more difficult to undo). Being left alone for an hour in a hospital basinette (the input) immediately after birth (timing) can be much more traumatic to the infant's system (the response) than being left alone for an hour at the age of three months.

The Encoding Process

The imprint of the birth trauma will be encoded by those parts of the nervous sytem sufficiently developed to record the shock. One of the ways to tell which structures are developed is by observing the degree of myelination: myelin is a fatty sheath which covers the nerve fibers and signals a readiness for operation. The imprint will be laid down throughout the nervous system itself and in the various key structures that handle sensory input.

The nervous system at birth records pain, pressure, gravity, rotation, smell, temperature, touch, and some vision and hearing. The sensory roots, acoustic nerves and optic radiations have all started myelination at birth. Skin movement information is already well developed before birth.

These sensory impressions are not experienced by the baby in terms of ideas and concepts but in terms of pure sensation. An adult reliving his birth in the delivery room may see the people, react to the light, see steel objects, feel the pressure and then, with his late-developed cortex, realize in the Primal that it is part of the delivery scene he has been reexperiencing. This is the interface between newborn sensations and adult perceptions, and it permits integration and understanding of disparate sensations which occurred early on when the nervous system was not fully developed.

The sensations that the baby registers will be fixed in the system though in a disconnected way, so that under later stress the adult will feel a certain pain in the back or neck, a pressured feeling in the head or in a particular joint or muscle group—but will have no idea of any specific cause. The adult's nightmares will also register these sensations, and the second and third levels of consciousness will weave a story around them to make them both symbolic and logical. The sensations may, as we shall see later, form the stuff of epileptic seizures or even the material for psychotic hallucinations.

Research on Pain

Confirmation of the fact that Pain is literally an engraved process is demonstrated by the work of Morpugo and Spinelli.* They discovered

---

*C. B. Morpugo, and D. W. Spinelli, "The Plasticity of Pain Perception," *Brain Theory Newsletter,* Volume 2, No. 1, October 1976, p. 15.

that the anatomic areas of the imprint in the brain become larger with more pain: pain takes up a larger brain surface and may even dominate most brain functioning. New neutral brain circuits are engraved by the ongoing painful experience so that "more and more of the neuromachinery is prepared to recognize as painful stimuli that which would go completely unnoticed in a normal subject."

What this means is that the originally uncommitted neurons become part of the neuromachinery of Pain so that there is a "filter" of Pain through which we begin to view the world. That filter of Pain shapes our perceptions, attitudes, beliefs and gives meaning to outside events. More and more of the brain is converted to the Pain system and less is left to do the real work of solving everyday problems of life. The brain itself is being warped and distorted so that it no longer functions normally. There is change in the frequency and amplitude of the brainwaves, and a change in the relationship between the right and left hemispheres of the brain. When the early traumas are relived, these relationships are righted again. These changes can be and have been measured by neuroscientists.*

Another implication of Morpugo and Spinelli's research is that the threshold for reacting to pain is lowered. This means that even a very minor stress can evoke a traumatic response. For example, the imprint leading toward an asthmatic attack could be triggered by a rude waiter; or the imprint for an epileptic attack could be set off by a clap of the hands or a loud shout.

The research shows that early Painful experiences are physically larger than neutral experiences, actually change the structure of the brain and alter our very perception of reality. The characteristics of even single neurons in the brain depend on the nature of our early experience; and the way the brain as a whole works later in life is a product of those very early shaping experiences. Morpugo and Spinelli state that "the neurocircuits that perceive pain are *themselves* structured, both in quality and number, by past experience." As I said in *Prisoners of Pain:*

> The imprint of Pain fixes a permanent imbalance in brain biochemistry—an imbalance that arises to meet early life stress. . . . The lopsided biochemical arrangement continues throughout life and forces the person to construct a neurotic environment so as to remain in synch with his altered system. For example, his personal tempo is speeded up to meet an activated brain. Thus, an environment constructs a new brain system which produces a new environment. (pp. 117–18)

*Hoffman, Eric, University of Denmark, "Report on the Hemisphere Changes in Patients Undergoing Psychotherapy," 1980, in association with Professor Leonid Goldstein, Rutgers University.

I believe that under the impact of the birth trauma the vulnerable cells may have to recruit a great number of "neutral" neurons to absorb the insult. The trauma, then, affects an inordinate amount of brain space and is another way that it comes to dominate our behavior. The recruited neurons form a barrier surrounding this imprint, insuring that it does not reach consciousness. If this did not happen—if there were not gates that operate in the brain to keep us repressed and unconscious—the newborn, the infant and the child would be awash in catastrophic Pain which could lead easily to either total fragmentation or death.

The work of E. Roy John, an important investigator from New York Medical College in the field of neurophysiology, is also instructive concerning imprints. He put animals in traumatic situations and conditioned (paired) a neutral stimulus such as a buzzer to the trauma. Later just the sound of the buzzer evoked a facsimile of the early trauma in the brainwave patterns of the animals. In short, the animals responded to their imprinted history rather than to current reality. This indicates how previously stored memories, when triggered, direct responses that have little to do with what is going on in the present. Being held back from what one wants to do can produce a rage in a person who has a stored memory of being held back by a nurse at birth. The latent rage reaction is part of that old imprint. Again in *Prisoners of Pain* I wrote:

> The trauma is stamped in so that an exact duplicate of that original event lives on in the brain. The body and brain then react "as if" the original situation were always there and the biochemical imbalance is maintained. (pp. 117–18)

But the imprint is not just in the brain. It is coded in just about every cell of the body. So, for example, cells genetically programmed to mediate feelings become altered to mediate repression. New nerve pathways, rerouted ones, are utilized to shunt the Pain message away from centers that are overloaded, and cells change in their permeability, firing patterns and reactivity. These processes are how the memory is fixed. The genetic program has been aborted. Under the blitz of Pain the DNA molecule which transmits the genetic code may become a new template so that the cell utilizes a different code. Pain has indeed "changed the rules."

There is another way we know about imprinting. In certain brain diseases with extensive cortical damage there often is a "release" phenomenon which immediately plunges the person into the fetal birth position. It is one more way we know how low in the system these birth events are coded. To put it another way, the infant inside of us is always waiting to get out and this infant is held down by the cortex. When this inhibition is interfered with, what we see again are the birth movements.

The writhing and paralysis of the hands and wrists indicate again what a primitive nervous system we are dealing with. The mid-line abdominal muscles working in a kind of sine wave rhythm in conjunction with the para-spinal muscles (the muscles to the right and left of the spinal column) produce the salamander movements that we see in the newborn—the same movements that we see in the fish and the snake. All of this is under the mid-line nervous system control which is the innermost interior portion of the brain, the portion which is fully organized even before birth. The fact that higher functions do not work during the birth sequence tells us what kind of nerve tissue we are dealing with.

The brain must rely for its survival on its most ancient structures when, for one reason or another, its most recently acquired structures cannot function. In the case of massive trauma, the cortex is overwhelmed and cannot do its job. In Primal Therapy we have found ways to temporarily impair the functioning of the cortex to achieve the "release" phenomenon. It is then that one sees the infantile posturing, the baby crying or infantile grunts, the abnormal head and hand postures. That release behavior represents a combination of memory together with a "peeling back" of higher levels of neurologic functioning. It must be emphasized that one gets this primitive reaction whether the neocortex is knocked out physically or psychologically. The release is due to the *imprint* and not to the cause of the impairment. There is, in short, an intrinsic infantile organization and through that organization the imprint is released. It is not just a memory; it is a group of behaviors which occur when a certain level of brain organization is utilized. This is a rather complex but important point: the imprint is released once the upper layers of consciousness are peeled away, allowing the lower organization to behave on its own terms.

At the beginning of a Primal experience there is a tremendous input of electrical energy from inside which blocks the cortex from acting, thus automatically causing the body to retreat to the next level down.

There is in the brain a structure called the hippocampus which acts as an inventory for all of these Pains and provides access to these memories. One can actually slice away this library of "file cards" through surgical procedures and abolish those early memories. Further, the memories are laid down sequentially in the hippocampal structure from the earliest memories to the later ones. This index system allows one to have access to memories that are recorded all over the brain in holographic fashion so that almost any aspect or any area of the memory can, in what is known as "reminiscence," reactivate the entire memory sequence. Thus, in Primal Therapy, a smell of ether or the sight of white gowns or whatever other isolated sensory stimulus is pertinent may reactivate an entire early sequence of the newborn's experiences of the surgery room.

Recently there was a series of hypnotic experiments with young chil-

dren in which they were able to describe their births in details consistent
with their official birth records and with the memories of their parents.
These findings were reported both by David Chamberlain at the American
Society of Clinical Hypnosis Meetings in 1980, and by David Cheek, a San
Francisco obstetrician and well-known researcher in hypnosis.

Chamberlain said that "birth memories may provide a breakthrough to
understand or help complete a picture from around other efforts that have
been faithfully gathered." He documented one hundred cases of pur-
ported birth or womb memories and concluded that the "usual rituals of
obstetricians are in urgent need of humanization."* Chamberlain emphasized that birth memories are real and true.

Clearly, the memory of birth persists and is retrievable. The children in
the above experiments recalled events that occurred at their births even
though they had no words or concepts to describe these events at the time
they happened. As newborns, they saw bright lights, shining objects,
white gowns and surgical masks—but only as wordless impressions. It is
only later, with the development of the cortex, that they were able to put
words to all the disparate impressions and come up with a single picture of
what occurred.

The point that I wish to make here is that the entire *experience* of the
trauma also lives on and has an effect on the system. The memory of
suffering operates on a different level of consciousness than the memory
of the scene itself. Thus it is possible for someone to easily recall a
traumatic childhood event, but the recollection is a totally neutral one
because the suffering component is still repressed. It is the suffering
component of the memory that remains unresolved, and it is the suffering
component of the memory that eventually must be retrieved for final
resolution of the imprint.

The registration of the imprint and the quantity of its energy or affect is
determined by the amount of threat to the life system of the organism. The
greater the threat, the deeper the Pain and the more widespread and
deeper the imprint. This kind of imprint is graphically illustrated in the
clinical work of our staff neurologist. The following example brings out the
point.

A meter reader for a gas company was attacked during his rounds by a
dog that grabbed him by the abdominal muscles and would not let go. The
man knocked the dog almost unconscious with a stick and as he began to
recover, the dog attacked again, grabbing his thigh. No matter how much
the dog was beaten he would not let go, and the man's thigh was ripped to
shreds. The man realized that his life was at stake and if he didn't do
something soon he would die. He managed to fall on the dog, crushing it.

---

*From *Brain/Mind Bulletin,* January 20, 1981, Vol. 6, No. 4, p. 2.

This was an imprint and such a strong one that whenever the man later closed his eyes, he saw the dog attacking him and had all of the anxiety and fright appropriate to that experience. He was awakened many times during the night with exactly the same nightmare of that dog hanging on viciously to his thigh. It was a kind of movie "cut print" in which the event is registered for all time. One again can see here how a massive trauma at birth can also produce the kind of flashback phenomenon with recurring nightmares, poor sleep and so on. That memory is a reverberating circuit.

The birth imprint leaves a different kind of sequelae—not visual scenes but "feelings." A small or crowded elevator, for example, can reawaken the birth experience with its feeling of claustrophobia. This early *connected* fear becomes amorphous anxiety later on when a person rides in an elevator; the connection to its roots has been lost. After reconnection, anxiety becomes fear and terror related to the original specific trauma.*

It would take something like an encounter with a mad dog to come close to the imprint of birth in severity. In all of these situations the energy is locked in the limbic system which then acts as a capacitor, discharging energy in a variety of ways—whether it be via tics, crying jags, screaming, temper tantrums, epilepsy or stuttering. These are the ways the limbic capacitor unloads part of its burden so that the organism can maintain some kind of balance and stability.

Some new research has shown that the closer one goes along the neural pathways toward the limbic system, the greater the number of opiate receptors. These opiate receptors are equipped to handle repression biochemically and they indicate how gating or blocking increases as one approaches the limbic system. Thus, this system seems to be designed to handle overload. The closer one gets to overload the more necessary it is to gate and repress. The limbic system must protect the organism against catastrophic Pain so that it will not go into shock, death or chronic seizures.

Effects of the Imprint

Because the imprint of trauma involves a complete system, first-line Pains distort or impair many functions. Thus we have seen already how there can be chronic stomach distress, for example, or rapid heartbeat, high blood pressure or slightly elevated body temperature. There may be

*There is new evidence indicating that nerve cells secrete a substance which determines which other nerve cells will connect with them. The identity of the material is as yet unknown but the evidence for its existence is firm. In the disconnection process between feelings and its conscious counterpart, certain neural circuits can no longer "recognize" each other. In reconnection the brain's biochemistry is normalized so that the nerve projections find each other at long last, completing its circuit as originally intended. This is analogous to the recognition of an antigen by a specific antibody in the immune reaction.

hormone distortions leading to diseases such as hypoglycemia and diabetes. In short, all kinds of physical afflictions can have their roots in early trauma. The dislocations of function and the subsequent afflictions are part of the memory of the trauma. The afflictions are entwined with the imprint as a single response unit. Chronic hypersecretions of stomach acids leading to ulcers are part of an imprinted memory circuit. Constriction of the bronchioles leading to asthma is another example.

This means that "memory" is not just something we think about and recall. Bodily memory is always there, reminding us that something terrible happened of which we are not aware. The affliction is now part of the memory. This point must be kept in mind when we consider resolution; for we need to go back and reexperience all of the memory in a trauma, and that includes hypersecretions. Since the memory is psychobiologic, the resolution by reexperience must be psychobiologic. Mere psychotherapy is not enough. Because biologic processes reflect that imprint, there is a change in the relationship of the various stress hormones; there is an alteration of the sex hormones, a continued constriction of various blood vessels and a permanent but slight increase in all vital functions such as body temperature, blood pressure and pulse.

The imprint is "held" by these biochemical and neurophysiologic changes. It is so difficult to root out precisely because it is a memory of an adaptation. And the body is reluctant to give up its life-saving memories.

The effect of imprinted but inaccessible memory is that personality development must form around the imprint. Blocked feelings then direct development. Those feelings are not utilized for one's maturation. Major segments of the brain are "off limits" and consciousness must struggle along without the help of all its potential faculties.

The fact that neurons and biochemistry are conditioned very early in life means that one sees the world thereafter through the screen of one's history. Perception of reality is circumscribed by those transmuted neurons from birth onward. What the neurotic then sees is old meanings in new situations. He is always in the right feeling but in the wrong context. That is the meaning of neurosis.

A neurotic person, in order to remain in synch with the imprinted imbalance, creates an environment that approximates the early stress situation. For example, struggling to get out of the womb may create the kind of person who creates many, many struggles in his life. A person who never finished the birth process properly may have many beginnings, many projects left undone. Clearly, the therapeutic focus must be on the brain imprint which holds the neurotic imbalance steady. Resolving its force changes the inner environment so that the brain can finally right itself. As less and less cortex becomes involved in Pain, defenses diminish, the mind clears, perception is lucid and one sees the world as it is.

Indeed, being "open-minded" is a biologic state, not just an attitude or a value.

12
Illusion vs. Reality: Rebirthing vs. Reliving

Going back and undoing history is an amazing concept. But history isn't undone in a few minutes or even a few weeks, and it cannot be undone in any way different from how it was laid down in the first place. No gimmick, technique, machine or drug can alter that history, because events stored biologically can only be undone by the same biologic process that imprinted them in the first place.

In reliving the birth trauma, the person dips into an unconscious that holds many secrets of his life. It is not the Freudian unconscious that refuses to yield up its libidinous mysteries; rather it is a friendly unconscious that will tell us everything we ever wanted to know. It is gentle in all aspects and tells us only when we are ready to hear. It will hold the rest in store, releasing the secrets like a good friend—not so quickly that we might be overwhelmed, but soon enough to keep us interested.

The experience at the beginning of life tells us so much about the rest of it that we can only be in awe of such precise and sweeping information; information conveyed not by words but by the body which speaks a language all its own. Indeed, the body is talking all of the time in its own way: it says "I'm under pressure" in its hypertension and migraines; it says "I am suffering" in its ulcers, colitis and asthma; it says "I am fearful" in its phobias and paranoia; it says "I am trapped" in its compulsions and obsessions; it says "Pain is killing me" in its cardiac attacks, suicidal depressions and catastrophic diseases. The miracle of it all is that the exact picture of the original, traumatic birth scene is held in storage. It is the exact birth scene which, when repressed, results in all the ailments, fears and illnesses. But the birth picture must be decoded from all its various sensation points which when put together form a coherent imprint of the total experience undergone decades before. That "decoding" process cannot be predicted or prescribed, for the elements of each person's birth trauma are unique. The exact constellation of sensations that eventually cohere into a total reexperience for the person is his and his alone. No other pattern would "fit" his internal reality. Like the fingerprint, the individual's birth trauma cannot be duplicated.

Sensations are primary in the birth trauma. They are the language appropriate to the time-period being relived. No words occur during a birth Primal and no words can really describe it. As adults, we must come to grips with the fact that clarity does not always mean words. Perhaps the clearest perceptions we have (outside of Primals) are in our dreams; the colors, sights and sounds of the dream images have a freshness, a vividness, an intensity that we cannot duplicate in waking life. That same kind of clarity exists on a different level of consciousness during the birth experience. There is a clarity of sensation that even later images cannot match, for sensation is the most direct, immediate and physical aspect of the experience. The sensation of emptiness just after birth when removed from one's mother is a powerful input that is felt later on as a kind of Primal emptiness in one's life. To be saturated with this wordless sensation during a Primal is precisely (and paradoxically) what triggers the flood of insights that produce understanding, clarity, consciousness.

One has to take into consideration the neurology of Pain and the evolution of the brain when working the birth trauma. Any approach to this intense experience must not try to defy this evolution for the sake of dramatic happenings. It is a serious business, and no less than the integrity of the human mind is at stake. The reexperience of that trauma is like unwinding a tape recording of an event: it always rewinds to zero and starts again. As the sequence of birth is run off over months, the zero point is moved ahead so that each Primal begins where the last one left off. The body always seems to know just where that point is.

For more than a decade we have been accumulating validating evidence for both the Primal and the original trauma, but anyone who has had the experience doesn't require the evidence—it is within them. The importance of the research and the corroborating evidence is to place the birth trauma and the birth Primal within a neurologic context so that: (1) it is understandable in terms of neuroanatomy and neurophysiology; (2) we begin to have an understanding of the deepest origins of neurosis and of neurotic behavioral traits; (3) we can begin to quantify the amount of residual tension laid down by it and to correlate this tension with later personality development; (4) we can discover a means by which neurosis and psychosis can be reversed through the undoing of this original trauma; and (5) we can ensure that the birth Primal is neither a forced nor suggested experience, but rather flows directly out of neurologic reactivity.

The Primal theory about birth trauma is in accord with what is now known in neurology. Primal theory explains how Pains are laid down on the various levels of consciousness within the developing nervous system.

In terms of the traumas imprinted, Primal Therapy works with this evolution in reverse: that is, we work with the final representations of the birth trauma first—the outer brain and its cognitions; then with the middle, feeling brain, and ultimately with the inner brain where the Painful sensations of birth are to be found.

Our extensive research into the birth trauma has taught us several important things. First, that memories are concrete realities, stored and awaiting access to consciousness, for how else can we explain why a patient lying quietly on the floor in a totally non-threatening environment would show significantly mobilized system and brain functioning merely as a result of a painful or traumatic memory? Second, we observed that the closer the memory of the traumatic event came to consciousness the higher the vital signs and brain wave amplitudes became. Third, the higher the valence of Pain from the original experience the greater the increase in all of these indices. Fourth, the Pain was directly related to brain wave amplitude and vital sign functioning, as indicated by the lowering of these indices with the resolution of the Pain, both in the acute phase of a Primal and permanently over time. (This means that birth Primals resulted in qualitative changes in physiology that endured.) And fifth, the changes were correlated with other significant changes in the biochemistry of the person, including a normalization of the levels of stress, growth and sex hormones. To summarize all this: we found that the amount of dislocation of function on any level of consciousness depended on the degree of Pain, and that the greatest Pain measured by our instruments was that of birth.

The Rebirthing "Industry"

Ever since I wrote of the possibilities of reliving birth many years ago, a whole "rebirthing" industry has sprung up. I want to discuss the problems with this and its dangers. As with everything else a little bit of knowledge is dangerous; in the case of rebirthing exceptionally so. Taking any one aspect of the Primal process and building a system around it is unwise. Neurosis is built out of a lifetime of Pains. They must all be taken into consideration.

Because birth Pains are found in the innermost depths of the nervous system, they must be reexperienced at the end of a systematic continuum, not at the beginning. That does not mean it isn't possible to get someone into a birth Primal very quickly, because it is. But the results are almost always deleterious; and the frightening part of it is that both rebirthing therapists and patients are often unaware of, or choose to ignore, these effects.

On theoretical grounds alone it should be clear that in reversing neurosis one must deal with the most recent, less severe Pains, working methodically toward the deeper, highly charged ones. This is in accord with how the brain is developed. The greater intensity of the deeper Pains has been measured. As I have noted, we have also seen what happens when patients get to very early trauma too soon in their therapy. A degree of disconnection and disintegration occurs. When that happens special measures should be taken to see that it does not go on. It is very easy for a groove to develop between third- and first-line Pain, bypassing the second level so that baby reactions are used as a defense against really feeling the connecting Pains of later childhood. Thus, all the thrashing, screaming and writhing can look like a real birth Primal when in reality it has become just one more defense against feeling. In short, it is one more form of acting out for a neurotic patient anxious to do something magical to resolve his neurosis. Because he is dealing with a highly charged Pain, and because he has not felt enough on the higher levels, he cannot have a fully integrated, connected feeling. The result is another overload and symbolization; but it is the kind of symbolization that sometimes looks deceptively connected.

One patient wrote:

> The first times I cried like a baby were early on in my therapy. My therapist sometimes took a long time to come to me in group, and I would cry about needing him and then drop into hard baby crying. I used to discount these experiences because they seemed disconnected; I shied away from the "baby place" because I felt a danger of circumventing my mass of childhood Pain.
>
> After about a year of therapy, however, my Primals started to connect more satisfactorily to my birth and baby material. Whatever the feeling was that I was experiencing—needing Daddy, needing Mommy, "Help me," "Love me," etc.—there would be a point when I could just drop back and baby-cry. I also started to feel real relief at this point after Primalling.

There are many varieties of rebirthers, but the best known begin with a swimming pool or tub heated to 100 degrees or more. The patient is stripped and placed either floating on the water or immersed in it, sometimes with snorkel and nose clips, until panic seizes him. This is done on the first day, indeed the first hour. The patient is then encouraged to get in touch with his birth feelings. Some begin flailing around as if in birth feelings and some do touch on the periphery of birth and experience many of the sensations that someone reexperiencing Primal Pain would—bodily tension, inability to breathe, choking and gagging, the eruption of phlegm and so on.

One variation is to have prospective patients (who usually do not undergo any preselection to rule out serious pathology) read a story about birth. This is to get them into a proper frame of mind for the birth experience. The aim, one group claims, is to reactivate the birth trauma. The patients then select a number in which they will take their turn getting into birth. They then lie back and try to let birth take over. Obviously, many people cannot do it. But others can; and those are the very ones who should not. If they are that close to real birth feelings, their defense system is too shaky. They need anything but a shattering experience; particularly since most are only indulging in a weekend experience and not undergoing systematic therapy where there is careful follow-up.

Many of the rebirthers use the breathing techniques first described in *The Primal Scream*. They get the patient to breathe more and more deeply until he loses control of his body and ostensibly gets into birth. We rarely use those techniques anymore precisely because they can bring up Pains out of sequence; when we do, it is in very selected cases and only under special circumstances. But rebirthers are usually engaged in the random application of fixed techniques and some seem unconcerned about the consequences of what they do and conduct no follow-up studies on their patients. Some even hold stage shows in which anyone from the audience can volunteer for the birth experience. Tragically, this is being done by persons who have no idea about the background of the volunteers. What may be a fairly harmless catharsis of sensation for one may cause serious mental disintegration in another.

What nearly all of the rebirthers have in common is a somewhat mystical orientation. And herein lies an important danger. If the therapist has a predilection for the mystical, a patient's bizarre or unreal ideation will escape his notice. When the patient touches on birth and it is too much to integrate, it will lead him to develop strange ideation. It will not be considered strange or symbolic because the therapist may be ready to believe in this ideation too.

Some natal therapy is incorporated into the Freudian framework. Therapists make the claim that they do not want to overwhelm the ego but rather use the cognitive abilities of the patient to aid his progress. In six sessions of traditional Freudian verbal therapy, the patient's psychosexual history is outlined and the focus is on the Freudian stages of development. In the next session the patient lies down, eyes on the therapist and arms folded. He takes three deep breaths and is then passed to another group member. He begins to move and sink deeper into himself until he reaches a different level of consciousness. Then he has his "rebirth." In other words, after a few hours of psychosexual discussion the patient transcends levels of brain organization to reach the deepest level without ever feeling a single interconnecting Pain beforehand. It is impossible under conditions such as this—being passed around, breathing and sinking—to have a connected birth experience. The Pain would simply be too much. If there ever were a situation capable of overwhelming an "ego," this would be it. The rebirthers do not know how to protect the patient because they have neither a systematic theory nor a proper understanding of the brain's organization around which to build one. More often they simply substitute dogma and ritual for a natural approach to reexperiencing Pain.

One doesn't just lie down and have a birth Primal. For all those thousands of Pains which came after and on top of the birth trauma, there are also the corresponding repressions. It is unthinkable that one could simply transcend all that repression after six sessions of talking and go to something which will shake the system to its roots. Indeed, even our patients usually need some kind of present-day shock to the system that makes the defenses more vulnerable—a vulnerability that will only be there after months or years of feeling. One way that we know the Pain is on the way is that the feelings pushing upward provoke the person often to create a "crisis." He will do something that is either impulsive or upsetting to his life and then this upset (of the defenses) will help him to get to the real birth feeling. He may start an argument over nothing, for example. In any case, it is the patient who decides when he's ready, not any therapist; and it isn't even that the patient "decides" anything.

When a patient comes close to birth in his therapy, and many patients never do, a number of characteristic symptoms arise. There are telltale pathognomonic signs. We watch for them and then help ease the patient into feelings he is already in touch with. He is in touch by virtue of having had months of Primal experiences to prepare the way. When he arrives at a reexperience of birth and early infancy he can then integrate what he undergoes. Usually the first birth Primals, or even the first ten of them, are shortlived because the Pain is so intense that the body shuts off immediately, as it should.

The patient should never be pushed beyond this point. And it is crucial that the therapist know where this point is. For example, there are some obvious telltale statements a patient might make during the stages of a Primal, such as, "I think that the struggle with my boyfriend isn't worth it. I'm just going to crawl back in my hole so that I never see the light of day." Whether or not the patient is ready to "crawl back in her hole" depends on many factors. First, the past history of her Primals. Is she far enough along and has she resolved enough from childhood? Second, are there other physical signs that foretell the impending birth experience? Third, has she indeed resolved enough on the second line this particular day to be able to go deeper? After knowing or sensing the answers to these questions and many more, the therapist must time his probing just right and as a logical consequence of what went before. The techniques must be specifically cued to the statements made. The therapist uses his specialized techniques but must follow the lead of the patient. And he must know the second the patient is not ready for the experience; for there are telltale signs of this as well. One never fits the patient into a pre-set mold—another hallmark of many rebirthing therapists. (In the natal therapy I've cited only three birth experiences are considered necessary. There is no set number in Primal Therapy and it is absurd even to talk of average numbers.)

I have stated elsewhere that the hallmark of the pseudo-therapist is an authoritarian approach wherein the therapist makes crucial decisions for the patient. In natal therapy, for instance, the speed and type of movement of the birth experience are controlled and directed by the therapist in an effort to alter the birth sequence in favor of a happy ending. The benefits are then supposed to pass over into daily life so that we no longer act out our neuroses. This is magic, not science; what is important about reliving the birth experience is that it must be run off exactly as it happened without interference. The experience itself is resolving. That is why one cannot decide to superimpose a good ending over a particular Primal trauma with the hope of resolving it. When the rebirthing therapist does this he is tampering with a precise neurological circuit—a memory imprint as unmodifiable as one's past history. That history is a prepotent reality. The original trauma did not end well; that is the truth. There is no way to make a Primal experience end well. Since adults are stronger and more mature when they come to relive the birth trauma, they can integrate an experience that the neonate could not. That integration ends the sequence.

Interrupting a sequence by an attempt to alter it is actually dangerous. The person will be trapped in a phony solution with his memory circuits rerouted and diverted into unreal channels. This is no more than what happened originally when early *real* Pain was diverted into unreal, symbolic spillways. The rebirthing therapist is thus compounding the problem; he is literally making more work for the patient's neurological system. For the original circuit, now detoured by the therapist's imposed solution, must develop a new groove to encode all the misconnections of an imposed and unreal birth experience. The person thus avoids the real Pain but imagines that he has had a real experience. The new, artificial ideation becomes a fixated superstructure to house and contain the further disconnected Primal energy. Far from resolving the birth trauma, the rebirther has interfered with the normal repressive processes and the natural unleashing of Pain. He is then obliged to offer an ideology or rebirthing benefits, lest the patient be left without some formalized, defensive framework.

There is another approach to rebirthing which I consider more dangerous, involving the use of LSD to facilitate the process. Any consciousness-altering drug such as LSD throws birth Pains out of sequence so they cannot possibly be integrated. The body seems to know what can be integrated, for when left to its natural devices it offers up Pains in sequence; thus it produces only that which can be integrated and no more. The result of unresolved Pains brought up in "rebirthing" is an exacerbation of neurosis. That is what symbolism is all about; it takes one farther away from oneself and the result is a belief in mystical experiences and events—including those which are literally far away in the cosmos, as in the militant belief in UFOs. I believe that what happens with mind-altering drugs is the production of severe neuroses and inchoate psychotic states— albeit a controlled or benign psychosis in which the delusions fit into some kind of socially acceptable scheme.

Unfortunately, one doesn't get over LSD experiences easily. Indeed, it is my observation that some of their effects may be permanent. By opening the limbic gates and depressing third-line consciousness, one is fully flooded without the help of the intellect to keep the flooding within cohesive boundaries. It is no accident that the former acid-takers stay hooked on UFOs, out-of-body astral projection, bizarre Eastern philosophies, pyramid power, religious conversion, etc. They must continue to be unreal because they have no way to be real. They have been driven crazy by unleashed Primal energy which must be constantly cloaked in ideation. By contrast, when the release of Primal energy is treated with care, no ideology is necessary. The cortical representations (precise ideas related to the actual experience) will constitute the endpoint of the original circuit and will become part of that circuit. The sensation now has a name, a context and a personal meaning.

When mystically oriented types become our patients we usually give them tranquilizers to act as first-line blockers; interestingly, they quickly lose their mystical views. What we have done is to bring the activation level of Pain down to manageable proportions. Then the patients can begin to feel about the real experiences they didn't even know were bothering them.

Reliving the Birth Sequence

It is very important for those who are about to experience first-line Pains in Primal Therapy to know that they exist, that they are "feelable," that it could take months to feel all of it, that it is normal to experience only bits of it at a time, that they are nonverbal and require no explanation or scene, and that feeling feelings is the specific preventative for psychosis. The patient must be reassured that there is no danger if he is properly supervised.

Just knowing that the Pains of birth are there and have been all of one's life, that they need to be experienced for the resolution of great tension is a great relief to patients. That nameless dread they have previously suffered is no longer nameless. They can go into that black, empty void and have the experience for what it is without having to elaborate upon it in any way. The body must acknowledge its Pain. Indeed, it is when one tries to make "intellectual" sense out of the experience that psychotic symbolism can appear. Trying to make sense is exactly what drives people crazy . . . another of those dialectics. Feelings, and words about those feelings, are organized at different levels of the brain and by different structures. They are not interchangeable and cannot do one another's work. Feeling "helpless" is an interpretation of experience that exists only with the development of language. But the experiential feeling of helplessness— that powerlessness of the infant to shut off Pain—precedes its label by years.

There are no words during a birth sequence because there were no words originally. To have someone talk or even think during a birth sequence is to immediately transform it into a contrived, abreactive experience. When a therapist says anything to a patient during these experiences he is taking the patient off the track, bringing him into the present to think about the past rather than letting him be in the past, fully. But the truth is that we cannot relive the past from the mental vantage point of the present.

Trusting the inner process—trusting those precise neurophysiological mechanisms that link mind and body—is what therapy is all about. The brain and body know the unfinished tasks. Phlegm will be produced during a sequence that involves drowning in fluid, but it will not be produced once that aspect of the whole sequence is run off. Tears will not arise during a birth Primal and there will be no childlike scream triggered off during the reliving of a time when the newborn was incapable of such a sound. Patients who are writhing in rhythmical fashion on the floor cannot begin to imitate those movements or sounds once they are out of the feeling.

One question must be asked: where was all the mucus, all the phlegm, all the gasping, all the choking, all the unique movements, for all of those years? How is it that such concrete physical concomitants of a trauma decades old can be reproduced? How can a throat fill with phlegm now, how can a nose fill with mucus now, in response to a memory of birth?

We need to understand that there are tracks leading from the nasal passages and throat to the brain and back again, in the very low centers of the brain neuraxis. It is there that old memories are triggered which somehow produce mucus. It is a reflexive action. The cupfuls of mucus that come up during Primals are, literally, unthinkable. Apparently, all of the physical reactions that accompanied the trauma are stored as part of the memory circuit. That is why a patient in the grip of an anoxic reexperience of the birth trauma will actually turn blue and be unable to catch his breath. The lungs seem to stop working and the person has tremendous difficulty breathing. This again cannot be faked: when patients are asked to duplicate the same kind of symptoms out of the birth feeling they cannot do so.

A number of patients have noted that after birth Primals dealing with mucus they no longer have to clear their noses and throats each morning. That fullness was yet another reminder of an old memory. Usually patients are not aware that they are memories until the symptoms go away with the reliving of the past.

But birth Primals do more than just remove specific symptoms; they also produce an overall sense of physical and emotional well-being. One patient wrote:

> A friend once predicted that I would go through Primal Therapy "like a red-hot arrow," and I think this has turned out to be partly true. However, even though I was feeling my childhood Pains fast and furiously for about a year, this was largely an act of faith on my part. For the real relief did not come until I started connecting to my first-line, birth Pain.
>
> I have now been feeling for two and a half years, and I'm glad to report that I don't need to Primal as often as I used to. I can get away with once a week, whereas before I used to have to Primal two, three times a week—and sometimes every day. The feeling of well-being I have now is a total body feeling. When I was only Primalling about childhood Pain I would feel some emotional relief afterwards, but feeling the baby feelings really started to give me back my body. My body feels relaxed now in a way that was absolutely not possible for me to experience before I went into therapy. This good feeling cannot be overemphasized, because it's the only good reason for going back and dealing with all the horrible unfelt feelings, with all those traumas of early life.

And another:

> Well, I could go on and on. But I'm very happy to have finally relived my birth and to be feeling the feelings that have been causing me so much trouble all my life. I am also happy to realize that though I have been through a lot, I still have the real me left. I'm a good and gutsy person, and I like myself! I will never sell myself out to anyone again. Now I've got to start to work on trusting and following my feelings, which are so often correct. I got into a lot of trouble one weekend because I did not follow what I felt, and, of course, I had to lie down and feel those feelings afterwards. I realize that I will have to

do this a lot until the connections are strong. But I am getting stronger and clearer every day. I know it's just a matter of time and feeling. I'm very optimistic now, and feel that I can control my life and make it the way I want it. I'm very grateful to all the therapists who helped me, and I also deserve a pat on the back because I've put in a lot of hard work over the past two years to get where I am now!

The aim of Primal Therapy is to retrieve the suffering component of repressed memory. That suffering component operates on different nerve tracts from the verbal component, which is why it is sometimes possible to remember very far back to a traumatic event and yet be detached from the memory in a complete way. It is the suffering component of repressed trauma that must reach consciousness to be released as a connected experience. When that happens the trauma takes its place solely as stored information, no longer acting as a force that the body must continually contend with. It is now accessible information rather than circulating Pain. It remains in the memory and can be recalled at will, for it is the suffering that leaves the body, not the memory.

I have pointed out that for every traumatic memory there is a defense against it. The defenses are biologic requirements which come into being so that we will not be overwhelmed by the past. Altering those defenses in any artificial way without regard to the sequential ordering of Pain is dangerous. To be more specific: liberating the suffering component of memory by deep breathing, by hot pools, by having patients assume birth positions, etc., can flood consciousness, forcing it to "stretch" itself into the strange and the mystical.

One could probably not build a computer that would unravel in such orderly fashion Pains ranging from low valence to high. It is very much like the mechanism that holds many plates in a stack at one time: as the top plate is removed, the whole stack is pushed up. Trying to reach for the bottom plate too soon would send all the plates above it crashing to the floor.

The drama and power of the birth event can be seductive for both patient and therapist. The therapist can delude himself into believing that he produced the experience—that it came about in his patient by virtue of his own power and ability. This is not true. The therapist must guard against taking such personal credit. It is the patient's past history that "creates" the birth trauma; the therapist only provides the support and guidance for its reexperience.

Both patient and therapist often want to believe in magical and instantaneous cures, and so turn to this technique or that. But in the end, there is no shortcut to the unconscious and thus no shortcut to consciousness. The unconscious was constructed out of the slow accretion of experience, and consciousness arises in the same way: by the slow, sequential probing of the unconscious. There is no single Primal, no magical transformation, no weekend breakthrough that will suddenly thrust one into health. There is not a "vomiting out of the mother," a "thrashing out of the Pain," and the like, that gets one well. There is only the day-to-day reexperience of what happened to us. We must trust in our own evolution—even in the evolution of our Pain—for it is how we got to where we are.

Conclusions

The treatment for the effects of birth trauma involves months and years of therapy, and even then may not be totally effective. A change in birth practices, however, involves far less time and is far more effective. In my opinion it is the most important action we can take in the field of mental health. No other single factor can alter neurosis or psychosis on such a fundamental level; no diet, no conditioning, no manipulation of external circumstances, no massage, no lecture, no philosophy, no ideology, no religion, no amount of love and affection can do what a proper birth can do.

I am not talking about the millions of dollars it would take to develop widescale therapeutic programs to treat the results of bad births but about a simple, elemental change in procedure. I am not talking about training thousands of new therapists but about utilizing the gynecologists, obstetricians and pediatricians we already have in a coordinated effort to change attitudes, approaches and procedures. The tremendous impact of such changes could be as significant as birth itself, for they would greatly diminish the vast array of mental health problems we are now confronted with: the learning disorders, the psychosomatic illnesses, the phobias, compulsions, perversions—and yes, even some of the catastrophic diseases. Ultimately, a simple change in birth practices would affect our social structure, our penal institutions, our mental hospitals and the values by which we raise our children—the next generation to inherit the earth.

I have been in practice for more than thirty years and have seen every possible combination and permutation of mental illness. I have seen what bad families can do, what orphanages and rejection can do, what rape and incest can do; and it is still my opinion that birth and pre-birth trauma are prepotent over almost any later kind of trauma. For in that birth process is stamped the way we are going to handle our lives thereafter. Personality traits are engraved, ways of looking at the world are imprinted, attitudes are shaped. What we will become is found in the birth matrix.

The best testimony I know of to the importance of altered birth practices is the qualitative difference between children born naturally and nontraumatically and those born under conventional circumstances. The second best testimony I know of is the enormous change that takes place in Primal patients who have relived the traumas they underwent at birth. Those changes tell us about the scope and impact of the birth trauma in the first place—a trauma we now know is woven into the tissues, cells, bones and blood of almost every human being. That is why I believe that a decent birth is at least half the job of child rearing and may be equal to years of positive experiences with parents. To put it another way, a proper birth can buffer the effects of adverse experience later on, whereas an improper birth leaves one vulnerable to even the most benign events.

The birth trauma is a reality, yet it is still a most difficult reality for many to accept—particularly those in the psychological and psychiatric sciences. Many still believe it is nothing more than an untested theory. On the contrary, the concept of the birth trauma did not develop as a theory to be superimposed over reality, but rather evolved out of observation and measurement of that reality. It is not a theoretical invention; it is a discovery. It came about because we found concrete ways to quantify the unconscious; we found ways to evoke, observe and measure what is inside the human mind at its most profound depths. Moreover, working with thousands of patients from most of the countries of the world has led us to the inescapable conclusion that the birth trauma is a reality that cuts across culture and geography and is wholly independent of language. It is universal.

In one of society's great paradoxes, our supposedly most advanced methods have produced the most primitive consequences, and in the most primitive societies we find the most advanced (that is, natural and beneficent) birth practice: the simple stoop-squat-deliver method. Modern technology must not interfere with natural processes but should be used instead to aid those processes. Parents must not be intimidated in their search for a doctor and hospital that can give their child the best entry into the world. Parents need to insist on the best possible birth practices available. They must not be defeated by established hospital procedure, by authoritarian doctors or by the rigidity of long-standing policies. It is a human life they are fighting for, and they have every right to do so assiduously. For at the same time, they are fighting against the physical disease of their infant, against the later learning and behavior problems of their child, against the later neurosis and mental illness of their child as an adult. Indeed, to fight against improper birth practices is to fight for life— and in the most constructive and enduring way possible.

We have seen what a poor birth can do in our clinics. We have had a chance to see what a proper birth can do. No professional has the right to remain ignorant when the stakes are so high. There is no social program, no therapeutic approach, no kind of institution that we could create or construct that would be as beneficial for humanity as a simple change in birth practices. We are talking about preventing the root, generating cause of so many personal and social problems. We are talking about minutes or hours of care with years and decades of consequences. A radical change in society is possible by the natural retreat to our origins. It is as simple as that.

Appendix A: Research on Fetal Stress

To understand how and why stress has such an impact on the fetus and its later life, we have first to grasp the awesome, complex and intricate process that is gestation. We also must come to a new understanding of stress itself, not only as something which impacts us from the outside, but as something which is imprinted as an environment inside the body. That stress imprint is the duplicate of the early traumatic situation. With the entire panoply of sensory input constellated by the feelings into a cohesive whole, it forces the whole system into a position of continuous reactivity.

The process of gestation is the process of creating and shaping life. When that process occurs in the context of a stressed system, there are going to be consequences. We now know that during the nine months of fetal growth, the developing fetal brain recapitulates the evolutionary history of the human species: a single cell differentiates into myriad cell groupings, which in turn form into complex organ and tissue structures, all of which finally coalesce into the whole human baby. Each specific phase of this development—each specific organ, system and structure—has a precise and preordained schedule of unfoldment. In order for that schedule to proceed as planned, all the necessary raw materials from the mother's system must be available at just the right time. Timing, in fact, is almost as critical in healthy fetal development as are the "building blocks" of raw materials. This is because there are critical growth spurts for each organ system; failure in the logistics of the entire system will be fatal to whatever brain substructure is implicated. That substructure will never be properly completed.

What happens is that the resources ordinarily earmarked for the development of an organ system will be employed differently, with a resulting deficiency to that developing organ system. I believe that any major negative stimulus—physical or emotional, internal or external—can interfere with this delicate genetic unfoldment. If, for example, a particular growth spurt of an organ occurs during the time that a mother is extremely anxious, fearful or angry, the fetus will be affected in that system just as surely as it would be affected by malnutrition or illness. The mother's biochemistry will be altered by the hormonal adjustments to her emotions and much of the energy intended for fetal development will be shunted off into repressive processes.

In order to generate the cells required to form a human brain, tens of thousands of neurons must be produced and differentiated throughout each day of fetal development. We can only dimly imagine what happens to this vast production and differentiation of cells when there is malnutrition, repression or alteration of biochemistry during gestation. Neurons are being generated and organized into complex neuronal nets. The brain has an extraordinarily high demand for oxygen during this time because of the enormous energy outlays required to synthesize, organize, unite and regulate those billions of cells into a human being. It is clearly the most delicate and vulnerable period of growth.

There are long-term implications when fetal brain development is interfered with. For example, the brain has a number of back-up systems which are depleted by any lack or insufficiency in brain cell production. The entire brain system will then be affected by the deficiency in its back-up processes. This means that traumas which would usually be diffused to and processed by back-up duplicate cells cannot now be so handled because those back-up cells are deficient in number. In other words, there would not be enough cortical brain material to handle Pain. Indeed, many children and adults are more susceptible to chronic anxiety states simply because they do not have the neuronal wherewithal to handle trauma. That neuronal deficiency begins in the womb.

Stress in the womb can account for many types of birth traumas, birth defects and birth deficiencies. Stress to the fetus comes in many ways. It may come from the physical condition of the mother—how well she eats, whether she smokes, drinks or takes drugs; it may come from her emotional and psychological state—how she feels about herself, how she feels about her baby, how she copes with life; and finally it may come from whatever environmental conditions she is exposed to.

Until recently it had been assumed that the placenta acted as a buffer to screen out or at least dilute noxious stimuli from impacting the fetus. Now researchers are finding, not so surprisingly, that the opposite is true. One researcher wrote:*

> Almost any biologically active substance (such as nicotine, alcohol, caffeine, etc.) can behave as a pollutant. For the pregnant woman these substances act as for any other individual; however, the fetus may be more sensitive to such effects. Because the placenta is permeable to essentially everything taken into the maternal organism, the fetus is exposed despite its apparent sequestered locus within the uterus. In some instances the fetus may even concentrate the toxins.

We must also remember that "biologically active substances" transmit the mother's psychological state as well as her physical condition. What this means is that the fetus concentrates the toxins caused by the mother's Pain as surely as it concentrates toxins from alcohol or nicotine or from environmental pollutants. Pain is a biologically active and toxic substance to which the fetus is continuously exposed.

When we look at the research on stress to understand the effects of particular causes, first we must bear in mind that the bottom line of all these different stressors is, in many cases, the mother's Pain. It is that Pain which compels her to smoke, drink or to take tranquilizers. It is Pain that elevates her blood pressure, alters her hormone levels and may ultimately drive her to reject the child growing within her.

External Stressors: What the Mother Takes into Her Body

Current research has established the deleterious effects of smoking, drinking, drugs and malnutrition on the growing fetus. The consequences of these effects are far-reaching, so far that much of what happens to us in later life can be traced back to them. Lifelong patterns are laid down during gestation in an environment that no one can see. Intrauterine injury is incorporated into the entire psychophysiologic makeup so that the baby begins life injured. It adapts to this injury atuomatically, making its later inordinate reactions, both physical and psychological, appear normal. As an infant it may cry and whine excessively; as a young child, it may behave hyperactively; and as an adult it may be forced to use antihistamines on a chronic basis—all to compensate for events that occurred four months before it was born.

The point is that whatever injurious state is normal—i.e., most frequent

*Longo, Lawrence D., "Environmental Pollution and Pregnancy: Risks and Uncertainties for the Fetus and Infant," *American Journal of Obstetrics and Gynecology,* 137 (2): May 15, 1980, pp. 162–173.

or predominant—for the mother becomes stamped in as "normal" biological behavior for the baby. How? The portion of the fetal nervous system
that is mature enough to learn is that portion that mediates species-
specific, unmodifiable behaviors such as coughing, gagging, vomiting,
sneezing, urinating and defecating. Any significant stimulus occurring in
the intrauterine environment of the developing fetus is going to be
registered and learned in the nervous system with a permanence analogous to the permanence of behaviors like gagging and choking. Thus the
baby learns that certain types of "environments" in the mother's bloodstream are associated either with pleasure and a sense of well-being or
with pain and a sense of threat. It learns, for instance, that the only time its
mother is calm and relaxed is when there is a certain level of alcohol—or
nicotine or morphine or fat—in the mother's bloodstream. The state that is
calming for the mother then becomes calming for the baby. This is called
state-dependent learning: the mother's state of being is learned and
incorporated by the baby. It is a type of learning that has nothing to do
with genes or heredity, only with the intrauterine environment. That is
why the mother is not just lowering her baby's body weight by smoking or
drinking during her pregnancy; more, she may be setting up conditions
that will predetermine whether or not her child becomes a chain smoker,
an alcoholic or a drug addict in the future.

Anoxia

Anoxia is the medical term for oxygen starvation. It is commonly
known to occur during labor and birth, but it can also occur throughout
gestation as a possible side effect in many of the stressors discussed in this
chapter.

Anoxia can be caused by what the mother takes into her system—by
tobacco, drugs and fatty foods; and it can be caused by the mother's own
internal state—by the presence of anxiety, tension and Pain in her. But
whatever the cause, anoxia has the same deleterious effects. Ashley
Montagu explains in simple terms how the process of oxygen transfer
should occur from mother to unborn baby:

> The oxygen that is so necessary to [the baby's] survival and to the
> orderly development of his body reaches him by way of his mother's
> bloodstream. Her blood, which carries oxygen molecules along with
> it, bathes the hundreds of thousands of little rootlike villi that extend
> from the surface of the placenta. The oxygen molecules pass, rather
> slowly, through the walls of the villi and into the tiny blood vessels
> within. These lead to the placenta proper, then to the umbilical cord,
> and finally to the blood vessels in the body of the developing child.
> The oxygen molecules travel in his bloodstream to his heart, and from

there are pumped out through the body to all the growing and developing tissues where the oxygen is needed in order to carry out the work and division of the cells.*

Anything that interferes with this delicate process will threaten the developing baby. Precisely how the baby will be affected is determined by whatever critical growth spurts are underway when the anoxia occurs, and by the severity of the anoxia itself. Known effects of anoxia are brain damage, cerebral palsy, epilepsy, mental retardation and possibly the later onset of mental illness.

Sometimes the damage is not at all obvious. It is now known that even mild anoxia may cause subtle forms of brain damage. Later, reading difficulties, behavior problems such as hyperactivity, and slightly lowered intellectual capacities may all be caused by brief bouts of oxygen deprivation before or during birth.

Another possible consequence of mild anoxia is diminished repressive capabilities. There are certain cells in the limbic (or emotional) system which are very sensitive to oxygen loss. These cells have to do with the repression of Pain. Damage to the fetus in this area may not be obvious for many years, but it does make the individual more sensitive to trauma and less able to deal with it. It can mean an almost constant anxiety state in the child and adult due to faulty repressive mechanisms.

How? There are a series of "gates" in the brain that work both neuronally and biochemically to shut down Pain—that is, the consciousness of Pain. One of the key areas for this gating process is the limbic system, which deals with memory. It stores experience and holds it in abeyance for later integration. Meanwhile, emotional memory or at least the energy from its unintegrated components, travel round this system in reverberating circuits, spewing out aspects of the memory such as fear, terror, anger, sadness and tension, but out of context.

Faulty gating is unable to hold down this effluvia so that it makes its way into consciousness; we see the results in persistent nightmares, inexplicable fears, phobias and anxiety states. Montagu has noted that "several mental disorders have been shown to appear much more frequently in individuals who have had anoxia at birth than in those not born anoxic. The mechanism of this may be that the central nervous system is damaged by the anoxia while it is developing, with the consequence that in later years it is more susceptible to the stresses of life."†

Many times the damage from prenatal anoxia goes completely unrecognized. Researchers Haesslein and Niswander noted

*From *Life Before Birth,* Signet Books, New York, 1965, p. 48.
†Op. cit., p. 62.

... the frequency with which unrecognized hypoxia/asphyxia during pregnancy and before the perinatal period results in early brain damage to the fetus, usually unrecognized, which then is attributed to perinatal asphyxia. Prenatal conditions in the [pregnant] woman that might cause such damage are often difficult to identify and are frequently completely unrecognized.*

In their study of seventy-five newborns who had registered fetal distress from oxygen deprivation during birth, the deprivation did not lead to neurologic damage unless there had also been chronic distress in the womb:

Since evidence of chronic intrauterine distress was identified in five of six of our neurologically damaged infants, it seems likely that the chronic [fetal] distress was the major contributing factor.†

They noted that other researchers also

... observed no increased risk of brain damage in a group of severely asphyxiated neonates, compared to nonasphyxiated neonates, unless the asphyxiated neonates also had suffered intrauterine growth retardation.‡

The importance of all this research is that it indicates how conditions in the womb influence the impact of trauma at birth. Certainly a baby who has been well nourished with oxygen throughout gestation is better equipped to handle the trauma of decreased oxygenation if it occurs during labor and birth. It only makes sense that trauma is cumulative. A nervous system that has received plenty of oxygen throughout its development is more fortified to handle a lack of oxygen at birth than one already stunted and underdeveloped by nine months of chronic oxygen deprivation. The problem with this research, however, is that it also suggests that infants can undergo oxygen deprivation during birth *without harm* if fetal conditions were satisfactory. I disagree: experiencing oxygen deprivation is always traumatic. What varies is how well the newborn is equipped to handle it. Fighting for oxygen—the single most critical element for life—is inherently traumatic. It could not be otherwise. If you have ever gasped for air from staying underwater too long, you know how Primally frightening it is. To the infant struggling to get born, it is immensely more frightening because he or she can do nothing about it.

*Haesslein, Hanns C., and Niswander, Kenneth R., "Fetal Distress in Term Pregnancies," *American Journal of Obstetrics and Gynecology,* 137, 1980, 245–251.
†Ibid., p. 249.
‡Ibid., p. 249.

What it comes down to is this: womb experience can turn a mildly traumatic birth into a severely traumatic one and vice versa. But no matter how good conditions were in the womb, trauma at birth is still traumatic, is still imprinted, will still reverberate throughout the system and will still have repercussions on all levels of consciousness.

TABLE 1

Proven or correlated effects of poor eating, drinking, and drug habits on the developing fetus and newborn.

1. Alcohol........................Fetal Alcohol Syndrome
   birth defects
   facial dysmorphology
   intrauterine growth retardation
   lowered birth weight
   mental retardation
   nervous system damage
   Infant cancer
   Spontaneous abortion
2. Caffeine ....Birth defects
   "Hyperized" hormonal set-point
3. Drugs ....Anoxia (oxygen starvation)
   Brain damage
   Postnatal chronic lethargy
   Prenatal addiction
4. Malnutrition...................Adrenaline excess
   Glucose shortage
   Lowered birth weight
   Mental retardation
   Predisposition to anorexia nervosa
   Prematurity
   Reduced number of brain cells
5. Tobacco ....Anoxia
   Constricted blood flow
   Intrauterine growth retardation
   Lowered birth weight
   Nicotine predisposition
   Prematurity
   Stillbirth
   Toxic poisoning

Alcohol

Alcohol and pregnancy don't mix. The Federal Drug Administration is now warning expectant mothers about the hazards of drinking. There is indication of what is now called the "Fetal Alcohol Syndrome" (FAS), a group of developmental abnormalities in the fetus and newborn associated with maternal alcohol abuse. These developmental abnormalities comprise quite a long list: low birth weight, small head size, characteristic facial dysmorphology (abnormal facial features), intrauterine growth retardation, congenital anomalies and abnormalities, central nervous system impairment resulting in irritability and depression in infancy, retarded motor and intellectual development, hyperactivity in childhood and a short attention span. Fetal alcohol syndrome is now known to be the third most common cause of mental deficiency.*

So serious are the consequences that the Research Society on Alcoholism Executive Committee presented the following statement on the fetal alcohol syndrome in October 1979:

> Observations of human babies and of experimentally treated animals have made it clear that a mother's heavy drinking can severely damage her unborn child. We do not know the exact amount or timing of drinking that causes these effects. We cannot say whether there is a safe amount of drinking or whether there is a safe time during pregnancy. We do know that heavy drinking can be damaging. Women should therefore be especially cautious about drinking during pregnancy and when they are likely to be pregnant.†

There is now no question that alcohol retards the general growth and physical development of the fetus. It is known, for example, that alcohol reduces fetal brain weight, and, not so surprisingly, that it alters the cerebellum which mediates balance and coordination. What alcohol does to the adult it *imprints* on the fetus: balance and coordination may be permanently altered because the structure itself is permanently altered by alcohol.

Just how the damage occurs at the tissue and cellular levels has not been clear. Now researcher James R. West and his colleagues at the University of Iowa College of Medicine have discovered a possible mechanism.‡ Through experiments with mice they found that alcohol dramatically altered the nerve fibers of the hippocampus—an area of the brain mediating memory, learning and feeling. West and his team concluded that such hippocampal nerve anomalies may be responsible for the more blatant

---

*Clarren, S. K., and Smith, D. W., "The Fetal Alcohol Syndrome," *New England Journal of Medicine,* 298, 1978: 1063.

†As quoted in "A Clinical Perspective of the Fetal Alcohol Syndrome," an editorial for *Alcoholism: Clinical and Experimental Research,* Volume 4, No. 2, April 1980, p. 121.

‡West, J. R.; Nornes, H. O.; Barnes, C. L.; and Bronfenbrenner, M., "The Cells of Origin of the Commisural Afferents to the Area Dentata in the Mouse," *Brain Research,* 160 (2), January 1979, 203–15.

central nervous system abnormalities that occur in infants subjected to their mothers' alcohol during gestation.

Research is also linking various types of infant cancer with the fetal alcohol syndrome. Kinney et al.* discovered adrenal cancer in an infant whose mother had drunk heavily throughout pregnancy. The infant died at three months of age. While there is insufficient evidence at this point to prove that the fetal alcohol syndrome causes infant cancer, the researchers concluded that their case, in addition to other cases reported in the literature,† "suggests a possible relation between maternal gestational alcohol abuse and neoplasia (cancer) in the offspring. In the future, clinical and pathological documentation of cancer in infant patients with fetal alcohol syndrome would help in clarifying the role of alcohol as a fetal carcinogen."‡

What all this means is that stress in the womb via alcoholic toxins may cause infantile cancer. It also may suggest the possibility that more moderate amounts of alcohol during pregnancy might be linked with a more gradual onset of cancer in adulthood.

Another link between cancer and alcohol was found with the discovery of the presence of a poison called aphlatoxin in alcohol. On a weight basis, aphlatoxin is one of the most potent carcinogens known to man. Aphlatoxin develops in grain that is stored in warehouses without air conditioning. The grain becomes moist and is infected by a mold; as the mold utilizes the grain for its own growth, it secretes two kinds of aphlatoxin into the grain. Several years ago a researcher pointed out that the ten leading brands of alcohol on the market in the United States were significantly contaminated with aphlatoxin. Aphlatoxin causes liver cancer in all vertebrates in which it has been tested—from trout to man—and is known to be able to cause that cancer in picogram quantities—that is, in quantities of a billionth of a gram. So, in addition to the inherently harmful ingredients of alcohol, the drinking mother is exposing herself and her baby to yet another, highly toxic carcinogenic drug: a drug that might in fact predispose an unborn child to fatal childhood cancer.

In a study by Sokol and his team,§ alcohol abuse during pregnancy was found to result in a 50 percent risk factor for "adverse perinatal outcome"; that is, a baby born of a drinking mother stood only a 50 percent chance of being born normal—a 50 percent chance of being born

*Kinney, Hannah; Faix, Roger; Brazy, Jane, "The Fetal Alcohol Syndrome and Neuroblastoma," *Pediatrics,* Volume 66, No. 1, July 1980, pp. 131–133.

†Hornstein, L., Crowe, C., Gruppo, R., "Adrenal Carcinoma in a Child with History of Fetal Alcohol Syndrome," *Lancet,* 2, 1977, 1292.

‡Kinney, op cit., p. 132.

§Sokol, Robert J.; Miller, Sheldon, I.; Reed, George, "Alcohol Abuse During Pregnancy: An Epidemiologic Study," *Alcoholism: Clinical and Experimental Research,* Volume 4, No. 2, April 1980.

free of the dysfunctions and abnormalities associated with fetal alcohol syndrome. In other words, the baby of a drinking mother is forced to begin life with odds against him of two to one.

Another finding of this study was that the mother who drinks and smokes is quadrupling the chance of risk to her baby:*

> . . . Alcohol abuse and cigarette smoking appeared to contribute independently to intrauterine growth retardation, each approximately doubling the risk for birth of a small-for-gestational-age infant. . . . In the current study, the effects of alcohol abuse and cigarette smoking on intrauterine growth retardation appeared to be additive, together increasing the risk about fourfold.

They concluded by suggesting that what is currently known about the fetal alcohol syndrome is probably only the "tip of the iceberg."

The National Institute of Alcohol Abuse and Alcoholism recently conducted an exhaustive survey of the scientific research as it relates to alcohol consumption during pregnancy. The main conclusions of the survey, as reported to the Congress in November of 1980,† were that (1) pregnant women who drink as little as one ounce of alcohol twice a week show an increased incidence of spontaneous abortion; (2) three to four ounces of alcohol consumption per day contribute to birth defects; (3) excessive drinking leads to the fetal alcohol syndrome which includes mental retardation, growth deficiencies, facial abnormalities, cardiac and other organic problems and central nervous system disorders; (4) and finally, that alcohol enters breast milk and is transmitted to the nursing infant—yet another possible imprinted association beween calm (read *love*) and alcohol.

Beyond the "tip of the iceberg" are the long-term implications, the least serious of which might be a predisposition to alcoholism for the same reasons as occur in smoking. And indeed, many alcoholics will tell you that they don't really feel healthy until they've had a couple of drinks.

Maybe that is why the treatment of alcoholism has been so unsuccessful; and why most conventional treatments, when they "succeed," require the recovered alcoholic to never take another drink. Any return to alcohol, it seems, may reevoke a very early memory that provokes the compulsion all over again. Primal patients who were alcoholics are able to drink moderately on occasion, usually only after a good deal of very early first-line (read birth) trauma has been reexperienced. Rooting out the real source of the compulsion—and compulsion it is—eliminates the force

---

*Sokol, Miller, and Reed, op. cit., p. 144.

†As reported in the *International Herald Tribune*, July 20, 1981, in an interview with John Deluca, Director of the National Institute on Alcohol Abuse and Alcoholism.

behind it and allows the person to taste alcohol without having to continue drinking in order to blot out all of the Pain evoked by that first drink. Again, the first drink evokes a memory with a force. That is the central problem. Blotting out Pain feels good, therefore drinking feels good.

Caffeine

Caffeine is a stimulant and can thus be a stressor. It speeds up the mother's system, puts an added load on it and probably affects the fetus on a cellular level. In August of 1980 the U.S. Food and Drug Administration issued a warning to pregnant women to limit their consumption of coffee. They reported that caffeine (which is the central stimulant in coffee) force-fed to animals results in a much higher incidence of deformities in the offspring. A few cups of coffee a day results in a faster heart rate and a general agitated state for the mother. When it occurs while the fetus is organizing its nervous system and hormone output, it could lead to an altered "setpoint" in activation levels of the fetus, i.e., a tendency toward higher levels of activating hormones and an increased metabolic rate. As an imprint this may lead to hyperactivity in the baby both at birth and in childhood. Accompanying this is a hypermotility—a speeding up of some of the bodily processes—with the eventual result of disease. The general personality development may well be of someone who is constantly "on the run"—someone who maneuvers his life into a hectic pace so as to rationalize, unconsciously, his hectic metabolic rate. More importantly, a "hyper" state experienced so early in the development of the embryo may determine how the birth process is reacted to, and that in turn reinforces the stamped-in personality tendencies. For example, the "hyper" baby is going to fight harder to get out and that again will make aggression and assertion the primary tendency against obstacles and opposition later in life. This is most likely to occur because the hypothalamus (the ancient structure regulating reactivity) and the reticular activating or alerting system are organized early on.

Indeed, any artificial substance taken frequently enough and in strong enough doses may produce cellular changes in the fetus, setting up conditions for later disease which appears with sudden but inexplicable onset in adolescence or adulthood. The effects of childhood-compounded stress may finally constitute the last straw, pushing the system over the brink and into serious illness.

Drugs

All drugs are capable of crossing the placenta from mother to child. Drugs are especially dangerous to the unborn child. For one thing, they are prescribed based on adult body weight: a dosage suitable to a 130-

pound woman is hardly suitable for a 3-pound baby. For another, drugs require fully developed systems to break them down. The adult liver produces enzymes that cause chemical changes in the drugs so that they can be assimilated into the bloodstream. The unborn baby's liver cannot produce these enzymes, so the drug remains unchanged in its system and has altogether different effects on the baby than it has on the mother.

A tragic example of this occurred in the early 1960s with the thalidomide disaster. Thalidomide was a highly effective sleeping pill. It had been tested on animals and had not caused any harm. Especially attractive to pregnant women was the fact that it lessened the nausea and vomiting of the early stages of pregnancy. It was cheap and even sold over-the-counter in Europe and Asia. (It was not sold in the U.S. because it failed to meet the FDA's standards.) Eventually, it was discovered that thalidomide—so pleasantly effective for the pregnant mother—resulted in a severe and rare birth defect called phocomelia: a malformation or even absence of the bones of the arms and legs.

It has been difficult to pinpoint damage due to drugs because, in many cases, the damage does not become apparent until years later—and then usually it is not attributed to the real cause. A weak kidney that becomes evident in a 35-year-old adult may have been damaged by drugs in the womb.

Anoxia is also a common side effect of drugs; most drugs reduce the amount of oxygen in the mother's bloodstream and depress her respiration. A mother who takes tranquilizers or painkillers (including barbiturates and sleeping pills) is reducing the oxygen flow to her baby. In fact, researchers have found that drugs which produce "peace of mind" may be anything but peaceful for the fetus. A University of Rochester study found a long-lasting lethargy in the offspring of tranquilized mothers. The infant animals were dull and had low energy levels weeks after birth. The investigators believed that brain damage was a possible cause, since they had been unable to find even a trace of the tranquilizer (Valium) in the newborn. It had apparently affected their brain functions in a permanent way.

Babies born of mothers addicted to heroin during pregnancy are born with a drug addiction. They must be cured of the addiction after birth by the administration of more drugs. When a nursing mother begins to use heroin after her baby is born, the drug appears in the breast milk and the baby shows withdrawal signs if its feeding is delayed.

Again and again, research is showing what is really only common sense: what goes into the mother goes into the baby; and what is already in the mother is also transmitted to the baby. Drug addiction and neurosis are not far apart. They are both ways of blunting Pain; they both alter the system chemically and biologically; they are both addictive—watch a neurotic trying to give up his defenses to see what withdrawal from neurosis looks like—and they are both passed on.

Reliance on drugs is really only a mainfestation of neurosis. Drug usage and neurosis are not two separate things. A pregnant mother who needs drugs—even mild sedatives—is probably hurting her baby on two counts: through the effect of the drug itself and through the effect of the Pain she is trying to blunt with the drug.

Malnutrition

Malnutrition can mean anything from anorexia nervosa to obesity. It means overeating, undereating, eating too much fat, eating too little protein. The effect of a mother's malnutrition on her developing baby is profound. It may even be the single most important factor for healthy fetal development. Study after study has found that women on proper diets give birth to healthier babies, are much less likely to have premature births, have shorter labor times, and have no miscarriages or stillbirths. A good, balanced diet is essential, and the longer the mother has herself been properly nourished, the better it is for the baby. Even when the mother shows no signs of deficiency or disease from chronic poor diet, the fetus is likely to be affected. Iron-deficient mothers, who may not register as "clinically" anemic, may nevertheless produce anemic babies.

Does the fetus "react" to what the mother eats? In a way, yes. The fetus makes swallowing motions, and indeed, does swallow some fluid during the last trimester of gestation. Its taste buds seem to be fairly well developed *in utero:* modification of the flavor of the surrounding amniotic fluid it lives in produces a grimacing reaction. It has been found that malnourished fetuses make less swallowing motions than those fetuses carried by well-nourished mothers. Even during gestation it seems that our general appetite and eating behavior is being imprinted.

A study by R. A. McCance and E. M. Widdowson* demonstrated that any growing organism is sensitive to variations in nutrition. When nutrition is inadequate, as for example in rats, there are "permanent consequences" if this trauma occurs during critical periods of growth.

A research team at UCLA has demonstrated that pregnant rats deprived of protein produced offspring with a reduced number of brain cells; and the malnourished mother rats usually produced smaller and lighter placentas than nourished mothers. It works the other way as well. Pregnant rabbits with very well nourished placentas were likely to give birth to babies who had a greater number of brain cells than normal.

In humans it has been found that nutritional supplementation of the

*"The Determinants of Growth and Form," Proceedings of the Royal Society of London, 1974, Series B: Biological Sciences, 185: 1–17.

diets of low-income women (who ordinarily might not eat all that is required for a healthy pregnancy) resulted in increased birth weights of their male offspring. It is believed that this is because the male fetus grows more rapidly than the female toward the end of pregnancy, and is therefore more susceptible to external circumstances.*

A study conducted at the University of Manchester, England, demonstrated that pregnant rats exposed to even mild malnutrition during the time when the cerebellum portion of the brain was developing gave birth to animals with a reduced number of brain cells in that area. The rest of the brain, particularly the cerebral cortex, which has a slower level of development during gestation, showed a less pronounced deficit of neurons.

Certain kinds of mental retardation may also be linked with malnutrition. It has been found, for example, that retarded children have a lower birth weight than other children, even though they were full-term babies. This suggests that some kind of malnutrition found its way into brain development, literally retarding and reducing its growth. Another important research finding, particularly in animal studies, has been the discovery that malnutrition in the mother not only extends to the baby she gives birth to, but to *its* offspring as well. The babies of malnourished mothers are smaller and less developed, and in turn *their* babies are also smaller and less developed.

Malnutrition is usually associated with poverty and ignorance. But it has another common genesis in the United States and that is the extreme and faddish diets of overly weight-conscious women. Mothers who go on faddish diets are actually starving their babies. If the mother gains less than sixteen pounds during her pregnancy, she has a much greater chance of giving birth to a brain-damaged baby. That the fetus is being starved by a diet-conscious mother is an experience like any other social experience it will have outside the womb. The fetus is "learning" something about how its mother feels about it—and the general message is starvation—i.e., deprivation, lack, withholding. Starvation is a memory that is reacted to for the rest of one's life, even though there is no conscious recall of any trauma. Indeed, during early, nonverbal Primals patients have reported inexplicable sensations in their stomachs, often not aware that the sensations are those of fetal hunger.

The memory can cause one to eat voraciously at the least hint of hunger later on so as to keep that starvation feeling away (a feeling often compounded by starvation during infancy due to scheduled feeding), or it can set up a prototypic pattern of eating and vomiting so as to maintain the

*Mora, José; Sanchez, Ricardo; De Paredes, Belen; and Herrara, Guillermo, "Sex Related Effects of Nutritional Supplementation During Pregnancy on Fetal Growth," *Early Human Development*, 5, No. Holland Biomedical Press (February 1981), pp. 243–251.

original imprint—filling up and emptying out in a ritual that continues for years. The real feeling is starvation and the minute there is a full feeling vomiting ensues.

Anorexia nervosa is the medical name for self-imposed starvation. It is almost always found in young girls and women. It means a severe loss of appetite and results in serious and even fatal weight losses. Freudian interpretations for the cause of anorexia are common: the young girl is afraid of her emerging sexuality or is reacting to incestuous feelings between her and her father. Less Freudian interpretations are also common: the victim is crying out for attention, or she feels she has no identity; therefore, she literally starves her body into obscurity.

However, we have found that, not so surprisingly, it may begin long before the so-called Oedipal complexes or identity crises—it may actually begin during that nine-month nightmare in the womb. One patient wrote:

> My mother didn't want me; she tried to abort me. When that didn't work, she starved herself for seven months so that she wouldn't look pregnant. She finally started eating during her *(my)* seventh month because she had started to show. When I was born I was anorexic and couldn't keep anything down. I feel now that I keep myself on the brink of starvation and then finally eat something, because I've had that feeling from the very beginning.

Her struggle to get even basic nourishment in the womb led to a lifelong struggle to get basic emotional nourishment, no matter what the cost:

> I'm a struggler. I don't let go of people even when I know they don't want me. I struggle to survive, even when it means staying with the person I'm with, no matter what, so that I feel safe. I see now why I always fell in love with someone I really had to struggle for; where I would try and try and try up to the very end, then quit, give in and submit.

Not eating enough during pregnancy affects more than just the baby's physical development. It is a way of rejecting the baby, of withholding love during the time it is most needed. And lack of fulfillment of any need is remembered.

Yet another patient who was subjected to toxemia *in utero* experienced a lifetime of anorexia and suicidal feelings as a result:

Adult symptoms   I have been anorexic all of my adult life and I've just found out what it is all about. When I think about it, really all of my vegetative functions have been out of order most of the time: I have trouble sleeping, trouble

fucking, trouble keeping food down and trouble defecating. The feelings I've been going through recently
have helped clarify all of these problems at once.

Prototypic trauma:
fetal toxicity

Before I was born my mother lost a baby during its
fifth month. She became toxic and just poisoned the
fetus. The same thing happened to me, only I was
somehow strong enough even as a fetus to survive.
Today I felt that same toxicity, and with it the death
feelings that have plagued me all of my life.

Protoypic response:
a lifetime of nausea
and anorexia

I have always had a slight sensation of nausea,
especially just after eating, so that my impulse has
been to regurgitate anything that came into my body. I
see now that I have been reenacting that poisoning
experience in the womb. I must have had the impulse
to regurgitate to survive in the womb—and maybe it
was even that impulse, or a primitive version of it, that
did keep me alive. Yet that impulse almost killed me
later on when I began to lose so much weight.

Overflow of trauma
into sleep and sex

Whenever I am in a situation of stress or vulnerability those same early death feelings come up and my
body is obliged to push them down. In sleep I sink
down to what feels like a baby level of consciousness;
as a result, I get terrified and have trouble getting to
sleep at all. In sex I'm vulnerable, so I just shut off
when I get too excited. I guess feeling deeply is the
problem—it seems to bring up that early trauma.

Preoccupation with
death and suicide

My life has been a living death because I've lived so
closely to those early death feelings in the womb. I
have been suicidal for years, preoccupied with it, and
now I see why. Even before I was born I was surrounded by death and having to fight it off!

Somatic derivatives

I kept myself close to death with my anorexia, or at
least I stayed close to that feeling of death. Pushing
down against that trauma also kept me constipated.
The way I know this is that I'm not constipated
anymore. None of my body processes functioned right
because my body held the death feeling always cap-
tive. Somehow those death feelings had to be taken
care of before my body would work again.

Blocking in therapy

I followed the same pattern of blocking my feelings
in therapy. As feelings would come up I would get
overwhelmed, push down the feeling I was dealing
with in the present, and just kind of abreact or release
helter-skelter all of that energy trapped inside me.

I was always regarded as an "hysteric." I couldn't
focus on any one feeling because I had a volcano inside
of me to be dealt with.

Resolving the im-
print

I now see that death has been uppermost in my mind because it was really lowermost—it was really so deeply *buried* in my mind. It has bubbled up most of my life, so it's no wonder I was always nauseous. I had an imprint of toxicity before I was even born, and I've spent a lifetime getting over it!

When a mother is chronically undernourished, her body secretes more adrenaline than normal at all times because extra adrenaline is needed to utilize her own fat and convert it into blood sugar. The fetus is thus constantly under the influence of a higher-than-normal adrenaline level, which might be logged up by the baby's nervous system as the normal level. Later in life the individual might not feel normal unless he or she is hyper. A certain biological state—in this case, a hyper-adrenaline state—is established as the norm.

Conversely, if a mother overeats during pregnancy as a way of quelling her own Pain, then high blood levels of fat might come to be associated with emotional calmness and well-being—which the baby learns, because of its intrauterine experiences, is only associated with eating a lot of fat. This might lead a person to be obese or to crave a high-fat diet later on because, through state-dependent learning, the high-fat diet has become associated with a sense of well-being. What looks like heredity from mother to child is more simply the result of sharing the same early experiences.

The role of fat as a blunter of Pain is not widely known. Eating fat is, medically, an insult to the body, no matter what one's weight is. Fat hurts the body at a cellular level. The body responds to the inflow of fat in the bloodstream as an emergency situation, and defends against it. I believe part of that defense process involves the release of endorphines. This would nicely account for why it is that people will reach for ice cream out of tension or anxiety, eat it and then feel mellow. Why is eating ice cream relevant for the baby *in utero?* Because the ingestion of fat reduces capillary blood flow by 50 to 60 percent: the baby gets 50 to 60 percent less blood flow while the mother is eating and digesting ice cream.

Fat in the bloodstream also causes a decrease in glucose delivery to cells. How? Fat impairs the action of insulin, which is the substance that gets glucose out of the bloodstream and into the cells. Glucose is a key substance in maintaining cell metabolism. If a mother is eating fat, her insulin isn't working so well and she has to secrete more of it than normal to get the glucose out of her blood and into her cells. But if she produces more insulin than normal, then she automatically develops reactive hypoglycemia. Everything is fine for twenty to forty minutes after eating while the insulin is acting to bring the glucose level in the bloodstream down by transferring it into cells. The problem comes when that extra insulin continues to act, thus lowering the blood sugar content down below normal levels. At that point the body (especially the brain) goes into an emergency state because there is not enough glucose to maintain cell metabolism. This can bring on migraine, muscle ache, anxiety attacks, trembling, a feeling of asphyxiation and so on.

If a pregnant mother drank, say, five Cokes a day, her blood sugar would go through roller coaster changes of very-high-to-very-low to very-high-to-very-low levels of insulin and glucose. What does all this mean for her baby? It means several things. First, it means that the baby does not get enough oxygen while the mother is hypoglycemic—which is almost any time after she has been drinking Cokes or eating sweet or fatty foods. The research of Carson et al* showed that sustained insulin infusion (which is the same thing as being hypoglycemic) of pregnant lambs resulted in significant decrease in oxygen flow to the fetal lambs. We shall see in the next section how even mild decreases in oxygen can lead to minimal brain damage in the developing fetus.

Second, in a hypoglycemic mother the baby is getting too little glucose in addition to too little oxygen. Oxygenation of tissue and glucose utilization of tissue are intimately and reciprocally connected: if the glucose level is too low, the cells cannot properly utilize oxygen since that requires energy; and vice versa, in the presence of asphyxiation the cells cannot properly utilize glucose. Glucose and oxygen are both centrally and critically important for the health of cells, and if either gets too low certain brain cells will die.

Third, fat in the mother's bloodstream means that the baby is being subjected to excessive levels of adrenaline: when the sugar level gets too low in the bloodstream (the bottom half of the hypoglycemic roller coaster), adrenaline is released to convert fat into sugar and this produces an exceedingly nervous state. What this may mean ultimately is that chronic adult nervousness may begin in the womb with the stamped-in alteration of glucose utilization processes.

Tobacco

The fetus must receive all of its nutrients and its oxygen from the mother's bloodstream through the placenta. What this means to the unborn baby of a smoking mother is five minutes of suffocation and poisoning each time the mother smokes a cigarette.

Suffocation occurs in two ways. First, tobacco robs the blood of oxygen

*Carson, Bonita S., Philipps, Anthony F., Simmons, Michael A., Battaglia, Frederick C. and Meschia, Giacomo. "Effects of a Sustained Insulin Infusion Upon Glucose Uptake and Oxygenation of the Ovine Fetus," *Pediatric Research, 14:* 147–152, 1980.

so that the mother's blood is forced to take up the gases in the tobacco at the expense of needed oxygen. This can result in oxygen starvation to the fetus with many serious side effects. The possible source of suffocation arises from the fact that tobacco acts as a vasoconstrictor—it literally constricts the size of the mother's blood vessels so that they carry less blood.

Researchers have found "degenerative changes in the umbilical blood vessels" of smoking mothers, which means that that delicate bridge of life between mother and infant is being permanently altered by the smoking.*

The importance of blood flow to the fetus is obvious, and anything that inhibits that blood flow, such as cigarette smoking, must be viewed as a threat to the fetus. It was found that the volume of uteroplacental blood flow in mothers with "intrauterine growth retardation" (their fetuses were smaller than normal for their gestational age) was one-quarter of the volume of blood flow in mothers with normal pregnancies. In other words, the babies showing retarded fetal growth and development were receiving 75 percent less blood from their mothers than normally developing babies.†

A study of 17,000 British children indicates that the child of the heavy smoker (someone who smokes ten cigarettes or more after the fourth month of pregnancy) is in poor physical condition at birth and shows inadequate social development as a child.‡ There is evidence here too that the smoking depletes vitamin C levels. This can affect the cellular structure as well as adversely affecting the synthesis of collagenous tissue of the body. Smokers need twice as much vitamin C as nonsmokers. Mothers who smoked during pregnancy lost their babies 30 percent more often than those who did not. The babies in this study who survived were measured at the age of seven. They were one-half inch shorter on the average than children of nonsmokers. They were also less skilled in reading and presented more psychological problems in school. They seemed less physically coordinated and showed impairment in copying simple drawings.

The fetus is really getting a kind of double-barreled deprivation: it gets less oxygen from the mother's bloodstream, and it gets a lower quantity of blood because the mother's blood vessels are constricted. And new research shows that even the thought of smoking a cigarette changes the mother's physiology. When she anticipates having a cigarette her blood

*Asmussen, I., and Kjeldsen, K. "Intimal Ultrastructure of Human Umbilical Arteries," *Circul. Res.*, 36: 579–589, 1975.

†Lunell, N. O., Sarby, B., Lewander R., and Nylund, L., "Comparisons of Uteroplacental Blood Flow in Normal and in Intrauterine Growth-Retarded Pregnancy," *Gynecologic and Obstetric Investigation*, 10: 106–118, 1979.

‡"Gravida's Smoking Seen Handicap to Offspring," *Ob. Gyn. News,* June 15, 1970, Volume 5, 12, p. 16.

pressure and heart rate change adversely. It is no less than the fact that the anticipation of Pain brings physiologic change.

While the fetus is deprived of oxygen during this five-minute cigarette, it is being ingested with poisons: tobacco contains numerous toxic substances (nicotine, carbon monoxide, methyl alcohol, carbonic acid, alkali, pyroline, hydrocyanic acid, arsenic, collidine, furfural, pyridine and various tar products) which are all, in some degree, poisonous to the tissues of the human body.

Carbon monoxide "poisoning" has particularly harmful possibilities. Carbon monoxide is known to have highly detrimental effects on cell functioning in human beings of any age. Researchers have found that smoking produces a significant concentration of carbon monoxide in the blood. What does this mean for the fetus whose cells are just being formed? Montagu writes:

> Carbon monoxide in the blood is believed to slow down several important chemical changes that occur during a child's prenatal life. In the tightly organized schedule that governs his development, an unscheduled change in any single aspect can have far-reaching effects on the child's entire body and mind.*

Research has shown again and again that smoking during pregnancy leads to premature births and to lower-than-average birth weights; it can cause a delay in the breathing of the newborn and there is some indication that the newborn's respiratory apparatus is somewhat retarded.

Probably the largest single study on this subject was conducted by the U.S. National Institute of Health Perinatal Research Project. The study began in 1958 and is still continuing. Several years after the study began, intermediate findings were reported from data that had already been compiled on some 30,000 pregnant women and their 24,000 offspring. The data showed that premature births occurred more frequently for women who smoked than for women who did not smoke, and that the more cigarettes a woman smoked, the smaller her child was likely to be.

The long-term effects of being born prematurely and of growing up smaller than average can be serious. In later chapters I shall show the myriad repercussions of prematurity, but I want to state here that the effects of prematurity do not end once an infant is considered out of danger; neither do the effects of oxygen deprivation or toxic poisoning. These physiologic alterations are imprinted into the developing fetus as they occur and become an integral part of his physiology and personality for life. The imprint endures and it endures partly through these alterations in function. The baby has been smoking too, and the warning on the

---

*Op. cit., p. 112.

pack of cigarettes is no less applicable to him. We must take the attitude that there is a human being inside, a most vulnerable creature, who is much more affected by what the mother is doing than she is herself.

What is more, the mother may be predisposing her child to nicotine addiction. Adult smoking patterns may well begin in the womb: nicotine is a powerful blunter of Pain, and when the mother blunts her own Pain by smoking while pregnant she is also affecting the fetus. The fetus is getting "used to" a level of nicotine in its system. This level is a memory that associates a calm inner environment with a certain level of nicotine. Mother is biologically more relaxed in this state. Thus, apart from the biologic effects of nicotine on cell growth, protein metabolism and cholinergic synapses on the developing nervous system, there is also a "learning" taking place; there is a learned association between nicotine and relaxation. The adult chain-smoker is responding to a physiologic memory stamped in prior to birth. We must keep in mind that just because an event takes place in that internal world away from view does not mean that it is not having its effects. The fetus doesn't *see* its mother smoke and thereby learns the pattern; it *feels* her smoking and thereby learns it.

Internal Stressors: The Mother's Emotional and Psychological Condition

Not only is the fetus affected by what the mother takes *into* her system—it is equally affected by the *state* of that system: is the pregnant mother easygoing, relaxed and calm; or is she chronically tense, depressed or agitated? Is her life situation quiet and stable or is she encountering crisis after crisis? Not so surprisingly, both animal and human research is showing how the mother's inner state profoundly affects the development and personality of her baby.

The kind of effect any trauma has on the fetus depends on the time it occurs during gestation. As mentioned previously, there is a timetable of critical growth spurts during which various functions of the nervous system are being organized and the hormones that regulate those functions are being newly manufactured. Traumas during these times greatly affect those critical organizations.

TABLE 2

Proven or correlated effects of stress-induced emotional and psychological imbalances in the pregnant mother on the developing fetus and newborn.

1. Anoxia (Stress-induced) . . . . .Brain damage
                                    Cerebral palsy
                                    Crib death

                              Epilepsy
                              Learning and behavior problems
                              Mental disorders
                              Mental retardation
                              Psychogenic abortion
2. Anxiety........................Autism
                              Childhood emotional disorders
                              Decreased resistance to infection
                              Higher stress and adrenaline levels
                              Infant hyperirritability
3. Blood Pressure and Heartbeat.....Hyperirritability
                              Abnormal heart rate
                              Lowered birth weight
                              Nutritional deprivation
                              Oxygen deprivation
4. Hormonal Imbalances............Growth deficiencies
                              Hyperthyroidism
                              Hypothyroidism
                              Low stress threshold
                              Neurological damage
                              Prematurity
                              Sexual and gender abnormalities
                                 behavioral
                                 structural
                              Stillbirth
5. Unwanted Pregnancy............Malformations
                              Spontaneous abortions
                              Stillbirth

Anoxia (Stress-induced)

We have seen that anoxia can be caused by drugs, tobacco and high fat levels in the mother's bloodstream. It can also be caused solely by the mother's emotional state, regardless of what she ingests. Fear, anxiety and Pain constrict blood flow to the fetus and reduce the oxygen content in its blood. The anxiety and Pain of the mother can even kill the fetus. There is a class of mothers known clinically as "psychogenic aborters," meaning that their abortions have no organic basis but are caused by the mothers' emotional state. How can emotions kill a baby? It is known that these women have extremely high stress levels. Individuals with high levels of Pain produce their own internal painkillers, serotonin and endorphine. The aborting mothers have exceptionally high levels of serotonin which tends to be a vasoconstrictor and thus may reduce oxygen levels to the point where death to the fetus results. Haesslein and Niswander note:

Maternal anxiety may also be an important cause of prenatal neurologic damage to the fetus. It has been observed that exposure of a

gravid (pregnant) woman to anxiety-producing stimuli results in a decrease in uterine blood flow and simultaneous changes in the fetal cardiovascular system consistent with fetal asphyxia.*

In animal research, investigators Greiss and Gobble† found that triggering excessive adrenaline in pregnant ewes caused "profound uterine vasoconstriction" to the point where almost all blood flow to the fetus was cut off. And working with rhesus monkeys, Myers‡ found that fetal asphyxia occurred when the mothers were subjected to psychological stress.

The evidence with both animals and humans is clear: maternal stress to the fetus can cause all manner of problems from slight neurologic damage to death by asphyxia.

Anxiety

Anxiety is Primal fear—that is, a fear derived from past trauma which seeps into one's present life. It is the sum total of the mobilization processes of the body against the rise of Pain to consciousness. The consciousness of Pain is what is threatening and all of the repressive forces of the system are set in motion to stop it. When those repressive forces are insufficient for the task, terror seeps out and is experienced as amorphous anxiety. But that is only the first stage of a Primal A consciousness overwhelmed by early Pain is in danger of psychosis. The system, wise as it is, rushes in to prevent it through its gating systems. It is the faulty gates that are the problem. Thus, anxiety is a signal of Pain on the march. It is the disconnected physiologic aspect of the early experience. When the scene in toto meets consciousness, anxiety turns into Pain, then into pure feeling and finally is canceled out.

Meanwhile, anxiety perpetuates a vicious cycle. To avoid it we call upon external aids—drugs, alcohol, tobacco and food. To process it our systems are forced to produce excessive amounts of stress hormones. For the pregnant mother the situation is doubly dangerous.

It has been observed that anxious mothers ask for more drugs during pregnancy and require more drugs during birth. They are more likely to have higher stress hormones and higher adrenaline levels in their bloodstreams, which "hyperizes" both mother and baby. Anxious mothers tend to smoke and drink more and the healthy nutrients they do ingest are not broken down well due to the anxiety. There is a decreased resistance to

---

*Haesslein and Niswander, op. cit. p. 245.

†Greiss, F. C., and Gobble, F. L., "The Effects of Sympathetic Nerve Stimulation o the Uterine Vascular Bed," *American Journal of Obstetrics,* 97, 1967, pp. 962–967.

‡Myers, R. E., "Production of Fetal Asphyxia by Maternal Psychological Stress," Pavlov, *Journal of Biological Sciences,* 12, 1, 1977, pp. 51–61.

infection which affects the fetus and there is an added motility of the womb which batters the fetus.

Autism may also be linked to maternal stress. A study reported at the 1977 Meeting of the American Association of Psychiatric Services for Children found that mothers of autistic children were two times more likely to have psychiatric problems than mothers of normal children. This is not to conclude that stress is the sole cause of autism, but researcher Alan J. Ward noted that "an unusually high percentage of mothers of autistic children are subject to 'family discord' while they are pregnant."* Ward suggested that his findings supported the notion of a link between prenatal maternal anxiety and children with higher levels of anxiety, higher rates of emotional disorders and slower rates of development.

Many studies have correlated emotional disturbance in the mother with hyperirritability, restlessness, vomiting and feeding problems in the newborn. Lester Sontag, a leading investigator of the effects of stress on newborns, writes:†

> Such an infant (born to an emotionally stressed mother) is from the beginning a hyperactive, irritable, squirming, crying child. . . . He empties his bowels at unusually frequent intervals, spits up half his feedings and generally makes a nuisance of himself. He is to all intents and purposes a neurotic infant when he is born—the result of an unsatisfactory fetal environment.

The system of an anxious mother is itself constantly running. Stress literally churns us up. For a tiny fetus floating helplessly in the uterine sac, that churning turns its environment into something more like a storm at sea than the gently rocking cushion it is meant to be. Clearly the dialogue between mother and child begins at conception and not at birth and that dialogue is one of stress and turbulence when the mother is upset.

Montagu provides a clear and simple explanation of how the mother's state of being is transferred to her growing baby:‡

> A pregnant woman . . . can share a portion of her emotion with her child. This is because a portion of any emotion is physical, expressed in changes in her body that can be transferred to her child. The beginning of an emotion is the original perception—that a fire is raging, for instance, and that it constitutes a danger. The second stage is a set of physical and chemical changes in the body that immediately follow the perception of danger. . . . These changes are quite specific and are of two kinds: chemical substances manufactured by the nerve

---

*Reported in *Science News*, Volume 112, December 3, 1977, p. 374.
†As quoted in Montagu, op. cit., p. 164.
‡Montagu, op. cit., p. 159.

ends and hormones released by the endocrine glands. It is these substances—chemicals and hormones—that form the connection between the perception of danger by the mother and its effect on the growth and development of her child. When these substances enter her bloodstream, they are on the road to the child's bloodstream; when they have crossed the placenta and begin the journey through his system, he is receiving in a visible, measurable form the force that began as a subjective feeling in his mother. And it is by these chemicals and hormones that he can be affected.

A neurotic mother carries the danger—the fire—within her. Unconscious Pain is a continuous, inner activator of the chemicals and hormones Montagu refers to. It is the "visible, measurable force" that crosses the placental barrier and alters the very makeup of the baby developing within. Indeed, researcher Lena Martensson at the University of Lund, Sweden, doubts that there is such a thing as a placental barrier. Almost all substances pass from the mother to the fetus, including whatever atmospheric pollutants she is subjected to. The fetus suffers from Los Angeles smog, from pesticides (she is studying pesticidal effects on guinea pig placentas) and from factory emissions.

Blood Pressure and Heartbeat

What happens during gestation can greatly affect what happens during birth. The mother's blood pressure is an important determinant of fetal growth. Elevations in the mother's blood pressure during pregnancy are accompanied by decreases in blood flow to the fetus. This means that the baby gets a reduced supply of oxygen and a reduced supply of nutrients which profoundly affect its growth and development.

Researcher Woodson and his team* found that the fetuses put under the stress of high blood pressure during gestation were less able to withstand the oxygen decreases that occurred during labor and showed more frequent and more pronounced decreases in heart rate during labor than those newborns whose mothers had had normal blood pressure levels throughout pregnancy.

The fetus is clearly affected by what goes on with the mother's blood, but does it also feel and experience traumatic variations in that blood? Apparently so. One patient wrote:

Adult symptoms   On Christmas day several years ago I awoke with a feeling of deep suffering filled with death-awareness.

*Woodson, R. H., Blurton Jones, N. G., Woodson, E. Da Costa, Pollock, S., and Evans, M., "Fetal Mediators of the Relationships between Increased Pregnancy and Labor Blood Pressure and Newborn Irritability," *Early Human Development,* 1979, 3/2, 127–139.

Trigger My pulse rate had dropped to 40 beats per minute. My mother had sent me a book of nature photographs in color called *The Sun's Birthday*. Awash in Pain, it seemed to mean only "the son's birthday."

I lay on my bed and aimlessly looked at the pictures. There was a caption under a picture of a book that read: "All living things need water to survive." I turned the page and there was a two-page color photo of a giant storm wave in a typhoon.

Reliving: "Red everywhere" What happened next was an eruption of the earliest Pain I ever encountered in over three years of Primalling. I felt the Pain come from my pelvis, not my belly. I tasted bloody, amniotic fluid. All my vision went red— red everywhere. I reexperienced total weightlessness and I knew with certainty that I was dying and that my mother was dying.

A profound calm My "crying" didn't sound like baby crying, but was more like the coarse, harsh cry of a wounded animal. It went on and on for about thirty minutes. Suddenly the feelings were gone, and I experienced a profound calm and stillness, and I was filled with wonder at what I'd just been through.

Later I called my mother and said, "Sometime before I was born you had an episode of bleeding. How soon before my birth was it?"

She replied, "How did you know I bled?"

"I'm certain you did, now I just want to know when it happened."

Objective verification "It happened about two weeks before you were born," she said.

Since I was born six weeks premature, the vintage of that trauma was in the first third of the third trimester. All I can conclude from my experience is that a baby in the womb *knows* what his or her mother is feeling—at least during the third trimester.

Another direct emotional connection between mother and fetus occurs through the mother's heartbeat. We know that the mother's heartbeat is "heard"—experienced—by the fetus. The rhythmic beating of the heart is an intrinsically comforting sound—as long as the beats occur rhythmically and at the right pace. Neurotic heartbeats tend to be faster—"speedier"— and less rhythmic, which may have something to do with the imprinting of "speedy" reactions in the baby that affect it from birth onward. Research shows that when people are asked to set a beat which makes them feel most comfortable, they choose something around their own heart rate. Having been conditioned by mother's heart rate in utero, the rhythm becomes imprinted on the baby's consciousness as the "normal" rhythm. There is evidence that a very fast heart and respiratory rhythm can be imprinted into the unconscious of the fetus, which then has a direct effect on how fast the nervous system reacts from then onward: it will affect how highstrung the child is, how fast the adult drives his car and how fast he sets the general tempo of his life.

Montagu described an interesting experiment that "showed conclusively that when a newborn child can hear the sound of a normal heartbeat, he is quieter, he is healthier and he gains weight faster than when he cannot (hear the heartbeat)."* The experiment dealt with newborns, but it seems safe to assume that the effects are qualitatively similar for the baby *in utero*.

In the experiment, which was conducted over a sixteen-week period, two loudspeakers were set up in the nursery of a hospital to project the sound of an authentic, normal heartbeat. The heartbeat sound was played continuously, day and night, over alternate four-week periods: the sound was played for four weeks, turned off for four weeks, played for four weeks and turned off for four weeks. During the entire period, the weight of the babies and the frequency of their crying were regularly measured. All of the infants in the experiment were "normal" infants who stayed in the nursery for four days immediately following their births.

The results were quite clear: the heartbeat sound enhanced weight gain and diminished crying in the infants who heard it during their four-day stay. It was also observed that the "heartbeat infants" breathed more deeply and more regularly than the other infants.

To see what would happen if the quality of the sound were changed, the investigators increased the recorded heartbeat from 72 to 128 beats per minute. The result was a noticeable increase in crying and restlessness among the infants.

The investigators believed that the weight gain in infants who heard the heartbeat sound was due to the fact that they cried less: their energies were used to grow, whereas the energies of the other infants were used to cry. The implications for the baby *in utero* are, I am sure, exactly the same. A comforting heartbeat enhances all the baby's growth processes simply by virtue of allowing them to take place, undiverted. A stressful heartbeat, on the other hand, diverts the growing baby's energies away from growth and onto stress. That we each "march to the beat of a different drum" is indeed true.

One of our staff members related the following pertinent description of what he feels are "bits and pieces" of his earliest experiences in the womb:

*Montagu, op. cit., p. 191.

The feelings and sensations I want to describe really seem more like disconnected patches of information than like the feelings and sensations of one, cohesive experience. I think that's because I've only reexperienced bits and pieces of my birth and the time just before it, and much of it is still inaccessible. So far, the bits and pieces don't seem to have much coherence, other than the fact that they have an enormous impact on me.

Birth feelings and sensations

The other day I was feeling some feeling when I noticed that my left hand started making this thrub-dub-thrub-dub sound as it struck the carpet. I made the motion with my left hand in such a way that the initial hit was the strongest "thrub" sound, and the slight bounce that came after made the weaker "dub" sound. The action of doing this was quite involuntary. I wasn't aware of starting to do it or of *deciding* to do it. At some point I simply realized that I was making this sound, and that it was synchronous with what I was feeling—in fact, it tended to *reinforce* the feeling.

Involuntary hand motion: a heart-beat?

It struck me that the sound resembled a heartbeat, but I stopped myself from thinking about whether or not it was and just went with the feeling. Afterwards, I asked my wife, who had sat with me while I was feeling, if the drumming sound reminded her of anything. Before I could even finish my question, she replied with a knowing smile, "It sounded like a heartbeat." The knowing smile was because she had often heard me drum my fingertips in that particular pattern, but I apparently had not noticed it myself.

I then connected the fingertip drumming sound with this peculiar sound I make in my throat. [He now makes a very unusual and indescribable sound in the back of his throat that vaguely resembles the sound of a heartbeat through a monitor.] I have always been fascinated by that sound, but never really connected it to anything. Now it occurred to me that I would drum my fingertips only when I wasn't able to make the throat sound for one reason or another—for instance, when I'm into a feeling and crying.

Idiosyncratic throat sound: a heartbeat?

But both the throat sound and the fingertip drumming feel the same inwardly—they both seem to express or reinforce the same basic feeling. They also both feel connected in some way to my birth and prebirth experience, as does my very strong phobia of dying from a heart attack. I haven't felt these connections clearly yet, so all I can tell you is what I "know"

Same basic feeling

of my history. What I'm trying to say is that although I haven't felt the *exact* connections, I do clearly feel that there *are* connections.

Birth history

During the latter stages of pregnancy, my mother had toxemia. (When I asked her as an adult what "toxemia" was, she said it occurred when the baby's wastes poisoned the mother's blood. Medically, this is not entirely correct.) Anyway, in an effort to improve her condition it was decided to induce labor. Ten days before I was born she was given twelve injections of a labor-inducing drug at one-hour intervals. Still I did not budge!

Endurance of birth sensation

To this day an injection will make me pass out. When I got my shots at school as a child the nurse would notice how pale my face became and she would immediately lead me out into the fresh air. A dentist once jammed his knee into my rib cage because he thought my heart had stopped after he had given me an injection.

It's not the needle prick—I can give blood easily— it's the feeling of a strange fluid rushing into my bloodstream. That feeling of the fluid rushing in can still make me faint.

Adult symptom: al- coholism

As an adult I became an alcoholic, and I now feel that the alcoholism was a way of keeping my system poisoned just as it had been poisoned before I was even born.

Hormonal Imbalances

Hormones control and regulate cellular activity. Hormone glands produce secretions which are carried in the bloodstream to their target cellular systems. Each hormone has a specific function: it "tells" its group of cells what to do and how to do it. Growth hormones help cells to grow and differentiate; sex-related hormones give sex cells the messages to be masculine or feminine; and stress-related hormones help cells react to and handle stress.

The mother's hormonal system is a mirror of her emotional state. It is one key way the mother passes on her Pain. If a mother is chronically nervous, depressed or agitated, her hormones—which pour out continuously into her bloodstream and then into her baby's bloodstream—will be out of balance. Her baby will be subjected to a continuous oversupply or undersupply of the various hormones.

In my previous book, *Prisoners of Pain,* I discussed how hormones change under stress, and it is not unlikely that we soon shall have precise measurements of the mother's Pain and the degree of dislocation of her hormone functions. One thing is certain from our long-range research: there is dislocation of hormone functioning when Pain is present and a normalization of many key hormonal secretions when Pain is "extracted" from the system via Primal Therapy. These dislocations exist even in the absence of diagnosed disease. It sometimes takes decades before symptoms appear, but when these deviations from normal exist in a mother, overt disease or not, they will have an effect on the fetus—the fetus no longer is living in a "normal" environment. We can understand a disturbed child who has had a bad home environment but it is more difficult to comprehend that the fetus is likewise disturbed by a bad biochemical environment.

The thyroid controls growth, development and metabolism. It guides and controls all the processes that build up and break down protoplasm, the most basic life substance. That is why thyroid alterations are so significant. Chronic stress can change the secretion rate of the mother's thyroid which, in turn, alters the baby's entire metabolic "gauge." The baby's thyroid gland begins its production and secretion of thyroxin a few weeks after gestation begins, so it will be affected throughout most of the nine months by any imbalance in the mother.

If the mother is *hypo*thyroid (meaning her thyroid produces too little thyroxin), she will be chronically tired and will have less physical resources to meet stress. Her baby may then be "born tired," with hypothyroidism stamped in as the "normal" metabolic situation. It is as if the baby's life processes are conditioned to function in slow motion. (It also may be that the baby's system works harder and oversecretes to meet the mother's deficiency.) As a result of hypothyroidism, there may be a greater tendency toward passivity in later life, toward giving up under stress and a "what's-the-use" attitude that pervades everything one does. (Hypothyroidism is not always evident as a clinical condition. There can be just a small reduction in output which is enough to shape personality but not enough to register on tests.)

Similarly, a *hyper*thyroid mother may pass this on to her growing baby. It becomes "hyper" in the womb so that the predisposition for a heart attack in the mid-forties or mid-fifties may be imprinted long before the baby's heart ever takes its first independent beat. The baby may even respond to its birth trauma differently—with more *push*—because it has been "hyperized" weeks or months before. It is going to push more because it has got more "push" in the form of thyroxin. The hyper adult then often arranges his life as if drive and pressure are necessary. He doesn't think anything is wrong with his manic pace. His life becomes one big rationale for his imprinted gestation experiences.

Before I am accused of riding one horse into oblivion, let me hasten to add that I am writing in order to underline the effects of early trauma on development. My purpose is to emphasize what fourteen years of observation has taught us and to bring into view an area that has been overlooked for a long, long time. Clearly there may be many other reasons for hormone imbalance later in life, and heredity may well be an important one. But even hereditary predispositions may need specific traumas to make them overt; and conversely, without those traumas the tendencies may remain latent.

There is now a good deal of research indicating that stress during gestation may alter patterns of sexual functioning. In one recent study with animals, it was found that stress to the mother in the form of conditioned anxiety, crowding, immobilization and temperature extremes permanently altered the structure or function of sexual behavior in the offspring. Female offspring suffered ovarian irregularities, experienced a fewer number of conceptions and a greater number of spontaneous abortions, had longer pregnancies and gave birth to fewer viable infants than non-stressed offspring. The stressed mothers showed radically reduced nursing behavior and produced insufficient amounts of milk. The sexual behavior of male rats from stressed mothers was feminized to the point where they were unable to exhibit normal copulatory behavior. The researcher concluded:

> Prenatal stress therefore seems to affect later reproduction not by disrupting postnatal rearing conditions but by altering the fetus possibly by changing the hormonal milieu.*

Why are the hormones altered? Because severe stress triggers large amounts of steroids, the stress hormones, which are secreted by the adrenal glands. Disturbances in the gonadal and adrenal hormones at the time when sexual differentiation is occurring in the fetus disrupts and alters that differentiation:

> Prenatal stress therefore may influence the exchange of gonadal and adrenal hormones between the mother and fetus or the balance of these hormones in the fetus alone during a critical stage of hypothalamic differentiation, thereby producing reproductive dysfunctions in adulthood.

It is particularly noteworthy that the development of the hypothalamus, one of our most important brain structures, was implicated in the re-

*Herrenkohl, L. R., "Prenatal Stress Reduces Fertility and Fecundity in Female Offspring." *Science,* Volume 206, November 1979, 1097–1099.

search. This means that many of our vital functions—from hormone output to pain thresholds to growth and sex patterns—may be permanently altered for the worse during those first nine months.

It has been demonstrated that the female hormone estrogen, administered just after birth to male rats, feminizes them for a lifetime. That same hormone administered later on does not produce such changes. There are critical times when hormone imbalance can be catastrophic and prototypic. Thus hormone changes that take place even in early childhood may not be critical in setting up lifelong patterns, whereas hormone imbalance during gestation may set up lifelong predispositions and imbalances.

Another study* discovered that women who took synthetic sex hormones such as progestin to prevent miscarriage later gave birth to masculinized babies: in 18 percent of the females born to these women there was a masculinization of their genitalia; and in both male and female infants there was an increase in aggressive behavior. The researcher pointed out that excessive hormones, in combination with the environment, may help to explain the problem.

Progesterone, a female hormone and ingredient in birth control pills, also can later influence the masculinity and femininity of offspring when given to pregnant women. A recent Columbia University study found that girls exposed to progesterone were quite "feminine" but so were the boys. When one considers that tens of thousands of progesterone prescriptions are written to prevent miscarriages, one understands the possible danger to the children.

Important new information on this subject has come from Gunter Dorner, head of the Institute of Endocrinology, Humboldt University, East Germany. Dorner investigated the connection between behavior and events in the womb; specifically, hormonal changes in the mother and her fetus and alterations in the brain. He has found that if mother rats are deficient in sex hormone (of which they were artificially deprived), permanent changes are caused in the hypothalamus. These changes affect later behavior in specific ways: when the hormone alterations are severe enough, homosexuality in their offspring can be a result. Dorner points out that female and male homosexuality are caused by deprivation or overabundance of the male hormone testosterone. "These [hormone] effects are written into the organism long before puberty. In fact, at various stages of fetus in the womb. They affect not only the form and shape that the body will come to have but also the way it will respond to hormonal influences at puberty.†

It is in the second month of pregnancy that gender differentiation begins. Prior to that point, the fetus contains the genitalia of both sexes.

*As originally reported in *Science,* reprinted in *Science News,* June Machover Reinish, Rutgers University, March 14, 1981, Volume 119, p. 166.

†As reported in *Playboy* magazine, April 1982, p. 146.

Changes in the mother's emotional state during this differentiation period can well affect the hormone balance and brain structure of the fetus. This means that future gender orientation is partially determined by events around the second month of gestation. Robert Goy of the Regional Primate Research Center of the University of Wisconsin has discovered that female rhesus monkeys given male hormone during pregnancy produce females who are likely to be the dominant members of the group. They are permanently more aggressive, tend to mimic male behavior by mounting other monkeys, play rough and may even have male genitalia.

The importance of this research linking changes in sex hormones to later development is that we have already found sex hormone changes in our patients with the resolution of stress. Thus, thinking retrospectively, we can assume that early stress in a pregnant woman has changed her hormone balance and that of her unborn child. If the resolution of Pain can normalize sex hormone output, the laying down of it ought to destabilize that balance. To put it differently, if the mother were "normal" during pregnancy we would expect her to have normal hormone balance. If she were quite neurotic or under stress we would expect some kind of imbalance which would later be reflected in the child—perhaps in the degree of his masculinity or her femininity. At the very least, this imbalance will help shape the way the child reacts to his later environment.

We must always take into account the "critical periods" of development when we discuss lifelong changes caused by hormone alterations during gestation. In one animal study, for example, testosterone (a sex hormone) was administered at different times to a group of female rats.* It was discovered that early administration had little effect, but that administration during a "critical period" (in this case, nineteen days) produced many permanent changes, including:

(1) alterations in structure of the external genitalia (a high percentage of the rats had modified vaginas);
(2) alterations in the functional state of the ovaries;
(3) abnormalities in the display of feminine and masculine sexual behaviors.

The conclusion of the researchers:

The data support the concept of a discrete prenatal period during which circulating androgen influences the development of tissues which mediate feminine sexual behavior in the rat.

*Huffman, Linda, and Hendricks, Shelton, E., "Prenatally Injected Testosterone Propionate and Sexual Behavior of Female Rats," *Physiology and Behavior,* 1981, Volume 26, pp. 773–778.

There seems to be a permanent change in sexual characteristics and tendencies once the inner environment has been tampered with during pregnancy.

A mother can undergo this kind of change without foreign injections, as our research has indicated. Again, we discovered that Pain dislocates sex hormone function and its removal normalizes output. This sexual deviation in the mother may be a significant factor in the sexual deviation (psychological) of the offspring later on. This doesn't just mean becoming homosexual. Rather, it means a certain character change so that the person is abnormally aggressive, passive, sexual or deviate in the choice of sex objects. We must, of course, never underestimate the importance of later childhood events on all this, but the basic tendencies upon which these experiences play are there from the start. They provide the "force" behind deviations.

Female offspring may be affected by maternal stress which alters hormone output in a most direct way: during the last trimester of pregnancy the mother's estrogen and progesterone levels rise to prepare for delivery. Among its other functions there seems to be a painkilling factor in these hormones, which drops radically once labor begins. This drop may unconsciously evoke the biologic memory of the same situation during the mother's birth when her bloodstream rose and dropped in the same manner as her mother's. Thus, a trauma is elicited which may make the childbirth painful and traumatic. That is, there is going to be a Primal anlage of Pain added to the situation that arises out of the mother's own birth memories. This seems also to be the case in painful menstruation: the monthly cycle re-creates the birth pattern of hormone output, with a rise in the middle and a drop as the period begins. We have found in many cases a regulation of the period as women have first-line birth Primals. The drop in hormones as the period begins seems to permit the ascendance of birth Pain. In Primal women with good access this will lead to birth Primals. In non-Primal women with no access it can and does lead to menstrual difficulties, irregular and painful periods, or even the lack of periods for months at a time. This is the assumed link between stress and menstrual problems. It is certainly hormonal at its roots. All of the above, however, remains hypothetical at this time.

To make the linkage more precise: the fetus is learning something as the sex hormones rise and fall in the mother. There may well be an association between discomfort and the drop in these hormones. Certainly, this is true at birth when the trauma begins as the hormones drop. Indeed, we have found that women in Primal Therapy have a much greater access to early Pain three or four days prior to menstruating than at any other time of the month. It is also the time when they are most likely to have first-line feelings. They seem to go back into that exact state just before birth when estrogen levels drop—which is why things like migraines and irritability are such common side effects of menstruating:

> Since I had my first period years ago I have had to stay in bed at least two days each month. I get deep cramps, weakness and pain. I usually vomit. Several days before my period I begin to feel a sense of agony and of not knowing what is going to happen. I also imagine that something bad will happen to me, like dying or losing someone close to me.
>
> During therapy my period would come up with the same fear. Then I began to experience a feeling where the fear around my period turned into the terror around my birth, with a tremendous feeling of impending death. During my birth Primal my head bashed against my mother's womb until I felt it would explode. The feeling arose of not knowing what was going on—the same feeling of confusion and fear I get before and during my period, compounded by the fact that my first periods were total mysteries to me. My condition got so bad that I often skipped many periods. Now as a result of my birth Primals, I have regular periods and I no longer have to go to bed with them.

Our assumption here is that the hormone drop associated with the original trauma left its residue so that later the same patterns of hormone changes during the menstrual cycle brought with them associated psychological reactions of fear, confusion and terror. The totality of physiologic and psychologic change was enough to disrupt the cycle and to make it painful. The Pain was an "add-on" of the original trauma plus all of the neglect and shame experienced by the patient during her teen years concerning menstruation. It wasn't that she was told it was "bad." Rather, the subject was never discussed—which amounts to the same thing.

I believe estrogen may function partly as an analgesic by working in conjunction with the endorphine system to keep Pain levels down during pregnancy and childbirth for both the mother and baby. Women do commonly report that they never felt better than when they were pregnant. It is only when estrogen levels drop sharply after birth that you get the "postpartum" depressions so debilitating to new mothers.

Researchers Haesslein and Niswander noted that women who have precipitous drops in estrogen during pregnancy are more likely to give birth to neurologically damaged infants.*

Hormonal dislocations may even be severe enough, it is now believed, to trigger premature labor resulting in stillborn infants. In one study,† the

---

*Haesslein, Hanns C., and Niswander, Kenneth R., "Fetal Distress in Term Pregnancies," *American Journal of Obstetrics and Gynecology* 137 (2): 245–253, May 1980.

†De Sa, D. J., "Stress Response and Its Relationship To Cystic (Pseudofollicular) Change in the Definitive Cortex of the Adrenal Gland in Stillborn Infants," *Archives of Disease in Childhood*, 53, 1978, pp. 769–776.

adrenal glands of forty-one stillborn infants were studied and a stress response pattern was clearly identified in the cellular composition of twenty-eight out of the forty-one glands. (The adrenal glands are located near the kidneys and produce hormones that regulate sexual and metabolic functioning.) In discussing the results of the study, the author wrote:

> The results presented in this paper are evidence of fetal reactivity to nonspecific stresses *in utero* . . . In particular, cystic changes and clear cell reversal represent the most extreme changes that may be expected. It is clear that the development of cysts constitutes a somewhat special fetal reaction to stress and is best seen in the most immature fetus. The cells undergoing cytolysis show the ultrastructural and histochemical features of stressed cells and it is tempting to speculate that this represents a biochemical immaturity in cells of the infants' adrenal cortex. Thus such an immature infant might not be capable of responding in a controlled and sustained fashion to an espisode of stress. . . .
>
> It is tempting to suggest that in those stillbirths with a pronounced stress reaction in their adrenal cortex, the steroids produced probably contributed to the development of pulmonary maturation and possibly even led to the onset of labor.

In other words, *in utero* stress led to cell disintegration, hormonal aberrations and possibly to death for the fetus.

There is evidence to show that stress hormones penetrate the placental barrier and thus have a direct effect on the fetus. Further, adrenaline (one of those hormones) affects uterine tone and contractions. When in excess, it can, by itself, delay birth. Noradrenaline (another stress hormone) increases the frequency of uterine contractions and can thus create prematurity; or at least can alter the rhythm of the birth process, something again which is transmitted to the fetus. Depending on the kind of neurosis there can be an excess of either hormone during pregnancy. Because steroids enter the placenta, it is possible to produce offspring prone to diabetes by subtle but significant changes in the fetal hormone balance: the stress hormones alter the glucose tolerance of the newborn. A stressed mother can produce a baby with elevated glucose levels. Even if the mother is prone to high blood pressure (another usual indicator of stress) she will be more prone to produce a smaller baby. In some way, not yet detailed, this stress significantly affects growth hormones in the fetus. But this change in growth hormones has further and later implications as well: it will affect developmental and maturational processes, and, since the growth hormone plays a part in healing, it will also determine how effective the healing and repairing process will be in response to any bodily insult.

Hormonal alteration due to stress shows the unity of physiology and psychology. The very early events that shape physiology also shape personality. These events change the hormones that affect growth and sexual patterns, which in turn affect emotion, feeling and later attitudes, beliefs and ideas.

It is somewhat disconcerting to consider that sex drive and sex preference may well be formed in the womb. As already noted, an important way we know that this is true is that reversing early trauma in Primals results in a continuing normalization of hormonal output. Outer signs of this normalization process can be dramatic indeed: we have observed beard growth and chest hair occur for the first time in some of our male patients and we have observed breast development in some of our female patients, all with the reliving of very early trauma. These hormonal changes are accompanied by commensurate shifts in personality. The body and mind are of a piece. No shift in "mind" can be meaningful without a total shift in physiology as well, for mind evolves out of those specific physiologic processes that first comprise life.

Unwanted Pregnancy

There is probably no more pertinent stress to a fetus than not being wanted by its mother. We saw a personal account of the effects of such stress in the first part of this chapter. Research is at last beginning to document specific consequences of maternal rejection *in utero:* malformations, higher rates of spontaneous abortions and stillbirths and higher perinatal mortality rates.

Blomberg sought to investigate "whether emotional stress in a pregnant woman might have an adverse effect in the form of malformations on fetal development."* He used application for abortion as the operational indication of emotional stress: that is, pregnant women who had applied for abortions and were refused were assumed to be under emotional stress and were assumed to not want the pregnancy by virtue of having sought an abortion. All together, Blomberg investigated the babies of 1,263 women who had requested, and been denied, abortions. Based on the results of his findings, he concluded:

> The results may be seen as support for the hypothesis that emotional stress in a pregnant woman, operationally defined by the factor of unwanted pregnancy, may interfere with fetal development and result in a higher incidence of malformations.

Interestingly, he found an especially high incidence of cleft palate among the types of malformations that occurred.

Blomberg hypothesized that:

*Blomberg, S., "Influence of Maternal Distress During Pregnancy on Fetal Malformations," *Acta Psychiatric, Scandinavia,* 62, 1980, pp. 315–330.

Distress during pregnancy due to an intensive desire to terminate the pregnancy may directly affect the fetus via psychoendocrinal mechanisms or via disturbances in the circulation of the placenta.

In the following report we see a patient with a double-barreled trauma: he was born with a cleft palate *and* he was isolated in an incubator because of his low birth weight. He was born alone and disfigured, and has felt that way much of his life:

The original trauma, times two!

I was born at a normal time but weighed less than 5 pounds—I also had a deformity called cleft lip and palate. I was kept in an incubator for the first five days of my life. On the third day I started to die, and my parents rushed to give me a name so that I would surely go to heaven if I did die. I could not suck because of my cleft lip, and my mother was in such shock after she saw me that she could not nurse me.

Living it out

Later in life I was left alone a lot. My parents both worked full time. I have been alone nearly all of my life. I think I have created an isolated incubator in my present life. I work alone, I live alone, I don't go out at night, and I call my few friends on the telephone instead of seeing them. I sit in cafés alone and read. I am a very lonely person, even though I love to be with people.

Connecting to the feelings

Recently I have begun to feel the feeling "If no one is going to come I am going to die," and I have connected it to that experience in the incubator when I was really isolated at the time when I needed to be held and touched.

I have finally dreamt about my birth. In the dreams I am going through many rooms and I finally come out into the open air. There is a taxi waiting on the street, but no taxi driver, so I go back into the tunnel and feel like giving up. Before therapy, I always took the taxi in my dreams and drove away. Now I am beginning to feel the real feelings, and I realize that in real life I also always took taxis instead of driving because I wanted someone to take care of me. I don't need that anymore.

Not surprisingly, another investigator found a significantly higher incidence of malformations among infants put up for adoption,* again impli-

*Bohman, M., "A Comparative Study of Adopted Children, Foster Children and Children in Their Biological Environment Born After Undesired Pregnancies," from *Acta Paediat. Scandinavia*, Suppl. 221.

cating the mother's rejection of the baby as a causative factor in the malformations.

Other Deleterious Effects

It has been shown that the baby responds to changes in the placental temperature; that is, the mother's internal temperature. If the mother runs a fever, so must the fetus. Then again, if the mother's temperature is high because of being in a hyperenergetic, neurotic state, we must assume that this has some imprinting effect on the general temperature level of the baby. It is our experience that temperature is one of the best indicators of stress, as it shows that the body is working harder and producing more energy in the form of heat.

One could go on and on about all of the adverse effects. For example, stress affects acidity levels in our bodies, which in turn produces still other effects—a hyperacidic stomach, for one. This higher level of acidity makes the fetus hyperacidic and imprints a tendency toward this condition when stress occurs thereafter. The lucrative antacid business testifies to the millions who have this problem.

My point is a simple one: if one removes chronic Pain from the mother's system and if one provides the right kind of birth, nearly all of the adverse effects I have discussed can be avoided. It does help to have a decent birth, proper breathing, etc., as in the Lamaze method. But we must remember that these are no substitues for a "clean" physical system in the mother. Pain is the central culprit in birth trauma and in pre-birth trauma. It is dangerous because it is unconscious, unseen and unacknowledged. It therefore tends to be discarded as a force when it is in reality *the* force.

Crib Death

"Crib death" is the lay term for Sudden Infant Death Syndrome—the leading cause of infant deaths in the U.S. Infants die suddenly and unpredictably, during normal sleeping hours, generally between the ages of two to three months. No single factor has been found to cause the sudden deaths. Researchers are now finding, however, that symptoms which foretell crib death are detectable at birth*—which means that what happened in the womb may continue to play a crucial, if not fatal, role in the newborn's life.

Interestingly, it has been found that sibling babies born after infants who died from crib death stand a four to six times greater risk of also dying from this syndrome. In other words, if a mother loses her first baby to crib death, all the babies she gives birth to thereafter stand a much higher risk

*From a report by Rosenblith and Huntington in *Behavior Today*, April 18, 1977.

of also dying from crib death. It is easy to jump to the conclusion that some subtle genetic aberration must be responsible, but I think what it really means is that the subtle factors in the mother that cause crib death simply remain constant. Another study by Richard Naeye from Pennsylvania State University* reported that it was possible to use a checklist of factors to ferret out those newborns who were later likely to die from crib death. This again suggests that prenatal conditions may be more responsible than genetic encoding.

Evidence that oxygen deprivation may be the cause of crib death is mounting. Hoppenbrouwers and his colleagues found that siblings of crib death victims showed higher respiratory rates by the age of one week, which continued in varying degrees up until six months of age. They felt that the babies' breathing rates were higher to compensate for a chronic lack of oxygen, usually beginning in the womb.†

We have seen that anoxia is a side effect of several factors, including the mother's emotional state. If the baby *in utero* is subjected to chronically low levels of oxygen because the mother is chronically tense and anxious, it will be less able to handle stress later. Hoppenbrouwers et al. write along these same lines:

> The etiology of SIDS (Sudden Infant Death Syndrome) has been sought for a number of decades and is still obscure. The elusiveness of this disease suggests that a constellation of *minor* alterations, each of which alone cannot explain death, interacts to produce vulnerability to SIDS. Recent evidence indicates that risk infants may have already been challenged *in utero* . . . Minor aberrant stimuli in prenatal and postnatal life may trigger compensatory physiologic responses or aggravate existing minor abnormalities. These adjustments, while initially adaptive, when prolonged may initiate a sequence of events which perpetuates rather than limits abnormal functioning. In this model, increased respiratory rates represent such an adaptive response. The majority of infants would be expected to successfully compensate with little or no clinical symptomatology. For an occasional infant the accumulation of minor abnormalities or the occurrence of a sudden stress may present a challenge for which the infant cannot continue to compensate.‡

The Outer Environment

Studies are now showing that the fetus responds to all manner of outer environmental stimuli from an early age onward. Fetal reaction to sound is

---

*Richard L. Naeye, "Crib Death Factors," *Scientific American,* 1980, 242(4): 56–62.

†Hoppenbrouwers, Toke; Hodgman, Joan E.; McGinty, Dennis; Harper, R. M., and Sterman, M. B., "Sudden Infant Death Syndrome: Sleep Apnea and Respiration in Subsequent Siblings." *Pediatrics,* Volume 66, No. 2, August 1980.

‡Hoppenbrouwers et al., op. cit. p. 213.

a good example. Because the baby's Eustachian tubes are flooded with amniotic fluid in the womb, it was assumed for a long time that the baby couldn't "hear" sounds. Now it is known that the baby responds actively to sounds of all kinds from about the twenty-eighth week of gestation.

Pregnant women commonly report that their babies become extremely active in response to music, and, in fact, the babies' heartbeats and movement patterns change considerably. In one study, emotional music was played to the mother and measurements *in utero* were taken of the baby's vital signs and movements. The results showed that the fetus reacted in accordance with the mother's reaction. It moved more and had a faster heartbeat when the mother was emotionally moved.

It seems logical that some types of music would be calming to the baby while others would be stressful, overstimulating or whatever. If the baby responds to the sounds of music, it must also respond to other noise, perhaps even to the noise of arguments. Babies in the womb do produce a startle reaction in response to sudden noise. It is not unlikely therefore that they also respond to shouts and screams.

Animal research has shown that noise can have very negative effects on both adults and infants. In one experiment, newborn mice whose prenatal environment had been quiet and tranquil were larger and healthier than the newborns whose mothers had been subjected to varying degrees of noise. The rate of prematurity was also higher for the noise group. In fact, the proportion of poorly developed newborn mice and premature births increased directly with the increase of noise.*

"Noise" is also an internal process. There is a certain biologic background noise going on inside each of us all of the time—the "sounds" of the system at work. It is possible that a highly neurotic mother has a higher background noise inside of her, with all of its harmful effects. A frantic system must "sound" different, a sound that science has yet to measure or verify. A tranquil inner environment must be reflected in a "sound," it seems to me. This may in turn be manifested later on in certain sensitivities to noise. For example, some of us sleep very well with noise but not with light. Others wake up with the slightest noise but sleep well under bright sunlight. These proclivities come from somewhere. My assumption is that they come from experience—very, very early experience. The hearing of "noises" in certain states of psychosis may also come from experience of that kind.

Any stressful environmental factor will take its toll on a developing baby—usually a greater toll than on children or adults. Pollution, for example, is probably at least twice as harmful to a fetus as it is to us. A list of stressful environmental factors would be endless. Common sense and some degree of sensitivity can dictate to the pregnant woman what to avoid in the environment.

*Montagu, p. 190.

An important point to understand in this section is that the baby *in utero* learns a certain relationship to the world through his mother—through the quality of environment she exposes herself to, and through her responses to that environment. The baby forms its first impressions of the world through experiencing its mother's impressions. It is likely that these impressions predispose the baby to "expect" the type of world the mother has communicated. A mother who is angry and hostile most of the time communicates that reality to the baby. On some level, in some way, hostility may be imprinted as the baby's prototypic orientation to the world. Personality predisposition is probably not as genetically determined as we have thought. A baby "born cranky" may simply have learned crankiness in the womb as the predominant response modality.

The two-way relationship between the individual and the world clearly begins long before we are actually part of the world. We do indeed "see," "hear" and "feel" the outer world while in the womb, but all the perceptions are filtered through and mediated by the mother's own emotional responses. The baby *in utero* does not "see" an automobile accident, but it does experience the impact of that sight on its mother. The baby is learning to respond to the world from the moment it is conceived. From the moment it becomes part of the mother's life processes it is learning about life. And when that life is a neurotically lived one, the baby's first knowledge about the world it is to enter will be of neurosis.

Conclusions and Further Implications

The fetus is a tiny, developing human being. That it responds to all manner of input and is capable of coding and storing that input as memory is not commonly recognized. Many still believe the fetus is more protoplasm than person. But even if we consider it to be a primitive, undifferentiated life form, there is evidence of response and memory capacities in far more primitive life forms than the human fetus. The pea-tendril plant, for example, has been shown to react to stimuli, to store the information and to respond at a later time from the memory.*

What is clear is that even primitive cells react to stimuli, and code and store information. This is true not only of the nerve cells, but of all the different types of cells in the human system. This is important, as we shall see later, because there is a good deal of evidence for cellular memory in Primal Therapy—evidence such as the reappearance of bruises from forceps while a patient is reliving a birth trauma. This again points to why it is important to any psychotherapy aimed at profound biologic and psychologic change to consider all levels of memory. There is information

---

*Jaffe, M. J., "Experimental Separation of Sensory and Motor Functions in Pea-Tendrils," *Science*, Volume 195, January 14, 1977, pp. 191–192.

in all our cells to which we are continually responding, and much of that information was imprinted in the earliest days of life.

Is there nothing right that mothers can do for the babies they are carrying? "Getting along" with the baby within is probably the most important thing a mother can do. But she cannot really get along with her baby while she herself is neurotic. The matter really comes down to doing something about one's neurosis—and something can be done about that.

A neurotic mother tends to smoke and drink and take poor care of herself. Her own early Pain is an imprint that she cannot run from. It does no good to tell a neurotic mother who is carrying a child to avoid stress, for she can no more do that than she can run from her own body. Unfortunately, there is no act of will, no amount of motivation, no degree of sincerity that can, in itself, nullify the inevitable effects of the mother's neurosis. That is why the alternatives are fairly limited: a woman must either deal fully with her own Pain before conceiving a child, or run a very high risk of passing her neurosis on to the child. Trying to undo her neurosis while pregnant through some nine-month crash therapy program, however, will probably only make matters worse.

In vogue now is the "Right to Life" (anti-abortion) movement. The abortion issue is outside the scope of this book, but some observations can be made. The fetus is a living being. For it to be fully human it needs a cortex which comes along much later on. So abortion is killing a living creature but not a human being with a developed cortex; perhaps a splitting of hairs. But the right to life really should mean the right to a decent life, not a lifetime of defects, handicaps, Pain and agony. Those are the likely results of unwanted children. No one has the right, knowing all this, to sentence someone to a lifetime of misery. But, at the bottom, the matter is simple. A woman's body belongs to her. No one has the right to tell her what to do with it. Those who feel they have that right, those who claim to be pro-life, are often those who espouse death—the death penalty, higher production of the instruments of death for war, etc. Their cause is supposedly humanitarian, but to force a child to live without love, rejected and handicapped for all of his life, is hardly humanitarian.

The fetus, too, has rights: the right to a life of love and happiness, the right not to be placed in an institution for the rest of its life, the right not to suffer catastrophic disease or psychosis. Research has shown those to be the sequelae of forced birth, the legacy of being unwanted.

It is predominantly men who make these laws for women, and their consciousness of the implications of what psychologic stress in the mother does to the baby and later to that adult must be elevated.

The issue was pointed up in a recent article:*

*Longo, Lawrence D., "Environmental Pollution and Pregnancy: Risks and Uncertainties for the Fetus and Infant," *American Journal of Obstetrics and Gynecology,* 137 (2): May 15, 1980, pp. 162–173.

The New Jersey Supreme Court recognized the right of a woman to sue her obstetrician for failure to inform her of the availability of amniocentesis to evaluate the risks of bearing an infant with Down's syndrome and thus for "wrongful birth." What is the liability of a physician who fails to warn a patient of the hazards which tobacco, alcohol or drugs present to her unborn child? Will it be long before the courts decide that, indeed, providing such information constitutes the standard of medical practice? Might a fetus so damaged but born alive sue for "wrongful life?"

. . . [What about] the individual who develops hyperkinesis or mental retardation for maternal smoking, drinking or ingesting some drug? A "fetus" who later becomes a person may seek redress. Thus, what are the risks to the pregnant woman of suit from her own child for actions which she has taken that caused harm to that child? Although few would object to a woman's taking risks for herself, has she the right to make the choice for her fetus?

Appendix B: Measuring the Emotional and Psychological Effects of Birth

In 1979 we randomly selected a group of two hundred Primal patients for a follow-up questionnaire. All patients were asked to indicate the length of time they had been Primalling, the level of the Primalling (first-, second-, or third-line), and the degree of change, if any, in symptoms and behavior problems. Patients with several years of experience in Primalling (there were 62) were called the "Veteran Group." To achieve the first purpose of the study, we compared the Veteran Group to the total Primal population to determine if changes in behavior and symptoms increased over time as a result of Primalling. The second purpose of the study was to see if the level of Primalling significantly affected the degree of change and improvement. The results indicated that (1) improvements from Primal Therapy hold up over time; (2) there is an increasing rate of improvement the longer a person Primals; and (3) improvement significantly increases as patients Primal on the first line—as they relive their birth (perinatal) traumas.

The questionnaire contained a listing of over fifty symptoms ranging all the way from nailbiting to suicidal impulses in degree of severity and seriousness. It also contained a listing of emotional and behavioral problems such as excessive extroversion or introversion, workaholism, difficulty in functioning, in meeting people, etc. In evaluating the degree of change, patients could rate their symptoms and behavior problems as (1) more severe and more frequent, (2) unchanged, (3) less severe and more frequent, (4) more severe and less frequent, or (5) disappeared. Some specific results of the study:

Phobias

First-liners who began therapy with phobias showed a 70 percent improvement rate in the degree and frequency of the phobia compared with a 60 percent improvement rate for those patients having primarily second-line Primals. Most significantly, the Veteran Group (those Primalling from three to five years) showed almost a 100 percent cure rate for their phobias.

This finding clearly contradicts the belief that phobias are learned responses; that is, socially conditioned habits that you need only unlearn through various conditioning methods. There is no way to uncondition the birth trauma without addressing the trauma itself. This is why deconditioning therapies can only produce a kind of symptom substitution because in them one is working only on a symptomatic level and not dealing with the generating sources. Phobic symptoms have their attachment to deep-lying Pain and to drive away the symptoms without understanding those physiologic attachments can only ensure the eventual emergence of more severe forms of phobias—i.e., paranoia.

Symptoms have a biological function that must not be tampered with except in the specific context of that function. To detach a symptom from its cause is to try to rearrange the structure of the brain without understanding that structure. To unite a symptom with its cause is to automatically allow the brain to rearrange itself by allowing it to function in its natural mode, pre-Pain.

Nailbiting

One would imagine that nailbiting was a rather innocuous symptom. As it turns out it has first-line roots. Of the Veteran Primallers who reported feeling first-line feelings, 40 percent reported the disappearance of nailbiting, whereas none of those who felt only on the second line reported a comparable disappearance. Overall, after first- and second-line Primalling, there was an 88 percent improvement rate in this symptom.

What this points out is that even the simplest of symptoms may have complex and deep-lying connections. In Freudian terms nailbiting is anger turned against the self. We can see that this is not a sufficient explanation; and is again an imposition of theory upon psychological events rather than a straightforward correlation between facts. We can also see from this research the possible dangers in meddling with even as "mild" a symptom as nailbiting without regard for the underlying Pain. Taping a child's fingernails may force him to stop biting them, but it cannot force him to stop hurting.

Other Symptoms

There are a number of other symptoms that had more complete resolution with first-line birth Primals. These included hallucinations, depression, panic states and nightmares. Sexual problems such as frigidity, premature ejaculation and impotence also showed definite first-line roots: the more frequently patients Primalled on the first line, the more likely they were to resolve these problems. Chronic insomnia is another of those symptoms that is diminished by second-line Primals and resolved by first-line Primals.

The emotional and psychological changes resulting from deep-lying Primals are paralleled by important physiological changes as well: we found significant correlations between the reexperience of birth traumas and alterations in biochemistry, vital sign function and neurological function. There is a reduction of the stress hormone levels—an indication that the experience was biologically "real" and not faked; as well as a normalization of the growth and sex hormones and alterations in cholesterol levels. The overall amplitude of the brainwave alpha was reduced, and there was a consistent shift toward balance between the two hemispheres of the brain. The blood pressure, pulse and body temperature dropped and stayed low over the years. Lowered body temperature is a key sign because it, more than anything else, reflects the work of the body, the heat generated as it is mobilized against Pain. This index is one of the many ways in which we verify the physiological reality of birth Primals.

Index

300 IMPRINTS

Religion, 196–98
Reliving the birth sequence, 237–48
Repression, 112, 192, 197
    fetal, 27
    of sensation, 112
Research Society on Alcoholism Executive Committee, 258
Resolution of birth trauma, 225–97
    by discharging pain, 227–28
Respiratory disease, 90–91
Response
    to birth trauma, 140–50, 226
    to pain, 48–63, 228–29
    trauma-induced, 140–50
Rice, Ruth, 39
Richards, Martin, 42n
Rough handling at birth, 44
Rutgers University, 231n, 282

Sanchez, Ricardo, 264n
Santa Barbara New Press, 190
Sarby, B., 269n
Schizophrenia, 193
Science, 281n, 282n, 292n
Science News, 81n, 204n, 274n, 282n
Scientific American, 290n
Second-level body implications of birth trauma, 162–63
Second-level consciousness, 113
Second-level "stuck," 126–29
Seizure, 212
    grand mal, 205
Selye, Hans, 204
Sensations, 94, 110–12, 230
    of being stuck, 126
    at birth, 71–80, 238
    death, 217
    repression of, 112
    of suffocation, 111
Separation anxiety, 43–45
    adult, 146–48
The Seventh Seal (Bergman), 197
Sex, 94, 95, 107
    birth trauma and, 91–108
    compulsive, 96
    identity and, 96–97
    and need, 95–96
    social implications in, 106–8
Sexual behavior, 92, 106
Sexual identity, 96–97
Sexuality, 106
Sexual orgasm, 94, 107

Sherline, Harris, 42
SIDS. *See* Sudden Infant Death Syndrome
Simmons, Michael A., 268n
Sleep, 192–93
Slips of speech, 174
    see also Verbal slip
Smith, D. W., 258n
Smokers, 269
Smoking, 78, 92
    alcohol and, 260
    see also Tobacco
Social implications of birth trauma, 106–8
Sokol, Robert J., 259
Sontag, Lester, 274
Speech, 174
    see also Idiomatic expression; Primal expression; Stuttering
Spinelli, D. W., 230n, 231
Starvation, 264
    see also Oxygen starvation
State-dependent learning, 254
Staying put theme, 134–35
Sterman, M. B., 290n
Stop the battle nightmare, 110–11
Stress
    accidental, 26
    emotional, 287
    environmental, 291
    fetal, 251–94
    intrauterine, 26
    of mother, 281, 286
    personal, 26
    prenatal, 281
    reaction to, 81
    in womb, 252
    see also Stressors
Stress hormones, 286
Stressor(s), 253–89
    anoxia as, 254–61
    anxiety as, 273–75
    blood pressure as, 275–79
    caffeine as, 261
    drugs as, 261–67
    heartbeat as, 275–79
    hormonal imbalance as, 279–87
    malnutrition, 263–68
    tobacco as, 268–71
    unwanted pregnancy as, 287–89
Struggle of birth, 134
Struggle theme, 132–34